PRAISE FOR BETH KERY AND *WICKED BURN*

Winner of the *All About Romance* Reader Poll for Best Erotica 2009

"Truly hot enough to   e the pages smoke."

—Fallen Angel Reviews

"Kery gives readers beautifully written prose with amazingly descriptive sex scenes. But be warned—this is a very sensual tale. The well-crafted characters are full of raw emotions that are right on the page for the reader to experience." —*Romantic Times*

"After reading *Wicked Burn* by Beth Kery, I have a new favorite author! . . . With passionate love scenes, poignant romance, and a touching story, *Wicked Burn* is the kind of book that I will read again and again—it will certainly have a permanent place in my personal library." —*Wild on Books*

"A book you will never forget." —*TwoLips Review*

"[Kery] brings her characters to life with her descriptive prose and realistic dialogue . . . I held my breath as they came together in some of the sexiest love scenes I have read this year."

—*Romance Junkies*

"Beth Kery has written a tale filled with intense emotion and wickedly hot sex." —*Joyfully Reviewed*

"A poignant contemporary romance . . . filled with real characters."
—*Midwest Book Review*

"A remarkable tale that mesmerizes to the core."
—*The Romance Studio*

RELEASE

BETH KERY

HEAT | New York

THE BERKLEY PUBLISHING GROUP
Published by the Penguin Group
Penguin Group (USA) Inc.
375 Hudson Street, New York, New York 10014, USA
Penguin Group (Canada), 90 Eglinton Avenue East, Suite 700, Toronto, Ontario M4P 2Y3, Canada
(a division of Pearson Penguin Canada Inc.) • Penguin Books Ltd, 80 Strand, London WC2R 0RL,
England • Penguin Ireland, 25 St Stephen's Green, Dublin 2, Ireland (a division of Penguin
Books Ltd) • Penguin Group (Australia), 707 Collins Street, Melbourne, Victoria 3008, Australia
(a division of Pearson Australia Group Pty Ltd) • Penguin Books India Pvt Ltd, 11 Community
Centre, Panchsheel Park, New Delhi–110 017, India • Penguin Group (NZ), 67 Apollo Drive,
Rosedale, Auckland 0632, New Zealand (a division of Pearson New Zealand Ltd) • Penguin Books,
Rosebank Office Park, 181 Jan Smuts Avenue, Parktown North 2193, South Africa • Penguin China,
B7 Jaiming Center, 27 East Third Ring Road North, Chaoyang District, Beijing 100020, China

Penguin Books Ltd., Registered Offices: 80 Strand, London WC2R 0RL, England

This book is an original publication of The Berkley Publishing Group.

PUBLISHING HISTORY
Heat trade paperback edition / February 2010

Library of Congress Cataloging-in-Publication Data
Kery, Beth.
Release / Beth Kery.—Heat trade pbk ed.
p.   cm.
ISBN 978-0-425-23271-2
1. Triangles (Interpersonal relations)—Fiction.   I. Title.
PS3611.E79R45   2010   2009037784
813'.6—dc22

PRINTED IN THE UNITED STATES OF AMERICA

10   9   8   7   6   5   4   3

RELEASE

CHAPTER **ONE**

Genevieve ripped open the sealed envelope and withdrew the slip of paper. The security code to enter Sauren-Kennedy Solutions Inc. had been written in a bold, slanting hand. She recognized Sean's writing. She clenched her eyelids.

Slowly, the pain faded.

It had just been the unexpectedness of seeing his handwriting. She was shaken up—who wouldn't be after watching their house turn into a smoldering, blackened husk? Practically everything she owned had been destroyed tonight. She didn't have the energy to worry about what it meant to return to the penthouse after so many years.

Besides, Genevieve was in excellent practice at shoving any memory of the penthouse into the corners of her consciousness like a dirty, shameful secret.

She held up the paper and keyed in the numbers written in the familiar scrawl with a shaking hand. Sean had forwarded the updated security information through her lawyer about a year and a half ago. She'd never even opened the envelope, figuring she'd never use the contents. Thankfully she'd kept the code in the small safe at her boutique.

The code entry activated a retinal scan. The flash of light in her eye made a memory leap into her consciousness in breathtaking detail.

He'd taught her how to keep score at Cubs games. Sunlit gold strands of dark blond hair mixed with light brown as Sean leaned over and wrote on the program perched on his thigh. The bold, succinct strokes he made with the pencil contrasted so markedly with the instructions uttered in his mellow, New Orleans–accented voice—

The lock snicked open softly and Genevieve plunged into the office, acting as if she could run from her memories. It was the trauma of the night that was making her remember with such graphic detail. That's all.

The deep-pile carpeting muted her footsteps as she entered the posh reception area. Genevieve set down the bag she'd hastily packed at her Oak Street boutique and reentered the code, securing the doors once again.

Sean had made Sauren-Kennedy Solutions the most sought-after private intelligence firm in the country. These premises were nothing if not secure. Her husband, the former owner, might have been as knowledgeable and clever as any client could hope for when it came to intelligence work, but it was Sean who'd earned the trust that mattered. She knew from her lawyer that Sean had procured several lucrative government contracts over the past few years.

All was silent in the offices at two A.M. She looked around, feeling like an interloper instead of part-owner of the business. She took in the receptionist's circular mahogany desk and wondered if Carol still worked for them. She wouldn't know. All of Sauren-Kennedy business affairs were managed by her attorney. The offices had been redecorated since she'd last been there, but that wasn't too surprising. She hadn't set a foot on the premises for more than three years.

Her husband had been killed five days after Genevieve had last stood here.

For a few seconds, she wavered on her feet.

She shook off her doubts and marched toward the elevators. Why *shouldn't* she stay here? She owned the place, didn't she? Her step sounded more brisk and confident than she felt when her heels hit the polished granite tile.

The penthouse was on the top floor of the building where Sauren-Kennedy housed its offices. Max had insisted they buy a huge house on a wooded estate in the suburbs when they married, but he hadn't been completely immune to Genevieve's disappointment about moving out of downtown Chicago. She'd been such a city girl ever since she'd moved downtown during her college years. It'd been where she'd discovered what she was capable of as a clothing designer and entrepreneur; where she'd first found success. The penthouse renovation on the top floor of the high-rise where Max's company was housed had been for her—their city place, the weekend getaway.

Her phone began to ring as she stepped off the elevator. She drew her cell out of her purse and groaned softly when she saw the caller. Instead of ignoring the call from the man she'd been dating for eight weeks now—which is precisely what she felt like doing—she forced herself to answer.

"Hi, Jeff."

"Genevieve? A friend of mine who reports on the northern suburbs just called me about the fire. Are you all right?"

Genevieve lingered in the foyer, the phone pressed to her ear and her leather carryall clutched against her chest. "Yeah, it's been a hell of a night. And yes, I'm fine. Everything is going to be fine. *Please*, don't worry," she finished emphatically.

Jeff was a respected sports writer for the *Chicago Tribune*. He traveled a lot, and Genevieve knew he was in New York at the moment, covering the NBA All-Star Game this weekend. It didn't surprise her that one of his fellow reporters had called him about the fire. Given the fact that Genevieve and he were so far apart, she knew he would worry all that much more. They hadn't been seeing each other for long, but Jeff seemed pretty damn interested.

Genevieve had yet to decide how she felt about that.

"My friend said your house was . . ."

"It was completely destroyed," Genevieve finished evenly when Jeff trailed off.

"*God*. What happened?"

She slowly started to make her way toward the penthouse front door. "I don't know for sure. The fire chief said he'd get a report to me by tomorrow. Well . . . today, actually," she added when she recalled it was nearly two A.M.

"I'll catch a plane back in the morning."

"*No*." Genevieve made an effort to soften her voice when she realized how harsh she'd sounded. She didn't want to be rude, but she had enough on her plate at the moment without having to worry about Jeff hovering around and worrying about *her*. "You have the game to report on this weekend. Besides, you've heard we're supposed to be getting the snowstorm of the century starting tomorrow? I seriously doubt any flights will be getting into O'Hare for the rest of the weekend. And like I said, I'm *fine*. Things could have been much worse. No one was hurt. There's nothing in that house that can't be replaced." She sighed heavily and placed her forehead against the penthouse's wooden door. "To be honest with you, it would have been a lot harder on me if my boutique had burned down."

"Are you sure you're all right? Where are you going to stay?"

"I'm staying at a penthouse I own downtown."

There was a short pause.

"You never mentioned owning a penthouse downtown."

Genevieve straightened and began wearily searching in her purse for her keys. "We haven't really known each other for that long, Jeff. It's on the top floor of the building where Sauren-Kennedy is located." She found her keys and looked for the least used one on the keychain. "Listen, I'm going to go. I'm here, safe and sound, and I'm exhausted."

"Sure. I'll give you a call tomorrow, all right?"

She gave a small smile. He really was a nice guy. Good looking. Great job. Funny. She couldn't imagine why she was so . . . *uninspired* by him.

Of course, she hadn't been inspired by much of anything for years now. Not in the romance arena, anyway. She'd been hoping Jeff Winton was the one who would pull her out of the doldrums, but it seemed unlikely.

Not that it was much of a surprise that she wasn't feeling romantic at the moment, Genevieve thought wryly.

They said their good-byes and Genevieve inserted the key. The lock turned smoothly. She stepped into the dim, marble-tiled foyer. Without bothering to turn on the light, she removed her coat, her gaze never leaving the magnificent, luminous sight before her. She'd forgotten the stunning first impact of the penthouse view. She walked past the galley kitchen on the left and into the silent living room.

A different world existed outside the floor-to-ceiling windows. You became a denizen of the clouds when you came through that door, leaving behind the noisy, bustling world of sidewalks and traffic-filled streets. She stood next to the couch and the patio doors and looked down onto a different universe. She was like a bird perched on the top branches of a dense, metal-and-glass orchard of skyscrapers. That ground-world seemed so far away up here . . . so distant and muted.

The spires on the Sears Tower were partially obliterated by fast-moving, dark gray wisps. They were predicting a blizzard over the weekend. Genevieve had sensed the impending storm earlier in the heavy, oppressive air as she'd stood watching her house burn from a safe distance.

A woman moaned.

Genevieve froze. A man's low voice penetrated the thick silence, his mellow tone belying the firmness of the command.

"Don't strain for it. Let me give it to you."

She recognized that voice.

She turned around, her breath caught on an inhalation. She hadn't noticed the dim light at the end of the darkened hallway when she entered. Slowly, as though entranced, she walked toward the soft glow that spilled out of a partially opened door. Not the master bedroom, Genevieve thought. Not the same bedroom where she, her husband, and Sean had shared a carnal night of pleasure.

The night that had changed her life forever.

Genevieve's heart slammed against her breastbone as she approached the room. She couldn't have stopped herself from looking if she'd tried. It was as if she'd suddenly recalled with perfect clarity why her dirty little secret held so much power over her.

Because it was also exciting and forbidden. And at the core of that secret had been something neither time nor death nor harsh truths could diminish.

She peered into the room, her breath burning in her lungs.

The woman was naked and bound. Long blonde hair spilled down her back as she knelt on the floor. Her wrists had been restrained behind her back in a pair of leather cuffs.

Genevieve noticed all of this despite the fact that her attention was only for the man who stood before the kneeling woman. He wore a pair of faded jeans and a white collared shirt that had been unbuttoned, exposing an expanse of smooth skin gloving defined muscle.

The scar just above the waistline of his low-riding jeans was paler than the rest of his golden-hued skin. He'd been shot in Iraq, Genevieve knew; nearly died in an airless Army medical tent in the midst of the desert. When he'd finally regained consciousness in an Army base in Germany, they'd told him he'd won a medal for leading the successful rescue of a dozen soldiers being held hostage in a heavily guarded artillery station. He'd told them they could keep the medal and send him back to New Orleans for a reward.

They'd recruited him into the ranks of military intelligence instead.

Sean always used to say he should have just accepted the medal and kept his damned mouth shut.

His nipples were copper-colored. Genevieve could easily see the erect, flat discs through the smattering of curly, light brown hair on his chest. As usual, his short, wavy hair was tousled. It fell on his forehead as he looked down at the woman with a fixed, intent expression as he slowly pushed his cock between her widely spread lips.

Genevieve stared, held captive by the erotic sight. It was as if her brain had frozen right along with her muscles. She *felt*, she realized dazedly. It had become warm and achy between her thighs, but she was unconnected to her sexual arousal . . . as though she observed her body's response in the same bizarre, detached manner with which she watched the man she'd once loved with all her body and soul having sex with another woman.

Even though she throbbed in desire, Genevieve had gone numb.

When the woman strained forward with her head, drawing several inches of thick, veined flesh between her lips, Sean grunted in dissatisfaction. He tightened his hold on the handful of blonde hair he grasped at the woman's nape. Genevieve knew from experience the restraint of his hand would be gentle.

But firm.

The woman moaned in obvious protest when he withdrew his cock from her mouth. It made a popping noise as it cleared her lips. His penis fell at a downward angle, weighted by the heavy, tapered cockhead.

"I'm about to spontaneously combust down here, you bastard." Her voice sounded gruff . . . desire-roughened. Genevieve could see that the crests of her small breasts were pointed and hard.

He wrapped a big hand around his erection and stroked himself, his manner casual. "Didn't you say you were a trader at the Mercantile Exchange? Doesn't that job require the characteristic of patience?"

The woman tried to duck forward to get at his cock, but his hand at the base of her neck held firm. "Damn you," she hissed. She looked up at him, her expression both plaintive and irritated. He chuckled as he released her hair and stroked her jaw and cheek. The woman's lips curved in shared humor. No one could resist Sean when he smiled.

"I'm going to have to do something about that itch you have, or you're not going to play nice, are you, darlin'?" he teased with the soft New Orleans drawl that contrasted so sharply with all that hard muscle and brawn. Just the sound of his voice so close to her ear used to make Genevieve shiver . . . heat up her very core.

He helped the bound woman up from her kneeling position, his manner relaxed; his touch gentle.

Genevieve blinked, realizing her gaze had been glued to his glistening cock. It looked magnificent as it poked out from the fly of his jeans, a ready tool awaiting its master's bidding.

It didn't surprise her that he seemed so controlled. Not really.

Even when he'd allowed full expression of his wild, primitive nature on that New Year's Eve three years ago, even when he'd lost himself in the depths of intense passion, Genevieve had guessed Sean wasn't typically so expressive during lovemaking. He was usually so somber, so contained; his gaze alert, watchful. He lived like he was always ready for the other shoe to drop . . . like it was inevitable something was about to happen.

In Sean's experience, that *something* was usually never good.

His steel blue eyes didn't blaze with wild, inner fires like they had on that night so long ago when he'd looked down at Genevieve as he fucked her with long, powerful strokes. Genevieve hadn't been able to move a fraction of an inch from Sean's thorough possession of her body and spirit because Max had held her securely from behind.

Just like Sean had bid him to do.

Max may have been his boss. He may have been Genevieve's husband. But in the bedroom that night, it'd been Sean who was the undisputed master.

Hold her tight. Don't let her move. She's all mine.

No, none of that feral passion was here tonight. Sean seemed focused but calm as he led the woman over to an upholstered chair. He unhooked the leather cuffs from her wrists before he turned her around and seated her like a cordial gentleman. Genevieve stepped across the threshold of the room, still in the shadow of the door. She didn't want to lose sight of him as he walked behind the woman and the chair.

He drew the woman's wrists behind her head and bent her elbows, forcing her hands to fall behind the chair. He refastened the cuffs. The woman's sleek torso stretched. Her back arched, sending her small breasts into further pronouncement.

Genevieve bit off a soft moan when he reached down and gently tweaked a distended nipple. The woman's thighs clamped together and she squirmed in the chair.

"None of that now," he chastised softly. He came around the chair and leaned over her lap, pushing her legs wide and draping her thighs over the corners of the seat.

The woman pressed down with her pelvis, trying to get friction on her spread pussy. For a second, Sean's head lingered near the junction of the woman's thighs. The blonde tensed expectantly. Genevieve felt like a heavy stone dropped in her gut. She started to back out of the room, suddenly wanting to be *anywhere* but in that time and place.

But then he stood. Genevieve let out a shaky breath of relief, careful not to make herself heard. A distant, screaming voice shouted for her to leave. To escape. If Sean had glanced over to the door as he walked over to a bedside table, he would have seen her standing there like a stunned deer in headlights. The horrible thought couldn't galvanize her into action, though. It was like she was stuck in an emotion-filled, carnal dream.

An exciting, tortuous nightmare.

The woman cried out when he pulled out a flesh-colored dildo from the bedside table.

"No. I want your cock."

"You'll get it if you ever learn a measure of patience, darlin'," he murmured as he walked back toward the woman. She'd heard him call other females "darlin'" before, and it never sounded insulting. Instead, his low, resonant voice and New Orleans accent made it into a tender endearment.

Dawlin'.

Strangely, Sean had never called Genevieve that.

His penis was still erect and bobbing in the air before him. He set down the dildo on the arm of the chair, ignoring the woman's sound of disgust when he tucked his cock back into his underwear and fastened the first few buttons over the pronounced bulge.

He leaned over the arm of the chair and calmly, efficiently

inserted the rubber dildo into her spread slit. The woman bucked her hips back and forth when he fully sheathed the sex toy. She whimpered in rising excitement and desperation.

Sean left the dildo inside her and sat down on the cushioned arm of the chair, his long, jean-clad legs bracing him. He placed one arm along the back of the chair, his pose casual but also effectively preventing the woman from lowering her restrained wrists.

He began to caress her perspiration-damp torso. His hand looked big and masculine spread over the female's delicate, heaving rib cage. He caressed her ribs, belly, and waist languorously while the woman panted and moaned and flexed her hips against the penetrating dildo with increasing franticness. He played with her breasts, gently squeezing and stimulating the hard, small nipples until the woman growled in frustration.

"Make me come," she begged. "Please."

Her arousal felt tangible to Genevieve; as if she shared in it.

The female's hips bucked against the inserted dildo. When her bottom slid forward in the seat as she tried to stimulate herself, Sean's hand finally dropped, holding the base of the sex toy in place, giving her the resistance she required.

"That's right. Fuck yourself," he murmured as he watched her brace her feet on the floor, making her hips rise off the seat. She began to thrust her slit up and down on the rubber shaft.

"God damn it. Why are you making me work for it?" the woman squealed as she pumped wildly.

"You want something different?"

"I want to get it . . . *hard*," the woman spat out as she thrashed against the dildo.

"Well, since you asked so sweetly."

He stood and grabbed her splayed thighs, pushing them back firmly until the woman's pelvis rolled back. He pinned her spread knees to the back of the chair with a forearm. He leaned over the side of the chair, his profile to Genevieve. With his other hand, he began plunging the dildo into the woman's pussy, giving her the hard fuck she'd asked for. The blonde keened and thrashed her hips in wild excitement.

He slid the dildo all the way into her and turned the rectangular base until it hit the woman's exposed clit. His fingers pressed and circled, vibrating the hard rubber against the sensitive tissues.

The woman shook in orgasm. When her screams of passion quieted, he let go of her restrained legs. He leaned down and inserted an erect nipple into his mouth, his cheeks hollowing out as he supplied a firm suction. He vibrated the base of the dildo against her clit even more stringently than before.

The blonde woman cried out in agonized pleasure as her orgasm notched back up again to its original potent blast.

Genevieve must have whimpered in mixed misery and arousal, because suddenly Sean's head whipped around.

The woman continued to keen and moan while she gushed in climax, and Sean pinned Genevieve with his stare. His fierce, blue-eyed gaze hit her like a bolt of electricity. Her muscles jerked, the harsh movement awakening her from her trance.

The next thing she knew, she was flying blindly down the hallway. She heard him call out to her, his voice sounding flat with incredulity. He called out again, this time sounding closer . . . too near for her to make it all the way to the front door without him overtaking her.

She thought she might shatter into a million pieces if Sean put his hands on her at that moment. She fumbled for the master bedroom door and rushed inside.

"*Genny*. What the hell—"

His exclamation was cut off when Genevieve slammed the door and swiftly turned the lock. The handle jerked. His hand thumped on the door. She pressed her back against the wood, straining to hear in the taut silence that followed.

"Genny."

She clamped her burning eyes shut at the softly uttered plea. It must be a hollow-core door, because she could actually hear him quite well. It sounded like he'd spoken with his forehead pressed against the crack between the door and frame. They were only inches apart—

"You picked a hell of a time to come waltzing back into my life," he said, his low voice vibrating with emotion.

"I didn't know you'd be here."

"Obviously."

She licked her tear-spattered lips. For the first time, she realized her face was soaked. She must have been crying for a while now . . . maybe since she'd first heard Sean's easy drawl resounding from the depths of the penthouse.

"Go *away*, Sean." Her heart thundered in her ears in the pause that followed. The door gave slightly, as though he'd just pushed himself off it.

"I was here first."

"You can go straight to hell second, boy."

His chuckle sounded appreciative . . . amused.

Sad.

"Just give me a minute to tell her good-bye." For a second, she thought he'd walked away, but then his deep voice penetrated the crack of the door again.

"Are you okay? Did something happen?"

She stared at the enormous king-sized bed in front of her—the bed where the three of them had become drunk on pleasure three years ago.

Did something happen? She'd say it had.

Genevieve had been forever changed on the night Max had offered his young wife to his super-sharp, right-hand man . . . the night she'd burned beneath Sean's touch.

"I'm fine," she said blankly, her eyes glued to the bed as vivid memories played before her mind's eye . . . memories brought to the forefront by being in the room where it'd all happened.

"Yeah, right," she heard him reply wryly.

"Will you just *leave me alone*?"

"That's likely."

This time, she sensed for certain that he'd walked away. A minute later she still hadn't moved. They passed within feet of her.

"You're acting very rudely," the woman accused petulantly as she moved down the hallway.

"Yeah, I've been told I have a problem with that," Sean replied evenly.

"Is there someone here? Who were you talking to?"

But then their voices faded. She heard the front door open and shut, and knew Sean was escorting the female out of the tight Sauren-Kennedy Solutions security. He'd get her a cab. He may have grown up poor, friendless, and fatherless, one of the "conduct disordered" terrors of the mean streets of New Orleans, but Sean's manners were impeccable.

Genevieve still hadn't moved when he returned a few minutes later. She stood stock-still, her back against the door like she thought she was on the penthouse's window ledge with the city looming below her toes. Out of the corner of her eye, she saw the handle turn. He spoke softly again near the crack in the closed door.

"You'd better open up, girl. You don't really think that excuse of a lock is gonna keep me from you, do you?"

Her pulse threatened to leap right off her neck. She'd never heard him call another female *gull*, his drawl softening the "r" until it was only barely audible.

The sound of it on his tongue had always felt like a caress.

She spun around and flipped the lock. Her gaze remained fixed on the carpet as she stormed past him. She grabbed the bag she'd dropped in the foyer and reached for the handle on the front door. His hand rose behind her, shutting the door with a precise snap.

"What happened?"

"What makes you think something happened?" she asked irritably. She was hyperaware of him just inches away, leaning down over her. Heat resonated off his body.

"*Don't*, Genny. Haven't you punished me enough by avoiding me all this time? You know I'd never have wanted you to see what you just saw. Not in a million years."

Her soughing breath was the only thing that broke the silence that followed. Her chin dropped to her chest.

She *did* know it. She may have her doubts about him, but she knew instinctively Sean Kennedy would never purposefully hurt her.

The havoc he'd wreaked unintentionally on her life was another matter altogether.

"The house in Lake Forest burned down," she whispered. "It's . . . gone. Everything."

He placed his hands on her shoulders and spun her around. His tall shadow loomed over her. She blinked in disorientation when he switched on the crystal chandelier. He stared. The color washed out of his face.

"Come 'ere," he growled, taking her hand. Genevieve stumbled after him into the living room. A bar lined the north wall. He slid one of the suspended goblets from the rack and grabbed an open bottle of wine. The crimson liquid splashed into the bowl of the glass.

"Drink it," he ordered, all traces of his accent absent from the terse command. Genevieve hesitated before she glanced into his glittering eyes. She took the glass, draining half the wine in her first swallow. He pried the trembling goblet from her clawlike grip. He guided her over to the sofa and pulled her down next to him.

"Were you in the house?"

She shook her head as she released her hands from his warm grasp.

"I was working late on Oak Street. I drove home at around nine. I've been watching them try to put the fire out all night."

"Why didn't you call me?"

She just stared at the carpet sightlessly. He didn't seem to expect her to answer once he'd considered his impulsive question.

They both knew the days were gone when she would have leaned on Sean for support.

"Four engines were working on it when I got there, but they were just trying to contain the blaze at that point . . . keep it from getting to the trees and spreading. One of the firemen told me it had likely started in the garage and spread first to the kitchen. They had it out by the time I left. It was a nightmare. The police were there. The press . . ."

His body tensed for action but he remained seated beside her. She threw him an exasperated glance. Three years hadn't dulled her almost preternatural ability to read him. Never mind that he'd been trained by the United States Army to be an intelligence operative.

She'd known her fair share of spies. Max had held a top position at the CIA before he'd retired and started his private intel firm. But while Max had proved to be an enigma to her, Sean was pretty much an open book.

"Go ahead, call if you want to," she said. "There was a cop—Sergeant Gould. The chief from the fire department was a Martin McGruder."

"I'm not going anywhere right now. What about Jim? Is he okay?" Sean asked, referring to Jim Rothman, Max's longtime, live-in employee who did everything from house maintenance to grocery shopping.

"He's fine," Genny whispered. "He'd been out for the evening, like me. He came home from the movies at around eleven and stood with me, watching it burn." Her breath caught on an inhale. "He was more upset than I was. He kept worrying he'd left some appliance running or hadn't maintained the furnace the way he should. I must have told him a million times it wasn't his fault, poor man, and even if one of us *had* done something inadvertently, it wasn't intentional. He was worried sick. He's staying with his daughter in Niles."

"There was no indication it'd been set?"

"*Set?*" She sharpened her gaze on him. "Of course not. Who would have set my house on fire?"

His brows drew together as he studied her. His hand rose to cradle her jaw. "Was there a medical unit there? Did they treat you?"

"For what?"

"Shock." Their gazes met and locked.

He didn't try to stop her from standing. She returned to the bar where she lifted the wineglass to her lips. The crystal hummed when she set the goblet on the bar too forcefully. She saw him watching her in the mirror lining the back of the bar.

"Am I going? Or are you?"

"I think you know the answer to that, Genny."

She turned around. "You can't expect *both* of us to stay here."

He shrugged and leaned back, spreading his arms along the back of the couch. He'd buttoned the crisp white shirt, but not completely. When he spread his arms, the fabric parted. Genevieve found herself staring at the sexy triangle of exposed skin and curling, light brown hair. She blinked when he spoke.

"I'm working on a big project. My assistant will be here first thing in the morning. It's easier to sleep here when I'm staying so late in the office."

"*Sleep*, huh?" she muttered sarcastically.

"You couldn't expect me to know you'd show up here tonight. I said I was sorry about that." He waved toward the hallway and the bedroom. When she glanced out the window dismissively, he added, "Right—I forgot. You're good at ignoring my apologies. You're an expert at the business of ignoring me in general."

Heat flooded her cheeks. She opened her mouth to bring him to task for changing the subject but he interrupted her before a word left her tongue.

"I own this penthouse, too. Have you forgotten that?"

"No, I haven't *forgotten*. Fine. If you're staying, I'll be the one to go. I'll stay with my mother." Her eyes widened when he just shook his head slowly, his expression implacable.

"I'm sorry," he said. "But until I can get some more information about what happened with the fire . . . until I know for sure nobody set it with the intent of harming you, you're staying here. And so am I, Genny."

Her muscles felt as if they'd snap like rubber bands stretched too tight when he said her name again. He was the only person who called her Genny. The only one who *could* and make it sound so natural . . . like her true name. Once Max had tried to call her Genny. It had sounded forced and foolish on his tongue. She hadn't said anything, but Max had never done it again.

Max had encouraged her and Sean to spend time together. Her husband had confessed to her once that he felt a little guilty about the fact that he had so few interests in common with her, given their twenty-four-year age difference. Max had never shown an ounce of jealousy over the fact that Sean and she shared a love for taking in a Cubs game on hot summer afternoons or biking for miles along the lakefront. Sean had even taught her how to shoot at the Sauren Solutions in-house firing range.

It'd all been innocent . . . on the surface anyway.

Until that New Year's Eve three years ago, when Max had suggested the three of them indulge in a night of pleasure.

Until five nights later, when Sean had murdered him.

CHAPTER **TWO**

Sean watched her closely, seeing her indecision, her exhaustion. He sensed something else in her; something he strongly suspected was fear. The realization that it was *he* who was making her practically vibrate with anxiety made him feel like he'd just tipped pure acid down his throat.

He understood why she was so nervous around him . . . to an extent, anyway. He cursed himself at least once a day for his uncharacteristic impulsivity on that night three years ago. Genny had every right to avoid him like he carried a particularly potent version of the plague. When he'd been desperate to see her after Max's death, he'd sometimes catch her wincing when she looked at him.

He'd made a mistake. But that'd been years ago. How long did he have to suffer for caring about something beyond wisdom and circumstances?

Beyond reason?

He knew he wasn't good enough for Genny, but that simple fact had never once stopped him from wanting her more than he'd ever wanted anything. Besides, Sean figured he possessed some kind of deep psychological flaw that made him rebel against the obvious.

Stubbornness stiffened his backbone and he sat forward on the couch, elbows on his knees. He'd grown up knowing that if you wanted something, you had to do more than just fight for it. You had to go into that fight like it was your last volitional act on earth. You had to be willing to sacrifice everything before you went into that battle, whether it was a back-alley scrap with a bully or an Iraqi who hated you so much it was like a poison in his blood.

It hadn't been hard for him as a kid to live by that code. He'd had nothing of substance to lose but his own life—and hadn't he gotten the message from plenty of people that even *that* was a worthless commodity?

He still had nothing to lose at age thirty-seven, Sean admitted to himself grimly. But Genny had wandered into his domain again, even if it had been unintentional on her part. Mistakes and sins be damned. He wasn't going to let her go again without a fight. He just needed to work on regaining her trust.

If he could just spend some time with her, get her comfortable with him once again, maybe she'd open up.

"You're staying right here, Gen. There are two bedrooms. You can have your pick."

"I don't want to sleep in either one." Her usually soft, soulful gray eyes turned as sleety as the hovering gray clouds outside the window, but Sean pretended not to notice.

"The couch is nice and soft then." He stood and walked to the foyer. He locked the front door and keyed in the code for the alarm. She came up behind him as he finished.

"What are you doing?"

"Locking up for the night. Is this your stuff?" He picked up a huge leather carryall and peered inside, seeing hastily folded clothing and a bag of toiletries. "I'll put it in the guest bath." She ignored him as she stared at the alarm system mounted on the wall. She turned to him, an incredulous expression spreading on her face.

"That's a different system than the one downstairs. I've never seen it before. I don't know the code," she said slowly. "You just *locked* me in here."

"'Course I didn't. I locked everything else out."

Her mouth fell open at his terse reply. He resisted an almost overwhelming urge to crush her to him, to send his tongue between the tempting target of her lips. His lust for Genny had always been a given, but something about seeing her so unexpectedly and the knowledge she'd stood toe to toe with danger tonight added an extra edge to his hunger.

Her skin looked extremely pale next to the rust-colored knit dress she wore with a pair of leather boots. That dress highlighted every lush curve of her slender body while managing to look sophisticated at the same time. The clean lines and elegance of the garment made him suspect it was Genny's own design. Sean had never been much for fashion, but he liked Genny's style. He'd come to admire and respect her talent. Her face was still damp from tears and reddened from crying. Some mascara had smeared below her right eye.

She looked as sublimely lovely to him as she ever had, and it had nothing to do with a body and face that could alter the trajectory of a man's life. Sean'd known from the first time he laid eyes on her that Genny's beauty came from within.

He blinked, realizing he'd been staring at her breasts and thinking about how soft and shapely they looked pressed against the clinging knit.

Okay, so her beauty wasn't just spiritual.

He headed for the hallway. He was supposed to be rebuilding her trust in him, not gawking at her chest like a horny teenage boy, he thought irritably.

She followed him into the bathroom.

"You can't force me to stay here, Sean," she said when he deposited her bag on the granite countertop and walked over to the steam shower.

"Who said anything about *forcing* you?" He turned the faucet. "You're in shock. You'd be acting all kinds of irrational if you stormed out of a nice, warm, available apartment after your house burned down." He raised his brows and came toward her. She stepped back quickly, pressing her butt against the vanity to avoid him as he went past her in the narrow confines of the bathroom. She glanced up warily when he paused next to her, his hip brushing her belly.

"Give me one good reason why you can't stay here, girl," he demanded quietly.

She seemed too flabbergasted by his audacity to speak, so Sean steamrolled ahead. "Go ahead and take a nice hot shower. It'll help you to relax. I'm going to try to contact someone at the Lake Forest police and fire departments and then go to bed. Do you want another glass of wine?"

She glanced around, as though searching for a reason she couldn't stay at the penthouse hidden amongst the fluffy towels and rising steam. Her shoulders slumped suddenly, and Sean knew her shock and exhaustion had finally caught up to her.

"No. Just . . . just leave me alone." She brushed past him and grabbed her bag. She hadn't moved quickly enough for him not to see the tears that sprung into her eyes, though.

"Sure thing, girl," he said as though she'd requested the easiest thing in the world instead of the hardest. "I'll bring a pillow and blanket out to the couch."

He saw her frown furiously at the contents of her bag before he shut the door.

He lay in bed, his hands behind his head, thinking. The sun had been valiantly trying to come out for a half an hour now, but it was proving to be a weak opponent against the heavy snow that had begun to fall at dawn.

Genny had come out of the bathroom earlier wearing sweatpants and a huge T-shirt, her brown hair still damp. He'd stood in front of the sliding glass doors that led to the small terrace, dialing the number for the Lake Forest Police on his cell. She hadn't spared him a glance. She'd laid down on the couch and pulled the blanket almost over her entire head. She kept her back to him when he got off the phone after having a brief conversation with the Lake Forest Police desk sergeant.

She was making a point of ignoring him. He knew he'd pushed her defenses enough as it was, so he'd left her in peace.

She'd said she hadn't wanted to sleep in either bedroom, Sean recalled. How much had she seen of him fooling around with that woman—Suzanne? He shifted restlessly in the bed, made uncomfortable by the thought.

Why hadn't Genny called out to him? From the look on her face, she'd been appalled by what she'd seen taking place in this bedroom. Her face had been frozen in shock as silent tears rolled down her cheeks.

Funny, when he'd first heard her whimper of distress, he'd mistaken it for arousal.

Had she been shocked because he'd restrained Suzanne? Or had her distress been caused by seeing him with another woman? Sean suspected it was the former. Max had restrained her that New

Year's Eve at Sean's request. Maybe Genny didn't like seeing such a stark reminder of an event she regretted so greatly.

He understood why she didn't want to sleep in the master bedroom. He never slept in there, never took a woman in there . . . never went in there *period* if he could avoid it.

Genny still thought of that New Year's Eve, all right. She regretted it, but not for the same reasons Sean did. Genny would have wiped that night clean out of existence, if she could.

He, on the other hand, clung to the exquisite memories like a miser stroking his treasure. Sometimes, in the middle of the night, Sean would go over each detail, torturing himself. It hurt like hell, but it was a pain he wouldn't have sacrificed for anything. Once the memories were gone, he'd be left empty and hollow.

He relished the memory of burying his face against Genny's neck and breathing the scent of her arousal while her cries of pleasure vibrated into his lips. He thought of what it'd been like to have her shaking to orgasm in his arms while he poured himself into her.

His cock swelled and lurched against the sheets.

He hissed a curse and got out of bed. For once, he didn't welcome the pain of the haunting memories. Not when the dream-woman lay just feet away from him, soft and warm in sleep.

Ten minutes later, he'd showered and dressed, forgoing shaving to save time. He wanted to leave and get back before the storm made transportation impossible.

He wanted to get back before Genny awakened.

He checked on her before he left. She'd turned onto her back and slept with one arm over her head, her clenched fist opening slowly as the muscles relaxed. Her eyebrows drew together slightly, making her look like she was trying to puzzle something out in her dreams. Her breasts looked soft and inviting beneath the thin layer of her T-shirt as they rose and fell with her even breath.

Sean turned away, wondering if there'd ever be a time when he didn't look at her and feel regret.

He returned to the penthouse three hours later, glad to see Genny still slept. The snow fell so heavily it looked like a gray and white veil flickering outside the windows. With the storm and the light weekend traffic, he'd been able to drive up to Lake Forest with relative ease in his SUV. The plows and salt trucks had been surprisingly efficient for once.

But the snow had started falling heavier on the Edens Expressway on the return trip. It was just a matter of time before the city became immobilized until Mother Nature had her say.

Fatigue overcame him as he removed his coat, gun holster, and boots and keyed the code into the alarm. When he was here alone, he rarely bothered with added security. No one could enter the penthouse without first getting into Sauren-Kennedy, and that was a near impossibility. Certainly nothing the Lake Forest fire chief had told him had raised Sean's hackles or made him suspicious the fire had been set purposefully.

But Genny was here now, and it never hurt to be cautious.

It'd been three years since Albert Rook had attempted to blackmail Sean with knowledge that could potentially send Genny to prison—three years since Sean had threatened Rook in return and sent the former Sauren Solutions intelligence operative packing.

Sean's intelligence contacts informed him that Rook was in Indianapolis, Indiana, where he owned an outdoor hunting and fishing store that served as a front for laundering money for a local drug kingpin. Sean wished the slimeball was a hell of a lot farther than Indianapolis from Genny, but Rook had never done anything to make Sean think his threat held strong. Sean had meticulously kept an eye on the man over the years.

Although he had to admit, when Genny had said her house had burned down, Sean's thoughts had leapt immediately to Max's old lover.

He hesitated in the living room, his gaze on Genny curled beneath the blanket. He told himself to go back to bed.

He found himself sinking into the cushy leather chair instead.

As his relaxation grew, the barriers faded. Memories flooded his brain. He stared at Genny as the snow fell silently outside the windows.

And Sean remembered.

He'd first met her at a company party that he'd looked forward to about as much as he might a trip to the dentist to get his teeth drilled. Making nice-nice just wasn't Sean's thing. Manners were like the sport of a world-class athlete. It was necessary to have it hammered into you from an early age for it to become as natural as breathing. Sure, he'd attended his fair share of social events during his military career, and he'd learned how to comport himself. But he was usually ready to leave a shindig like this before he'd ever crossed the threshold.

Besides, Army brass had nothing on Max Sauren.

He'd reminded himself repeatedly as he drove to Max's Lake Forest estate that he had only himself to blame for the unpleasant errand. He'd understood what he was getting into when he'd taken the position of chief operating officer at Sauren Solutions Inc. eight months before. The corporate world was a whole new adventure for Sean Kennedy—one he wasn't entirely certain he was equipped to navigate.

He'd sighed dispiritedly when he'd walked onto the huge, terraced deck that overlooked a lush garden and manicured lawn. Dozens of small cocktail tables had been set up on the deck, each of them adorned with a single white orchid and a tea light. An elaborate, built-in bar and a buffet table were being well patronized by Sauren Solutions employees.

Two white-jacketed waiters weaved amongst the partygoers, tables, and enormous pots of lush flowers. Amy Brighton and Jess Cheaver, two young surveillance experts, greeted him cheerfully. From their eager expressions at seeing him, Sean figured Amy and Jess were relieved to have something break the monotony. The long faces of the partygoers only strengthened his suspicions.

Max was schmoozing a gray-haired man who Sean recognized as Senator Joseph Carmichael from Ohio. Sauren Solutions had managed to bail Senator Carmichael out of a sticky situation involving illegal hiring practices in the senator's home state. It'd been before Sean's time, but he'd perused the file. Not that the file gave much away. Somebody at Sauren Solutions had obviously found some dirt on Carmichael's chief rival in the senate, Mycroft Stokes. Stokes had been the one pushing the investigation against Carmichael.

Following the hiring of Sauren Solutions, Stokes had suddenly discovered much more pressing matters with which to make headlines, and the Carmichael illegal hiring practices scandal had slowly evaporated.

A waiter passed and handed Sean a small plate and a glass of champagne. He was staring dubiously at the contents of the plate when a woman spoke.

"The fork is small enough to get the meat out of the shell."

He grinned and glanced over his shoulder to the speaker.

He forgot what he meant to say.

Her brown hair was parted on the side and fell in shiny waves past her shoulders. She wore a white, sleeveless sheath dress that fastened at her neck. The dress was simple, and her accessories spare, but the woman gave the impression of effortless chic. It was the look of uncertainty on her heart-shaped face that mesmerized Sean from the first glance—the way her vulnerability contrasted so greatly with her innate sense of style.

It hadn't been just because it was the first time he'd been exposed to her beauty that Sean had forgotten his glib comment. Genny had *never* ceased to have the power to knock rational thought clean out of his brain.

"I know how to eat escargot," he said, firming up his sagging grin. "I was just wondering what the hostess was thinking, serving it at a Fourth of July party."

He knew he'd erred when he saw her expression falter.

Shit.

On *so* many levels. *She* was the hostess. He just knew it all of a sudden. And if she was the hostess, than she was Max's wife. And wasn't it just his luck that Mrs. Max Sauren and this incredible creature were one and the same woman?

"It was a stupid thing to serve," she mumbled, looking stricken.

"Are you *kidding* me?" Sean asked as he walked over to one of the white tablecloth-covered tables and began to eat with relish. He was relieved to say that she followed him over to the table. "My mama was a waitress at the Bourbon House for a spell. I lived like a king for ten months or so, eating leftover escargot, oysters, and clams. When I first ate escargot, I thought I'd lose it f'sure. But I was bound and determined to eat every last slimy bit of it. Didn't Mama tell me it was the equivalent of eating money? Took me about three bites before I realized rich people weren't the idiots I'd started to think they were when I saw snails on my plate."

He'd relaxed a little when she laughed. She put out her hand.

"I'm Genevieve Bujold, Max's wife."

"Sean Kennedy," he returned, taking her hand in his.

Her eyebrows shot up on her forehead as she took a seat next to him. "Max's new chief operating officer? I've heard so much about you."

He paused in eating when he saw that she studied him curiously with eyes that were the color of storm clouds when sunlight starts to break through them.

"What?" he asked.

She grinned. "Oh . . . sorry. Max said you were a war hero."

"That's not what you were thinking, girl," he chided softly before he resumed eating.

She looked nonplussed for a second but then she laughed. "No, you're right. He said you were ruthless."

"It's true. That's why he hired me. I show no mercy to the administrative staff when they try to skip out early from work and I'm a tyrant about keeping down office supply shortages."

She chuckled as she accepted a glass of champagne from a passing waiter.

"You're like Max. So secretive about what you *really* do at work every day." She took a sip of champagne. "My mother still doesn't believe me when I tell her Max is a spy."

"Sounds a bit melodramatic."

"But it's easier to say then 'private sector intelligence operative.' "

"Now that's a fact," he replied with a grin.

Talking to Genny was the easiest, most natural thing he'd ever done. He didn't know how it happened, but a half hour slipped by like a second. Every once in a while, a Sauren Solutions employee would stop by and greet him and pay respects to Max's wife, but thankfully no one lingered long. The sky softened to a lavender color and lightning bugs begun to spark out in the garden as Sean found himself telling Genny about his mother. She listened without interrupting, her expression somber and intent.

"I hope your mama will find peace someday," she said in a hushed voice after Sean'd finished explaining about his mother's long history of alcohol and cocaine addiction. It was a fact he'd told precisely two people in his entire life: a kind priest with a great sense of humor who used to visit him in the hospital when Sean had been wounded in Iraq.

And Max Sauren's wife.

"She goes through periods where she seems okay . . . hopeful."

"You take care of her, don't you?" Genevieve asked quietly.

"If you count sending money to the manager of her residential facility taking care of her, I guess so. She won't accept much else. To her credit, to my knowledge she's never finagled a dollar of the money I've sent for her care to go on a binge."

"It's more than most sons would do, Sean."

He shrugged, suddenly feeling like a major idiot for having spilled his guts to this gorgeous stranger.

Genevieve sighed and leaned back, seeming to sense his discomfort.

"I didn't grow up having it as rough as you did, but this type of thing"—she waved at the mansion behind them and the lush grounds—"was about as familiar to me as Mars growing up in Gary, Indiana. My dad was a steel worker, but with all the layoffs and plant closings . . . well, things were never too certain for us. He'd go through long stretches being out of work. He either worked himself raw, worrying the entire time about layoffs or was unemployed and fretting about not getting a paycheck. I blame the steel industry, at least partially, for the fact that he was dead at age fifty-three." She met his gaze and smiled wistfully. "You *must* be a spy. You got me to reveal my secret so easily."

"Which part was the secret?"

"The part about where I grew up."

"Why's growing up in Gary, Indiana, such a secret?"

She shrugged, the movement diverting his attention to her smooth shoulders and lithesome arms.

"It's not *really* a secret. But you have to admit: only the daughter of a steel worker from Gary, Indiana, would ever think of serving something as pretentious as escargot at a Fourth of July party." She gave him a wry look and he knew that she hadn't really fallen for his hasty cover-up of his earlier slip.

"It's the first event I've ever planned for Max without any professional catering help. I wanted it to be perfect for him. It was stupid of me. I should have had a barbecue or something. Not a stuffy cocktail party." She glanced around the deck sadly. "People don't look like they're having a very good time."

"You'll have a barbecue next time. As for tonight, I think you did a fantastic job. Best party I ever went to. I'm having a great time."

"Do you know what I think?" she asked.

"What do you think?"

"I think Max knew exactly what he was doing when he hired you. You notice things about people. You noticed something about me, didn't you?"

"You think it takes some kind of spy instinct for a man to notice the most beautiful woman at the party, is that it?"

For a few seconds, she looked taken aback by his compliment, but then he laughed softly. She shook her head.

"No. I think you recognized how nervous I was. I think that despite all her hardships, your mama managed to teach you some very nice manners, Sean."

He leaned forward and held her gaze. "I was speaking the absolute truth. I'm having the time of my life, Genny from Gary, Indiana."

Her smile gave him a glimpse at something he'd never been taught to hope for.

"I didn't hire you to charm my wife, Kennedy, but I never complain about anything that makes her happy, so you go right ahead."

Genevieve looked a little startled but recovered immediately when she glanced up into her husband's face.

"Max," she murmured warmly. Max Sauren stroked his wife's shoulders with long, elegant fingers and extended his other hand to Sean in greeting.

As usual, Sean's boss looked movie-star handsome with his wavy mane of silver hair, perfectly proportioned, chiseled features and deep-set, dark brown eyes. His cream-colored pants and jacket might have been borrowed from Gatsby's closet, but Max added a degree of careless elegance and sophistication that even surpassed those of the fictional character.

Sean had instinctively understood upon first meeting Max Sauren that a methodical, cold-blooded killer resided in his depths. The knowledge didn't detract from the fact that Max was also a pleasant, extremely clever, stimulating companion. They had a good working relationship, and respected each other's strengths.

In Sean's mind, Max Sauren and he were like two different species—a canine and a feline forced to share the same environment. Sean didn't have to trust the wily, sleek big cat in order to like him.

"Kennedy."

"Max. Al, how are you?" Sean exchanged a handshake with the dark-haired man who'd approached the table with Sauren. The smile on Albert Rook's thin lips didn't match the hard glitter in his green eyes as they shifted from Genevieve, to Sean, and back to Genevieve again.

Rook had been one of Sean's first challenges when he started work at Sauren Solutions. Rook had been with the company since Max had started it. Max had recruited him after he'd retired from the Navy, where Rook had served as a weapons systems analyst in Navy intelligence.

At first, Sean'd thought Rook's sullen animosity toward him stemmed from that old Army–Navy rivalry. It didn't take him long to understand Rook's resentment went deeper than that.

Much deeper.

Rook was angry that Max had hired Sean from the outside, believing he should have been offered the position of chief operating officer instead. Sean had pulled Rook aside one day last spring and confronted him about his sullen attitude. He'd given him two choices: get over the fact he'd been passed over for the position or walk. Sean seriously doubted Rook had completely gotten past his resentment, but he acted a good deal friendlier. Which was fine with Sean.

As long as he did his job.

"Did you see Carmichael?" Max asked Sean. He tapped his forehead as he recalled. "Oh, that's right. Carmichael was before you joined us, wasn't he?"

Sean nodded. "Sauren must have done a hell of a job for him. That whole illegal hiring scandal blaze fizzled into nothing."

A smile tilted Max's sculpted lips. "I handled that myself, you know."

Sean recognized the knowing sparkle in Max's eye. It was the type of case that Max would never pass up, of course, involving high-level people and bartering secrets. Max loved the moment when his opponent realized he'd been cornered with no escape.

Mycroft Stokes was well known on Capitol Hill as being a cantankerous, lovable old coot. His off-the-cuff, emotional diatribes to the press in defense of the "common man" had endeared him to his constituents. He was loud, uncouth, and extremely powerful— exactly the kind of man Max would have delighted in putting in his place.

"Is that a fact?" Sean tipped his glass in a small, grudging salute before he drank. Given the degree of the uproar over the hiring scandal, Max had done one hell of a job in not only getting the charges dropped against Carmichael, but in silencing the uproar. The way Max relished this nasty aspect of his job so much turned Sean's stomach a little, but he grudgingly respected a job well executed, nonetheless.

Stokes's secret hadn't been revealed in the file Sean had perused. Max guarded his methods and contacts carefully. From what Sean knew about Mycroft Stokes, he could make an educated guess about his weak point, however. He'd wager that Max had laid evidence before the aging senator regarding his proclivity for keeping company with teenage, nubile females who didn't seem to mind his gray hair, wrinkles, or the fact that he was married.

Sean wagered his wife of forty-four years and the voters in Stokes's state would take a different opinion.

Forget cash and fuck position. In Sean's world, *knowledge* was the essence of power.

The four of them chatted as full night settled. Sean absorbed it all without any conscious intent to do so: the way that Albert Rook looked at Genevieve with a cold sort of appraisal, like a man who sat down to a five-star meal with no appetite; Rook's furtive glances at Max, to which Max seemed entirely impervious. He saw the teasing, easy manner in which Max treated his wife; the way he stroked her dewy-looking skin with distracted appreciation, like a man who petted the silky coat of his favorite dog.

He noticed Genny practically glowed every time she looked up at Max. The initial roar of jealousy that resounded in Sean's skull eventually faded to a rumble. He realized that she looked at Max like a proud daughter might gaze at a father. He thought of what she'd said earlier about her dad—*I blame the steel industry, at least partially, for the fact that he was dead at the age of fifty-three.*

It looked as if Genevieve Sauren had married a father figure as much as she had a life partner. It was a cold sort of comfort, but Sean knew beggars couldn't be choosers.

Genevieve obviously worshipped her husband. Sean wondered just how much she actually knew about Max.

Not much, he thought as he studied her radiant smile when Max teased her. He was a little surprised to realize he had no desire to ever see her disillusioned in regard to her husband . . . to see Genevieve Bujold disillusioned *period.*

If he hadn't known for certain she was serious trouble to him when he first laid eyes on her, Sean knew it for a fact when he made that realization.

CHAPTER **THREE**

For a moment, Genevieve thought she was dreaming when she awoke to see Sean Kennedy sleeping in the chair across the room.

She lay curled beneath the blanket watching his motionless form for several minutes, afraid to move because she didn't want to disturb the peaceful moment. Warmth and drowsiness gave her a reprieve from her troublesome thoughts. She looked her fill while Sean was unaware of her hungry gaze.

He'd changed clothes since last night, she realized. Had he ever gone to bed? His long legs were bent at the knee. His jeans didn't cling to him tightly, but they managed to outline his strong thighs and narrow hips to perfection.

Max used to grouse about the fact that Sean occasionally wore jeans to work, saying it lowered the standards for professionalism among the employees. Max had stopped complaining after observing the effect of Sean's easygoing management style combined with a work ethic that stepped up the performance of every employee at Sauren. Sean may be exacting, but he demanded more from himself than anyone. Everyone from the secretaries to Max's top operative gave Sean not only their respect, but their genuine affection.

His wasn't a classically handsome face, but it was full of character. Someone had broken his nose once in a childhood scrap. His mother hadn't had a job at the time, or any insurance, so it'd never healed properly. The slight crook in it only added to his stark, masculine appeal.

His mouth was perfection, the lips firm, their shape hinting at his stubborn, determined nature as much as his innate sensuality.

When he smiled, he could make a female's heart skip two beats.

She snuggled farther into the soft blanket as if to hide her small grin from herself. He'd once said something similar about the way her smile affected him, but Sean was a born flirt. Never mind the somber, serious façade he usually showed people.

Her gaze skimmed across a heather gray mock turtleneck that emphasized a powerful chest and wide shoulders. His reserved persona was what Sean typically presented to the public at large, but she'd witnessed his fierce, volatile nature on a few occasions. It'd both alarmed and strangely thrilled her when she'd caught that glimpse of his personality in the past.

Now it frightened her.

She recalled one occasion.

They'd attended several Cubs games together the summer and fall before Max had died. One hot September day, a fan sitting behind them at Wrigley Field had become loud and disorderly as he argued with his female companion. Everyone in the vicinity grew uncomfortable as their argument escalated both in volume and vulgarity. At one point, Sean had turned around and politely asked if they could take their disagreement elsewhere, but had received a rude gesture and instructions to *fuck off* for his efforts.

When the man threw his beer in his female companion's face,

some of it splashed onto Genevieve's hair and soaked her shoulder. But that wasn't enough for the irate fan. As his girlfriend cursed and threatened him, he'd lunged for *her* beer, obviously intent on serving it to her in the same manner that he had his own.

Sean grabbed the bully's wrist lightning quick, halting him. The man dropped the cup and quickly transferred his ire to Sean, snarling and cursing and whipping his fist free from Sean's hold, prepared to strike. Sean stood and spun.

The next thing Genevieve knew, the man was sprawled back in the seats, squalling, blood pouring from his nose and reddening his face and shirt with alarming speed.

It'd been hard for her to stop Sean from going after the man to give him more. She'd grabbed his arm and felt his muscles straining, tight and hard. For a few seconds, her voice hadn't seemed to penetrate his thick anger. Finally he'd blinked and glanced over at her.

His gaze had been so cold; it'd been as if he'd never laid eyes on her in his life.

She'd managed to get him to leave the crowded ball game. The guy he'd hit had been a drunk bully, but Genevieve was worried Sean might get arrested if they stayed.

It'd all happened so fast, Genevieve later had trouble recalling the exact sequence of events. What she did perfectly recall was the cold, blazing fury in Sean's face. She'd never seen him look that way. It was bizarre to consider this other side of his character—this shadow side—that she'd never before caught a hint of until that moment.

The chill in the penthouse penetrated the snug blanket. Her stomach growled. How long had she slept, anyway?

She blinked, breaking her intense study of Sean, and glanced out the windows. No wonder it'd seemed so dim in the living room. The storm had started. The thick, falling snow and low clouds acted like a curtain. For a few seconds, she watched the motion of the fat snowflakes. Their vertical trajectory and rapid fall indicated just how dense the flakes were with moisture.

She felt like she was being slowly buried in the onslaught of snow . . . imprisoned here with Sean. The realization of how pleasant the fantasy made her feel caused her to spring up from the couch, jarring her out of her reveries.

Even though Sean couldn't have seen her abrupt movement, he moved restlessly in his sleep and shivered. She lifted the blanket she'd been using and draped it over his long, bent legs and torso, careful not to wake him. She flipped on the gas fireplace, hoping it would warm him.

She hesitated for a moment by the arm of his chair before she turned away.

She grabbed her cell phone and headed toward the kitchen. Genevieve hoped her Bujold Designs manager, Marilyn Marks, hadn't tried to drive downtown from Skokie to open the store. When they'd spoken last evening before Marilyn left, Genevieve had warned her about the predicted snowstorm and made her promise not to come in if conditions got too bad.

From the looks of things outside the penthouse window, Bujold Designs would likely remain closed this Saturday along with hundreds of other businesses in the city. But Genevieve had no other choice but to go out into the storm.

Staying here with Sean just wasn't an option.

Thinking of Sean made her mind turn guiltily to Jeff. It was ridiculous to feel guilty about anything, of course. Jeff and she hadn't even slept together yet. It'd been a very loose, casual dating relationship.

Still, she felt guilty enough that she tried to call him. Relief swept through her when he didn't pick up. She set down her cell phone on the kitchen counter after she'd left a brief message, and glanced around.

She needed sustenance before she wandered out into the storm. Sean could sleep a bit longer while she ate, showered, and dressed. She'd wake him before she left so that he could unsecure the door. She'd have to call her mother and let her know she was going to stay with her and her aunt over the weekend.

Where the hell was she going to stay after that? For a few seconds the image of the flames leaping from the dark outline of the mansard roof of the mansion sprung into her mind's eye. Sean must have been right. She must have been in shock last night. Because even though she'd kept telling herself she *must* be upset, she'd felt entirely detached as she'd stood there watching her house burn.

Watching *Max's* house burn.

It'd been like watching a neighbor's house go up in flames. She'd been more worried about Jim than anything.

When had it happened, this feeling of disconnection with that lovely, rambling house? Had she *ever* felt she belonged there? She felt more at home in her Oak Street boutique and design studio than she had in the mansion.

Strange to think she'd hardly considered the fact that she was homeless the entire time she'd watched Sean sleeping.

She was going to have to decide where to live. But first things first. Food and caffeine were required.

And quickly.

A few minutes later she'd done a quick survey of what Sean had available in the kitchen and started the coffee. As for food, there wasn't much, but she did find some bagels in a bakery box in the refrigerator along with a few packages of cream cheese. There were apples in the crisper. When she pulled out a bagel, however, she discovered it was as hard as a hockey puck. She was debating whether or not the bagel would be edible if she toasted it when a phone rang.

Genevieve started in surprise. It wasn't her ringtone. In fact, it sounded like a residential phone. She hadn't realized the penthouse even *had* a phone. No one had ever stayed here long enough to have a line installed. Apparently Sean had changed that, she thought as she picked up the receiver tucked behind a phone book on the kitchen counter.

"Hello?"

"Oh . . . hello. May I speak with Sean, please?" a woman asked.

Genevieve imagined the blonde who'd worn the handcuffs last night. "He's sleeping right now. May I leave a message?"

"No, that's all right. This is his assistant, Carol. I'll just try to reach him later. He must have had a late night, huh?" Carol asked dryly.

"Carol? Carol Fallia?"

"Yes, who's this?"

Genevieve smiled as she clutched the phone to her ear and walked to the corner of the kitchen farthest from Sean. She didn't want to wake him, if she could avoid it.

"So . . . you got a promotion? The last time I knew, you were our receptionist."

There was a long pause. "Genevieve? Genevieve Bujold? Is that you?"

"Yes."

"Well, what in the world . . . ? How *are* you?"

Genevieve laughed. "I've been better, but I'm surviving. How about you? And how are those kids? God, Blake has got to be in high school by now, right?"

"Yes, a sophomore, can you believe it? And what a heartbreaker. Every inch his father—well, before Jamie gained forty pounds and lost his hair, anyway. That's just like you to remember his name, Genevieve. What are you doing at the penthouse? We haven't heard from you since . . ."

"Since Max died," Genevieve finished when Carol's voice faded off. A silence ensued. Max's employees—and most Chicagoans, for that matter—knew Genevieve had been the primary suspect in Max's murder investigation for a period of time. There had never been sufficient evidence to prosecute her. The murder weapon had never even been found, and a motive could never be established.

There was no *obvious* motive that could be established. But none of that made the awkwardness any easier when Genevieve unexpectedly encountered one of Max's old acquaintances.

"Sol Green, my attorney, handles of all the Sauren-Kennedy business affairs for me," Genevieve explained.

"Right," Carol agreed, sounding relieved that the tense moment had passed. "Sean told me about you being a silent partner. I can understand how you wouldn't want to be reminded of Max all the time, like you would be if you took a larger part in the company's affairs."

"I thought it was for the best. Hearing your voice makes me feel guilty though . . . for not maintaining friendships, even if I wasn't going to be involved in the business."

"Well, it's not like you haven't had your reasons! I read that article they did on you in *Chicago* magazine last month. You've been busy. Your little boutique firm has really grown, hasn't it? The article said your designs are being sold all over the world. I read that Michelle Obama ordered almost everything in your spring line! What's she *like*?" Carol asked excitedly.

"As nice and down to earth as your best girlfriend."

"And what about—oh, listen to me, gossiping away when there are more important things to discuss. Like what you're doing up at the penthouse, for instance?"

Genevieve considered providing a vague explanation, not really feeling up to rehashing the events of the fire. But then she thought of what she'd said about feeling guilty about not maintaining friendships. It'd been selfish of her. So she explained to an increasingly alarmed Carol about the destruction of the Lake Forest mansion and answered all her questions.

"I can't believe it. Such a gorgeous home. I remember several lovely parties that you and Max hosted at that house. And to think of it . . . ruined," Carol murmured. She sounded dazed. After a pause, she asked, "Does Sean know about all this? I'm only asking because . . . well . . . he'd want to. Know, I mean."

"Yes, he knows."

"You said Sean was sleeping. So . . . he's there?"

"Yes," Genevieve said, trying to sound matter-of-fact; as if it were the most natural thing in the world for her to have spent the night in the penthouse with Sean. She found a cup in the cabinet and poured freshly brewed coffee into it. The rich aroma seemed to brace her. "He was here when I arrived last night. He said he's been staying here while he works overtime on some project. I know he said he was expecting you, but surely you're not going to try to come in, given the weather."

There was a short pause. "I'm not sure I know what—"

"Is that Carol?"

Genevieve looked over her shoulder to see Sean standing in the entryway of the kitchen.

"Yes," she replied, a little knocked off balance by the unexpected sight of his big, male body in the small galley kitchen. His dark blond hair looked sexily sleep-tousled but his blue eyes were sharp and alert. He came into the kitchen and held out his hand.

"Can I talk to her for a second? I want to tell her not to come into the office like we'd planned. The weather's gawd-awful."

"Carol? Sean wants to speak with you. It was nice hearing from you. I promise not to be such a stranger this time around. I'll give you a call in a couple weeks after I find a place to live. Maybe we can get together for lunch sometime?"

"Oh, I'd love that. I still can't believe it, about the house. How awful for you," Carol sympathized.

"I'll be fine. Jim and I are safe, and that's the most important thing. As for the house—well, that's what insurance is for, I guess. All right then. Here's Sean. Good-bye."

She added powdered creamer to her coffee and listened to Sean talk while she stirred, glancing cautiously at his profile every few seconds.

"I'm sorry. I meant to call you earlier, but I fell asleep," he said into the receiver. "Yeah, well, don't worry about any of that now. No one should go out in this weather, anyway."

A long pause ensued while Carol spoke. Genevieve noticed that Sean seemed to be making a point of not looking at her.

"The Skyway, too, huh?" Sean asked. "Well, it's only gonna get worse. They say it'll be coming down like crazy all weekend. We might get three or four feet of snow before Sunday night, and the temperature is supposed to drop. The wind is going to pick up as well. I'll be giving everyone a call if they say conditions are too bad on Monday to come into the office. Don't worry about it. Believe it or not, I used to make my share of deadlines without an assistant. I'm *not* saying I don't need you, darling," he scolded after a pause, his handsome mouth curving in amusement. He suddenly glanced over at Genevieve and caught her staring. She ducked her head and took a sip of coffee. "Yeah, we both know I'd be stumbling around blind without you. Okay. You, too."

He hung up the phone. Genevieve handed him a coffee cup and a spoon and slid the sugar bowl and creamer along the countertop. She remembered how he took it: strong and sweet—Sean's version of what he called *regulah* coffee. He murmured a "thanks."

A tendril of burnished hair had curled at his nape, she noticed, as he bent his head to pour his coffee. She resisted an urge to straighten it with her fingers . . . to feel the texture of soft, thick waves.

This kitchen was too small.

"I'm going to shower and dress," she said briskly. She picked up her coffee and started to leave.

"You remember Carol lives in Hammond?" he asked in an almost offhand manner as he prepared his coffee. She came up short and turned. He finished stirring his coffee and faced her, leaning against the counter. Genevieve noticed the ledge hit him at the top of his thighs, just below the curve of his taut ass. She yanked her gaze from the enticing sight.

"Yes, I remember." She leaned against the counter as well, trying to be as nonchalant and comfortable as Sean appeared to be.

"She just told me they've closed both I-94 and the Skyway between here and Indiana. If you were thinking about staying at your mom's, think again. We've already gotten a ton of snow, and by all accounts, this storm has barely started."

She studied the tiny clumps of creamer swirling around in her coffee. "There's always a hotel, I guess."

"You know I'm not going to let you check into a hotel. This place is yours to stay in for as long you need it. Hell, you can take up permanent residence here, for all I care."

She glanced up, moved by the earnestness of his tone. It wasn't *his* fault her house had burned down, after all. It wasn't *his* fault she'd watched him having sex with another woman.

"I'm sorry about all this," she began. "I know it's an inconvenience for you. And about last night, I'm sorry I—"

He straightened from the counter and came toward her. "You don't have to apologize for any of it. Just consider it an unfortunate turn of events. Let's just get things settled as far as the house and finding you a new place. *Forget* about last night."

Forget about it? She wished she could. She sensed his almost palpable concern. God, she must look like a wreck for him to be looking at her like he was. She touched her hair self-consciously, recalling she'd gone to bed with it damp. It probably looked wild—

"Just do me a favor, okay?" Sean asked, interrupting her stupid ruminations about how she looked to him.

"What?" He came closer yet. He leaned his hip against the counter, the fly of his jeans lightly brushing her hip.

"Let me stay here for the next few nights, as well."

She could see the thousands of cobalt, sapphire, and steel blue dots of pigment that colored his iris like a pointillist painting. His lashes were long enough to make a female jealous. His spicy, subtle male scent filtered into her nose. Sean always smelled so damn good. Just his scent used to make her wet, like her brain recognized him on some deep level where words and logic couldn't penetrate.

The surge of heat between her thighs told her nothing had changed.

"I'll think about it," she told him gruffly before she hurried out of the kitchen.

"Wait, Genny."

Against her better judgment, she paused again on the threshold. This time, she kept her back to him, resisting the urge to look her fill of him . . . to touch him. She knew it was unwise, but the fact of the matter was, Sean was a temptation unlike anything she'd ever known in her life.

And the past three years had been so cold.

So empty.

"They finished their preliminary report on what started the fire. I spoke with the fire chief this morning up in Lake Forest."

"You did?" she asked, turning in surprise. "I didn't realize you'd left."

He nodded as he folded his arms beneath his chest. "McGruder said the fire was started by faulty wiring in the wall between the garage and kitchen. That house was built over fifty years ago. Sometimes those ol' power boards and wiring can't support some of the modern energy demands made on them."

"But why now?" Genevieve asked. "What happened that was so different last night?"

He shrugged. "It was a weak point in the house. It was bound to start a fire at some point. We had that cold snap last week. Must'a reached its limit after all this time. I'm just glad you and Jim weren't asleep in the house when it did."

"Jim will be so relieved it wasn't anything he did," she murmured.

"I brought a copy of McGruder's report for your insurance claim. Have you called your agent yet?"

"Yes, I called her last night. Thank you for getting the report, Sean. Everything is going to halt to a standstill with this snowstorm, so it's helpful to have the report in hand."

"If you give me your agent's card, I'll fax the report downstairs."

Genevieve nodded and set down her coffee. He came and stood at the threshold of the kitchen while she stepped into the foyer and dug in her purse for her insurance agent's card. She wasn't used to having someone do an unwelcome task for her when she was tired or overwhelmed. It felt nicer than she'd expected.

Too nice.

She handed him the card and moved past him to grab her coffee, all the while hyperaware of how close Sean stood.

"Genny?"

She glanced up to meet his eyes. He hesitated.

"I'll fax the report, and then go around the corner while you're in the shower and get us something to eat."

"Okay," she said. She got the distinct impression that wasn't what Sean had been planning to say when he'd said her name.

"And Genny? Just . . . just think about what I said. About me staying for a couple nights."

"Sean, I want you to know that I'm seeing someone."

Her cheeks flushed with heat when she realized what she'd just said. It'd suddenly felt imperative that she put up some kind of boundary between them—no matter how flimsy that boundary was.

His expression flattened. "Seriously?"

"Of course I'm serious."

"No . . . I mean are you serious about this guy?"

Genevieve pretended to consider. "I don't know. We haven't been seeing each other for that long. I like him, though. Are you serious? About that woman . . . from last night?"

His brows knitted together in puzzlement.

"What? No . . . *no*, that was just a . . . a . . . you know." He shut his eyelids briefly when he noticed the way she examined him. "Christ, Genny. I can't even remember her last name. I just met her at the bar when I took a break from work and went to get something to eat over at McClinty's."

Genevieve stared down at the floor. She'd never done the things that Sean was doing with that woman last night in her entire life, let alone done them with someone she'd only known for a few hours. Sean and she were worlds apart when it came to sex. Bitterness seemed to rise in her throat until it burned her vocal cords like acid.

"I can't say that I *do* know, Sean. You're the one who regularly has casual affairs, not me." She started when he put his hand on her jaw. He tilted her face up to meet his gaze. His manner seemed urgent.

"Genny . . . that woman . . . on the night that Max was killed. It *wasn't* what you're thinking. You never let me explain to you."

Genevieve blinked. She was stunned. How had he known her thoughts had gone to Ava Linley—Sean's alibi for Max's murder?

On a purely practical basis, Sean'd had more to gain by Max's death than anyone—even Genevieve. Max and she had a prenuptial agreement, which had provided well for Genevieve, but she wasn't designated as the controlling shareholder of his lucrative intel company in the event of his death. Genevieve held the minority interest. It'd been in Sean's hiring contract that in the case of Max's retirement or death, *Sean* would be offered first rights on purchasing the majority interest in Sauren Solutions Inc. Sean had done precisely that after Max's death. He'd proceeded to make the intel firm nearly four times as valuable as it had been under Max.

The only reason the police hadn't focused on Sean as a potential suspect was the simple fact that he'd possessed a hard and fast alibi for the time period in which Max had been shot.

Sean'd been with another woman on that night.

Genevieve knew Sean had gotten the woman to lie for him. The fact that he *really* hadn't been with Ava Linley didn't comfort Genevieve in the least. Women acted a little nuts when it came to Sean—how well she knew. That woman had been one of his besotted lovers. She wouldn't have blinked an eye about lying for him. Whether Ava'd actually slept with Sean on the night Max died or not wasn't the point.

Sean'd had another lover when he'd had sex with her on New Year's Eve three years ago. He'd seen Ava shortly afterward. Just thinking about it made Genevieve's stomach roil.

She straightened her spine. "Your love life is none of my business, Sean."

Her eyes flew up to meet his when he made a bitter noise of disgust. "You're the only person on this planet whose business it *is*, if only you'd take an interest."

His words and the profound frustration in his expression

combined to freeze her lungs in her chest. She gazed at him in dawning wonder.

"It's *true* that Ava and I had been casually involved before that New Year's Eve. But I wasn't intimate with her on the night of Max's murder, Genny. Or *any* night after that New Year's Eve. That's a *fact*. I wouldn't have. Not after what happened with us on that night . . . not that soon. *Not* before it came crashing down on me that you were locking me out of your life."

Her heartbeat started to pound like a throbbing siren in her ears in the taut silence that followed.

"I may have my faults, but I'm not *that* callous." His fingertips brushed her cheek. "Do you believe me?"

She searched his expression long and hard. Maybe she was a fool, but she'd never known Sean to mislead her purposely.

She nodded her head. He closed his eyes briefly, obviously relieved.

"Everyone's different about how they behave in a casual relationship," he murmured a few seconds later. He studied her face just as intently as she'd been examining his. "All I want to know is whether or not you think of this guy you're dating as something serious or not."

She found it difficult to lie to him while she was staring into his lasering eyes. She always had.

"*He's* serious. I'm not so sure that I am."

"*Good.*" He noticed her raised eyebrows. "Uncertainty is a damned sight better than nothing, from where I'm standing."

For several seconds neither of them spoke. His hand seemed to emanate heat into her skin.

She nodded her head once, turned and fled.

It frightened her a little, to think of how much power he held over her. She'd known by some instinct that Sean'd been asking her to think about more than whether or not he could be her roommate in the penthouse for a few days. She'd *known* that, but she'd agreed to consider it anyway.

Stupid. Idiotic.

But a heavy sensation pressed on her chest, constricting her breath, when she thought of walking away from Sean one more time. He'd shot her husband in a fit of rage. He'd never been punished for it, and never would be, if Genevieve could help it. She was still shocked at Max's betrayal.

But that didn't mean he'd deserved to die for his machinations.

She'd kept her silence about what she knew, but just because she'd do anything to protect Sean didn't mean she condoned murder.

What else would you be doing if you ran into Sean's arms? a brutally honest voice called out in her brain. Another thought joined it, this one just as upsetting.

You're as much to blame. You might not have pulled the trigger, but you didn't do enough to stop the events that led up to it.

She shut the bathroom door and searched her reflection in the vanity. What sort of a person was she, to want to be with a man who put cuffs on a woman during sex, a man whose eyes blazed with love for her, but who had also consented to share her with another man in bed?

Sean'd never said the words, after all . . . never once said he loved her. She might have been deluding herself.

Even though Sean and she had never so much as kissed before that New Year's Eve, their attraction toward each other had grown so thick it seemed to weight the air around them. Sometimes she'd been surprised that other people seemed so oblivious to the prickly, charged atmosphere whenever she and Sean were together.

Even toward the end, when neither of them bothered to hide what was in their hearts even though they never spoke the words, Genevieve suspected that Sean wasn't celibate. Women gravitated to him like metal filings to a powerful magnet. She recognized the gleam of fascination and lust in many a female's eyes whenever Sean was near. His rugged good looks, unfailing manners, soft drawl, quick smile, and a somberness many mistook for shyness, all combined to create a powerful aphrodisiac.

Was she really so self-centered as to believe that if New Year's Eve hadn't happened and Max hadn't been murdered that Sean would eventually have declared himself exclusively for her? Sean'd just implied that was the case, there in the kitchen. But Sean was a man who could have just about any woman he chose on any given night.

Genevieve *wanted* to believe him, but perhaps it was her naïveté at work. She'd married too young and too impulsively, mistaking security and respect for love. She'd never really mastered the sophistications and subtleties of the adult world of dating and mating.

But if Sean didn't care about her in the way she suspected, would he have become so angry with Max? Furious enough to kill?

She exhaled shakily and went to turn on the shower.

Did any of the circular logic that never got her anywhere even *matter* now? She'd seen Sean again, heard his voice, inhaled his scent . . . experienced his touch. And it suddenly felt like an utter impossibility to keep up the struggle. She was so tired, her spirit worn so thin.

Damn Sean for awakening this hunger inside her once again.

CHAPTER **FOUR**

She paused upon leaving the hallway after she'd showered and dressed, her gaze drawn to the falling snow outside the windows. The gas fireplace had chased off the chill. Sean had turned on a lamp on an end table. It cast the living room in an inviting glow. She approached the floor-to-ceiling windows and searched futilely for the shadows of spires and towers that she knew were just yards away, but the storm prevailed.

The snow fell thick and silent. The city, the millions of people, the webwork of their lives—all of it seemed so far away from her.

She turned at the sound of the front door banging against the jam. Sean entered, his wavy hair dampened from melted snow, his arms stretched around three paper bags. She met him and removed the cardboard carton he held precariously in one hand.

"Where'd you get all this stuff?" she asked bemusedly, walking ahead of him as he herded her into the kitchen. He deposited the fat bags on the counter. Genevieve set down the carton with two coffees in it and peered inside a sack. She drew out a plastic bag of homemade pasta.

"There's an Italian market and deli around the corner. Thought I'd better stock up on some supplies. They're predicting blizzard conditions later. Most of the Loop will shut down."

"You don't think you can survive off rock-hard bagels and whiskey from the bar, huh?" she asked wryly, making a point of not including herself in the scenario. She hadn't officially decided to stay here, after all. Although, considering the conditions outside, she really had no idea where else she could go. There was always a hotel, but—

"*Be prepared*. That's my motto," Sean said as he removed his damp peacoat in the foyer. Genevieve tensed when she saw the leather gun holster he wore, but then he took it off and hooked the strap beneath his coat.

He attacked his wet boots next, moving with a brisk jauntiness, as if he'd been infused with energy. She considered saying something about not being certain yet about where she'd spend the next few days.

But he seemed so *happy*. She found she didn't have the heart at the moment for bringing up such a tense subject.

"You were never a Boy Scout, *boy*," she murmured humorously instead as she removed a small white bag and appreciatively sniffed at the rich ground coffee inside. She glanced into the foyer and saw Sean had paused in the process of removing his black leather lace-up boots. He smiled at her, the effect as potent and warming to Genevieve as swallowing a slug of premium brandy.

"Nah, but it was even more of a crucial motto to live by where I grew up," he teased as he kicked off his boot. He turned and started keying in the code to the alarm system. She watched him over his shoulder, her hand frozen in the process of removing a round loaf of seeded Italian bread.

"Sean, is that really necessary?"

He shrugged before he hit the final button and the mechanism beeped softly.

"I'm paranoid. It's one of the hazards of the profession. *Lawd*, it's coming down out there," he said cheerfully as he entered the kitchen. He noticed her amused expression. "What? Is there some law I'm not aware of that says I have to be in a bad mood because of a snowstorm?" He reached into a sack and withdrew a bottle. "We've got wine. We've got coffee. We've got Salvatore's good olive relish so I can make you some muffuletta. Mmm, mmm. *Good* food," he enthused as he withdrew a small paper bag and handed it to her. "Look what they had at the market, girl. That'll cheer you up. I won't say a word if you eat every one of 'em while you're all snuggled up out there on the couch, either."

Genevieve paused in the process of withdrawing some romaine lettuce. Her eyes leapt up to meet Sean's. He wore a crooked grin as he watched her, his blue eyes lambent and warm. She hastily took the bag of gourmet bing cherry chocolates and set it on the counter, averting her gaze.

She didn't know what to say. He knew they were her favorite treat, knew she craved them whenever she was a little blue. She'd once told him how she occasionally bought the treats and ate a whole bag of them while she read a trashy novel in bed. She recalled how he'd been fascinated by her revelation of that small intimacy.

The fact that he'd remembered—the repetition of that benign, personal secret in his husky voice—made her lose her already unsteady emotional footing. It had struck her as sweet. Precise. Intensely sexy.

So *Sean*-like.

Genevieve couldn't tell if Sean knew he'd struck a chord deep inside her or thought he'd erred somehow, but he didn't say anything else as they unloaded the remaining groceries, both of them careful not to run into each other or make contact in the small kitchen.

Heat rose in Genevieve's cheeks. Tension grew in her muscles.

She exhaled in relief when she finally put away the last item—a plastic bag of Italian tomatoes. She hurried into the living room, sighing in disappointment when she realized that thanks to the fireplace, it was no cooler there than the kitchen.

The frigid windowpane felt wonderful pressed to her flaming cheek. She saw him approach in the glass, his reflection cast from the golden glow of the lamp onto the gray gloom of the stormy day. Her mind shouted out a last desperate warning to flee.

But there was nowhere else to go.

She couldn't run from herself. Her desire followed her wherever she went, how well she knew.

She closed her eyes, blocking out the faded reflection of his sober, concerned face when he wrapped his hands on her upper arms and massaged the muscles through her sweater.

"What are you always runnin' from?" he murmured softly.

"You know." Suppressed emotion caused her chest to spasm when he pressed his mouth to her jaw. She felt his body ghosting hers from behind.

"I know you better than you know yourself, girl. You've got nothing to be ashamed of. And while you're here with me, you don't have to do anything you don't want to do," he rumbled near her ear. She shivered and he drew her into his arms . . . softly, like he thought she might break.

"Genny."

She lifted her head slowly, letting it fall back on his chest. If only she was as comfortable—as at home—with her desires as Sean. She opened her eyelids. Meeting his gaze through the hazy reflection in the window somehow seemed more manageable than looking at Sean himself at that moment.

"Why didn't you let me near you? Why didn't you ever let me say I was sorry?" he asked.

Dread swelled in her chest. "For what?" she rasped.

He turned her gently. His blue eyes looked aflame. "You'll never know how much I regretted it."

"Don't. *Don't* say anything else."

The plea had popped out of her throat. Her heart hammered out a wild warning. Another convulsion seized her rib cage and he pushed her cheek to his chest while she shook in a paroxysm of emotion. He pressed his mouth to the top of her head.

"You were far too precious to be treated like that. I wouldn't have wished that for you, Genny. Not for us. And it was the first time I'd touched you. Gawd, girl, I'm *so* sorry. I just wanted you so much. It'd been so damn hard not to have you . . ."

She'd clenched her eyes closed when he'd started speaking, as if to shut out the truth, but she opened them now slowly.

It hadn't been the confession she'd expected.

She lifted her head off his chest. His face looked rigid with strain.

"You said I didn't have to do anything I didn't want to do. Well, I don't want to talk about that night, Sean. I don't."

"We've got to talk about it *sometime*."

She took a deep, steadying breath. "Do you want to stay here with me for the next couple nights?"

His mouth fell open. "You *know* I do, but—"

"Then don't plan on talking about what happened on that night, not about Max . . . *any* of it." She met his incredulous stare without flinching. "I *mean* it, Sean. The minute you say a word about it, I'm leaving. Those are my terms. Take it or leave it," she said sternly.

"All right."

She blinked, a little surprised by his quick concession.

"Well . . . all right, then," she muttered dubiously. Her eyebrows shot up when he gathered her closer in his arms. Genevieve suddenly became aware that she was pressed tightly against the length of a long, hard male body. Sean kissed her temple. His lips felt warm and firm next to her tingling skin.

"What d'ya want to do now that that's all decided, girl?" he asked gruffly near her ear.

He still ached a little, but Sean forced a smile when he saw Genny's dazed expression. He'd been trying to tease her out of their somber mood, desperate to do anything that would remove that haunted expression in her storm-cloud eyes.

Sure, he'd been teasing, but if she'd said she wanted to begin a sex marathon then and there that only would have ended when he had to be hospitalized for dehydration, Sean would have been happy to comply.

And all too ready, he thought wryly when he realized he'd grown stone-hard as he held Genny in his arms. Never mind that she'd looked fragile enough to shatter just moments before. Sean knew from personal experience that he became nothing better than a beast when he inhaled the fragrance of Genny's clean hair or caught the sweet, womanly scent at her neck. Genny'd always made him hyperaware of the drastic contrast between his need to be tender, to cherish, and a primal mandate to make her completely his own.

He knew for certain he wasn't a beast though, because animals weren't capable of regretting their hunger.

He reluctantly backed away from her, releasing her from his embrace.

"Don't . . . don't you have to go down to the office?" she asked when several feet separated them. She touched her cheek distractedly and gazed at her wet fingertips, her brow wrinkled perplexedly.

Poor girl. She hadn't realized she'd been crying.

"I need something to eat first." He stretched. What started as an affected yawn turned real. "Then maybe a little nap. I never really slept last night."

His words seemed to make her awkwardness and confusion evaporate. "I'll just heat up the coffee you brought and fix us something for breakfast, then."

He stayed in the living room when she passed him, sensing she needed some time to herself. He wasn't exactly thrilled at the prospect of allowing her the opportunity to rebuild her defenses, but what choice did he have? None, if he didn't want to hurt her more.

Just like he hadn't had any choice in agreeing not to talk about the night Max, Genny, and he had spent here together.

Seeing her like this—so fragile and sad—made him feel like pulverizing whatever it was that upset her. Too bad *he* was the no-good trash who was responsible for her distress.

A familiar bitterness had seized his gut when she'd said earlier that she was involved with another man. First Max, now some other asshole was claiming what nature had clearly decreed was *his*.

What the hell? Was he cursed or something? For most people, actually finding a mate who perfectly suited them was an unattainable fantasy. Sean had been lucky enough to find Genny, but fate always seemed to dangle her just out of his desperate reach.

'Course it hadn't been *fate* that had alienated Genny on that New Year's Eve. No, *Sean* had done that in spades.

He collapsed onto the couch and dug his fingertips into his eye sockets. His eyelids burned with fatigue.

You can't go back in time and change it all. Childish to wish it, so better just stop it right now.

Genny might have responded like a man's fantasy come to life that New Year's Eve in bed, but Sean knew as well as anyone there had been an unhealthy franticness to her desire; that she'd behaved in a manner that wasn't consistent with her beliefs and values.

He knew it, because it'd been the same for him. Not because he'd broken a personal code—not in the general sense. He'd enjoyed a couple of ménage à trois in his wild, hell-bent youth and the radar on his moral consciousness hadn't even blipped.

But because it'd been Genny—because it'd been *them*—yeah. It'd been a sacrilege of sorts.

She'd been another man's wife and he'd never so much as kissed her. But somehow, it hadn't been Max who had allowed Sean to make love to his wife that night. It'd been *Sean* who had permitted another man to touch her in his presence.

Sean had seen her hesitation on that night, but he'd sensed her inner fires even more. He'd made a conscious choice to quiet her uncertainty by feeding the flames until all doubts were burned to dust.

He hadn't been satisfied until he'd created a fever of lust in her. He'd treated her like she was the most experienced, voracious female he'd ever bedded, forced her to submit again and again to the desire that raged between them like an unquenchable inferno.

And every time he saw a trace of the uncertainty in Genny's eyes, he'd coaxed the flame higher yet again, never content until her ravaged, reddened lips shaped a plea for more.

Sean hated himself for that. It'd been his own doubts he'd seen mirrored in Genny's soulful eyes. But he'd let his baser instincts rule him instead. And he'd paid for it.

Genny had even more.

Max had paid for his machinations with his life, but Sean had a hard time feeling sorry for him.

Max Sauren . . . whose clever, cool gaze had seen so much.

Max.

The man who was never truly content unless he held a trump card over everyone that was close to him.

Sean should have suspected that Max had been up to something. He'd come to understand Max's obsessive need to collect secrets. Max was fond of keeping the more crucial ones—his greatest treasures—in a leather-bound, high-security carbon attaché case he'd been given upon retiring from the CIA.

Max used to be uncommonly proud of that particular gift.

He'd been told by the director of the CIA that the attaché case was a replica of the "football," the high-security, bulletproof case that followed the president of the United States everywhere he went. The president's contained the codes for a nuclear missile launch. Max's secrets may not have been crucial to every living creature on the planet, but they were explosive enough when it came to certain individuals.

Sean'd been so preoccupied by his feelings for Genny that he'd been blindsided by what Max had pulled on that New Year's Eve. He'd been caught in the big cat's trap, and he'd unintentionally dragged Genny into it with him.

He knew Max had planned to use the videotape he'd secretly made of them making love that night to blackmail him. What Sean didn't know was whether Max had planned to use it to control his wife, as well.

Had Max shown Genny that recording? If Max had, it certainly would explain the disquietude and anxiety he saw in Genny's eyes sometimes when Sean looked at her.

The question of what Max had said or done to Genny in those days following that New Year's Eve haunted him. He may have his doubts about the evidence Albert Rook had shown him after Max was killed, but Sean dreaded the idea of questioning Genny about it.

And if Max *had* shown Genny the videotape?

Well . . . Sean figured he might have killed Max for less.

CHAPTER **FIVE**

The pleasant aroma of eggs, toast, and coffee, the warmth from the fire and encroaching drowsiness caused Sean to abandon his morbid thoughts for more practical matters.

He drifted off.

His stomach growled, rousing him just minutes later. He cracked open his eyelids and saw a vision.

Genny walked toward him wearing a soft-looking light blue sweater and tight jeans that showed off coltish long legs and the enticing curve of sashaying, feminine hips. He reluctantly removed his heavy-lidded gaze from the juncture of her shapely thighs and looked upward.

And to top off this unearthly vision of loveliness?

She carried a plate with an egg, cheese, and ham sandwich and a steaming cup of coffee in her hands.

"Angel of mercy," he murmured.

"Where your stomach is concerned, anyway," she replied dryly before she set the food on the coffee table in front of him.

He caught her hand and pulled her down in his lap when she

tried to walk away. A little yelp of surprise popped out of her throat when her ass thumped down on his thighs. He wrapped his arms around her ribs and pressed his mouth to her throat, as if to soothe those jostled vocal cords. He felt the tension in her sleek, soft body, but he kept on holding her anyway.

Selfish. Kids who never had anything always were.

It never struck him that what he said next was in direct opposition to his thoughts, despite the fact that he'd never been more honest in his life.

"I'd do anything to make things right for you, girl."

She went still in his arms. He held his breath when he felt her hand move. Her fingers stroked the hair at his nape, furtively at first. A shiver of pleasure rippled up his spine when a fingernail scraped his scalp.

"Just don't . . . don't *fret* about it anymore. Okay, Sean?" He pursed his lips against her skin, feeling her earnest plea vibrate from her flesh to his.

"I won't if you won't."

Her fingers stopped moving in his hair when she recognized the hint of a dare in his tone.

He twisted his face, rubbing his whiskers into her neck. She jumped in his lap. Her initial shriek of alarm segued into hysterical laughter. He played her ribs with his wriggling fingers. Her squirming ass in his lap consisted of the sweetest kind of agony. Her loose hair swished around him as she giggled and struggled, perfuming the air with its clean, fruity scent.

Sean released her after their little tickle and tussle match when he realized his intentions were turning to things besides getting Genny to relax at his touch. He planned on touching her a lot in the next few days, and the sooner she acclimated to that fact, the better.

She scrambled out of his lap and stood unsteadily. Her glare of condemnation didn't bother him overly much. A grin fought against a scowl on her pretty mouth.

She wasn't going to run—at least not right now. He could just tell. The opportunity to spend time with her, to coax her back into his life beckoned to him like a whispered promise.

Genny's expression turned suspicious when she noticed he was grinning like an idiot. "You know I hate to be tickled."

"I seem to recall something about that . . . yeah." He was distracted by how soft and firm Genny's heaving breasts looked beneath her sweater. The shine in her gray eyes that had been so wary and sad just minutes ago made him happy beyond reason.

She snorted and picked up the cloth napkin she'd placed beside his plate and tossed it at his chest forcefully. "Just eat your sandwich before it gets cold, boy."

"Yes, ma'am," he said, his gaze fastened on her swaying ass as she stalked away. He shook his head as if to clear it when she passed out of his vision.

Damn, he thought appreciatively when he bit into the chewy toasted Italian bread that surrounded scrambled egg, asiago cheese, and thinly sliced prosciutto.

The woman knew how to cook almost better than she knew how to walk.

Genevieve became consumed with the idea that she and Sean needed something to *do,* some sort of activity or purpose. If she spent too much unstructured time alone with him in this penthouse during the biggest snowstorm in five decades, thoughts and feelings were inevitably going to turn in the direction of sex. They certainly had earlier, when Sean had teased and tickled her. She didn't need to be an expert on human behavior to know what that heavy-lidded gaze he'd been giving her while he stared at her breasts meant.

And the growing hardness between his thighs when he'd held her against him didn't require interpretation, either. Neither did the dampness in the crotch of her panties that grew more and more noticeable the more time she spent with him.

When Genevieve had agreed to allow him to stay there with her, she'd accepted the inevitability of making love with Sean. Some things were fated to happen, and her and Sean exploring the depths of the singular passion they'd shared since their first glance was one of them.

Genevieve just wished she knew if their coming together finally on their own terms was a fate of the happily-ever-after genre or the plane-crash variety.

Not that there could *really* be a happily ever after with Sean. Not with Max always standing between them.

She wished there was a guarantee that she'd made the right decision in letting Sean stay there, but there wasn't one, so she'd just have to live with that. She'd come to terms with the fact that she couldn't fight her need for him any longer.

But now that they'd finished eating, the rest of the day and night loomed like some kind of vast, frightening chasm that needed to be crossed.

She inspected the television set in the living room while Sean cleaned up the breakfast dishes. Watching TV was the only distraction she could think of in the midst of a snowstorm. Unfortunately, the penthouse didn't have cable installed, but at least there was a working DVD player. She hadn't been the one to furnish the unit; Max had done it all. She couldn't recall ever watching a movie here. They usually were too busy attending social events or the theater. The penthouse had never been used for lying around and being lazy. It was ideal for weekend city activities.

Or illicit affairs.

Apparently, that's what Sean used it for. Not that his affairs were illicit, necessarily.

Her heartbeat escalated at the volatile thoughts. What was so terrible about being Sean's next conquest in the penthouse? She'd wanted to be with Sean practically since the moment she'd first seen him. Maybe she hadn't been conscious of it then, but some nameless, formless thing had clicked into place when she'd first looked into his eyes. She'd already accepted what would happen between them over the next few days was an inevitability.

But that didn't stop her insecurity from zooming off the charts.

She'd only been to bed with four men in her life. One of them had been a guy she'd dated seriously in college; the other a man she'd gone out with for two and a half years named Dave. She'd actually been on a date with Dave when she met Max at a party given by a socialite who owned the Oak Street building she rented for her boutique.

The other two men she'd slept with had been her husband and Sean. She'd been planning to sleep with Jeff at some unde- fined point in the future. It was obvious Jeff was more than inter- ested, but he'd also been willing to be patient. He knew she was a widow . . . seemed to guess she was unsure about becoming inti- mate with a man again, although he couldn't understand the true circumstances of why that was.

Jeff knew she was hesitant, but he more than likely was wrong about why she was so unenthusiastic to jump into bed with another man.

The truth was, something about having sex with Sean had changed her, *transformed* her on some deep level until she no lon- ger recognized herself.

No longer trusted her desires.

She kept thinking about the orgy of pleasure they'd indulged in on that New Year's Eve night. Her inhibitions had been dampened by champagne and a desire denied for too long. She'd *needed* to release it, or she would have eventually gone mad. When she'd finally touched Sean, when he'd kissed her, it'd been like lighting a fuse to dynamite.

Sean probably thought she was like that all the time in bed. Wild and uninhibited. Shameless. He'd probably be shocked to know that while Max's and her sex life had been satisfactory, if not spectacular, initially, toward the end of their four years of marriage, it had dwindled into nonexistence.

For all she knew, Sean thought she and Max were swingers. Max had proposed the whole thing so casually on that night. Genevieve had never protested, and just stood there frozen in shock. Sean and she had never discussed the events of that night afterward.

Genevieve wouldn't allow it.

Why *wouldn't* Sean make the assumption that she made a regular practice of going to bed with two men?

The fact of the matter was, before that New Year's Eve night they'd spent with Sean, Max and she hadn't had sex for almost a half a year. Initially, she'd worried Max was having an affair, but he always seemed so warm with her, so interested and proud of her work, so kind. And there was never any indication of a lover— no furtive phone conversations, or even a particularly attractive female at the office who had made Genevieve suspicious.

Then she'd met Sean, and the issue of being intimate with her husband had slowly faded in importance. She'd told herself it was natural for married couples to become less active in regard to sex. Besides, Max was in his fifties. He didn't have the drive that a younger man did.

Or a younger woman.

Genevieve hadn't known the depths of her sexual desire until she'd met Sean. Hadn't known what she was capable of in bed. Or what she was capable of allowing someone to do *to* her.

Not just anyone, she corrected herself. *Sean.*

Heat flooded her cheeks as graphic memories played across her brain—looking up at Sean while his cock had been in her mouth and Max had been behind her. Fucking her.

Slower, Max, I want to savor this, and she's going to explode at the same time I do.

She had, and so had he. Exactly in the manner Sean had orchestrated it.

"What's wrong?"

She started at the sound of Sean's voice. She'd been so lost in the charged, erotic memory she hadn't realized he'd finished cleaning up in the kitchen and reentered the living room.

"I . . . nothing. Why?" she muttered, flustered. She opened up one of the cabinets on the television console and peered inside, even though she'd already discovered it was empty.

He studied her speculatively for a few seconds with eyes that were far too alert for Genevieve's comfort. "You had a funny look on your face."

"There's no cable and no movies for the DVD player, either."

Sean yawned and plopped down in the leather chair. "There's a place around the corner that delivers DVDs, but I noticed on the way to Salvatore's they were closed. Probably because of the storm."

She stood from her kneeling position and walked over to the couch, her anxiety building as Sean continued to watch her. She picked up the remote control and turned on the television.

"Maybe there's something on one of the networks. I'm not used to watching television at this time of day. We could watch a football game, but you know I'm not much of a sports fan except for baseball. But maybe there's a movie, or—"

"Genny," he interrupted her blathering.

Her gaze shot over to him.

"What's wrong?" he barked.

It was on the tip of her tongue to tell him that he shouldn't expect much from her. She *wasn't* that woman he'd had hand-cuffed last night. She wasn't even that woman he'd made love to with such ruthless precision on New Year's Eve three years ago.

Was she?

But she'd told him she didn't want to bring up that anxiety-provoking topic, the night she'd lost all her illusions about Max . . . and about Sean, too.

The night that led to Max's murder.

She closed her eyes briefly. She felt trapped in a prison built by her own desires and insecurities.

Trapped . . . but afraid of the consequences of release.

"Nothing's wrong," she told Sean gruffly. She flipped the channels with the remote control, not really taking in much on the screen. An image suddenly penetrated her distraction. Her jaw dropped open.

Sean's head swung around when he saw her reaction. He sat forward in the chair. Neither of them spoke as they watched the local news story—the gold and orange flames leaping ominously against the shadow of the roof, the black night sky, and the out-line of the thick, surrounding forest. Genevieve saw herself on the screen—her eyes looking huge in a face that had been washed out by the camera lights, the surrounding emergency vehicles, and the rising anxiety for Jim, who stood next to her.

"The owner of the Lake Forest mansion, thirty-three-year-old Chicago fashion designer Genevieve Bujold, was not in the house at the time of the fire. There were no fatalities, despite the complete destruction of the multimillion-dollar home."

The footage altered to several hours later. Snow fell and the gray light of dawn illuminated the image of firemen carrying a few blackened items out of the smoking skeleton of the house and laying them out on the front lawn.

Genevieve hastily changed the channel. She didn't want to see any surviving remnants of her life with Max.

She flipped the channel to a black-and-white rerun of the *Andy Griffith Show*, not really aware of what she'd chosen, and settled back into the corner of the couch.

It somehow seemed fated—sad, but appropriate, too. Her marriage to Max had gone up in figurative flames three years ago. The destruction of the Lake Forest mansion by fire was like a long overdue period at the end of a story that never should have been told.

Sean kept his eyes on the television, but he was aware of Genny unfolding the blanket and curling up in the corner of the couch, her posture stiff and guarded. Seeing her house burning on the television screen hadn't been the only thing that had gotten her uptight, although it sure hadn't helped matters any.

What'd happened while he was in the kitchen? She'd been starting to relax around him. He'd even gotten her to laugh once while they ate when he'd reminded her of the time he'd taken her bowling and she'd thrown her ball into the adjacent lane—and got a strike.

The guy next to them had been thrilled.

But then he'd walked into the living room and she'd had the strangest look on her face. Her gaze had been far off and her cheeks were stained bright pink. It'd been a damn distracting sight, because Genny had looked exactly like a woman who had been thinking about sex. Hot, incredible, mind-blowing sex. The kind of sex they'd had on that New Year's Eve.

He kept his eyes trained on the guileless antics of the citizens of Mayberry on the television, but his thoughts were the polar opposite of innocent.

This time when he remembered that night, it was different. He sifted through the carnal memories and wondered. That look of heated arousal on Genny's face when he'd walked into the living room made him suspect for the first time that maybe . . . just *maybe* Genny remembered that night with more than just shame and regret.

CHAPTER **SIX**

Sean's eyebrows went up in amazed amusement when Max exploded with laughter at Sean's joke. He continued to guffaw as Sean, Genny, and he got off the elevator and headed toward the penthouse, the sound echoing harshly off the granite-tiled walls. Sean'd never seen Max drunk. The older man was the consummate professional, smooth, clever, and controlled.

Sean figured Max's unregulated secret fetish was why he'd never seen Max drunk. Drunkenness and secrets didn't tend to go well together.

Sean had suspected from the beginning that Max had very good reasons for hiring him as his secondhand man at Sauren Solutions. Now that he'd seen Max operate, now that he'd met Genny and observed Max and his wife's relationship, Sean thought he understood Max's motivations pretty well.

What Max saw in Sean's background wasn't just the toughness and edge that came from a poverty-stricken, crime-ridden childhood in New Orleans, his distinguished service in the Army during Desert Storm, or his recruitment and rise within the ranks of Army Intelligence.

No, like any good intelligence operative, Max had taken special note of Sean's occasional write-ups for insubordination, contrasting with the honors and medals won for uncommon—maybe even foolish—bravery. Sean had rebelled against authority as a general principle most of his youth, but when he made exceptions because of genuine respect, he served not only with fierce loyalty, but was willing to risk danger and death to do so.

That was the kind of man Max wanted working for him; the type that would have thrown his body on a live grenade in order to save his boss's life. Sean figured Max wanted his own personal version of the President's Secret Service agents.

He thought it said a lot about the shortcomings of narcissism that Max actually believed *Sean* was that man.

He figured there wasn't any harm in Max's mistaken assumptions about his psychological profile. If Max felt safer because he believed he controlled some emotional deficit in Sean's psyche, far be it from him to tell him he was way off base.

Genny smiled widely at Sean over her shoulder when he helped her out of her coat. She looked stunning, decked out in her New Year's Eve attire—a long, ivory knit wraparound dress that caressed and clung to her feminine curves in the most gawd-awful sexy manner. The sophisticated dress had a deeper V on the neckline than Genny typically wore. It'd been the biggest challenge Sean had ever faced to keep his eyes off the enticing valley between the swells of her breasts while they'd spent the entire evening together. It'd been both treat and torture to gaze upon the vision of her all night, to touch her body while they danced and made small talk that didn't begin to match the messages being broadcast in their eyes as they stared at each other.

After he'd hung her coat on a hook, he delved his fingers into her hair, carefully rearranging the gleaming waves on her back, savoring the feeling of the silky strands sliding along his skin. A man could only take so much temptation, after all, and over the past several months, Genny had started a fire in his belly—a fire that felt as if it would soon consume him.

She froze at his impulsive caress. He'd never touched her so intimately before. Sure, he'd put his arms around her as he taught her how to shoot. It quite possibly was the only reason they'd both become so enthusiastic about the activity. And once he'd discovered Genny was ticklish, he'd taken a great deal of pleasure in teasing her, using it as an excuse to touch her with seeming innocence.

But his fingers in her hair on such an intoxicating night?

That was different.

"Your hair was a little mussed," he murmured near her ear, releasing the soft strands reluctantly. He saw her shiver.

"Oh . . . thank you." She gave a nervous laugh and stepped away from him. But Sean knew the moment had been about as insignificant to her as it was to him. He knew it with a basic, primal instinct that he'd learned to trust long ago.

He followed her into the living room to join Max, a forced smile on his face. The evening had suddenly gone flat, feeling like a work chore instead of being any fun. Sure, it was titillating as hell to stare at Genny all night, to watch her laughing and to feel her body moving so sensually beneath his hand.

But who the fuck was he kidding?

He was the third wheel here. The thought of what might happen between Genny and Max after he left—how they'd likely take their New Year's celebration to the bedroom—made that old stubborn streak flame to furious life.

If staying prevented Max from touching Genny for a while, hell . . . he was *glad* to be the annoying third wheel. With any luck, the bastard would be too drunk to do the deed if Sean outlasted him, he thought acerbically when he saw Max uncorking yet another bottle of champagne.

"We already finished off three bottles at the Pump Room," Genny chided when they joined Max at the bar. They'd had a great time at the Chicago landmark restaurant, telling stories and laughing and ordering new dishes to try. They'd spent almost four hours there, Max playing the raconteur; Genny and Sean enjoying the older man's New Year's Eve high spirits and sharp wit.

Max's festive mood had surprised Sean a little, as his boss had indicated they would be mixing business with pleasure when he'd asked Sean to join them. They'd been hired by a Fortune 500 company's CEO to investigate the shady dealings of its chief financial officer. The suspect covered his tracks extremely well, however, and Max had said he wanted to pick Sean's brains about hiding funds in off-shore accounts. Sean had picked up a lot of related knowledge when he'd been a Foreign Affairs Officer in Iraq and, later, Germany.

But Max had barely mentioned two words about methods of hiding money all night.

"Well, we're celebrating, aren't we?" Max asked jovially as he filled three flutes. In his tuxedo and with his handsome head of silver hair, he looked as natural pouring champagne as he had dancing with Genny earlier that evening. Sean had to admit they made a striking couple as they moved gracefully among the other dancers. He'd shared a couple of dances with Genny as well, but he knew he could never measure up to Max in the sophistication department.

Not that he'd given a rat's ass about how he looked dancing, as long as he got to touch Genny, to feel her body gliding sensually beneath his appreciative hands.

Max handed them their flutes and raised his own in a toast. "To another record-breaking year for both Sauren Solutions and Bujold Designs," he said, referring to Genny's boutique and design firm. Sean smiled at Genny. He liked that she'd kept her maiden name. She'd told him before that since she'd already gained a modest reputation in the fashion community when she married Max, she didn't want to alter her name.

Sean was just happy that Max hadn't succeeded in putting that particular stamp of ownership on her.

Genny's eyes met his over the rim of her glass as they drank. Her red lips curved as she tipped the icy fluid between them. Sean watched her through a narrowed gaze. He'd been getting erections off and on all night while he stared at Genny across the table from him or held her in his arms while they danced. After one dance he'd had to excuse himself and go to the men's room to cool down, not treasuring the thought of returning to the table where his boss sat, his wife on his arm, with such an obvious boner pressing against the pants of his tux.

But now as he stared at Genny sipping champagne and thought of the warmth and sweetness that would reside between her lips, a rush of heat and blood pounded into his genitals. His cock swelled and ached, and even though Max started talking, Sean couldn't interpret what he said or tear his eyes off Genny's lush mouth.

He'd never known desire could tear at a man so much. The need to touch Genny—to possess her—felt as if it clawed at him from the inside out.

She slowly lowered the flute. Her eyes looked unnaturally glassy as she returned his stare. Sean was hyperaware of the throb of her pulse at her elegant throat and the gentle rise and fall of her full breasts.

He became vaguely aware that Max chuckled as he set down his champagne on the bar. Max removed the flute from Genny's hand, but still, Sean and Genny couldn't pull their gazes off each other.

Somehow Sean knew exactly what was going to happen next,

even though just this afternoon he would have scoffed at the idea. He found himself skating right on a knife's edge of dread and wild anticipation.

Blood pounded both in his ears and in his cock when Max spread a hand over the side of Genny's hip and rubbed.

"You look beautiful tonight, Genevieve."

Her lips opened as if she would speak, but she swallowed convulsively instead.

"Doesn't she look amazing?" Max asked, turning his attention to Sean. He continued to stroke Genny's hip as he spoke, letting his fingers delve into the firm flesh of her buttock. She stood as though frozen, her elbow still bent in the same position it'd been in when she held the champagne flute.

"I've never seen anything lovelier," Sean replied, his gaze still locked with Genny's. He studied her expression, searching. After spending so much time with her for the past six months, Sean understood that while Genny wasn't necessarily a sexual innocent, she was far from being a player.

Did she understand what was happening here? He'd back off if she showed an ounce of disgust or fear, but he was so desperate for her, so crazed with need, Sean admitted he might only see what he wanted to see if it gave him the opportunity to make love to her.

"I've seen how much you admire my wife. I've seen how much she reciprocates the feeling."

Sean tore his gaze off Genny's face and looked at Max.

"Nothing has ever happened between us."

Max laughed softly, the sound resembling a low, vibrating purr. "I believe you. If it had, perhaps the air wouldn't be so thick with pheromones. You'll forgive an old man for being so affected by it, I hope?"

Genny started slightly, as though she'd just awakened from a trance. "Max—"

"Hush, Genevieve. I'm not complaining," Max soothed. He dropped a kiss on her forehead. "Perhaps it's too much to ask, but it would give me so much pleasure to share in all that passion. Just for one night? That's all I ask. You wouldn't deny me that, would you, sweetheart?" he coaxed near Genny's ear. He nuzzled her hair aside and pressed his lips to her neck.

Genny stared at Sean as Max kissed her, the glassiness of her wide gray eyes striking him once again. He'd thought it was an effect from the champagne before, but now he knew it was a sort of fevered excitement. The knowledge made his cock lurch next to his thigh.

But Sean saw the uncertainty, as well; the way she looked at him for guidance, some indication of what he wanted . . . what he thought was right.

Max continued to stroke her body more intimately, sliding his hand along the outer swell of a breast. He cupped his palm, shaping her flesh to his. A snarl shaped Sean's mouth even as lust stabbed through his cock. It was a damn erotic sight, but a feral fury rose in him as well as he watched Max finesse the firm flesh.

It was the strangest combination of emotion he'd ever experienced in his life. It did something odd to him, caused some kind of volatile friction inside him. He'd had a brief, potent impulse to wrap his hands around Max Sauren's throat and squeeze. It should have been a glaring warning for him to get out of there.

And fast.

But he'd ignored it, chose not to acknowledge it, because he couldn't bear the idea of walking away from Genny at that moment.

Perhaps Genny read some of the ambivalence that suddenly overcame him because when Max's hand shifted down to the belt of her wraparound dress, her hand rose to stop him.

"Max . . . *no*. Wait."

"It's only fair, isn't it, love?" Max murmured silkily. He knocked aside her hand. His long fingers unfastened the knot that secured her dress. "The type of thing going on between you and Sean can't be denied for long. As your husband, I'd rather be there when it happens, than not. In fact, I'm looking forward to it."

Genny looked a little desperate when Max slowly parted the two sides of her dress, exposing her body to Sean's gaze. But her lips and cheeks had deepened with arousal and her pulse fluttered rapidly at her throat.

"Well, Sean? What do you say?" Max asked, removing his hand and stepping back . . . allowing Sean to look his fill at his wife.

Sean just stared for a long moment while his blood surged wildly in his veins. She wore an ivory demi-bra that left the tops of her lush breasts bare, a tiny pair of matching bikini panties and pale thigh-highs that were only slightly lighter in shade than her lustrous skin.

Sean forced his gaze from her curving hips and smooth, taut belly.

"Genny?" he asked gruffly.

She looked like a woman who stood on a very narrow ledge who couldn't even see the ground it was so far down. Sean had never wanted to hold her more, but he needed her to decide on her own, without his influence.

He felt her small nod in every cell of his body.

He transferred his gaze to Max. "I call the shots."

Max smiled. His small shrug seemed to say both *but of course* and also carry a hint of noblesse oblige.

That was Max for you. The perfect manners—even when sharing his wife. The thought galled Sean, but he quieted his doubts by looking back at Genny. She trembled slightly as she stood in her high heels.

He placed his glass of champagne on the coffee table and went to her, stopping just a foot away. He held out his arms.

"Come here, girl," he said quietly.

She stepped closer, placing her hands on his chest. He smoothed her hair with both of his hands, using his thumbs to tilt her face up so he could fully see her. The sensation of her hands sliding along his chest enflamed him.

"It's gonna be okay," he whispered.

"Sean—"

But he never knew what she was going to say next, because he covered her mouth with his own, slaking his monumental thirst for her. Six months of pent-up desire went into that kiss. He placed one hand on the back of her waist, steadying her as her spine arched. He leaned over her and drank deeply. He probed the sweet cavern of her mouth with his tongue again and again, establishing that sacred domain as his.

His.

The fact that she returned his kiss with wild abandon made it all that much more explosive of an experience. One hand swept along her side, tracing the swell between waist and hip, the feeling of her silky skin and firm flesh making him mindless with lust. He couldn't get enough of her responsive mouth, but if he didn't feel her naked skin sliding against his sometime soon, he'd go right over the edge into insanity. He broke their kiss reluctantly.

Max watched them with gleaming, dark eyes.

"Let's go," Sean told the other man grimly before he took Genny's hand and led her to the master bedroom.

Genny stared at a commercial for car insurance, but all of her attention was on Sean as he straightened and shifted in his chair, causing the tautly drawn leather to make a crackling noise. The wind had picked up. It made a low howling sound as it swept across the windows. The snow no longer fell straight but swirled around the glass in a wild, frantic dance.

She pushed the blanket off her when she realized she was sweating. Sean glanced over at her abrupt movement. She held her breath in her lungs when his gaze fixed on her chest.

On that New Year's Eve night when he'd released the restraints of his passion, Sean'd made no secret of the fact that he loved her breasts. He'd worshiped them with his hands; made a feast of them with his mouth. Even immediately after he'd climaxed, he'd kissed and licked and sucked at her nipples with a hunger that stunned her.

She pictured him looking up at her with fiery eyes, his cheeks hollowed out as he applied a firm suction around the tip of one breast. When she'd started to whimper and writhe in Max's hold, Sean had kissed her wet, erect nipple with firm lips.

I could eat you alive, girl.

Liquid heat surged into her pussy as the graphic memories flooded Genevieve's brain, whisking her out of the present and firmly into the carnal embrace of the past.

CHAPTER **SEVEN**

THREE YEARS AGO

Genevieve had never felt this way before. She felt detached and separate from herself, as though she were an observer watching events unfold on a stage. And yet ... she'd never been more aware of her body: the heart beating madly in her chest, the sensation of the cool air on her tingling, bare skin, the tight achiness that plagued her nipples and sex, the feeling of Sean's warm hold on her hand as he led her down the hallway to the bedroom.

His touch steadied her. She'd been shocked at what Max had proposed—knocked off balance. The disorienting experience of having her husband say something so unexpected and volatile in such a calm, almost playful manner, too much champagne and most of all her raging desire for Sean—all of it was like a wicked combination of blows.

She knew it was selfish, but one thought kept penetrating her haze. She would have the opportunity to touch Sean—to discover the full meaning of that fierce, possessive gleam in his blue eyes whenever he looked at her.

He turned on a lamp on one of the bedside tables and turned

to face her. Max's body pressed against her from behind. She took comfort from Sean's heated gaze as Max pushed her dress off her shoulders and down her arms. It fell in a soft heap around her ankles. Max's fingers slid beneath her bra next, deftly unfastening the clasp. Her bra fell on top of her dress.

"Exquisite, isn't she?" Max murmured as he captured her breasts with his palms and lightly stroked the sensitive skin along the lower curve.

Sean's nostrils flared. He stepped forward and shaped her lips to his in a quick, hot kiss.

"Hold them up for me," he said against her mouth. His head lowered. Genevieve whimpered when she realized he'd been speaking to Max.

Max cradled her breasts in his palms from below, causing the crests to thrust forward. Her fingers delved into Sean's thick hair when he slipped a nipple into his mouth. Fire tore through her like lightning, following a path from the tip of her breast where Sean suckled and lashed with his sleek tongue all the way to her pussy, where her flesh swelled with pleasure.

Max's hold tightened as she moaned and writhed.

Nothing . . . *nothing* Max'd ever done to her sexually seemed so forbidden . . . so exciting as when he held her steady for Sean's hot, tormenting mouth. He kneaded the breast that Sean suckled. Genny could sense him looking over her shoulder, as if he enjoyed the sight of Sean pleasuring her.

Sean drew on her more tightly and she called his name, her fingernails scraping his scalp. Her nipple popped out of his mouth, the crest pebbled and reddened from his ministrations. He pressed his lips to her ribs, exploring the sensitive tissue between the bones. He knelt before her and took a small tender bite from her waist then soothed it with his tongue. She shivered uncontrollably.

"Steady, girl," he whispered as he glanced up to her face. She wondered what he saw there because his facial muscles tightened. She reached for him, desperate to feel his body next to hers, reassuring and solid. But he caught her wrists and pushed them behind her back.

"Max," he said. Max seemed to immediately comprehend what he wanted, because her husband caught her wrists and pinned her forearms into the small of her back. Sean ran his hands along the back of her thighs, soothing her, but also seeming to relish the feeling of her stocking-covered legs.

"Your hands on me make me a little crazy," Sean explained, his tone gruff and warm. Perhaps he'd seen the uncertainty on her face. "I only want to make you feel good, girl. You know that?"

Genevieve nodded, struck mute by desire.

"Good. Now"—he slipped his hands beneath her underwear and drew them down her thighs—"let's have a look at your little pussy."

She shut her eyes, his words and the sight of his head in front of her genitals overwhelming her with a blast of sexual anticipation unlike anything she'd ever known. Her vagina clenched painfully. She sensed Sean's heated gaze at the juncture of her thighs as her panties fell to her ankles. Her trembling amplified when she felt him part her swollen sex lips with his fingers.

"Ain't that a pretty thing?" he whispered, awe spicing his tone, his breath brushing against her exposed clit. He swiped his tongue once over nerve-packed flesh. She whimpered.

"Gawd, you're sweet, girl."

He put his mouth on her, his manner focused, intent, and unapologetically greedy. A growl rumbled his throat, vibrating into her. He ate her like he'd been waiting for the feast forever.

If Max hadn't been holding her elbows, steadying her, her

knees would have buckled at the onslaught of pleasure that swept through her. Sean continued to hold apart her labia, giving him free reign to agitate and torment her most sensitive flesh.

His tongue was a gift sent straight from heaven.

He lapped and suckled with his hot mouth and pressed and stabbed with his stiffened tongue until Genevieve no longer knew up from down, right from left . . .

Right from wrong.

She only knew delicious, dizzying pleasure.

She cried out in stark protest when the amazing sensations ceased for a moment. Her eyelids blinked open. Sean looked up at her, the lower part of his rugged face slick from her juices.

"Hold her steady, now," he told Max.

Max transferred her wrists to one hand and pressed close behind her. He put his arm around her waist and pushed her back into his body. Genevieve could feel his erection pressing against her bare ass. Her husband kissed her on the ear and spoke to her softly as Sean found her slit with a thick finger and penetrated.

"Did it feel good, love? It looked like he knew what he was doing."

Genevieve moaned as Sean finger-fucked her, making a wet noise as he moved in the tight, lubricated channel. He pressed the flattened joint of his forefinger against her clit, moving it in a circular motion. The precision of his movements left her reeling— as though he was inside her mind and knew the optimal amount of pressure to send her right over the edge. She gritted her teeth together in an agony of deprivation when Sean twisted his hand, corkscrewing his fucking finger, and then withdrew.

"Genny?" Sean prodded.

She pried open her eyelids and looked down at him.

"Answer him. Did you like it?"

"Yes."

"Then ask for it, girl," he whispered gruffly. "Tell me you want it."

She quivered as Max kissed her ear and pressed his cock against her ass. She couldn't recall ever feeling Max so rigid and swollen with excitement. She couldn't take her eyes off Sean.

"Put your mouth on me. *Please*," she entreated in a whisper.

He smiled tenderly. He placed his hands on her hips and parted her labia with his tongue. She pressed her hips against him, wild with cresting desire.

Climax tore through her, electrifying every nerve in her body. For a few moments, her identity left her. She was transformed into nothing but a live wire, a conduit for pure, pulsating pleasure.

She came back to herself with the sensation of Sean's hands on her thighs, pressing them apart insistently. She realized that Max had tipped her back farther against his body, taking most of her weight and granting Sean the angle he required to send his tongue deep inside her slit. Her husband had released her wrists while she climaxed and now held her hips as he ground his cock between her buttocks.

Genevieve whimpered while Sean drank thirstily of the fruits of his labor, thrusting his tongue along her post-climactic, tingling nerves again and again. She wondered how long he would have stayed there, eating her, sucking her juices, if he hadn't become aware of Genevieve's cries of reawakened arousal and Max's increasingly excited thrusts against her.

Sean seemed so focused . . . so lost in his need, and yet determined at once.

Sean eventually lifted his head slowly, his gaze remaining on her wet, spread pussy. He stood, still not meeting her eyes. He removed his tuxedo jacket and tossed it over a chair, then tore at his bow tie impatiently. His fingers clawed at the top buttons of his shirt, but before he could make any progress, both of his hands seized Genevieve's jaw.

He leaned down and ravaged her mouth, pillaged it with his tongue. Their combined flavor struck her brain, and Genevieve understood that no matter how rough Sean's kiss, it was the sweetest sort of caress, the highest tribute he could pay her. She was so transported by the power of that kiss that she didn't realize until Sean finally sealed it that she was completely in his arms, and that Max had removed his clothes.

She caught a glimpse of her husband coming toward them before he moved behind her. His eyes looked darker than usual, liquid and hot with arousal. His body had always pleased her. He was as tall as Sean. Max was meticulous about his workouts, and it showed in the lean, long lines of his well-muscled body. He always shaved his testicles. When they'd first started sleeping together, he'd asked Genevieve to shave as well, and she had. Her pubic hair had grown back in the months of their abstinence, however, although she was careful to keep her curls neatly trimmed.

Genevieve had been right. She'd never seen Max quite so aroused. When he pressed against her from behind, his mouth hot on her neck and shoulder, and her breasts crushed against Sean's hard chest, it was easy to silence her doubts about why sharing her with Sean would arouse him so much. Max shifted his cock, sending it between her thighs and rubbing it against her outer sex.

"What about a condom?"

Genevieve blinked at Sean's terse question. She glanced up into his face. He looked hard. Angry? Genevieve couldn't be sure. She could feel that his muscles had stiffened.

In fact, Max usually did wear a condom with her. She never understood why, since she was on birth control. She'd finally just determined that he was a little fastidious when it came to sex. But they hadn't made love in quite a while, and he was out of practice, she supposed.

When Max didn't move from behind her for a few seconds, she wondered if Sean had overstepped his bounds. Tension rose in her as Sean continued to stare at Max. She looked over her shoulder to see Max's face, but then he moved away. He found a condom in the drawer on the bedside table and returned. Genevieve exhaled a sigh of relief when she saw that while his handsome face was glazed with perspiration from arousal, he didn't seem angry about Sean's question.

Sean looked pacified, if not pleased.

"Come here, Gen," Sean coaxed softly. He pulled her over to the bed, pausing to unbutton his shirt and whip it over his shoulders. Genevieve stared at his naked torso. It was a sight she'd fantasized about . . . hungered for. His muscles struck her as succulent. They flexed as he removed his shirt. She could perfectly imagine sinking her teeth into the hard, rounded flesh of his shoulder. His golden-hued skin seemed to carry the sun around in it. It gloved his delineated abdomen muscles tightly. He wasn't deeply tanned, living in Chicago, but she imagined his skin would soak up the sun's rays thirstily.

His gaze leapt up to meet hers when she reached out and placed her fingertips on the scar above the belt of his low-riding tuxedo trousers.

Max cradled her hip. She felt the heat emanating off his body. The tip of his penis brushed her bottom. Arousal stabbed at her pussy but doubt also flickered through her awareness.

"Shhh," Sean soothed. He bent his head and kissed her once softly. She went willingly enough when he pulled her onto the bed. He lay on his back and she straddled his hips. Sean put his hands on her shoulders and pulled her down to him. He kissed her cheeks and her nose and her brow, taking his time. She was more impatient for his kiss, seeking him out with fevered lips . . . so hungry.

So desperate for Sean's taste.

She felt Max move behind her on the bed. Sean's hands transferred to her jaw as Max positioned her hips to receive him.

Sean's mouth settled on hers in a possessive kiss at the same moment that Max drove his cock into her pussy. He consumed her cries of pleasure, voraciously swallowed her moans as Max fucked her.

Her head swam as a friction mounted in her flesh. Sean's essence overwhelmed her. Ruled her. Sensations mixed and melded in her desire-drunk brain. It might have been Max's cock in her, but it was Sean mastering her at that moment, releasing her desires, setting them free.

"Touch me, Genny," he said next to her seeking lips a moment later.

She didn't need coaxing. Her hands were all over him, wild for the sensations spread out before her like a tactile feast. Her lips followed her eager fingers, charting the planes and ridges of muscle and bone covered in thick, smooth skin. His shoulder muscle felt every bit as succulent between her front teeth as she'd imagined it would.

"Genny," Sean hissed. His fingers delved into her hair, holding it back off her face so that it didn't get in the way of her explorations. Max continued to fuck her, stoking her fires higher and hotter.

Sean grunted in dissatisfaction when she tried to reach an erect nipple with her mouth, but was brought up short because of their positioning.

"Move her back on the bed," Sean said. Max paused in his thrusts and withdrew. Genevieve gave a little squeak of surprise when he tightened his hold on her hips and buttocks and slid her knees down on the slick duvet.

Her face hovered over Sean's belt. He reached down and began to unbuckle it.

"Down just a little lower, Max," he murmured.

Genevieve's muscles began to tremble again in acute anticipation.

CHAPTER **EIGHT**

All the memories of that New Year's Eve had been branded indelibly into Sean's brain, but recalling the look in Genny's eyes when he'd slid the tip of his cock between her lips had never ceased to make him hard and restless.

He shifted uncomfortably in the leather chair, his eyes flickering off the ending credits of the *Andy Griffith Show* over to Genny. She glanced at him, her eyes shiny and wary, and her cheeks bright pink. He stood and went over to the fire.

"Why didn't you say something about being so hot," he muttered irritably as he flipped off the switch, quenching the flames.

"What are you so pissy about?" She sounded every bit as uptight as he was.

His eyelids narrowed as he studied her from his kneeling position in front of the fireplace. Her cheeks and lips were even more flushed than they had been before and her face was glazed with a light coat of sweat.

"Are you feeling okay? You look like you have a fever."

"I'm fine. It's like you said. It's too hot in here."

Sean'd been thinking about going to her. But despite the fact that she'd claimed she was hot, she pulled up the blanket around her in a defensive gesture, rebuffing the advance he'd been considering. He returned to the chair, feeling momentarily defeated. He couldn't understand what'd got her so tense all of a sudden.

For the time being, it seemed, all he had were his memories.

THREE YEARS AGO

He shoved his black tuxedo pants down around his thighs. His boxer briefs followed. The sight of Genny's pink tongue whisking anxiously across her lower lip as she stared at his cock caused a pang of desire to go through him. His cock lurched. He wrapped his hand around it, soothing the sharp ache. She reached for him.

"Don't touch me now. Max? Hold her wrists behind her back," he said, sharper than he intended. He was sure he'd lose it if he was forced to feel both her hands and mouth on his cock at that moment, and he wanted this to last.

Wanted it to last forever.

She gasped when Max sunk his cock back into her pussy, grunting in appreciation as he did so. Sean could only imagine how hot she was, how tight and sweet. He steadied her at the shoulder when Max gathered her wrists behind her back and resumed fucking her.

Genny stared up at him, her breasts trembling as Max plunged into her body. Sean cringed inwardly when he saw that although her eyes were glazed with desire, uncertainty had entered the stormy depths once again.

"I only want him to hold you because I'm gonna come sooner than I want if both your hand and mouth are on me." He lifted his penis between their bodies and brushed the cockhead over her lips. They parted. She moaned feverishly when he slicked a stream of pre-ejaculate on her lower lip. "It's going to feel so good, girl. Slowly now," he instructed as he slid the head of his cock into her mouth. He ground his teeth together at the sensation of penetrating the tight ring she'd formed with her lips and feeling her humid warmth.

He gathered her thick, silky hair at her nape and bunched it in his fist. When she started to slide him farther into her mouth, he restrained her gently.

"Hold still," he whispered, his tightly leashed restraint making speech difficult. "I want to give it to you."

The sound of Max's pelvis and thighs smacking against Genny's buttocks grew more rapid . . . more frantic. Max's movements jostled her, but she held her head as steady as possible as he slid his cock along her tongue. He shuddered in pleasure.

"That's right, girl. Such a sweet mouth," he praised. It pleased him beyond measure that despite her obvious desire, she allowed him to control the movements. He flexed his hips, dipping into her delicious heat, before he pulled back, dragging sensitive, stony flesh along her tongue and the ridge of her widely spread lips. Her tongue lashed at the head before he plunged back into her.

She glanced up at him. For an electric few seconds their gazes held as he fucked her mouth.

"Slower, Max," he said. "I want to savor this, and she's going to explode at the same time I do."

His command was terse enough to pierce Max's increasing excitement. He slowed in his fucking motions. Genny drew on his cock with a steady, mind-blowing suction. He experienced her hunger firsthand, even if she didn't duck her head down and consume him greedily.

He held her head steady and thrust his cock between her tight lips. He grimaced in both regret and pure pleasure when the tip touched her throat. She calmed her gag reflex as he withdrew, keeping her head motionless. She didn't look up at him, but Sean sensed her determination. He used his hold on her to gently push her head down. Her suck grew even stronger, telling him what she wanted.

"Nice and easy," he said as he watched her, only vaguely aware that Max had paused, sheathed all the way in Genny's pussy, and watched as Sean attempted to breach the barrier of her throat. When he felt the sensation of her throat muscles constricting around his cock tip, he hissed in pleasure. He drew out of her quickly, not wanting to take advantage of the trust she'd put in him by letting him control the movements.

"Gawd, you're sweet, girl," he murmured as he resumed fucking her mouth shallowly. "She deserves a little treat for that, doesn't she, Max?"

Max purred an agreement. Genevieve's moan vibrated along the length of his cock when Max transferred her wrists to one hand and reached between her thighs with the other. He massaged her clit and began fucking her again. For several rapturous moments Sean's entire awareness narrowed down to the heat of Genny's hungry, hot mouth and quick tongue. His thrusts into her humid depths increased until they matched Max's feverish strikes into her pussy. Her vocal cords vibrated almost unceasingly as she moaned in mounting excitement.

"One more time, girl. Let me in one more time, and then we'll come together," Sean promised through clenched teeth. He hissed a curse as she held steady while his cockhead pressed into her throat. The sensation of her squeezing muscles overwhelmed him.

He shouted out as climax ripped through him. His semen jetted directly into her throat before he withdrew, unblocking the passage for her breath. He thrust into her shallowly, the strength of his orgasm verging on pain. He was vaguely aware of Genny's clamping hold on his cock loosening.

He opened his eyelids.

A spasm convulsed her face as her own climax hit her. A stream of his cum leaked from her lips as he continued to fill her mouth. Max shouted out gutturally as he, too, found his release. Genny closed around his cock again, even in the midst of her own pleasure.

He pushed her head forward and loosened his hold on her hair, granting her permission to move. She ducked her head, the fact that he'd restrained her before seeming to heighten her hunger. She sucked and swallowed everything he had to give her. Sean's head fell back on the pillow and he grunted in ecstasy when she lodged him deep yet again.

Another shudder of pleasure shook him as he poured his last drops into Genny's throat.

He lay there and panted for air. Slowly he became aware that the sound of his harsh breath twined with that of Max's. He could feel Genny's exhales striking his hip in short, ragged gasps. Her eyes looked dazed and unsure when he leaned up and grasped her shoulders, pulling her on top of him. Her breasts felt soft and delicious pressed next to his heaving chest.

Max moved with her, falling over her body, sandwiching her between them. Sean realized his cock was probably still embedded in her pussy.

He chased away the disturbing thought, brushing the hair out of Genny's damp face and kissing her temple.

"Okay?" he murmured as he pressed his lips to her hot cheeks. She nodded, but Sean noticed she didn't meet his eyes. It struck him as ominous, that averted gaze. Was it all over so quickly, then? He hadn't had near enough of her, and already regret was settling.

He knew what would quiet her uncertainty; what would extinguish his. He drew her head down to him and kissed her softly, coaxing her waning fires back into full flame. When she moaned and slipped her tongue between his lips, his desperate desire swelled. He'd have never guessed he'd just had a thunderous orgasm moments ago.

He slid his fingertips across the exquisitely soft skin at the sides of her breasts. His fingers brushed against Max's. Sean spread his hands, forming the firm flesh to his palms, claiming those patches of skin as his.

Stupid reaction. Max was her husband, after all. But for right now . . . for these next precious minutes, the laws of nature, not man, would prevail.

Genny was *his*.

It barely penetrated his awareness that Max's stroking hand on the side of Genny's torso brushed his abdomen and hip, he was so caught up in kissing Genny's sweet mouth. Besides, her small, caressing hands on his shoulders and along the sides of his ribs captured his attention completely, enflaming him.

When he sealed her lips closed a moment later, he was gratified to see that all the hesitancy in her eyes had been replaced by heat. His gaze flickered over her shoulder to Max. The older man wore a satisfied expression that galled him a little.

"I want her on her back," Sean said. "Hold her for me."

Max's enigmatic eyes sparked with interest.

"No, lay on your back. Lay Genny on top of you," Sean instructed when the other man started to move toward the head of the bed. Max seemed to understand. He quickly removed the condom, placing it on the bedside table, before he lay down on his back. Max rolled Genny into his arms, her back to his chest.

Sean stood and removed the rest of his clothing before he crawled back onto the bed. Max had leaned up and was kissing Genny's shoulder. As Sean straddled Genny's naked body, he heard what the other man was murmuring near her ear.

"It felt so good, love. Your pussy has never felt so hot. If that's what Kennedy does to you, we'll have to do this more often, hmmm?" he purred next to her skin as he nibbled at her neck.

Sean cursed mentally when he saw the doubt that crossed Genny's face, stronger than he'd seen since they began making love. He knew she looked up to Max like a father figure . . . respected him. She had once, anyway. What was she thinking of how Max was behaving?

What was she thinking of Sean? What *would* she be thinking tomorrow, when the heat of the moment had passed?

For a few seconds, he considered stopping . . . calling the whole thing off. But then Max glanced up at him, his eyes hot and knowing, before he grasped Genny's wrists and pinned them to the bed. The older man shifted his legs, hooking his feet around her ankles, fixing them to the mattress.

Damn him. Max'd obviously guessed Sean's proclivity for restraining a woman during sex. He wanted Genny so greatly that it was too tempting to just imagine that Max was a substitute for cuffs or a dildo . . . another means of giving Genny pleasure.

He looked down at her wearing nothing but her stockings and high heels, bound by Max . . . awaiting pleasure. He shoved aside all his doubts as his pulse began to throb in his cock. Her breasts looked soft and inviting, round and full, rising and falling with her breath, tempting him beyond reason.

He gathered her breasts in his hands, pushing them together until the fat, dark pink nipples were only an inch apart.

He lowered his head and began to feast on her tender flesh like the beast that he undoubtedly was.

As Sean replayed that heated memory while a winter storm raged outside the windows, he knew for a fact that he would have never been able to turn away from Genny that night. He could mentally flagellate himself as routinely as he brushed his teeth, but none of that mattered.

The truth couldn't be denied, Sean admitted as he looked over at Genny huddled up in the corner of the couch.

He stood and walked toward her.

CHAPTER **NINE**

Genny's heart seemed to hesitate for a second in her chest when Sean looked over at her and stood. She glanced down over his body anxiously. She knew he was coming to claim her in that moment just as surely as she knew her own name. What *else* could that hard gleam in his blue eyes or the delineated column of his cock pressing against the denim covering his left thigh mean?

She rushed off the couch. Her sudden movement caused him to pull up short.

"I have to go to my studio."

"What?" he asked, his brows knitting together.

"My *studio*. My boutique. I just remembered that you said the temperature was going to drop. The plumbing there is ancient. If I don't turn on the faucet in the bathroom, the pipes will freeze."

He stared at her, looked out the window, and then glanced incredulously back to her face. "It's dropping about an inch of snow an hour out there. If we take out one of our cars, we'll just get stuck, Genny. I doubt there are many cabs operating, either."

"I'll walk then," she said with forced casualness. "I brought some tennis shoes. I need the exercise."

He halted her as she moved past him with a hand on her elbow. "You *can't* be serious. Your feet will get soaked if you go out without boots on—"

She jerked her elbow out of his hold, feeling a little desperate. "I *have* to go to my studio."

His mouth opened to argue.

"It's all I have now, Sean."

His words froze on his tongue. He clamped his mouth shut into a grim line.

"All right. I'm going with you."

"I thought you had work to do in the office."

"I'm going with you."

Genevieve just stared at his retreating back. She knew better than to argue with Sean when he used that tone of voice.

The cool air felt wonderful on her flushed cheeks at first. It didn't take long before desire-warmed flesh grew frigid, however.

A plow had cleared Wells Street perhaps an hour ago, but the sidewalks were thick with untouched snow. They walked on the side of the street, because there wasn't a car in sight. The el tracks over their head and the high-rises gave them a small measure of protection against the swirling, stinging snow for the first part of their trip, but north of the loop they were more fully exposed.

They finally turned right from Dearborn Avenue onto Oak Street. Sean grabbed her hand to keep her steady as the brutal Lake Michigan wind cut through her wool coat as though it were made of tissue paper. The wind came off the lake at Oak Street Beach and zoomed between the buildings, creating one of the most unpleasant wind tunnels in the city.

While shoppers patronized Michigan Avenue for the more famous stores, the block on Oak Street between Michigan and Rush was prized for smaller, high-end fashion boutiques. When Genevieve's father had passed away, she discovered that he'd named both her and her mother as the beneficiaries on his modest life insurance policy. Genevieve had used it as start-up money for her business.

She'd wanted to succeed in her own right, but part of what had propelled her manic hard work in those early days was the desire to show her father she'd made good on his legacy. She'd burned to make his life worthwhile . . . to make the ghost of him that resided in her brain proud.

She noticed as they plodded along the snow-laden street, their shoulders to the wind, that very few shops were open. She shivered and squinted at Sean. Snowflakes clung to his eyebrows and whiskered jaw. His dark blond hair had been streaked with white. He looked resigned to his frozen discomfort.

"Whose idea was this, anyway?" she asked.

He threw her a dry glance. "Had to have been some crazy girl from Gary, Indiana. Boys from N' Orleans are too fragile to go out in a blizzard."

Keeping up with Sean's long legs in the thick snow had got her heart pumping. She snorted between pants. "Fragile, my ass."

"Too smart, then," Sean added with a rakish grin that told Genny she'd been forgiven for her foolishness.

She sighed in relief when they finally reached her canopied storefront. Her boutique and design studio were housed in a renovated limestone town house. The original structure had been built in the early nineteen hundreds. She hadn't been completely lying when she said she was worried about the pipes freezing and bursting. It had never happened before, but it *could* happen. The building was old enough, after all.

She drew her keys out of her coat pocket. Her hands were numb. Sean was right. She *was* crazy for insisting they wander around the city in near-blizzard conditions because she was worried about whether or not she could actually measure up to Sean's expectations of her in bed. When she couldn't seem to work the key into the lock, Sean took the keychain from her frozen, stiff fingers and unlocked the door.

They spent several minutes stomping snow off onto the entryway floor mat and wiping flakes off each other's shoulders and back. She glanced behind her when Sean swatted at her butt several times.

"There's no snow there anymore," she scolded.

"Who said anything about snow? I'm giving you a spanking for dragging us out in this mess. I'll give you a more thorough one later."

Their gazes met and held. Genevieve realized she'd thawed out in a second, all from seeing the heated gleam in Sean's blue eyes as he teased her about a spanking.

He *had* been joking, hadn't he?

She entered the showroom of her boutique and flipped on the lights, trying to seem businesslike. She turned around next to a rack of dresses when Sean called out to her, all traces of his former humor and warmth absent from his voice.

"Stop, Genny. Come here."

She spun around.

"What?" she asked in rising confusion when she saw Sean's rigid expression as he stared at the carpet.

"Know anybody who should be in your store who wears men's size twelves?"

Genny stared at the muddy boot prints on the carpet—prints that were most definitely not hers or Sean's—and met Sean's gaze. She shook her head. He unbuttoned his peacoat and shoved his hand into the opening, withdrawing his gun. In the periphery of her stunned brain, she noticed he still carried the 9mm Beretta preferred by intelligence operatives—both ex-military and CIA. Max had also carried a 9mm Beretta.

They said he'd been murdered with his own gun.

"Get behind me. Refresh my memory. What's in the back?" Sean asked quietly as he nodded to the door behind the checkout counter.

Genevieve blinked, chasing away the anxious memories that seeing Sean's gun evoked.

"Genny?" Sean prodded when she didn't answer immediately.

"My design studio and a bathroom."

"There's a back door, right?"

"Yes," Genevieve replied. "It leads to the alley."

"It's a little chilly in here. Looks like your visitor wasn't considerate enough to shut the door before he left." Genevieve saw him peer around the showroom, his sharp eyes taking in everything. "Stay here."

He followed the tracks behind the counter and disappeared down the hallway. She heard a door close, and Sean returned a moment later, his gun sheathed in his holster once again.

"Whoever it was is gone. Got your cell phone?" he asked. Genevieve nodded and held it up. "Go ahead and call the police. You'll need to have a report made for the insurance."

"Why?" Genevieve asked anxiously, pausing as she dialed 911. She'd never had a break-in since she'd first rented this space seven years ago. "What did he take?"

"I don't know. You'll have to come and look. There's nothing obvious missing, but he's ransacked your studio."

The call to the police took longer than she would have expected. Because of the storm, they were only sending out officers to true emergencies. Most of the information regarding the break-in had to be taken over the phone. Sean had disappeared down the hallway while she talked. She assumed he was canvassing the area, conducting his own investigation.

She hung up, braced herself for seeing the wreckage before she followed him.

"*Shit,*" she said emphatically when she stood on the threshold of her studio.

"Genny?" Sean's voice echoed from the back of the building. He must have been inspecting the intruder's point of entry.

She didn't look around, although she was aware of him coming up behind her. All the despair she *should* have felt last night as she watched her house burn crashed down on her now.

She stared at the bolts of fabric, tipped over metal files, and loose paper strewn all over the floor. Everything in her desk had been spilled onto the carpet. A horrifying thought struck her and she hurried over to her desk. Her keyboard had been knocked askew, but the screen flickered to life when she touched the mouse.

"Thank God. I didn't back up my work last night before I left. The computer doesn't seem to be damaged."

"Do you notice anything missing?" Sean asked.

She glanced around, frowning when she saw that dirt from a fern had spilled all over a bolt of muted green silk crepe de chine. How could someone be so mindlessly violent?

"A common criminal isn't going to think most of this stuff is valuable," she muttered as she bent and lifted the bolt; dirt and clumps of leaves slid off the exquisite fabric. "He must have been looking for money. Maybe it was some drunk idiot who wandered over from Rush or Division," she said, referring to the restaurant and bar-lined streets just blocks away that were so popular from everyone from college kids to the affluent professionals who lived downtown.

"Whoever broke in here wasn't a drunk college kid."

Genevieve looked around when she heard the conviction in his tone. His firm lips were pressed into a grim line.

"What do you mean?" she asked, noticing his irritation.

"Did Max know you had that joke of a security system in your store?"

Genevieve bristled. "It wasn't any of *his* business." She sighed, exhaling her short-lived pique when she saw Sean's eyebrows go up in a wry expression. She felt too overwhelmed to be irritated at Sean. Besides, he probably was right. "It was the system that was here when I took possession of the place. I rented it before I ever met Max. It's always worked just fine in the past."

He rolled his eyes. "That's because you never had anyone try to break in until now. Not too difficult to have a perfect performance record when it's never been challenged. Still, joke of a system or not, whoever disabled it knew precisely what he was doing."

"Who would possibly want to—"

"We'd get a better handle on that if we knew what he was looking for," Sean interrupted. He glanced at the contents of the drawers of an antique bureau, which were now dumped all over the carpet. He walked over to the table where she did her sketches and flipped back the cover of one of her sketchbooks. "Do you think one of your competitors could have hired someone to break in here and steal some of your work?"

For some reason, the question struck her as funny; maybe because it was asked by a private intelligence operative. "*Fashion espionage?* Come on, Sean. I'm not *that* big of a name."

His sharp eyes flickered over to her before he set down the sketchbook. "What'd the police say?"

"Squad cars are only being sent out to true emergency situations because of the bad conditions. I'm supposed to call again after the streets get cleared and an officer will come over to make

a report," she said dully as she looked around her once pleasant, cozy workspace. Had it just been this morning that she was
thinking how her studio seemed more like a home to her than the
mansion? She blinked in surprise when Sean touched her arm. He
moved as silently as a stalking wolf when he wanted to.

"We're going back to the penthouse."

"I'm fine, Sean. I want to get this place straightened up."

He shook his head. "Just leave everything as it is until the police
get here to take the report. The lock was busted on the back door,
but I've jerry-rigged it for the time being. It'll hold for now."

Genevieve sighed, seeing his point about not altering things
until the police made the report. She tightened the belt on her coat
and started to walk out of the room.

"Genny?"

She turned. Sean watched her intently.

"You're sure there's nothing missing?"

She shrugged and glanced around the studio again. "Nothing
I notice right off the bat, especially with everything being such a
mess. The only things a burglar might want to take are the two
computers and my stereo, and those are all still here. Marilyn went
to the bank yesterday and made a deposit, since it was Friday.
There was no money on the premises."

"And you were the last one to leave last night?"

She nodded.

"You didn't notice anything unusual when you locked up?"

"No," she said after a moment of rehashing her memories. "I
left at a little after nine. Everything was quiet."

Until she'd gotten home, anyway, and seen all the fire trucks
and emergency vehicles at her house. Her gaze shot to Sean's face.
She wondered if he wasn't thinking the same thing when his blue
eyes narrowed into slits. He didn't seem too happy about the turn
of events. Not that she was, either.

"Genny . . . is there anything you're not telling me? Anything I should know?"

A chill skittered down her spine. "What's that supposed to mean?"

"You've got to admit, it's kind of strange. Your house burns down one night and then your store is broken into the next afternoon. Those tracks out back are fresh, you know. Not a half an inch of snow has accumulated in the guy's footprints out in the alley. My guess is that he was in here at about two o'clock—at about the same time we left the penthouse.

When he saw her stunned expression, he shook his head, his eyes never leaving her face. "Come on. Let's get you back to the penthouse. I think you've had enough surprises in the past twenty-four hours."

CHAPTER **TEN**

Sean hung up his cell phone and stared thoughtfully out the window into dense, swirling snow. Genny had been shivering uncontrollably by the time they had returned. The rosy bloom that had been in her cheeks when they'd left the penthouse had entirely faded, leaving her wan and pale. He'd hustled her off to take a hot bath the second after they'd removed their coats.

He'd just spoken to Joe McMannis, an ex-Army buddy of his who worked as a private investigator in Indianapolis. Maybe he was paranoid, but Sean suddenly had a burning need to know the exact whereabouts of Albert Rook.

He knew it didn't make sense, but the hackles that had been raised by the report of the fire at Genny's house had turned into a sudden, sure prescience when he'd seen those muddy footprints on the floor of her boutique and felt the draft of cool air emanating from the back of the building.

Something wasn't right. Genny was in danger. And when he thought of Genny being threatened, his mind automatically went to Albert Rook. Maybe it was because part of him had been waiting for the other shoe to drop ever since Max Sauren had been found shot dead in his car in an abandoned warehouse parking lot on the north side of Chicago.

The police had never been able to make an arrest, although Genny had been their primary suspect. The fact that Max's own gun had never been located had indicated he'd been murdered by his own weapon.

And any detective worth his salt knew that a man shot by his own gun was probably shot by someone close to him. If that was a fact for a normal gun owner, it was three times true for Max Sauren. Max had lived a dangerous life, beginning with his days in the CIA and ending as the owner of a private intel firm. Max had accumulated quite a few enemies over the years. No one knew that fact better than Max himself. No stranger or mere acquaintance could have slipped inside Max's defenses easily.

Plus there was the fact he'd been shot in his own car. No prints had been found inside the car that shouldn't have been there, given Max's associations. Genny certainly qualified as a Max Sauren insider, just as Sean himself did. But so did Albert Rook.

Rook was like a cockroach—you could make him disappear from sight for a while by sending out a warning to his existence, but he'd eventually come sneaking out of the cracks of the dark corners of your life.

Sean just wanted to know one thing: What had made his threat to Rook wear thin?

He thought back to two nights after Max had been found dead. Sean'd just left the Sauren mansion. He'd been fulminating because Genny had sent word through an apologetic Jim that she was too exhausted to see him. It'd been the fourth time he'd been turned away from seeing her, and she refused to return his phone calls.

Sean hadn't shared more than three sentences with Genny since New Year's Eve.

He'd just cleared the front door of the mansion when his cell phone rang. He frowned when he saw the name on the caller ID. He'd experienced a feeling of foreboding not unlike the one he had three years later after seeing those footprints on the carpet of Genevieve's boutique.

"What do you want, Rook?"

"Is the *grieving* widow refusing to see you again?" Rook asked snidely.

Sean paused on the front steps, making a quick survey of the wooded area surrounding the circular drive. Rook and his car were nowhere in sight.

"I told you we need to keep business going as smoothly as possible at Sauren. Clients are going to get cold feet when they hear about Max's death. We need to show them we're as on top of their cases as ever. I assigned you to the Singleton account. What the hell are you doing spying on *me* instead?" Sean muttered furiously.

"You weren't the only one who was friends with Max. So what if I want to see his murderer brought to justice?"

"You and I both know you and Max were a hell of a lot more than *friends*."

"You can't prove that," Rook said silkily. "Not like I can prove just how close you, Max, and his wife were five nights before Max was killed. I have incontrovertible evidence—extremely *graphic* evidence—that illustrates just how amorous you were with Genevieve Bujold in the penthouse on New Year's Eve. Don't you think Detective Franklin would be fascinated by that proof? No?" Rook goaded with mock innocence when Sean went silent in shock.

Fuck.

"What do you want?" Sean stood on the front steps of the mansion, as rigid and furious as the two carved limestone, roaring lions that guarded the entryway to Genny's home.

"Aren't you listening, Kennedy? Justice."

"*Justice?* I guess some have mistaken justice for revenge, but I've never heard of justice being mistaken for cold hard cash before. Leave it to you to make that interpretation, Rook. Or maybe it's shares in Sauren that you want? You never could stand the fact that Max agreed to let me buy in to Sauren when I signed on as his chief operating officer, could you?" Sean murmured, his light tone belying the ache he felt growing in his gut.

Someone had taken *video* of the three of them in the bedroom that night, Sean thought as panic tickled at his awareness. But who? Rook? Max?

And why?

The only thing he knew for sure was that the knowledge of that video would decimate Genny. Not to mention be a volatile piece of evidence if the police got their hands on it.

"What's that supposed to mean—*what do I want*?" Rook actually had enough nerve to sound insulted when he asked the question.

"Stop beating around the bush. What do you want?"

The fact that their fragile surface peace had been shattered seemed to suddenly light a match to Rook's anger. "Max always acted like nothing could ever faze his decision-making, but he clearly let his cock make his choice when he hired a redneck like you to run his company."

"Yeah? He sure as hell wasn't letting his brains rule him when he let your ass get anywhere near his dick, was he? *Shut it*," he said sharply when Rook started to shout into the phone. He glanced back at the brick Tudor mansion and continued more quietly. "Just get it over with. What do you want from me?"

"I'll tell you what I want when we meet," Rook snarled. "I have solid evidence to show you in regard to your girlfriend—evidence that'd put her behind bars for a very long time if I showed it to the police."

Sean loosened his clenched jaw. It hurt; he'd been clamping it so tightly while he waited for the attack to come. "Meet me in my office in an hour and a half."

"I want you to know I've taken measures to make sure this evidence will come to light if you do anything to harm me."

Sean bent his head and spoke into the receiver softly. "I know you're somewhere around here, Rook. You'd better turn around, get in your car, and drive away, because I want *you* to know something. If you so much as glance at Genevieve Bujold before we've settled things downtown in an hour and a half, you'll be seeing Max a lot sooner than you think."

He hung up the phone and walked to his car. His muscles felt stiff with shock and rising fear, but his mind moved agilely as he worked all the angles.

Sean had assumed he was attending a blackmail meeting on that gloomy winter day three years ago, and he hadn't been wrong. Sean'd played the hand that had been dealt to him on that day with Albert Rook. He might not have had the best of cards, but Sean had learned early on that even the worst hands had the potential to be winners.

Max had once revealed to Sean that Albert Rook had sold secrets to the Chinese during his stint in the Navy as a weapons systems analyst. Max possessed hard evidence of that powerful secret.

Sean didn't.

But that hadn't stopped him three years ago from using the information in a bald-faced bluff in order to protect Genny.

After a bit of theatre involving a fake version of Max Sauren's infamous leather-bound attaché case and a threat to expose the evidence of Rook's treason to the United States government, Rook had backed off in his blackmail scheme.

Rook himself might well have been bluffing about the evidence he showed Sean in regard to Genevieve—digital photos of Max's gun, two bullet shell casings . . . and the real kick in the ass: Genevieve's prints on those shell casings.

They'd never been able to pull prints off the two bullets that killed Max, but the fingerprints on the brass shell casings were definitely Genevieve's. Rook was able to prove at least that much to Sean. Before they'd updated to retinal scans, Sauren Solutions had used fingerprints for several security entry points. They had an archive of employee and several key family member fingerprints, so Sean had been able to cross-check the prints on his computer during that blackmail meeting with Rook.

Sean'd never truly possessed the hard evidence of Rook's treasonous activities, although thanks to Max, he knew it existed—and he knew *Rook* knew it existed. Max had likely enjoyed dangling that volatile knowledge over his lover's head. Hell, for all Sean knew, he'd used it to get Rook to have sex with him. Neither man had ever struck Sean as overtly gay or bisexual, but in the world of secrets and espionage, that was the type of personal knowledge that would be held close to the chest.

Very close.

Sean suspected Max kept the evidence of Rook's treason with the rest of his volatile secrets—inside his high-security attaché case. Chances were, Rook believed that's where the evidence was, as well. Sean'd seen Max subtly flaunt that attaché case too many times in rivals' and enemies' sweating faces in order to think otherwise. He'd searched the Sauren Solutions premises after Max died, but he'd never been able to find the attaché case.

But Rook didn't need to know Sean'd come up short.

The air in Sean's office had seemed to pop with fury and animosity when Rook had entered on that day three years ago. Sean had sat at this desk and watched the other man silently, waiting for Rook's opening move.

Rook's thin, hawkish face looked rigid with tension as he approached. He wore what Sean had come to identify in his mind as the *Rook uniform*—one of many dark, well-made European suits, a white shirt, black leather briefcase and conservative tie. Sean'd never seen the knot loosened, never seen a brown hair out of place on Rook's head. Not having any sexual interest in men himself, Sean wasn't sure what Max found appealing in his lover. Sean guessed that some might find Rook's intense manner and lean, wiry body attractive.

Personally, Sean thought the guy was an oily creep.

As he approached Sean's desk, a small smile grew on Rook's thin lips. Sean ignored the urge to change the shape of that insolent grin with his hammering fist. He waited silently while Rook set down his briefcase on Sean's desk and opened it.

"Everything you need to see is on here," Rook had said as he withdrew a thumb drive. Sean took the drive and inserted it into his computer, still fantasizing about planting his knuckles in Rook's smug face. "As I'm sure you already know, that's just one of several copies. I have all the hard evidence and other copies secured in a safety-deposit box. I've left instructions with my attorney for how to proceed if something should happen to me."

Sean's smile was a thinly disguised snarl. "Little worried about your safety, Albert?"

"You're the one that should be worried."

"We're about to find out which one of us has more of a right to his anxieties," Sean murmured.

"Why don't you open up the file that says *penthouse video* first," Rook had challenged. "That ought to make you *sweat* a little . . ."

Rook had seemed to enjoy Sean's fury as he'd watched the video of himself making love to Genny while Max held her. He'd certainly relished informing him that Max had planned the whole taping incident to keep as a ready resource should Sean or Genny ever get out of hand in their love affair, or make any onerous demands on Max. Sean could only imagine Genny's reaction if Max had threatened to show the video to someone like Genny's mother.

You knew Max. He always wanted something tasty to pull out during a tight spot, Rook had taunted.

Sean had known that the police were hungry to pin Max's murder on Genny. Whether she'd done it or not, Rook's evidence had the potential to get her arrested at the very least. That was a possibility Sean refused to allow to happen. So he'd played the hell out of the hand that he'd been dealt, and it'd worked. He'd sent Rook running scared.

But now the asshole might be back.

Sean blinked, temporarily rising out of his memories, when he heard the water start running in the guest bathroom again. Genny was heating up her bath. He kept his gaze trained down the hallway and set his phone on the coffee table. Something told him she was stalling about leaving the bathroom . . . about their being together in these intimate surroundings.

His instinct was hollering another unwelcome message in his brain. Genny was in danger once again—just like she had been three years ago.

And for some goddamned reason Sean couldn't divine at the moment, he suspected that slimeball Albert Rook was at the bottom of it all. Sean'd been waiting for the day he'd come back ever since he'd sent Rook packing three years ago.

Still . . . the thought plagued him. *Why now?* Why would he have stopped believing in Sean's threat to turn over evidence that Rook was guilty of treason against the United States?

One thing Sean felt entirely confident about was that Genny was safe here in the penthouse. Rook may be good enough to disable

Genny's security system at her boutique. But the bastard wasn't going to get anywhere *near* her while she was within the multiple, high-tech security measures Sean'd had personally installed both for the intel company and the penthouse following Max's murder.

He walked over to the bar and drew down a glass.

There was something else he knew for a fact. Whether you wanted to call it fate, luck, or chance, *something* had brought Genny back to him. He poured wine into the glass.

It'd be easier to protect her if he'd established a firm claim. To hell with Albert Rook, and fuck Genny's supposed boyfriend.

It was way past time for him to make Genny his.

He flipped off the lights, leaving the room in darkness except for the orange glow from the flames in the fireplace. He walked down the hallway toward the bathroom.

CHAPTER **ELEVEN**

Genevieve's bath water began to cool around her. She should get out before she became as cold as she had been when they'd come in from the snowstorm. An image of her ransacked studio leapt into her mind's eye. She thought of Sean out there in the penthouse . . . waiting. A delicious thrill of anticipation went through her body, but so did a tremor of anxiety.

She reached for the hot water tap and leaned back again in the tub.

It would all be so much easier if she'd never slept with him—if she didn't know about his demanding manner of making love . . .

If she hadn't responded so wholeheartedly to Sean's dominant nature in bed.

It was strange, but somehow her submission to Sean—submission to her own desire—on that New Year's Eve night had become all mixed up in her mind with Max's manipulations, and later the horror of being told he was dead. It was exciting beyond belief to think of making love to Sean, but it also caused dread to expand in her belly.

It'd been her desperate need for Sean that'd been at the root of all the grief that followed, all the ugliness. It'd been the basis for her sexual submission on that night. Her love for Sean had also been the match that had ignited an explosion of deceit and violence.

She sat up abruptly, sloshing the water around in the tub when the bathroom door opened. Sean walked in. He shut the door and leaned against it. For several tense seconds, they stared at each other across the expanse of the warm, humid bathroom. Genevieve swallowed convulsively when she saw the fierce blaze in his blue eyes.

She remembered that look all too well.

He pushed himself off the door and came toward her. "I brought you a glass of wine. I thought you might need it. To relax a little."

Her eyes widened when she took in his low, intimate tone. He paused next to the tub and glanced down at her body. His gaze seemed to scorch her wet, naked skin. Her nipples prickled and tightened. Her eyes were on the same level of his long, strong, jean-covered thighs. He handed her the wineglass. She reached out for it automatically. Her gaze traveled up his body to meet his stare.

His facial muscles had pulled tight with desire—and determination.

"You said I'm not aloud to talk about that night, Genny, so I won't. But I want you to know something: I won't bow down to guilt. Not mine. Not even yours. Do you understand?"

Her eyes burned as he held her stare. She nodded.

"Good," he said softly. He touched the fingers wrapped around the glass. "Drink some, girl."

She watched him as she drank and her pulse throbbed at her throat. He looked magnificent to her at that moment. For the life of her, she couldn't imagine how she'd managed to stay away from him for three years.

He took the glass from her a moment later and set it at the edge of the large tub. He waited.

She leaned forward and twisted the tap, shutting off the water. She stood before him, water dripping off her body. His heated gaze raked over her, lingering on her breasts before he looked up at her face.

"Our first time wasn't what either of us would have wished for, but it's over and done, and we can't change it. I know you're nervous. I am, too, a little, so I'm going to make this as easy as possible. You're going to get out of that tub, I'm going to dry you off, and then we're going out to the couch, where it's nice and warm. I'm going to take off my clothes," he murmured, his voice growing gruffer with each word he spoke, "and I'm going to put myself inside you, girl—where I belong. Nothin' fancy, I promise. Just me and you. Do you think you can handle that?"

Her heartbeat throbbed in her ears as she stared into his blazing blue eyes. Anxiety? Guilt? No.

Nothing existed but Sean at that moment.

"Yes." She put out her hand and he grasped it, steadying her as she stepped out of the tub. He drew down the white towel from the rack and unfolded it. He dried her off with a gentle thoroughness that had Genevieve's breath coming raggedly by the time he reached her toes.

"Turn around," he said without looking up.

She did, and the whole excruciating, exciting process continued. He wiped off her calves and the back of her knees. He stood and covered his hand with the towel before he dragged it across a thigh. When he dried the other one, he pressed lightly with his hand, urging her to spread her legs. She whimpered softly when he parted her buttocks with one warm hand. He dried not only the cheeks, but the crevice between them. He squeezed a buttock tautly in his palm before one long finger reached.

He slicked a fingertip across the sensitive tissues surrounding her vagina. An electric thrill went through her. He gave a satisfied grunt.

"Warm and wet. You make things so damn easy, Genny," he rumbled near her ear.

"*Sean.*" She started to turn toward him, overwhelmed with need. He stopped her with a hand on her shoulders.

"Just a second now. You're not the only one who's in a hurry for this, trust me." He swiped the towel over her back, drying her thoroughly. He slung the towel onto the rack again.

Genevieve sputtered in surprise when he pushed her back into his arms and lifted her. His smile was as tender as his touch had been.

"I had to get you all dried off. You'd say I had ulterior motives if you caught a chill and were holed up here in the penthouse with me even longer," he said as he carried her out of the bathroom.

He paused in his progress down the hallway when Genevieve wrapped her arms around his neck and pressed her mouth just above his collar. His pulse throbbed against her lips, the rate of it every bit as rapid as her own. Her pussy had already begun to ache for him, but the sure knowledge of his reciprocal desire for her made it clench tight in need. She licked at his smooth skin, suddenly ravenous for his taste on her tongue.

"I may be nervous, but I'd be a liar if I said I wanted to be anywhere else in the world at this minute," she said next to his neck.

He resumed walking, this time more rapidly. He laid her down on the couch. The only source of light in the living room was the flames in the fireplace. Warmth and arousal weighted her flesh. She sunk into the soft velvet sofa and watched hungrily as Sean whipped his shirt over his head. Muscle stretched and flexed, leaving her spellbound. The flames played across his gold-toned, smooth skin, casting flickering shadows across the landscape of his torso.

His gaze traveled over her body as he unfastened his belt. His nostrils flared as he stared at the juncture of her thighs.

"Can you get pregnant?"

She blinked at the unexpectedness of the question asked in such a terse tone.

"I'm on the pill," she replied.

"I never have unprotected intercourse with a woman. Never. But I'm gonna come inside you tonight, girl."

"Aren't you worried about me? Who I've been with?"

"No. Should I be?"

She sighed. "No."

Heat sunk from her lower belly to her genitals when she saw his small grin. A drop of liquid trickled from her slit. She nodded her head in agreement to his proposal. Her vocal cords had gone numb when she read the message in Sean's fiery eyes.

Her acquiescence made him tear at the fastenings of his jeans with even more haste.

He freed his cock, jerking the boxer briefs down his thighs. It sprung from a thatch of dark brown pubic hair. His size and the stark evidence of his desire sent a thrill through her. He bent to remove his jeans, underwear, and socks and Genevieve was momentarily deprived of the awesome sight.

But then he straightened before her, the vision of him so beautiful it made her hurt.

She reached for his jutting erection even as their gazes held. He felt like warmed silk stretched tight over steel. The sheer weight of his cock in her palm stunned her. Her thumb traced a swollen blue vein. He winced in pleasure.

"You never really let me touch you. Before," she whispered.

"That's because you try me, girl. You're doing it again, right this second."

She sighed in sublime satisfaction when he swung one leg over her supine body and came down over her. Little detonations of pleasure went off everywhere in her flesh at the sensation of his skin sliding against hers, and then his delicious weight pressing her down into the soft couch.

He seized her mouth in a dizzying, hot kiss.

She craned up for more of the addictive taste of him when he lifted his head. He braced himself on one knee next to her hip. She realized he'd kept his other foot on the floor when he placed both hands at the small of her back and lifted her until her head slid down the couch and her spine bowed into an arch.

He held himself off her, bent down, and proceeded to consume her. His hot mouth felt like it was everywhere at once. He pressed firm lips to the bones of her ribs, making her quiver, and kissed her belly with a hot, open mouth. He scraped his teeth along her sides and nipped lightly at her hip.

But mostly he focused on her breasts—nuzzling them with his cheek, dragging his firm, warm lips across the sensitive skin as if to memorize her texture, slipping her nipples between his lips and drawing on her with a firm, steady suction that had Genevieve clawing her fingers through his thick hair and writhing in his hold.

Begging him.

Her pleas must have eventually reached him, because he released her captive nipple and leaned up. His eyes gleamed in the flame-lit room as he stared down at her. His biceps flexed as he pushed up her body and slid his stiff, burning cock along her hip and up over her belly.

"Sean. You *promised*," she whispered harshly, overwhelmed by the sensation.

A smile tugged at the corners of his mouth. "I did, didn't I?"

Genevieve shifted up her hips, applying pressure to his cock where it was sandwiched between their bodies. She ran her hands over his bunching back muscles and pulled him even closer. All traces of amusement vanished from his face. Genevieve opened her thighs, instinctively recognizing that feral expression.

He took his cock in one hand and arrowed it toward her slit. The steely head felt delicious against her wet, sensitive tissues. She spread her legs as wide as the couch would allow and pressed up against the hard pressure of his cock.

"I've waited for this for so long," he grated out as he held her gaze. He thrust his hips.

Genevieve made a choked sound of thwarted longing when he didn't get anywhere. She tried to open her thighs wider, granting him entrance into her body, but it was difficult with the back of the couch acting as a barrier.

"I'm sorry. I haven't . . . It's been a long time," she muttered, feeling foolish.

Since New Year's Eve three years ago, to be exact. And even then, when Sean had fucked her, Max had been there before him. It'd been a preparation, of sorts. Sean wasn't a small man.

She felt her heart sinking, despite her frantic excitement, when Sean just studied her intently for a few seconds. He'd sensed her nervousness earlier and tried to make things simple for their first joining. *And I can't even get* that *right,* she thought with rising frustration as she once again pushed against his cockhead.

"Don't apologize." He made a hushing sound when she cried out in protest as he moved off her and stood. He grabbed the folded blanket off the back of the couch and her hand at the same time. Genevieve stood next to him at his urging.

"It's my fault. Couches are kind of . . . restricting," he mumbled as he led her in front of the fireplace. He spread the blanket on the carpet and turned to her. One hand remained encircling her own while he cupped her jaw with the other. His head lower and she craned up for him, her arms encircling his waist.

As usual, Sean's kiss did a vanishing act on her anxieties.

They lowered to the soft blanket, never releasing each other from their mutual embrace. He pushed her back to the floor and came down over her, his mouth moving hungrily over her neck, cheeks, and seeking lips. She welcomed his weight, prized the feeling of him covering her more than any gift she'd ever received. She swept her hands over the warm, smooth skin of his back and buttocks, kneading dense muscle in growing desperation.

His mouth remained on her neck, hot and hungry, while he grasped his cock and positioned it next to her slit. He flexed. Genevieve moaned feverishly and spread herself wide, but he worked only the smooth, tapered head of his cock into her body.

He slipped an arm beneath her thigh and lifted her leg, sliding it along his forearm until he hooked her knee in the crook of his elbow. When he placed one hand near her ear on the blanket and reared up over her, he pressed on the back of her leg, prying her wide.

Genevieve cried out in amazement at the intense pressure as his cock slid into her body. He flexed his hips and grunted gutturally. He paused with his balls pressed tightly to her cunt. They stared at each other while their bellies heaved in excitement.

Genevieve had never felt so full . . . so volatile . . . so ready to burst into flame from a whispering touch in her life.

His tongue swiped at the coat of perspiration that had accumulated above his upper lip.

"Okay?" he asked on a puff of exhaled air.

Genevieve nodded. It was all she could manage with her knee

nearly hitting her chest and his large cock throbbing deep inside her. Her vaginal muscles convulsed around him. She felt his back shudder and a spasm went through his cheek.

"You're so sweet, girl. So tight. So . . . fucking"—he withdrew and then pressed his testicles to her again, grinding his pelvis against her clit—"*hot.*"

She cried out as the orgasm blasted through her body.

CHAPTER **TWELVE**

Sean's eyes crossed as heat flooded around his cock and Genny's vagina clamped around him. He'd already felt like he'd died and gone to heaven, being lodged inside the sweetest pussy he'd ever known. Then Genny started to come, and the primal mandate swelled inside of him to take her.

He looked down at the sight of her beautiful face pulled tight with pleasure, felt the shudders of orgasm coursing through her body. Her vagina writhed around his cock . . . taunting it.

He'd wanted her for so damn long. It seemed a little surreal that the time had finally come to make her his in this most basic of ways.

He made a small circling motion with his pelvis, grinding down on her. She whimpered and shook as another wave of orgasm hit her, vibrating into his near-to-bursting cock.

"Open your eyes," he muttered when her trembling had waned.

Her eyelids opened heavily She panted as she looked up at him. He saw her soul shining in her firelit, gray eyes. A spasm of emotion rippled through him, lighting a fuse. His cock swelled in her tight sheath, making him grimace in pain.

He started to thrust.

"Ah, girl . . . what you do to me," he grated out between clenched teeth. He slid out of her until only the cockhead remained fast in her clinging pussy then growled in ecstasy as he rocketed back into her. He watched her through narrowed eyelids as her breasts trembled from the impact of their smacking flesh and a whimper of pleasure popped out of her throat.

How could he feel so much tenderness toward her and yet want to fuck her like an animal all at once? The paradox created an untenable friction inside him.

"I'm gonna have to take you hard," he explained regretfully as he pumped. "I've waited so long, and you feel so damn good."

"Yes."

Just like that. Sweet, simple . . . generous beyond belief, even when the evidence was surrounding him that she hadn't taken a man in a very long time.

He drove into her again and again. Genny shifted her hips, sliding her pussy along his pistoning cock, meeting him stroke for stroke in their carnal rhythm. Sean didn't know if it was because so many feelings were involved when it came to Genny, or just the fact that her pussy felt like it'd been made for him, but the friction was perfect . . . optimal.

Mind-blowing.

A burning sensation tingled in his cock and went all the way up his backbone, pitching him into mindless excitement. He was like a waif who had unexpectedly arrived in heaven, a kid who feared his stay was an error and would inevitably be short-lived. He strove wildly to fill his greedy senses; raced to penetrate Genny's farthest depths before she was whisked away from him.

Genny, Genny, Genny. Her name resounded in his head every

time his flesh slapped against hers and she held him in her deep, tight embrace. He needed to prove she was right here with him, every bit as real as his own hot flesh, raging blood, and teeming cock.

"Sean," she moaned when he leaned down over her farther, altering the angle of his driving cock, desperate to feel every nuance of her embrace.

"You fit me perfectly, girl," he growled as their mating grew even more frantic. Sean preferred to be in control during his love-making, but here with Genny tonight, his monumental need ruled him. He'd find his control . . . but later.

Now he wanted to drown in Genny Bujold.

She screamed when he pushed her other knee into her chest, opening her body even more to him. He rode her climaxing pussy hard, lost in a frenzy of lust and clawing need, bucking into her as she chanted his name in a litany of ecstasy and his heart hammered wildly in his ears.

He stared at her clenched, perspiration-damp face, wanting to memorize the vision, before he drove into her high and deep. His climax ripped into him with hurricane force. He opened his eyes wide as he exploded, the force of his orgasm shocking him . . . shaking him. Despite the physical release, his tension and need didn't dissipate.

He slammed into her again and again as his cock erupted, feeling like he couldn't get enough . . . would never get enough.

Greedy bastard that he was.

Genny's heavy eyelids rose. For several seconds she just stared up at the awesome sight of Sean. He still held himself off her with his hands; her knees were still hooked in his elbows. He'd pried her body open just like he had her soul in those carnal, sacred moments . . . completely laid her bare for his ravishing spirit.

How could so much passion exist inside one man? she thought in wonderment.

His chest expanded and contracted rapidly; his head hung limp as he strove to get enough air in his lungs. The muscles of his arms and shoulders bunched tight and hard, like he'd just undergone a strenuous workout. She glided her hands over smooth, perspiration-damp flesh, relishing the sensation even as she attempted to soothe his physical agitation.

After a moment, his eyelids opened into slits. He considered her with eyes that glowed like banked coals. His cock lurched deep inside her, and Genny was left in little doubt that his fires would leap into full flame at just a touch. A message seemed to leap between them and Sean smiled.

He released her legs and collapsed on top of her with a loud groan. All the air whooshed out of her lungs.

"Sean, I can't breathe," she complained through choked laughter.

"Yeah, but you're not nervous anymore, are you?"

"How can I be nervous when I'm not getting any oxygen to my brain?"

"So my plan worked, huh?"

She dug her fingertips between his ribs. He jumped and rolled off her, bringing her with him in his arms until they were both on their sides, facing each other. They were looking at each other, laughter curving their lips, as his cock slid out of her body. All the humor Genevieve had been feeling faded at the poignant sensation of him leaving her.

For some reason it brought to mind the tenuousness of their joining, all the uncertainty and anxiety that had accompanied their first volatile lovemaking.

Unwanted tears stung her eyes. Why did their powerful attraction always have to be associated with heartache and impermanence?

"I'll be back inside you soon enough, girl," he said gruffly.

Just like Sean, to read her thoughts.

She formed his name with her lips but nothing came out. His hand rose to cradle her head when she buried her face in his neck. After a moment, her crisis faded, and she became hyperaware of his scent filling her nostrils and the movement of his fingers in her hair.

"I always loved your hair," he murmured. "How do you make it wave like this?"

"Same way you make yours wave, I guess," she said against his neck.

"Mother nature expressing herself, huh?"

She nodded. "For a guy, it's adorable and sexy. For a woman, it's horribly unfashionable."

He snorted. "You could have it straightened if you wanted. If you ever did, I'd turn you over my knee though." Genevieve figured it was safe to look at him now, so she leaned back and gave him a disparaging glance. He grinned. "Besides, you're one of the people who decide what's fashionable and what's not. If women could get their hair to look like yours, they would."

Genevieve shivered when he rubbed her scalp languorously and then ran his fingers through a handful of hair.

"So soft." His low, husky drawl made the back of her neck prickle and her vagina clench in renewed longing. "The first time I saw you I thought you looked like an old-fashioned movie star with all those gleaming waves falling around your shoulders"—his gaze settled on her mouth—"and those red lips."

She pulled a face, trying to diminish the strength of her physical reaction to him. "I never wear red lipstick."

He gave her a droll expression. "I never said you did. Your lips are always red. They get redder when I kiss 'em." He ducked his head and kissed her, quick and potent. "I get the worst erections every time I just think about your mouth." He slid his lips along her jawbone and down over her ear. He nuzzled her warmly. "'Course it's the same with your ears, and your neck," he added as he pressed his lips there and she shivered. His hand rose and lightly touched the front of her neck. "Best not to think about your lovely throat," he growled near her ear.

The memory of allowing him to fuck her mouth, of him breaching the barrier of her throat, rose up in her mind's eye in graphic detail. Heat flushed her cheeks and genitals. Sean stopped stroking her when he noticed her downcast eyes.

"Do you hate the memory of it so much, Genny?" he whispered.

Emotion tightened her throat. "I told you—"

"I know, I know," he muttered in rising exasperation. "You don't want to talk about that night. You want me to forget it ever happened. But I'm not like you, Genny. I don't want to erase it. I *want* to remember." He pushed her onto her back and leaned down over her. "It's all I had of you."

Genevieve stared up at him as volatile emotions warred in her breast. A heavy feeling of dread settled like a weight in her gut when she thought about discussing what had happened on that New Year's Eve ... and Max's murder five days later. But the haunted expression in Sean's eyes as he looked down at her made her hurt even more. She cradled his whiskered jaw in her palm and let her fingers run through his thick hair.

"I wish it'd never happened," she admitted. "But you're wrong to think I want to forget it all. I remember. All too well, Sean." Her hand rose between them. When he realized her intent, he shifted his hips, granting her access. She wrapped her hand around his moist cock. He wasn't as iron-hard as he had been before he climaxed, but he was still firm and delicious. A focused, feral expression came over his face as she stroked him. He placed two fingers on her lips and pressed into the flesh softly.

"You were so sweet, girl. So generous. You showed me so much trust on that night," he muttered gruffly. His gaze had been fixed on her mouth, but he suddenly met her stare.

"Do you still trust me that much, Genny?"

She swallowed thickly. "I believe with all my heart that you want me to be happy, Sean. And . . ."

"What?" he asked tensely when she faded off.

"I don't know why, but it brings me so much pleasure to please you."

"I know why," he rasped before he leaned down and replaced his fingers with his lips. He molded their mouths together in a lazy, decadently carnal kiss. Her movements on his cock matched the rhythm of their languorous exploration of each other's mouths. By the time he lifted his head moments later, Genevieve's body hummed once again with hot arousal and Sean's cock felt heavy and warm in her hand. She flicked her fingers over the thick ridge below the head, tugging at him gently. Fire leapt into his eyes.

"Oh, you're gonna have to pay for that, girl."

Her eyes went wide at his low threat. Still . . . she gave his cock another erotic tug.

He grunted, leapt up from the blanket and stood over her. Her mouth gaped open when she saw his cock from below. It was an awesome sight . . . if a little intimidating, she thought as she licked her lower lip anxiously. He wrapped his hand around his erection and stroked himself as he stared down at her naked body. "I don't think I've ever seen anything so lovely in my life," he murmured. "You tempt me something awful, you know that, girl?"

She tempted *him*? She watched, completely mesmerized, as he caught a stream of the clear liquid seeping from the slit on his cockhead and rubbed it into the skin until it glistened.

"You know what I want?"

Genevieve nodded. She never told herself to move, but suddenly she was kneeling in front of him, her hands on his muscular, hair-sprinkled thighs. Sean seemed every bit as hypnotized as her. One big hand slid down to the root of his penis. The other cupped her skull.

"Open your lips, just a little." Genevieve opened her mouth and stared up at him. The head of his cock felt warm and firm as he pressed it against her lips. She never breathed as he outlined her mouth, spreading a thin coat of pre-cum. She waited until he'd made a full pass. When he pulled away slightly, she whisked her tongue over her mouth, relishing his flavor.

He gave a low groan and stepped toward her. He rested just the tip of the smooth cockhead on her damp lower lip. Genevieve whimpered when she felt the weight of it press down on her lip.

"Don't move a thing. Not even your tongue," he muttered. His voice was hoarse with lust. He began to stroke the shaft of his cock with long, thorough strokes. This time Genevieve groaned. It was exciting beyond belief, but also a sexual torment to feel the weight of his cock on her lip, to inhale the scent of her pussy combined with his male musk . . . to have her mouth water in anticipation of his taste.

"That's right," he whispered as he continued to jack his cock, keeping the tip on the shelf of her lower lip. "Nice to let the excitement build, isn't it? Nice to savor it. Nice to know I'm eventually going to explode in your sweet mouth again after all these years." His entire arm moved as he stroked his long cock and stared down at her. "Is that what you want, too, girl?"

Did she *ever* want it. She looked up at him gave a small nod of her head. She swallowed the saliva that was building in her mouth as her craving for him became overpowering.

"You're so sweet," he murmured. He stepped slightly closer. "Just put the head in your mouth." He grunted in pleasure when she spread her lips wide around his girth as he pushed the heavy cockhead into her mouth. "Now use your tongue," he instructed as he resumed stroking the shaft.

Genevieve fluttered her tongue over smooth, dense flesh. She was so hungry for his taste she went straight for the slit. She pressed with the tip of her tongue firmly, and was rewarded with a rough groan from Sean's throat and the flavor of his pre-cum spreading in her mouth. When fluid stopped seeping onto her tongue, she gave the entire cockhead a hard polishing, never taking her eyes off the magnificent image of Sean as he watched her with a hyperalert focus.

He must have liked what she did, because he began to jack his cock faster. The sight was so intensely erotic that her nipples pulled tight in excitement. Not only her clit began to burn; the soles of her feet tingled in mounting arousal.

His eyes glittered dangerously when she began to draw on him as hard as she could, hollowing out her cheeks, hoping she could entice him to slide deeper.

She moaned when he flexed his hips and thick, throbbing flesh filled her mouth.

He tightened his hold on her skull. "Is that what you wanted, girl?" he drawled, a small smile pulling at his lips when he saw her eyes go wide. "If you tease, you'll pay the price." His fingertips pushed gently on her scalp. "Go ahead. Show me how you can suck on it." He halted her by tightening his hold on her skull when she started to dip her head forward. She met his eyes. "Just focus on the first half of it."

Genevieve nodded and drew back her head, sliding the delicious weight of his cock along her tongue. She fluttered her tongue over the smooth crown before she ducked her head forward, sinking him into her mouth to mid-staff. She closed her eyes and focused on the exquisite sensations of his texture, density, and taste on her tongue. Her lips tightened on him and she sucked thirstily.

He groaned when she maintained that hungry suction and began bobbing her head back and forth. She was so lost in the experience that she didn't notice for several strokes that he'd tightened his hold on her hair, restraining her.

"Keep still again," he grated out. She stopped with him lodged in her mouth, her lips at mid-staff. She opened her eyes and gazed up at him. She saw that a thin coat of perspiration glistened on his ridged abdomen and that his eyes looked aflame in his rigid face.

"Damn, you try me, girl," he whispered roughly before he began thrusting his cock between her lips. Her pussy throbbed in excitement as he made free with her. He always withdrew before he touched her throat, but he wasn't so gentle with her otherwise. He drove into her with increasing speed and force. The evidence of his excitement made her greedier. She drew on him and pressed up with her tongue against his throbbing, plunging cock until a low-level ache grew in her jaw and lips.

Still, she sucked hungrily . . . tempting and taunting him as he bucked between her lips . . . knowing if she was patient he would lose all restraint.

That was what she wanted, she realized dazedly as she held on to Sean's flexing buttocks with increasing desperation as he fucked her mouth. For him to feel so much pleasure, he forgot to be polite . . . for a brief, precious period of time, for *both* of them to be lost in his pleasure.

He filled her mouth with his hot, hard flesh. His other hand rose to hold her skull.

"Let me in now, girl," he rasped.

He pushed his cock another inch into her mouth. She jerked slightly when he breached her throat.

"Shhh," he whispered apologetically. One hand rubbed her scalp soothingly. Genevieve resisted an overwhelming urge to cough . . .

to eject him from her throat. She forced herself to breathe evenly through her nose, and the sensation faded.

"That's a girl," he praised. He slid back on her tongue only to penetrate her throat again. This time, she took him easier. He growled and slid out of her, fucking her mouth shallowly while her body recovered from his intrusion. His strokes became rougher and more irregular as he neared climax. Her pussy flooded with liquid heat when she felt him swell in her mouth.

Mindless with excitement, she grasped the root of his cock with one hand and a smooth, dense ass cheek with the other. She stroked him rapidly while he plunged between her lips. A shout erupted out of his throat. The flavor of his warm cum filling her mouth made her desperate with hunger. She plunged her head forward, heedless of the pain that came from resisting his restraining hold on her hair.

His shout grew louder when she took him deep. Her throat convulsed around him and tears poured out of her eyes, but she refused to dislodge him as he erupted.

His hoarse shout segued into a hissing sound. He pulled back. Semen pooled on her tongue in irregular spills as she sucked him until he could give her no more.

He panted like he'd just finished a sprint. One hand caressed her hair as he slowly recovered. Genevieve made a sound of protest when he slid out of her mouth.

"Sean . . . no," she whispered hoarsely.

He cradled her jaw with both hands and tilted up her face. "Lawd, did I do that?"

"What?" she asked, confused.

"Make your throat sound like you just swallowed sandpaper."

Genevieve smiled. "Tasted a hell of a lot better than sandpaper."

He chuckled and sunk to his knees before her. He gathered her in his arms and leaned back, making her knees rise into the air.

"Sean, put me down," she rasped.

"Kiss me and I'll think about it."

She laughed and kissed him. "What are you so happy about?" she whispered next to his lips a moment later.

"Why shouldn't I be happy? I've got a gorgeous woman in my arms, and she's the champion of giving head."

"Sean," she chided. Embarrassment heated her cheeks, although she had to admit she was more than a little pleased by his off-the-cuff comment.

He just laughed more and set her down. He kissed her mouth lustily once, and then lingered in a caress. "Why shouldn't I say it? It's the gawd's truth. And I want you to know something, girl."

"What?" she asked. His hand encircled her throat and he stroked her gently, as if he could soothe her agitated vocal cords from the outside.

"I believe firmly in fair play in the bedroom."

Genevieve went still in his arms. Her vagina clenched. Sean continued to stroke her, a sexy smile curving his firm lips.

"And I think I've got the perfect treat to pay you back, Genny."

"Sean . . ."

But he was suddenly gone from her embrace. She remained on her knees, watching him as he strode to the kitchen. Her mouth fell open in awe. He looked as natural and magnificent in his nakedness as a sleek, powerful male animal stalking around its den. The firelight cast shadow and golden light on supple, rippling muscle. She couldn't remove her eyes from the sight of his flexing ass.

He smiled at her a moment later when he returned. Genevieve saw the mischievous twinkle in his eyes.

Her brow wrinkled in confusion when he held up the bag of bing cherry chocolates.

"You know how much I love those things, Sean, but I wasn't really in the mood for eating chocolate right now."

He knelt next to her on the blanket. His hand rose to her breast, cupping the weight. He stroked her gently.

"Actually, I'm going to do the eating, girl."

CHAPTER **THIRTEEN**

He leaned down and placed a soft kiss on her nipple. Genevieve's heartbeat skipped into overtime when she saw all the amusement had vanished from his expression when he lifted his tawny head. "Lie down on your back."

She found it a bit difficult to take a full breath as she did what he asked. For a few seconds he remained on his knees, staring down at her. Genevieve noticed his sated cock lengthened next to his thigh.

"What are you thinking?" she whispered.

"I'm thinking you're beautiful."

She swallowed. "Thank you."

"Genny?"

"Yes?"

"I was also thinking I wish I could restrain you." She went entirely still at the casually spoken words. "But I said I wasn't going to get fancy, and I meant it. For now anyway. Just you and me." He jostled the bag of cherries. "These don't count as sex toys.

I'm just hungry," he teased, saying hungry with an adorable New Orleans–accented growl.

*Hon*gry.

She laughed. "You don't like chocolate cherries."

"No, but I love your pussy. Spread your legs, girl. Let me look at you."

Genevieve held her breath as she opened her thighs. He moved between her legs. For a few seconds, he just studied her exposed sex. She swore his gaze had weight; it seemed to tickle and heat her wet pussy. She moaned softly and shifted her hips. Her movement seemed to break his trance. He reached into the bag and withdrew one of the balls.

The gourmet cherries had been covered in chocolate, and then dipped in a thin coat of crispy, hard candy. They looked like small, bright red balls. Genevieve loved the sweetness of the chocolate contrasting with the sourness of the crunchy candy coating and cherry.

Never in a million years would she have considered the candies to be erotic in appearance, but her pussy clenched in rising excitement at the sight of one of the balls between Sean's thumb and forefinger. He lay down on his belly, his face hovering over her spread pussy.

He placed the cherry very carefully between her outer labia, wedging it between the lips directly on her clit. When she called out his name and shifted her hips in arousal, he stilled her with his hands on her hips and glanced up at her. She lifted her head.

"I want to make you feel good. But you have to promise me not to try to escape your pleasure, Genny. Stay still, now."

She nodded even though the level of excitement mounting in her made her doubt her ability to carry out his wish.

He leaned down, his eyes still on her face. He placed the tip of his long tongue on the hard shell of the cherry and began to press it down on her clit.

"Oh . . . Sean," she moaned shakily. It was an incredibly erotic sight, but it also felt delicious. Genevieve had thought before that his tongue was a gift sent straight from heaven, and she had that belief reaffirmed tenfold. He manipulated the ball of candy with expert precision, rolling it over her hypersensitive flesh just a fraction of an inch, back and forth, around and around, making it bob in and out, up and down . . .

Genevieve groaned and her head fell back. She lost track of time as Sean vibrated her clit with the hard surface of the candy, his firm, strong tongue a precise and relentless master. It felt decadent . . . voluptuous to lie there in that firelit room while such a beautiful man teased and tormented her pussy with a piece of candy. She cried out in excitement a while later when she felt his lips close on her labia and his tongue swiped over her clit.

She trembled on the edge of orgasm, but suddenly Sean was gone.

"I was about to come," she murmured in protest. She lifted her head and stared down at him. He watched her while he chewed the cherry with a cat-that-ate-the-canary grin on his face.

"Hmmmm," he purred. She saw his throat muscles convulse as he swallowed and had to resist an urge to put her fingers on her clit, her need to climax felt so acute. "Your pussy was melting the hard shell, so I had to eat it," he explained, unfazed by her scowl. He reached for the bag of cherries. "Besides, I want you to cool down a bit. I'm liking this way too much." She went still when he withdrew one red ball.

And then another.

Her hips shifted in restless excitement.

"You gotta promise to keep still, girl."

She licked at the coat of perspiration on her upper lip. Her clit pinched painfully, needy for stimulation.

"I promise," she whispered.

"Good." He placed both hard balls right over her clit. His head lowered.

"Oh, God . . . *oh*," Genevieve cried out. It felt unbearably exciting having both of the balls rolling and pressing against her clit, to have his warm tongue occasionally brush against her super-sensitized tissues. Her hips instinctively began to bounce up and down against the hard, rolling pressure. The soles of her feet burned nearly as hot as her clit. She bobbed her hips faster.

Sean made a low, growling sound that caused a shiver to run up her spine. His big hands spread along her hips and pressed them down firmly into the blanket. Genevieve began to keen uncontrollably. The sensation was so sharp that she struggled against his hold as bliss threatened to overwhelm her.

Sean held her without reprieve, though.

There was nothing to do but let go . . . to release all remnants of control.

She felt a slight give in the pressure of the hard balls, and suddenly Sean's hot mouth covered her. She vaguely realized that the friction and heat of her blood-engorged flesh and Sean's industrious tongue had melted the hard shell. Warm chocolate spread on her. Briefly, he closed his mouth, his lips still pressed to her labia and clit. She felt him moving as he chewed and swallowed the candy, the sensation keeping her right on the knife's edge of climax.

Then his heat was back on her. He applied a gentle suction that caused her to plunge into orgasm. Then he began to rub her clit briskly with his tongue and Genevieve's shout turned into a desperate scream.

He was merciless. Genevieve couldn't catch her breath as the orgasmic shudders kept blasting through her body, each wave seemingly just as powerful as the first.

"Stop . . . oh, *God*, Sean," she pleaded when he turned his head to get a new angle on her clit. He sucked and a fresh shudder of orgasm tore through her. Her actions belied her words. She raised her knees and clutched his head, keeping him firmly between her thighs, wanting to feel him . . . *needing* him to be there with her as she ignited again and again at the white-hot core of her passion.

Then he was crawling toward her as she panted wildly for air. Her heavy eyelids opened wider when she saw that his cock hung down from his body, firm and full. Without saying a word, he arrowed it into her soaking slit.

He gently took her limp arms and pinned her wrists above her head. He began to fuck her with long, thorough strokes as he stared down at her with a rigid expression.

He'd possessed her like this before—on that New Year's Eve night.

It was like being made love to by a force of nature: awesome, intimidating . . . indescribably beautiful.

She moaned softly, feeling helpless and overwhelmed as she faced her monumental desire. Her pussy was slightly tender from their previous joining, and she still hadn't fully recovered from thunderous, disorienting orgasm. But with every pass of his cock, Sean coaxed her sensitized nerves, soothed and fired them at once, until the prickle of vague discomfort became the burn of pleasure.

Her eyes rolled back in her head as he took her higher and higher. Her universe narrowed until it only encompassed the bubble of firelight and heat that surrounded them, her swelling pleasure . . . and Sean. Her sensations became a blur, but then sharpened when she heard Sean's voice.

"I'm never going to let you go again, girl."

She opened her eyes and saw the snarl of determination on his face as he slammed into her, fast and furious.

"*Never*," he repeated, before every delineated muscle in his body seemed to seize in a paroxysm of pleasure. It was the most awesome sight she'd ever witnessed in her life, all of that restrained energy suddenly exploding forth in one climactic moment. His penis jerked deep inside of her and she cried out at the exquisite sensation of him twitching and straining while he poured himself into her farthest depths.

He fell down over her several seconds later, breathing harshly. He buried his nose in her neck and fought to regain equilibrium. She raked her fingers through the perspiration-dampened hair at his nape, thinking of his fierceness as he'd made love to her.

I'm never going to let you go again, girl.

She shut her eyes and continued to stroke and soothe him. A feeling of great tenderness for him overcame her. Sean embodied male power, but in that climactic moment, he was vulnerable.

How strange, to think that when a man made love—*truly* made love—he showed his greatest strength and greatest weakness at once.

Her eyes blinked open when she registered the thought.

Sean loved her.

Of course he did. How could she have ever thought otherwise? Genevieve realized in growing wonder as she listened to his soughing breath. She'd seen him having sex with that other woman, but it hadn't been lovemaking. He hadn't exposed himself to that female, never let down his guard . . . never let go.

What she'd seen had been nothing like what had just passed between Sean and her. What she'd witnessed happening in the spare bedroom and what Sean and she had just shared here on the living room floor tonight were drastically different. One might as well compare eating to praying.

So strange. It was such an obvious, everyday thing. She'd first learned of the difference between sex and making love as a teenager, but Genevieve realized she'd never really *known* the profundity of the difference until that moment.

The rich scent of their combined arousal perfumed the air when she inhaled deeply.

"Sean?"

His head came up slowly. His tousled hair had fallen onto his forehead, and he still breathed heavily.

"You love me, don't you?" she whispered, awe spicing her tone.

A strange expression came over his face. He smiled slowly.

"From the first time I saw you, girl."

Genevieve just stared sightlessly at the ceiling when his head lowered again. He pressed his mouth to her neck. She knew he slept after several minutes when she felt the even cadence of his warm breath against her skin.

Sean'd given his heart to her tonight, and made no secret of it. Could she ever do the same?

Could the stain of Max's violent murder ever truly disappear?

Genevieve lay awake, forcing the shadows into the corners of her consciousness.

For a few precious moments, she just basked in the wonder of what Sean had been telling her ever since he'd stepped into the bathroom tonight.

She awoke sometime later, alone. The fire was still the only source of light in the living room. She glanced down at her body and saw that Sean had covered her in another blanket.

The sound of a pot rattling on the stove made her blink and sit up. She went to the guest bathroom, washed, and put on a short green satin nightgown. A minute later, she stood at the threshold of the kitchen and watched Sean while he stirred the contents of a boiling pan. She caught the scent of roasted tomatoes and spices. Her stomach growled. She hadn't eaten since the late breakfast she'd made for them.

She took a moment to appreciate the vision of a sex-rumpled, gorgeous man wearing nothing but a partially fastened pair of jeans cooking dinner for her.

"Barefoot and slaving over a hot stove. That's how I like my men," she murmured, affecting his Southern drawl.

His eyes sparkled when he glanced over at her. He tossed down the spoon he'd been using and came toward her. He landed a kiss on her mouth before he encircled her in his arms and lifted her off her feet.

"Your ol' stomach did what I couldn't do, huh? Woke you up?"

She hooked her hands behind his head and giggled. Yeah, *giggled*. Genevieve hadn't giggled in years.

"We've all got our priorities," she murmured before she kissed him on the mouth playfully.

And then once she captured his flavor on her tongue . . . not so playfully.

His blue eyes gleamed by the time she lifted her head.

"Keep that up, and I know what my priority's gonna be . . . and it won't be spaghetti."

Despite liking that hard, focused expression that overcame his face, her stomach growled again, louder this time. Sean's eyebrows shot up on his forehead. He set her down on her feet.

"Okay, okay, I can take a hint. Spaghetti over sex."

She chuckled and followed him into the kitchen, inspecting all the pans, cutting boards, bowls, spoons, and knives. She could barely see a square inch of bare counter.

"All this mess just to make spaghetti?" she asked.

"Heck no," he drawled, giving her a mock insulted look. He walked over to the refrigerator, opened the door, and pointed inside. "I made you some muffuletta. The flavors all soak up real good if it sits overnight."

"Why are there books inside the refrigerator?" Genevieve asked, staring at the stack of three thick books on top of the Saran-wrapped loaf of round, seeded bread.

Sean stared at her like she'd sprouted a second head. "You've had muff before. We got it at that deli on Taylor Street once, remember?"

"Yeah, it's some kind of yummy sandwich, if I recall. But that still doesn't explain why there are books in the refrigerator."

"Well, ya gotta *press* it, don't ya, girl?" He rolled his eyes as he flung the refrigerator door shut, clearly bewildered by her Yankee ignorance. He uncorked a wine bottle and filled a glass.

"Now you just take your wine and go on. I'll bring your dinner out to you. This kitchen's too small for two cooks. 'Sides . . . seeing you in that itty-bitty nightgown is just making me want to rip it off you, and the pasta'll go limp while I've you pinned down to the kitchen floor."

"Limp pasta. Can't have that," she said over her shoulder.

Sean swatted her rear. Her eyes popped wide.

"Go on now . . . 'fore you get a real one," Sean murmured, the sparkle in his blue eyes turning into a hard glitter.

Genevieve got out of there quick enough, wondering why in the hell the cracking sound of Sean's hand on her ass and the tingling sensation on her butt had caused heat to course through her genitals.

Genevieve set her nearly empty bowl of spaghetti with marinara and freshly grated Parmesan on the coffee table. She snagged her glass of wine with her fingers and watched Sean while he continued to eat with gusto.

He noticed the small smile on her face. "What? It's not too surprising I worked up a good appetite, is it? After all that great sex?"

"Not at all. I was ravenous."

"*Good,*" he said pointedly before he ate another forkful. "I'm looking forward to making you starved all over again."

She chuckled and stared out the floor-to-ceiling windows.

"Look," she said softly.

They watched the snow falling outside.

"Wind must have dropped off," Sean said. Genevieve nodded. The snowflakes once again fell vertically, thick and silent. She took a sip of her wine. A feeling of warmth and contentment weighted her muscles. It was nice, to sit there with Sean, with a fire and full belly and no place to go.

Genevieve should have known it was too perfect to last.

Her spine straightened when she heard the muffled sound of her cell phone ringing. She met Sean's gaze.

"I guess I should get it. Maybe it's something about the house . . . or Jim?"

Sean frowned. "Or your boyfriend?"

Genevieve avoided his gaze and sprung up from the carpet. She didn't know how to respond to Sean's obvious irritation. Besides, she was shocked that she'd completely forgotten about Jeff's existence. Sean was right. It may very well be Jeff calling from New York. She didn't particularly want to take a call from him in front of Sean, but she didn't want Jeff to worry about her either. She'd promised they'd talk today.

"Hello?" she asked breathlessly, barely getting to her phone fast enough before it sent the caller into voicemail.

"Ms. Bujold? Genevieve Bujold?"

"Yes, that's right."

"My name's Richard Ellerson, I'm an officer with the Chicago Police Department. I'm sorry to have to bother you on a night like this, Ms. Bujold."

"That's all right. Are you calling about the break-in at my boutique?"

There was a short pause. "No, ma'am. I'm not."

Out of the corner of her eye, she noticed Sean set down his bowl, his eyes trained on her. He stood. A minute later she hung up the phone and walked into the living room.

"What was that all about?"

"A storage locker that I rented out years ago—before I even married Max—has been vandalized," Genevieve murmured, feeling bewildered.

"Who called?" Sean asked sharply.

Genevieve said the Chicago police officer's name. "The police want me to go over to the storage facility. They want me to identify if anything is missing."

Sean glanced outside at the heavy snow falling, his brows crinkled in irritation and disbelief. "Are you kidding? They wouldn't send a patrol car over to your boutique, but they expect you to go out in this because a *storage locker* has been vandalized?"

Genevieve shrugged. She was highly unsettled by the phone call, and she could tell by the intense, worried expression Sean wore he was thinking about the strangeness of the fire, the boutique break-in . . . and now a storage locker vandalism. She remembered the way he'd looked at her this afternoon in her studio.

Genny . . . is there anything you're not telling me? Anything I should know?

She inhaled, shoving the intrusive thought out of her brain.

"I said I'd come. Officer Ellerson seemed to think it was impor-tant for some reason. It's only about six blocks west of here, on

Jackson Boulevard," Genevieve said briskly, trying to rid herself of the idea that Sean had been considering her with suspicion when he'd asked those questions earlier today, and quite possibly was doing it again right this second.

"Okay. I'm going, too. But first, give me your cell phone." When she returned with her phone, he took it from her and pressed the menu, looking for her most recent call. "Why don't you go and get ready?"

Genevieve nodded, even though she was mystified by his intentions. She lingered long enough to hear him identify himself as Genevieve Bujold's friend, and ask Officer Ellerson for his badge number. She stood near the hallway when he hit the disconnect button and started dialing again.

"Sean . . . what are you doing?" she asked when he began to dial another number.

"Just checking to make sure this guy Ellerson is who he says he is," he muttered grimly.

CHAPTER **FOURTEEN**

Genevieve looked at him suspiciously as they rode the elevator down to the Sauren-Kennedy Solutions parking garage.

"I thought you said earlier today that if we tried to take out our cars, they'd just get stuck in the snow," she said.

"I did. But that was before the city had a chance to plow and salt all the streets."

She gave him a narrow-eyed stare. Sean grimaced. "*Okay*, so what if I was trying to talk you out of going to your store this afternoon? I was right to try to discourage you. We froze our asses off walking to Oak Street and back."

"You lied to me on purpose," Genevieve accused. The elevator doors dinged open. She stalked across the concrete floor, the brisk clicking of her boot heels letting Sean know she was annoyed.

Just in case he hadn't gotten the point already.

She'd exited the bathroom five minutes after the call from the police wearing jeans and a sweater. She'd started to put on her wet tennis shoes in the foyer. Sean had halted her, insisting she put on those same high-heeled boots that now tapped out her irritation at him like some kind of universal female version of communication, like Morse code on estrogen.

He sighed.

Sue him for not wanting her to go out in a snowstorm again wearing wet shoes.

Sean followed her off the elevator, telling himself it figured things got a little rocky between them when they'd been going smooth as silk. He hadn't tried to defend himself as they got in his SUV. He was too busy worrying; first about this latest crime against Genny's property, and then later about safely getting them through the thick, snow-laden streets without getting stuck.

Not two minutes after they'd pulled out of the parking garage, Genny pointed at the two-story warehouse on the north side of Jackson Boulevard.

"That's it," she murmured, sounding more preoccupied than irritated at this point.

Sean followed the lead of a patrol car and a white, four-door Crown Victoria and put his SUV into park directly on the street. The unfortunate people who had parallel parked along the curb wouldn't be driving anywhere for weeks until the snow melted. Their vehicles had been buried in about five feet of snow, thanks to the passing plows.

They got out of his SUV and walked toward the storage facility. Even though the snowplows had probably already passed several times today, Genny and he still trudged through four inches of snow. He caught Genny's gloved hand, keeping her steady in her heels.

"What's wrong?" Genny asked quietly when she saw the way Sean inspected the white car as they passed.

"I can't wait to find out why it's necessary for both a patrol car and an unmarked to show up at a storage facility break-in during one of the worst snowstorms Chicago's had in decades," he mumbled. "What the hell did you have in storage?"

"Some furniture from my old Streeterville apartment, boxes of stuff from my college years . . . just a bunch of junk that didn't suit the Lake Forest house."

Sean studied her closely as they walked, taking in her perplexed expression. "You're sure there wasn't anything else?"

"Like *what*?" she asked, turning to him. Her movement caused her to slip. He caught her before she plunked down on the pavement. Sean pushed her long, tousled hair out of her eyes gently.

"Don't worry about it, okay? We'll find out soon enough."

She smiled, and the agitated, anxious expression in her eyes eased.

Despite his attempts to reassure Genny, he wasn't really shocked when they entered the unlocked entrance and he saw the figure of an imposing, bald black man wearing a long, dark blue wool coat standing next to two uniformed cops. He felt Genny freeze on the threshold of the door and pulled on her hand gently.

The door slamming shut behind her sounded unusually loud.

"Detective Franklin," Sean greeted the man who had headed up Max Sauren's murder investigation three years ago with a nod. "Things must be slow in the city tonight, if they're sending out homicide detectives to investigate storage locker break-ins."

Franklin flashed a white grin." Well you know what they always say, Mr. Kennedy. Storms have a way of bringing the rats out of their holes. I was having a boring evening at the station, and these two hard-working officers were kind enough to let me tag along."

Franklin's velvety, puppy-dog eyes shifted over to Genny. Sean resisted an urge to block her from the detective's seemingly benign gaze. Franklin glanced back at Sean again and his smile widened. He stepped forward and put out his hand in greeting.

"Imagine . . . seeing you two together like this. After so long. And in the middle of a snowstorm." A polite, slightly dazed expression overcame his jovial face as he shook Sean's hand.

Sean met the man's round-eyed stare and tried to hide his irritation. "We haven't seen each other in years. Ms. Bujold was at the Sauren-Kennedy Solutions office when the police called. So was I."

Franklin ignored Sean's glare and stepped toward Genny. "Ms. Bujold. So nice to see you again."

Genevieve's gray eyes flickered over Sean's face uncertainly before she grasped Franklin's outstretched hand. "Detective Franklin? I don't understand. What are you doing here? What's this about? It was an Officer Ellerson who contacted me."

Franklin nodded solicitously. Sean remembered the detective's style all too well—the deep, slow baritone, the expression of compassion in his dark brown eyes . . . the feeling you were talking to a social worker or psychologist instead of a man who had you on his short list for possible murder suspects.

Franklin was good. Too good for Sean's comfort. Maybe it was the fact that Franklin was a fellow Southerner. Sean knew firsthand how people tended not to notice the razor-sharp edge when it was coated in thick, sweet syrup. He'd used a similar device way too often to be unfamiliar with it.

He recalled trying to warn Genny not to fall for Franklin's mild manner. She was so trusting—especially with people who seemed sincere. He'd been worried to death she'd be lulled by Franklin's warmth and kindness. He'd tried to contact her in regard to that specific issue, but of course she'd made a point of ignoring his calls following that New Year's Eve.

Although, he guiltily recalled that she *had* tried to reach him several times on the afternoon of Max's murder. Sean had been in a meeting; his cell phone turned off. He'd often wondered why Genny had tried to contact him. He'd missed his window of opportunity with Genny while he'd sat through a boring, but crucial meeting with the Assistant Secretary of the Treasury of the United

States. Genevieve must have been desperate to try to reach him, but Sean hadn't been available to her.

And following Max's murder, she'd gone right back to avoiding him.

He examined a smiling Detective Franklin. Most of the detectives he'd known throughout his life didn't take too kindly to having an unsolved murder in their files. Sean had gotten the distinct impression Franklin could be downright relentless, despite possessing a face that any Southern mama worth her salt couldn't resist pinching. He'd been irritated when he saw Franklin standing there with the uniforms, but he wasn't surprised.

Not in the slightest.

"Yes, it was Officer Ellerson who called you," Franklin explained, waving at the youngest and burliest of the two cops. "And this is Officer Gonzalez. It's been quite a while since we've spoken, Ms. Bujold."

"Yes. It's been several years now," Genevieve replied. She glanced over at Sean and then back to Franklin. "Officer Ellerson? You gave me the impression that I was here to look into a matter of a storage unit that I rent being broken into. Isn't that correct?"

"That's right, ma'am," Ellerson said.

Genevieve once again glanced at Sean, bewilderment and a trace of anxiety written clearly on her face. "Well then . . . what are you doing here, Detective Franklin?"

"Apparently the detective is aware of the fact that your house burned down last night," Sean said dryly.

"Right," Franklin nodded. "Real shame, that is. I had an auntie whose house burned down to the ground in Mississippi. She lost everything. Terrible tragedy. I was so sorry to hear about you suffering something similar, Ms. Bujold."

"Thank you," Genevieve murmured.

"And it came to my attention that you called in a report just today about your store being broken into? I asked to be informed if your name came up in any other incidents." He spread his big hands and smiled engagingly. "And so here I am."

"What?" Genevieve asked, looking at him as if she hadn't heard him correctly.

"The detective is just following the tracks," Sean said.

"The tracks?" Genevieve mouthed. Her expression suddenly stilled. Her eyes flashed to Franklin. "Wait . . . you can't mean that this"—she pointed toward the entrance to the storage lockers— "and the break-in at my store . . . *and* the fire had something to do with Max's murder?"

"I 'spect that's exactly what the detective thinks," Sean muttered.

"Detective Franklin, is that true?" Genny demanded.

Franklin gave her an apologetic smile. "I believe I did tell you the last time we met a couple of years ago, Ms. Bujold, that an investigation such as this is *never* closed until the person responsible for committing murder is found, and—"

"Why don't we find some place to sit down and have this chat?" Sean interrupted in a hard tone when he saw every last vestige of color wash out of Genny's face.

Genevieve felt foolish sitting while Detective Franklin and Sean both towered over her. Not foolish enough to refuse the chair Sean had urged her toward—not with her knees having gone so weak when she'd heard Franklin mention that he was at the warehouse in association with Max's murder.

The owner of the storage facility—a Matt Michelson—had been contacted about the break-in and was sitting in his office filling out a form when Detective Franklin ushered them inside. Michelson was a young man who wore a goatee and wire-rimmed glasses. He politely gave them use of his office. After shaking hands with Genevieve and Sean, and giving his condolences to Genevieve about the break-in, he left them with Detective Franklin.

"I don't see how someone breaking into a storage facility has anything to do with Max's death," Genevieve said once Michelson shut the door behind him and Sean had eased her into a white plastic chair.

She'd been shocked at how much anxiety and fear went through her when she saw the detective's all too familiar face. Seeing him here so unexpectedly had made so many memories come back—so many feelings.

Having Sean standing by her side, her hand in his, made the whole experience that much more surreal.

That much more frightening.

Franklin leaned his large frame against the metal desk. Genevieve had always been amazed that such a tall, bulky man moved with so much grace. Despite the fact that he was at least six feet four and probably weighed two eighty, the detective looked quite elegant perched so precariously on the corner of the desk.

"Whoever broke into this facility was only interested in one locker, Ms. Bujold," Franklin explained.

"Mine?"

"That's right," Franklin said.

"But . . . still." She glanced up at Sean, whose sharp eyes were pinned to her face.

"It's the third thing that's happened to you in twenty-four hours, Genny."

Genevieve barely stopped herself from wincing when she heard her name on Sean's tongue. She wished he wouldn't seem so familiar with her in front of Detective Franklin.

"That's right," Franklin agreed. "First the fire at your house, then the break-in at your store, now this."

"The fire wasn't set, Detective." She glanced at Sean for confirmation.

"That's what I understand," Franklin replied. "Still . . . all of it is a bit strange, wouldn't you agree?"

Genevieve laughed. She couldn't help it. Both men looked so somber, and for the life of her, she couldn't figure out why.

"I'm obviously missing something here."

"It's too many coincidences," Sean stated.

"So what are you saying? That someone burned down my house and now is running around, breaking into my property for kicks, and then not stealing anything? That's ridiculous. And even if it were true, what would that have to do with Max?"

"How do you know nothing was taken from your locker?" Franklin asked.

Genevieve started at the unexpected question. "I don't. I just know there's absolutely nothing in there worth taking."

"No? No old bills or mail. Medical records . . . things of that sort?"

Sean's head turned slowly. Genevieve noticed his narrow-eyed stare on Franklin. A sick feeling swelled in her gut.

"I . . . I don't know. I suppose there are some old files—"

"Were any of Max Sauren's records kept in there?"

"No," Genevieve replied, her panic mounting. She blinked and answered more firmly. "*Everything* in that storage locker came from the time period before I married Max. There's no way it could relate to his—" She swallowed convulsively, unable to finish the sentence. "That's just preposterous."

Franklin shifted his polite gaze to Sean. "Well, maybe there isn't any connection. What do you think, Kennedy? Any ideas about all of this?"

Sean shrugged.

"Maybe I should ask you that question. You're the detective on the case. It's clear you have information that we don't."

What the hell is going on? Genevieve wondered in rising anxiety as the two men engaged in a staring match, all traces of easygoing, Southern amiability completely absent from both of their rigid expressions.

The only thought that kept arising in her brain was that she wished Franklin hadn't seen Sean and her together. Sean had been right when he'd warned her so long ago not to be too open with the detective. He may look like an enormous teddy bear, but Franklin was observant and smart.

What was he thinking about Sean and her arriving hand in hand? She wondered in rising panic. She'd been so careful to avoid Sean during the investigation, and for all those years afterward, as well. What rotten luck, for Franklin to see them together after all this time—

Franklin broke the tense silence, grinning broadly. "If I had as much information as the head man at Sauren-Kennedy Solutions, I'd be the superintendent of police by now."

Sean's expression remained stony.

"I don't like any of it, but I can't say I understand what's going on. I'm on as much of a fishing expedition as you, Detective." Sean hitched his chin toward the door. "Are you okay to take a look at the locker, Genny?"

She nodded.

"*Good* idea," Franklin agreed, suddenly all unaffected ease. He stood and held up his hand in invitation for them to pass in front of him. "I glanced at the police report you made over the phone this afternoon, Ms. Bujold. It didn't indicate if anything was taken from your boutique."

"I didn't notice anything missing. Whoever broke in just made a mess," Genevieve said as she stood.

"Hmmm, not too surprising, I guess," Franklin said.

"How's that?" Genevieve asked.

"If he found what he wanted, he wouldn't have to break in here, would he?" Franklin asked.

"Assuming it was the same person," Sean said as he went to open the office door.

Franklin nodded. "Right, right. Well, it probably is just a bunch of strangeness clumping together on the calendar. It happens that way sometimes. Either way, it was nice to be able to see both of you again."

Genevieve held her breath, her eyes glued on Sean's back. She was extremely glad that Sean didn't turn around at Franklin's casually spoken words. He continued walking down the hallway without pause. Her heartbeat began to throb in her ears as she followed him down the dim corridor, Detective Franklin bringing up the rear.

CHAPTER **FIFTEEN**

Sean pulled into his reserved parking space, switched off the ignition, and placed his gloved hands on the steering wheel. Neither he nor Genny moved in the tense silence that followed.

"Sean, I can't stay here anymore."

He exhaled the breath he'd been holding as he waited for her to say precisely what she'd just said. He'd actually been waiting for her to say it ever since they both got into the car and drove in silence back to the penthouse. Neither of them had uttered a word until that moment.

"You can. And you will," he stated quietly.

"Then *you* can't."

His head swung around when he heard her desperation. "Don't be afraid, Genny. There's no law that says we can't be together."

"But Detective Franklin—"

"Detective Franklin was fishing. He might have thought it was interesting to see us together, but just because we're together tonight doesn't make a case for something that happened three years ago. Besides, he didn't make a big deal out of the fact that you were staying at Sauren-Kennedy because your house had burned down."

She stared at him, aghast. "You don't really believe that. If he ever discovered what went on between us back then . . . what's happening between us now, he'd think he had a motive, Sean."

Sean shook his head. "*No.* Because we were together tonight because of the circumstances of the fire doesn't mean that you and I were having an affair back then."

"But we *were* together," she exclaimed, her eyes looking a little wild. It pained him to see her so afraid. He had to reassure her that just because Franklin saw them together didn't mean he was going to throw her into jail for Max's murder. He *had* to convince her, because he wasn't going to let her go off by herself until he figured out what was going on. The fact that Franklin had entered the picture again wasn't what Sean was most worried about at the moment.

He was more worried about the fact that someone was after something Genny had. And that someone just might hurt her if she got in their way.

He brushed a wavy strand of hair off her cheek, wanting to soothe the fear he saw in her big eyes. "He doesn't have anything, Genny. He's just a good cop who was following the trail of some unusual circumstances, hoping it would give him a lead that would help him break the case. I said it once, and I'll say it again. Seeing us together tonight doesn't mean anything substantial."

She opened her mouth to argue but he shook his head resolutely, halting her. "It doesn't. Sure, it might prick his interest, but us being together one night three years after Max's murder *doesn't* consist of a motive, especially when there's good reason for it given the fire."

He saw her swallow convulsively. "Are you sure?"

"Yes," he replied steadfastly.

"It just seems foolish for me to stay here, given what Franklin might make of it."

He closed his eyes briefly and sighed. "He can make of it whatever he damn well wants, it's not any proof of anything. Besides, I'm not going to let you stay anywhere else."

"You're not going to *let* me?" Eyes that were usually soft as a luminous gray cloud hardened to steel.

"Don't fight me on this, Gen. Please?"

"Sean, you can't really believe that someone wants to harm me. I mean . . . all this stuff with the break-ins is weird, but no one has tried to get at *me*."

"What about the fire?"

"You yourself told me that the fire chief thought it was caused by faulty wiring."

Sean shrugged and dropped his hand to her shoulder. "Yeah. But reports have been wrong before. I'm in complete agreement with Franklin about it—there's something going on. And I plan to make sure you're safe until I found out what that something is. Come on. Let's go on up to the penthouse."

Her sigh sounded frustrated, but Sean was glad to see that she didn't argue anymore. She reached for the door handle.

"And Genny?" he asked as they walked toward the garage elevators.

"Yeah?"

"I don't want you to go anywhere for the next couple days, unless I'm with you."

"*Sean,*" she scolded as she paused and gave him an irritated look. She didn't stamp her booted foot, but he got the impression she had.

"Please?"

She just studied him for a moment before she rolled her eyes and resumed walking. "Oh, all right. I'll stay put for now."

He raised his brows expectantly.

"I *promise*," she replied irritably when she realized what he waited for. "I still say you're being overly cautious. Everything I need to do is pretty much put on hold until this snowstorm is over, anyway."

"Great."

He wasn't going to let her go anywhere until he understood the landscape one way or another, but he figured it was best to ask politely for her agreement as opposed to locking her in the penthouse without her consent.

It seemed strange to walk back into the living room, to see the blankets on the floor and their bowls still sitting on the coffee table where they'd left them before going to meet the police. Everything looked the same, but Genevieve felt different. She pictured herself sitting there on the floor next to Sean, watching the snow coming down and feeling so peaceful. She recalled in breathtaking detail their heated, emotional lovemaking.

So much tension had risen in her muscles over the past hour, she couldn't imagine who that woman had been who had let go so wholly . . . trusted so completely.

She started slightly when Sean came up behind her and wrapped her in his arms.

"Shhh," he soothed. She shivered at the sensation of his warm breath brushing her neck. His hands transferred to her shoulders and upper arms, rubbing her muscles. "You're so tense. Everything's going to be okay, Genny."

"I don't see how," she whispered. She felt Sean's rib cage expand against her back as he inhaled slowly.

Regret coursed through her. Why was she being so selfish, saying things like that? Sean had to be ten times more anxious than she was, knowing that Detective Franklin was nosing around again . . . knowing Franklin had seen them together. She turned in his arms and looked up at him. "I'm sorry. I shouldn't dump all my jitters onto you."

He gave her a wry glance from beneath his lowered brow. "I forgive you."

She laughed and touched his whiskered jaw. "You look a little disreputable with all those whiskers. Sexy as hell, though."

"If you think so, that's all that matters," he murmured, turning his chin and nuzzling her hand. "You look tired. Why don't you go and get ready for bed. I'm going to go downstairs to my office for a little bit."

She traced one of his eyebrows with her fingertip. "Are you sure? You look exhausted yourself."

He gave her a lingering kiss. "You taste so good. I'd rather stay here with you, but I just need to do a couple of things, and I'll be right up to bed."

"Bed?" she whispered. Genevieve didn't know how he'd done it, but suddenly she was hyperaware of every point of contact between their bodies and their conversation had turned hushed and intimate.

"Oh right . . . I'll be right up to the *floor*," Sean rumbled, a small smile pulling at his lips.

She laughed and went up on her tiptoes to press her lips to his grin.

After Sean'd secured the penthouse and left, and Genevieve had prepared for bed, she turned on the light in the spare bedroom. Had it really only been last night when she'd stood here and watched Sean make love to another woman?

A mild feeling of nausea swept through her at the thought. Her gaze flickered over to the bedside table where she'd seen him pull out the dildo. Her cheeks heated when she considered what else he might keep in there—implements to torture a woman with pleasure.

The arousal that coursed through her confused and shamed her. How could she be both sickened by the thought of Sean touching another woman and turned on by it as well?

You wish he'd been doing those things to you, said a voice in her head.

She rushed into the room and whipped the padded comforter and two pillows off the bed. Her actions had been so hasty and pressured that she was panting slightly by the time she deposited the bedding on the living room carpet in a great heap.

Genevieve knew very well that people everywhere enjoyed adventuresome sex lives, and she thought that was great. It wasn't that she had some kind of hang-up about kink. But in her case, the only night of truly wild, uninhibited . . . experimental sex she'd ever experienced had become associated with a nightmare of murder, loss, and fear.

So yeah . . . might as well admit she had just a bit of a hang-up about the idea of letting go, about the prospect of releasing all her inhibitions. She'd been afraid about giving into her powerful attraction to Sean. But more important, she was afraid of her own desires. Afraid of the consequences that might follow.

And Genevieve didn't like being afraid by principle.

When she was a girl, she'd gotten into the habit of forcing herself to face her fears alone. It wasn't that her parents were negligent, by any means, but they'd had her when they were in their mid-thirties. Neither of them was college educated, and while they were proud of her accomplishments, they had little understanding of what was required of Genevieve to excel academically in one of the most crime-ridden public school systems in the country, the mountains of paperwork she had to fill out for scholarships, or the anxiety-provoking interviews she endured in order to get into a prestigious art school. Genevieve had learned early on that no one was going to hold her hand. She'd have to face her fears head-on, or admit defeat.

She walked down the dim hallway and stood outside the master bedroom. Her heart drummed unnaturally loud in her ears. She took a deep breath and plunged inside, flipping on the light before she had a chance to second guess herself. Her gaze immediately went to the large bed. She forced her eyes off it.

She slowly walked over to the built-in cherrywood wall system that took up the entire left side of the room. A vivid image played across her mind's eye—the image of Sean's powerful buttocks flexing as he fucked her, his hands on top of the custom-made, cherrywood headboard, supporting his upper body. The camera must have been to the left and several feet above the bed. She'd seen Max's, Sean's, and her own faces in profile, but it was Sean's image that was the most obvious figure on the screen.

The most dominant.

Genevieve sprung into action, grabbing a desk chair and hauling it over to the built-in shelving and cabinet system. She glanced back at the bed, trying to gauge the angle correctly, before she planted the chair and climbed on top.

She looked everywhere, opening cabinet doors and shelves, checking the two built-in closets, running her hand over nooks where her eyes couldn't reach. She wasn't really expecting to find anything—surely Max had removed all of the recording equipment when he retrieved the tape itself—but she searched anyway. Besides, with the type of expensive technology used by Sauren, Genevieve seriously doubted the camera was the type that would be perched inside a cabinet.

It was as much an exercise in facing her fears as it was a search for the camera that had recorded their ménage à trois that night.

When she'd exhausted herself by searching for something that wasn't there, she sat on the edge of the bed, panting.

It was perhaps one of the most painful, anxiety-ridden moments of her life, those minutes when Max had beckoned her to look at his computer screen.

The fact that he'd been dead within several hours of the event only made the memory that much more potent in her mind.

That much more *poison.*

Max had been in his study when he'd called out to her as she passed in the hallway, telling her to shut the door behind her. He'd smiled warmly as she entered. She recalled he'd been smoking a cigar, and the pungent smoke had made her eyes water as she approached his desk.

She had no hint of what was coming. If anything, Max had gone out of his way to be extra kind, careful and tender with her following that New Year's Eve, as if he'd sensed her confusion and agitation about them making love with Sean. In reality, he must have known she was considering leaving him.

But who really knew what Max Sauren was ever thinking?

She'd been relieved when he'd called her in to talk privately in his office. Their silence about that night had been like a toxin in her blood. Genevieve longed to clear the air, even if it did involve a difficult, heartbreaking ending with Max.

There's something I thought you might like to see.

His low, humming voice resonated in her memory.

Max'd turned the volume way up on his computer and pressed a key. Her own ecstatic cries and whimpers had twined with Sean's deep groans of pleasure, the volatile sounds filling Max's sedate, luxurious study.

She stared at the computer screen and then at her husband of four years in rising confusion and stark disbelief. She could still see the smoke curling around his face as he exhaled through a smile.

"It's so strange to think of it," Max reflected as he lazed back in his supple leather chair. "But Sean Kennedy actually threatened to kill me after the three of us spent New Year's Eve together." He wrapped his lips around his cigar and inhaled. "People will get the oddest ideas after engaging in a bit of meaningless fun."

Genny breathed in the pungent smoke and felt dizzy.

"I don't know what you're talking about, Max," she whispered hoarsely. "Why are you saying these things? What are you *doing*?"

He looked disturbed. "You don't believe me, love?"

"I don't know what you're *talking* about," she grated out, much louder this time. The situation started to feel as surreal as New Year's Eve had. More so, because Sean wasn't there to steady her.

Max leaned forward and plucked on several computer keys with his long, elegant fingers. A close-up of what Genevieve recognized as the back of Sean's tawny head with Max behind him, his face to the video camera. Through her haze of shock, she saw the top of her own head pressed to Sean's wide chest, her cheeks still sex-flushed, her eyelids closed in sleep.

What are you going to pay me for not killing you, Max? I assume you actually want *to live?*

Genevieve hadn't been able to see Sean's face when he uttered those words, but she'd recognized that cold tone—the tone Sean infrequently took when a frightening stranger seemed to take over his body. Part of her distantly wondered why Max didn't scurry off that bed and run for his life.

Panic had assailed her. She'd tried to flee Max's study, but he'd stood and grabbed her wrist roughly.

Don't hurry off, love. There's something else important I need to tell you.

Genevieve moaned softly, trying to clear that ghastly memory of being in Max's office on his death day out of her brain. Max'd taunted her on that day—given her crucial knowledge and then left her impotent to act on it.

"You were a *coward*, Max Sauren," she whispered with blistering heat. "If Sean hadn't killed you, maybe I would have."

She winced when she heard her own words, shocked at the depth of her anger. All right, maybe she would never have resorted to murder, but when she thought of Max's machinations, it left her feeling breathless with incredulity and fury, as if the blow had just been dealt.

But in that moment, she experienced the change, the difference in what she had been three years ago and what she was now.

Eventually, she stood and left the master bedroom. She wouldn't be so anxious the next time she entered it.

When Sean entered the penthouse, he immediately walked to the threshold of the living room, wanting to see Genny, needing to see she was okay. He smiled when he saw that she'd made them a more elaborate bed on the floor, adding more blankets and pillows. She'd turned on the fireplace again and slept facing the flames. He stood stock-still for a minute, not moving until he saw the subtle rise and fall of her blanket-covered breasts.

Idiot, a voice in his head scolded with dark amusement as he turned to activate the alarm. Hadn't he heard of parents doing the same thing with their newborn infants, standing over their crib to ensure the infant breathed while it slept? It both amused and amazed him that he did the same thing with a woman.

Maybe he shouldn't be surprised. Having Genny here with him

was a bit similar to what he imagined having a tiny little baby in your care might be like—the sense of wonder mixed with a profound anxiety regarding safety.

And then there was the sense of the fragility of their bond.

What he'd learned while he'd been down in his office only highlighted his rising anxiety. He'd spoken to his friend Joe in Indianapolis. Joe had looked for Albert Rook at his store and then at his apartment.

"He was here just last night, but there's no sign of him now," Joe had explained. "A couple people that work for him at that outdoor sporting goods store said he never came in today."

"How do you know he was there last night?" Sean asked.

"One of his neighbors saw him walking up to his apartment yesterday."

"What time?"

"She thought it was around six thirty P.M.," Joe said.

"Did anyone notice him leaving?"

"Nope."

Sean stroked his whiskered jaw, thinking. The first call about the Lake Forest mansion being on fire had come in at eight twenty-seven P.M. It took approximately three and a half hours to drive from Indianapolis to Chicago, and there was an hour difference in time zones. Rook *could* have done it, but it seemed highly improbable. There was always a chance he'd flown.

"Did the witness seem reliable?" Sean asked as he typed in a search for flight times from Indianapolis to Chicago on his computer.

"Hard to tell," Joe replied. "She had an ass I could have bounced a quarter off, though."

Sean had chuckled as his gaze ran down a column of flight departures. Joe had been insatiable during their Army days.

Looked as if nothing had changed. "Did she agree to go out with you, and that's why you're questioning her character?"

"Hell no, she turned me down flat."

"I'll consider her a reliable witness then," Sean'd murmured.

Genny rustled a little when he crawled beneath the blanket with her, but she didn't awaken. He put his arm around her waist and pulled her gently next to his chest. Her scent filled his nostrils. He tilted his head back on the pillow and watched the snow falling outside the windows while he breathed in Genny's fragrance.

He remembered what Detective Franklin had said earlier tonight.

Storms have a way of bringing the rats out of their holes.

Franklin was right. There was a rat nosing around. Sean suspected that rat was Rook. He'd give anything to know why the vermin dared to surface now.

CHAPTER **SIXTEEN**

Genevieve woke up in the middle of the night. She experienced no disorientation, despite the unfamiliarity of her surroundings. Maybe it was the feeling of Sean's long, warm, hard body behind her, his scent that grounded her in the moment. She turned to look, careful not to awaken him. She just stared for several seconds, appreciating the sight of his rugged, handsome face in repose.

That sense of contentment had stolen back over her while she slept, she realized. She glanced out the windows and saw the thick snow falling, heard the howl of the wind.

As long as the storm lasted. That's how long she had. As long as the storm held the city hostage, as long as they were trapped here, she wouldn't have to face Jeff, wouldn't have to face *herself* or question the wisdom of what she was doing.

She carefully slipped out from beneath Sean's arm and rose to use the bathroom. When she returned a few minutes later, she paused several feet inside the room.

The firelight made his eyes gleam as he watched her. He'd pushed back the cover and lay on his side. He wore only a dark blue pair of soft pajama bottoms tied low around his narrow hips. Her gaze trailed over the tantalizing slant that led from his taut belly up to a powerful chest. His elbow was bent, his head resting in his hand.

He said nothing when she dropped to her knees and immediately sunk her fingers into the curly hair on his chest. He didn't have a pelt, by any means, but his chest hair proclaimed his masculinity loud and clear. The crinkly hair felt delicious curling around her fingers while she touched hard, warm muscle beneath.

"Do you think I'm stupid for not wanting to sleep in the bedrooms?" she asked in a hushed tone as she continued to pet him.

"No," he replied hoarsely. He still hadn't moved as he watched her stroke him, but she felt the tension in his muscles. "I never sleep in the master bedroom, either. Not since New Year's Eve three years ago."

Her hand paused over a rounded, dense pectoral muscle. "You don't?"

He shook his head.

For a few seconds nothing could be heard in the still room but the low howl of the wind moving across the windows.

"I was thinking about what happened on that night . . . New Year's Eve," she said, her tongue feeling heavy and awkward, as if it had a mind of its own and disapproved of her topic.

"I don't regret it in the same way that you do. I can't. It's all I had of you, Genny."

"Until now."

"Until now," he conceded quietly. He didn't say anything else, but Genny sensed that he waited.

She cleared her throat and began to caress him again, watching the progress of her hand instead of meeting his gleaming eyes. "It's not just . . . It's not just what happened to Max directly afterward that makes me regret it, Sean."

Her hand moved as he inhaled slowly. "You regret it because of the way it happened . . . the way we—*I*—made love to you."

Genevieve nodded. She raised her fingers to his cheeks and lips, wishing she could make the guilt she saw shadow his rugged features disappear.

"I told you I was sorry, Genny. You have no idea how much. It was wrong to . . ."

"Share me with Max?" she asked when he faltered.

His blue eyes seemed to entreat her for understanding. "I know it's not an excuse. I just wanted you so much. I was a fool to let it happen. My punishment was to lose you for all those years. Don't make me suffer more."

Her eyes flicked up to meet his. "I'm not trying to make you *suffer*, Sean. It's not my place to *punish* you." Her breath caught in her throat. "I was just as much to blame."

"*No.* Don't say that."

Her rising misery must have shown in her expression because he pulled her into his arms. He fell onto his back, bringing her with him. She lay with her cheek pressed to his chest, his arms wrapped around her. The feelings she'd tried desperately to contain since first seeing him last night broke free. Tears spilled onto his skin. Suppressed emotion rose in her chest and tightened her throat unbearably.

"I'd never done anything like that before!" she exclaimed.

She clenched her eyes as mortification waved through her. It'd just popped out of her throat, as though the words had been waiting there in her vocal cords, impatient to be uttered for three long years.

Sean pushed on her shoulders. He stared into her face, looking flabbergasted.

"I never said you had. I certainly never *thought* it."

She shook her head and tears scattered down her cheek. "But Max seemed so comfortable about it all, and you acted like it was just par for the course for you, as well."

His hands closed over the sides of her head. "Haven't you been listening to me? Making love to you would never be *par for the course*. I hate myself for letting him touch you in front of me—I don't care if he *was* your husband," he roared, shattering the hushed, pregnant mood.

But Genevieve was so miserable that seeing the evidence of Sean's dismay and disbelief couldn't sidetrack her. The words just kept bubbling out of her mouth, as if a plug had been released and the contents burst forth under pressure. "I've tortured myself thinking about what you thought of me. It's become like a daily ritual I force myself to endure."

He sighed heavily. "Yeah . . . well, I'm familiar with that particular form of self-punishment myself."

"And . . . and when I think about what we did that night . . ." Fresh tears gushed out of her eyes. "It was so out of character for me. I'm so ashamed."

Sean blinked. A queer expression came over his face. "Wait . . . what do you mean?" he asked slowly. "Are you talking about the three of us having sex?"

"No!" she exclaimed heatedly. "I mean . . . *yes*, but not just that." She moaned as regret swamped her. "God, Sean, I *told* you I didn't want to talk about this. It was all so wrong."

He used his hands to tilt up her face. "Look at me, girl, cuz I don't think we're talking about the same thing."

She glanced up, meeting his gaze with difficulty.

"Not *all* of it was wrong, Genny."

She inhaled unevenly when she saw the return of his steely-eyed, determined stare. He used his thumbs to wipe away the tears on her cheeks.

"Are you saying you regret letting me take control of your pleasure on that night? *Genny?*" he probed when she glanced away uncomfortably. "Talk to me. This is important."

"I don't know why I did."

"Why you allowed it? Or why you liked it?"

She gave him a repressive glance. She didn't appreciate him speaking of her vulnerabilities so easily.

"Genny," he muttered, a trace of exasperation on his tone. "I had no idea this is part of what's been making you so nervous, girl."

"Do *not* make fun of me, Sean," she warned.

"I'm not making *fun* of you! I just meant—" He paused and seemed to gather his thoughts when he saw the insulted expression on her face. "I just meant it would have been a lot easier to assure you that you had absolutely nothing to be ashamed about if I'd known what you were thinking. You're an incredible, sexy, responsive woman. If you'd told me you were worrying about having submitted in bed, maybe we could have put this to rest a long time ago."

She just stared at him, left mute by his casual mention of such a volatile topic—at least volatile for *her*; she had kept it locked up inside her for so many years.

He stroked her cheeks lightly with callused thumbs. "It'll only be in the bedroom, Genny. You know me well enough by now to know I'd never even consider trying to control you outside of it. I know exactly what you'd do to me if I ever tried to boss you around in regard to other things."

His warm tone, slanting grin, and gentle caresses soothed her agitated emotional state, although she still felt far from certain.

"I've never liked the idea of having sex like that before," she whispered. "I never even *thought* of it. I thought women who wanted be tied up in bed—restrained and controlled—were weak . . . or sick."

Sean shook his head slowly. "It's not sick to understand your sexual nature—to do what turns you on—as long as you're consenting, and no one is getting hurt." His hands dropped to her shoulders. He rubbed her muscles in his palms. His low, cadent drawl relaxed her as much as his stroking hands and the heat of the fire. "You know I'd never hurt you. Just the thought of it makes me sick, and I'm not saying that in a figurative sense, either."

She gave him a wry look, and he smiled.

"It's true. But does it make me hornier than hell to think about restraining you so that you can't escape from the pleasure I give you, even for a brief reprieve? *Hell*, yeah."

He lowered his hands to her hips and shifted her completely on top of him. Genevieve's eyes widened when she felt his cock pressing against her belly. His heat penetrated her thin nightgown. She squirmed a little at the erotic sensation—or had her excitement stemmed from Sean's words?—and liquid heat surged from her core to wet her sex even more.

She had to face her insecurities full on when Sean's hands shifted to her hips, holding her immobile against his growing erection, and her clit twanged with arousal.

"See, girl?" he asked softly. "It turns you on."

She closed her eyes. Heat rose in her cheeks.

"There's nothing to be ashamed of. It's beautiful, the way you respond to me," he murmured thickly. She whimpered when his hands lowered to her ass. He palmed the cheeks and began to move her body in erotic little circles against his straining cock. "As a matter of fact, I've never experienced anything like you. It's like you were made for me, girl. That's why I would never have given up my memories of that night, despite the fact that I regretted it so much."

"But I've never felt this way with another man."

"That's fine and dandy with me," Sean said in no uncertain terms.

She opened her eyes. "But wouldn't I have known about it before? Wouldn't I have always wanted it that way in bed? Wouldn't there have been some kind of warning, some indication?"

He shook his head and laughed. "You make it sound like a disease or something. So what if you never had great sex until you were thirty years old? So what if you hadn't realized you like to submit in bed? Maybe you just never met the right guy."

He ran his hands up and down her ass, hips, and thighs, distracting her from the conversation at hand. Genevieve just stared at him for a moment with her mouth hanging open. His cock throbbed against her belly. She blinked when his smile widened.

"And I suppose you're the right guy," she said, both amused and irritated by his cocky, extremely sexy grin. How fair was it that he held so much power over her? "A man who likes to put cuffs on a woman and keeps a drawer full of sex toys."

"No other woman matters but you."

She gave him a disparaging glance, despite his earnest tone. He chuckled.

"It's the gawd's truth, girl. Do you want me to show you what I mean?" He cupped her bottom in both palms, the action striking her as lascivious and very exciting at once. He used his hold on her ass to rub their bodies together. Genevieve's cheeks grew even warmer.

"You've got an ass that could make a grown man cry," he muttered under his breath.

Her gaze raked across his face. "I don't see any tears. I wonder what that means?"

He laughed. Genevieve jumped when he popped one ass cheek with his palm before he continued massaging both buttocks with increasing greed. Her bottom tingled where he'd spanked it. A spurt of warm liquid seeped out of her slit when she heard the crack of flesh against flesh.

God . . . he was right. She really had been hardwired to like the kinky stuff. Or maybe it was more accurate to say she'd been hardwired to respond to Sean?

Either way, she ended up in the same place, Genevieve realized as she looked into Sean's gleaming, mischievous blue eyes. Better just to accept the inevitable . . . for now. Sean's potent sexuality made it difficult to worry about the right or wrong of her desires, and his tender playfulness made her anxieties shrink to almost nothing.

"So?" he asked huskily.

"So, *what*?"

"What about it? Would you let me make my point? About your nature? About how beautiful, and responsive you are? Come on, Genny. Just you and me," he coaxed gruffly.

She glanced out the window, feigning boredom despite the increase of her heart rate. "Well . . . seeing as I don't have anything else to do, with the snowstorm going on and all."

Sean chuckled before he rolled her onto her back and came down over her. "Hail to Mother Nature."

He covered her mouth with his.

Genevieve kissed him back hungrily, sliding her tongue next to his, teasing him just as heartlessly as he teased her, probing the depths of his mouth just as boldly. She was all too eager to forget her anxieties for a while, and nothing could make her do that as well as Sean's lovemaking. They both were breathless by the time Sean lifted his head.

"There's only one kind of woman who kisses like that," Sean murmured.

"The sexy kind?"

His mouth pressed into a hard line, but his eyes sparkled. "The kind that's so sexy her man has to cool her down a little bit, or pretty soon she'll be bringing down the place in flames."

Her eyebrows went up.

"Sorry. Bad joke, all things considered." He surprised her by leaping up from the blanket suddenly. He stood over her. "Take off your nightgown."

She sat up and whisked the light fabric over her head. She was naked beneath it except for a tiny scrap of panties. Sean nodded once at the patch of silk and she pulled them down her thighs. She slowly sunk back to a reclining position on the comforter.

He just stared at her naked body for several seconds before his hand sunk beneath the waistband of his pajama bottoms. He fisted his cock and shoved the fabric beneath his balls. It was an awesome sight to watch from below as he slowly stroked his long, thick erection. She took pride in his fixed, hungry expression as he looked at her body. It gratified her beyond measure to know that *she* had made his cock so swollen and stiff.

She hardly thought about what she was doing. Her hands rose and cradled her breasts. She massaged them slowly as she watched Sean stroke his penis. A warm torpor weighted her muscles. Her genitals began to ache deliciously. She held up her breasts from below, as though offering the tightening, pink centers to Sean.

He paused in jacking his cock and moaned. "You tempt me something awful. It's going to be so hard to go slow."

"Then let's go fast," she replied, her gaze glued to his big hand fisting his big cock.

"Uh-uh. I'm savoring you, girl. Every chance I get."

She lightly pinched her nipples, tempting him. Her vagina

flexed inward when she saw the flash of fire in his eyes. He groaned roughly and reached for her elbows, helping her to stand.

"You're not playing fair. I can see I *am* going to have to cool down that hot little body."

"Sean, what are you doing?" she asked in confusion when he took her hand and led her over to the glass patio doors that led to a small six-by-ten-foot terrace. Wind whipped across the frozen pane, swirling snowflakes chaotically through the air.

"Stay right here a second," he ordered before he headed for the hallway. Genevieve's eyes went wide in anxiety when he returned to the living room a few seconds later carrying a whippy crop with a two-by-two-inch leather slapper at the end.

"It's okay, Genny," he soothed when he saw her face. "I told you I'd never really hurt you. I'm just going to use it to enliven your flesh some . . . make your bottom glow just as bright as your cheeks are right now."

She looked up at him when she heard his teasing tone. Heat flooded her face again, but this time in arousal more than embarrassment. He stroked her cheek with a long finger.

"The first thing you need to understand is that seeing your trust firsthand is what turns me on, girl. I want to see you lose yourself in pleasure. I want to see you trust me enough to let go," he rumbled.

Genevieve bit her lower lip even as her gaze dropped to the awesome sight of Sean's cock. He'd left the drawstring below the thick shaft. It was a jaw-dropping sight to see it poking out from his body at a downward angle. She might be feeling uncertain about the crop, but seeing him standing there holding it in his big, capable-looking hand while his cock jutted out from his body, and the feeling of him stroking her cheek with so much gentleness . . . all of it went a long way to silence her anxieties.

His hand left her cheek. He touched the glass pane.

"Cold," he murmured, even though his eyes on her were blazing hot. "Do you trust me, Genny?"

"Yes," she whispered after a moment.

He stroked her hip from waist to thigh softly. "Good. It's not a gift I take lightly. Now . . . I want you to press your body up against the window."

CHAPTER **SEVENTEEN**

"What?" Genevieve asked loudly. She hadn't been expecting Sean to say something so crazy. "It'll be freezing, Sean!"

He grinned and ran his hand over her belly. Genevieve shifted her hips in growing arousal. She couldn't imagine why. How could pressing her body against a frozen windowpane be arousing?

Because Sean told you to do it, her brain answered automatically.

"I know it's cold, but your body is so hot right now," he coaxed with his soft drawl. "I told you I needed to cool you down a little."

"Sean . . ."

"Only do it if you want to, Genny. Always. But I should probably warn you if you decide to, I'm gonna have to use this on your bottom while you do it." He held up the leather slapper. "For purely practical purposes, of course. Gotta keep one side of you nice and toasty while the other side is so cold."

Her eyes went wide. She hadn't expected him to say that, either.

So why had her clit twanged with excitement, as though it'd known precisely what Sean was going to say in that low, sexy drawl.

"Gen?" he queried gently.

She swallowed thickly and nodded. Even though his proposal had struck her as a bit ridiculous, it had fired her flesh, as well. Still . . . she hesitated when she stood before the glass pane. It was going to be like pressing her body against a block of ice. The tips of her breasts stiffened at the mere thought. Sean stroked her back and then ran his hand lightly over her ass.

"Go on, girl. Press your pretty nipples up against it," he murmured. "You don't have to put your belly or thighs next to it. Lean into the glass. And don't put your forehead next to it. It'll probably give you a headache."

Genny stepped forward. She let out a loud gasp when she put her weight slightly forward and her chest and shoulders came into contact with the icy glass. A shock went through her and she trembled. She resisted a powerful urge to leap away. Her nipples drew into tight, sensitive darts against the cold, hard surface.

"Shhh," Sean murmured as he stepped closer behind her. She felt his hands on her wrists.

"Sean?" she asked shakily when he raised her arms until they were up over her head. He placed her palms next to the windowpane.

"Stay like that, girl. Don't lower your arms," he murmured, his warm breath near her ear causing her to shiver more. He put his hands on her hips and urged her to take a step back. When he'd finished positioning her, she stood with her shoulders, breasts, and hands pressed against the frigid glass. Her escalated breathing caused a patch of vapor to form an inch from her lips. Her hips and legs were farther back from her upper body, making her rear end stick out. She could see her reflection in the glass, and also Sean, standing behind her.

He caressed her bottom and moved to the side of her, his hand still on her ass. She groaned softly when she saw the reflection of his penis. Her gaze fixed on the sight of his other hand holding the crop. He tapped the end gently against his pant leg as he spoke.

"I think I'll spank you first. Just a little. Have you ever been spanked before?" he murmured as he spread his hand over her ass, the crack in the middle of his palm. He made a circling motion with his hand, massaging her flesh in such a way that she couldn't concentrate. Her nipples pinched tight against the glass, the sensation arousing her. But it just felt damn cold on the rest of her skin.

"No," she said, her voice sounding muffled as close as she was to the window. "And I'd appreciate it if you just got it over with. This glass is freezing."

"Sure thing, girl," he murmured. Her heart forgot its purpose for a second when she saw him draw back his hand.

Smack.

"Oh!" she exclaimed, the syllable popping out of her mouth in surprise. Her eyes went wide at the reflection in the glass. His cock had lurched up into the air at the same moment he'd cracked her bottom. She wiggled her hips, feeling a little dazed and desperate by the incredible surge of heat at her core. He slid his hand through the strap on the slapper, allowing it to dangle in the air as he stilled her wriggling ass. He grabbed a buttock and stretched the already taut skin even tighter.

"Hold still," he ordered, before he slapped the captive flesh several times. After he'd made one buttock prickle and burn, he turned his attentions to the other. He wasn't harsh, Genevieve realized. His spanks were designed to sensitize and fire her nerves more than anything.

It was a strange feeling to have part of her body tingle with cold while Sean concentrated all his efforts on making another part burn. And as in all things Sean did, his maneuvers were breathtaking in their precision.

She whimpered in rising desperation as he continued to crack his palm against her bottom. He paused and ran his hand over her ass, massaging the cheeks and soothing the flesh. She moaned when she saw him transfer the crop to his right hand. He lifted it and her muscles tensed in anticipation. But instead of popping her bottom, he ran the square piece of leather all over her ass. For some reason, his actions drove her crazy with excitement. It took her a moment to realize she wiggled her bottom, wild to feel more of the leather against her skin.

He chuckled and swatted her. Genevieve gasped at the sharp burst of sensation. Her bottom prickled where he'd popped it. He slapped her again and again, until all the nerves in her ass tingled with a low-grade burn. She bit her lip to prevent crying out in wild arousal when she noticed in the reflection that he stroked his penis slowly, his eyes fixated on her bottom as he popped it repeatedly. When she whimpered in rising desperation, he glanced up and spread the hand that had fisted his cock over her ass.

"Hot," he muttered thickly.

"*Sean*," she groaned. Her pussy felt drenched and enflamed. Her blood throbbed feverishly in her veins. The window pane no longer felt so cold. Her lust had prevailed, and the growing fire in her flesh heated the frigid glass.

His head came up. "What's wrong? Is the glass too cold?"

She shook her head.

"Does your bottom hurt?"

Again, she shook her head.

In the glass, she thought she saw his handsome mouth tilt.

"Good, because I'm going to make your gorgeous ass even pinker." He drew the crop back and swatted her several more times. The sharp cracking noise of leather against flesh made her vagina clench in agonized pleasure. A burning sensation plagued her clit. Genevieve thought she'd die at that moment if she didn't get friction on the nerve-packed, hungry little piece of flesh. She saw that Sean continued to stroke his cock slowly as he slapped her and that knowledge only enflamed her lust. *She* wanted to touch him.

She bit her lip to prevent herself from begging him to let her caress and suck on his beautiful cock.

Maybe he sensed the rising tension in her muscles because he paused and stroked her bottom again, soothing the fiery flesh.

"It feels nice and hot," he murmured.

She gasped when he raised his cock and rubbed the smooth head against one of her buttocks.

"Sean, stop teasing me, please."

"I'm sorry," he whispered gruffly. Despite his words, he ran the fat, shapely cockhead along the crack of her ass. He grunted appreciatively. "I just had to feel some of that heat. You're like hot silk, girl."

Genevieve came very close to pushing herself off the glass door at that moment and refusing to play. But something about the reflection of the transfixed expression on Sean's face as he slid the tip of his cock between her burning ass cheeks stopped her. She panted erratically as he buried the cockhead in her crack and palmed her buttocks, pressing the flesh around his burrowing cock. Her eyes went wide. He didn't apply pressure, but the warm, steely head of his cock pressed directly against her asshole.

"Sean? *Please.*"

He looked up. He sent one hand between her thighs. Her cry of rising desperation mixed with his groan of satisfaction when he ran two fingers along her slick outer sex. His fingers were just a fraction of an inch away from her clit. All she could think about was Sean touching her . . . how good it would feel to gush in orgasm, to find relief from the fever that plagued her.

"You're soaked. You're killing me, girl."

"I'm having a hard time feeling sorry for you," she replied in a choked voice.

He backed away and his penis fell from the crack of her ass. Genevieve sighed in mixed relief and misery when he grasped her shoulders and pulled her off the glass.

"It's a good thing it's snowing out there, or the neighbors would be getting one hell of a show," Genevieve muttered.

Sean laughed softly, but his amusement seemed strained this time. "Best for me not to think about how you would look from the other side of that door. Especially when I think about how you're going to look in a second."

"What?"

"Come over here," he said as he urged her to the patio pane next to the sliding door. "This window is still nice and cold. Look what you did to that one." Genevieve glanced at where he nodded. The heat of her body coming into contact with the cool glass had made moisture slick the pane. Sean smiled when he saw her eyes widen.

"Now we're going to have to cool off your ass." He leaned down and kissed her flaming cheek. "Not to mention that hot little pussy."

Her gaze shot up to meet his steamy stare.

"You know what to do," he murmured. "Bend over and spread your legs. Press your bottom next to the glass. While you cool off a little, I'll work on warming up the cold parts."

For a few seconds she just stared up at him. Her heartbeat throbbed in her ears. Why was she doing this? Why was she allowing him to turn her into someone she hardly recognized?

A lust-junkie.

She felt so excited at that moment, so alive, that she probably would have done anything to quench her raging desire. Sean's blue eyes blazed with arousal as he looked down at her.

That's why she did it, she realized with growing amazement. She craved that hot look in his eyes almost as much as she hungered for the blast of climactic oblivion. Some people might call that sick, but Genevieve accepted at that volatile moment that it was a personal truth she couldn't deny.

Sean must have seen the shadow of doubt that crossed her face because he cupped her jaw in his palm.

"You're not submitting to me, girl. You're submitting to the truth . . . and I know how hard that is for you. There's no room for shame here. Only us."

She nodded once before she turned her back to the patio window. She bent over and pressed her ass to the cold windowpane.

"That's right, girl," Sean praised as he leaned over her. He put his hands on the upper curve of her buttocks. "But come forward, just for a second."

When she came off the glass, he reached down, palming both her ass cheeks at once. He lifted. Her outer sex tingled as the tissues stretched slightly and were exposed to the cool air. "Now spread your legs farther and press your thighs to the glass."

Genevieve struggled to do as he requested, but she was distracted by the fact that he parted her ass cheeks as he held them up. Wintry air off the glass hit the sensitive flesh deep inside the crevice between her buttocks.

He's staring right at your asshole, Genevieve thought with nervous excitement.

"Now lean back," he instructed.

A spasm of mixed pleasure and discomfort went through her when she pressed back and her spread pussy came into contact with the glass. Her nerves seemed to zing and pop with the mixed message of hot arousal and bitter cold. Genevieve couldn't help it. She pushed back harder, enjoying the hard pressure against her pussy and clit despite the frigidity of the temperature against her skin.

Sean chuckled as he slid his hands off her ass. He urged her back with a hand on her shoulder and she pressed her bottom fully against the glass as well.

"I'm surprised I didn't hear any hissing and sizzling, you're so hot."

Genevieve moaned in unbearable excitement as his words penetrated her lust-befuddled brain. She squirmed against the cold, hard surface, getting pressure against her burning clit.

Sean cradled her jaw. His thumb swept over her cheek softly. "Jeez, you're on fire, girl." Genevieve glanced up to meet his gaze from her bent-over position. His cock was just inches from her face. She caught a whiff of his male musk and pressed her hips back more desperately against the glass. Sean's fingers on her cheek went still, and Genevieve knew he'd noticed her stare on his erection.

She'd never been cock-crazy before. When she'd first seen Sean's penis, though, she'd first understood the meaning of the term. The tapered, shapely cockhead drove her crazy. Just the sight of it made her mouth water. The thick rim below it felt sublime rubbing deep, secret flesh. She longed for the weight of it on her tongue.

As far as fellatio went, she'd always enjoyed it well enough. But when it came to Sean, her hunger stunned her. She recalled the erotic potency of sucking on him on that New Year's Eve night while he watched her with fixed intensity.

"Let me suck it," she whispered hoarsely.

"Genny," he groaned. His feet moved on the carpet. His cock inched closer to her face. She whimpered when he dug his fingers into her hair, drawing the long strands away from her face. His cock lurched upward toward her spread lips and he groaned again.

She cried out in protest when he suddenly dropped to his knees in front of her. Both hands delved into her hair this time. He held her head steady while he ravaged her mouth with his own. Her heart swelled in her breast. It did something to her to know for a fact that despite his tightly leashed controls when it came to his lovemaking, on the inside, Sean raged as hot for her as she did him.

He released her hair, letting it fall in a curtain around their melded mouths. His hands cupped her suspended breasts. He began to finesse them with deliciously warm fingers. He broke their tempestuous kiss and whispered next to her ear, "You're still cold. Your nipples are so hard." She pressed her forehead to his and panted softly as his skilled hands massaged her sensitive flesh.

She gasped as he lightly pinched the stiff crests. Before she could find the breath to respond, he put his hands on her shoulders and raised her upper body several inches. He ducked below her.

"Brace yourself on my back," he said, his warm breath striking a nipple. She barely had time to put her hands on his back, steadying herself, before he surrounded her chilled flesh in his hot mouth.

"Sean," she hissed. Sensation overwhelmed her. He gave her nipple a wet lashing. When she groaned loudly, he softened his strokes, laving the sensitive flesh with a firm, sleek tongue.

Prickles of pleasure tore through her breast as Sean heated and agitated the chilled flesh with his mouth, and normal blood flow began to return. The sensation was so potent that she pressed her pussy against the pane of glass and wriggled her hips, stimulating her clit.

When he'd tormented and warmed one breast with his mouth and massaging palm, he turned his attention to the other. Genevieve gasped at the exquisite sensation of him enfolding the sensitive, chilled tip of her breast in his mouth. He suckled and stimulated the erect crest for what felt like an unbearable eternity. All the while, her pussy pressed against the window, warming the chilled window with her hot flesh.

She grew shameless . . . lost in pleasure. Her hips made tiny, tight gyrations against the glass pane. Her fingernails dug into Sean's back muscles. He answered her desperation by sucking harder on her nipple, until her pleasure peaked.

But then his hot mouth was gone and he was standing again in front of her. He put his hands on her wiggling hips, stilling her clitoral stimulation against the glass.

She groaned in agony.

"Sean," she pleaded raggedly as she panted.

"It's okay," he assured gruffly. He used one hand to push her hair out of her face, gently placing it behind her ears. "Put your hands on your thighs and thrust your chest out. That's right," he praised. "Show me your pretty breasts." Her eyes widened when he raised the leather popper and ran it along the underside of a breast.

"Sean?" she murmured anxiously as he continued to run the slapper everywhere on her heaving breast but the distended nipple. The sensation was almost unbearably exciting, but she didn't want to have her breasts *spanked.*

He ran his hand along her spine, soothing her. At the same time, he ran the leather popper over an erect nipple. Genevieve moaned when he began to stimulate the hypersensitive crest by moving the crop in a tight circle.

"I'll do it gently, girl," he said quietly as he stroked her spine, concentrating on the six inches just above the crack of her ass. The caress struck her as highly intimate, both exciting and relaxing her at once. *How does he always know just where to touch me, just what to say?* she wondered dazedly.

"And if you don't like it, you just tell me to stop. That's how we'll always do it. Okay?" he prompted.

She nodded. Her heartbeat thundered in her ears when he brought back the crop and gently swatted the side of her breast.

It didn't hurt, but the whapping sound and the tingling sensation on her skin made her shift her hips against the cool glass. The pressure felt so good against her aching clit. She gasped when he popped the top of her breast, this time with a bit more force.

"Keep your ass still, girl," he said, his voice warm but firm.

She whimpered in rising sexual desperation as he continued to gently slap her breasts and she forced herself to remain still, her stare fixed on the awesome sight of his jutting erection. She became highly focused on each little slap, wondering each time he landed one if he came closer to a straining nipple.

Her nipples pinched unbearably tight. She found herself craving that low-level sting to alleviate the sharp, prickling pain that plagued the sensitive flesh.

Her eyes trailed up Sean's glorious, flame-gilded torso and fixed on his face. He looked so focused, and yet mesmerized, as well, as he watched the crop landing on her trembling breasts. She made a choked noise in her throat when the slapper came within a hairsbreadth of a pointed tip.

He glanced at her and their gazes melded.

"Please," she mouthed.

His expression turned rigid before he brought the slapper down on one nipple, then the other, then back to the first. Tap, tap, tap, the popper went rapidly back and forth between her breasts.

She called out his name as she climaxed against the glass pane.

CHAPTER **EIGHTEEN**

Genevieve was so lost in that first blast of pleasure that she hardly knew what was happening when Sean pressed back on her shoulders. She cried out in anguish when her stimulation was interrupted by him moving her on the glass. Her orgasm took on a tight, cramped quality. Sean pushed her farther back. A small slap on her inner thigh made her eyelids unclench.

"Spread your legs," he demanded.

She did so in rising disorientation. He placed the leather slapper over her labia and gave her a firm, hard, circular rub. She shouted out as the orgasm slammed into her full force once again. He held her against the glass with his hand on one shoulder and began to tap out a fast rhythm on her cunt with the crop.

Genevieve gave an anguished scream. It felt deliciously forbidden to have him slap her pussy, but she couldn't stop the waves of pleasure.

"It's all right, Genny," she heard him saying as her body jerked and shuddered. "Just let go, I've got you."

She tumbled headlong into pure bliss at his words. How long

he kept her there pinned against the glass while he alternated between gently tapping her climaxing pussy and applying a firm, circular pressure with the leather popper, Genevieve couldn't be sure. He kept her coasting at the crest of her orgasm, stimulating her with expert precision, ensuring that her climax lasted for a record-breaking period of time.

One thing was for certain: After that night, just the sight of the whippy crop would make her clit twang in arousal. Never mind how her body would react when she saw Sean holding that instrument of pleasure.

She felt wrung out by the time her orgasm waned. She was distantly surprised to realize that her throat had been scraped raw by her shouts of ecstasy. Her breath sounded harsh and ragged in the silent room. Sean tossed down the crop and pulled her into his arms. He dropped a kiss on her nose while she panted madly for air.

"Sexiest woman alive, that's what you are." She felt him grab her wrist. He placed her hand on his cock. It leapt at her touch. She encircled his girth instinctively. He felt iron hard as he throbbed in her hand. "See what you do to me, girl? Come here."

She followed him, still in a daze from being burned by the most intense sexual experience she'd ever had.

"Bend down over the arm of the couch," she heard Sean coax gently. "I can't take it anymore. I've got to be inside that pussy that melted right through ice." When she bent over and braced herself with her arms, he grabbed one of the large cushions from the back of the couch and placed it on the armrest. "Here. I know you're worn out. Put your weight on the pillow. Just rest your chest there. That's a girl. Now you just relax while I fuck you."

Despite her turned-inside-out state, Genevieve croaked with laughter.

Relax.

"Sean, you say the damnedest things." She took her first full breath into her lungs, however, once she rested with her chest, cheek, and arms on the cushion.

He chuckled as he moved behind her. All of her amusement faded when she felt him probe lightly at the sensitive tissues around her slit with his warm, steely cockhead.

"So hot, even though you were pressed against a frozen window," he said before he thrust, gently at first. Genevieve trembled at the sensation of his penis carving into her flesh, stretching her, forcing her to accommodate him. Instead of pressing until he was fully sheathed, he began to stroke her with small, electrical little pulsations, encouraging her to let him with his characteristic manner.

Gentle, but firm.

His rough groan told Genevieve he liked how she felt. Liked it a lot. She pressed her hips back, wanting to take him completely, to make him feel some measure of the intense pleasure he'd given her.

He responded by placing both his hands on her bottom.

"Hold still," he ordered. Maybe he regretted the edge to his voice because he inhaled deeply and sighed. "It feels so good. I want to make it last. Do you understand, Gen?"

She peered around, trying to see him in her bent-over position. Something in his voice made her want to see his face. She caught his eye before her cheek fell back to the pillow.

"Yes," she whispered.

"Good." The first several inches of his cock throbbed in her pussy as he leaned over and moved her mussed hair off her face. Then he grabbed her wrists and gently placed them at the small of her back. He held them with one hand, pulling back on them. His cock slid in another inch.

He groaned. She lifted her head again, wishing she could see his pleasure.

"Do you want to be able to see me, girl? Is that it?"

She nodded her head.

"Look in the window."

Genevieve shifted her head slightly on the pillow and gazed out the floor-to-ceiling windows. Her eyes widened. It wasn't as clear as a mirror, but she could clearly make out their reflection. Sean hadn't even fully removed his pajama bottoms before he started to fuck her. They still were up around his hips, covering his ass. The fabric was bunched down around his balls in the front. His jutting cock was partially buried in her pussy.

Her vagina clenched tightly at the erotic vision. Heat surged through her. She saw his head go back and his face clench, and she knew he'd felt her internal caress.

"Christ," he grated out. He held her hip and plunged his cock all the way into her, his pelvis making a whapping sound when it struck her bottom. He rapidly whisked down his pajama bottoms over his hips and ass, pushing them down to his thighs. Once his testicles were freed, he pressed them tighter into her. He used his hold on her wrists to pulse her against him, getting pressure on his firm balls.

He groaned gutturally. Genevieve cried out. He'd filled her to capacity and then pressed deeper. Her eyes shot wide at the sensation. Her gaze remained fixed on the delicious profile of his flame-lit ass, the large, round muscles tensed and hard, ready to hurdle them both into ecstasy.

"You really don't play fair, girl," he whispered roughly.

Genevieve gaped at the erotic tableau reflected in the snowy window. He held her at his mercy. She was completely helpless: bent over, her arms pinned behind her back, skewered by Sean's cock.

"I'm not doing *anything*," she replied.

He drew his cock slowly out of her and pushed it back in until his balls were once again pressed snugly to her ass. "You're you. And that's *everything*."

Genevieve barely had time to process those sweet words uttered in a low growl before he began to fuck her with long, thorough strokes. A little whimper pushed out of her lungs every time he drove his cock into her and their bodies collided. The air became filled with the brisk, rhythmic slaps of skin striking skin and Sean's unapologetic grunts of pleasure. She stared at him fixedly in the window, awe-struck by his pagan male beauty as he mated—hard, fast, and well.

Genevieve groaned. So *damn* well.

The thick rim beneath his cockhead rubbed deep, secret flesh . . . flesh that had never known a man's touch until Sean. Even though she thought it would be an impossibility to become aroused after her mind-numbing previous climax, she found herself becoming unbearably excited. His burrowing cock stimulated and fired her in a whole new way, causing an eye-crossing friction to build inside her. It created a tingling sensation all along her tailbone. She moaned as it built, turning her hot cheek on the velvet pillow.

Maybe his ability to read her mind was amplified since they were joined, but the hand on her hip moved, prying back one of her ass cheeks. She felt the cool air on her exposed rectum, amplifying the burning, tingling sensation that enlivened everything from her clit, to that secret spot Sean agitated with his cock so skillfully, all the way to her clenching asshole. His hold on her wrists tightened, as though in a subtle reminder that she was at his mercy at that moment. He sheathed himself in her and drew his pelvis in a tight little circle, making her cry out in rising ecstasy. His voice sounded low and desire-roughened when he leaned over her.

"I could fuck your little asshole right now, Genny." He pressed his thumb to her rectum and rubbed gently, threatening subtly to penetrate her. She cried out anxiously and panted in peaking excitement. "You're mine to do with as I want right now. You know that, don't you, girl?"

His cock jerked inside of her. She tightened around him and moaned helplessly.

"Answer me."

"*Yes.*"

He gave a satisfied grunt. "Now do you understand what I said before? When you let go . . . when you submit"—he drew out his cock and thrust back into her melting flesh—"I'm the one who's ruled by you, girl." He popped her bottom gently. "Do you understand?"

Genevieve stared at him open-mouthed in the window reflection. In that moment, she *did* understand.

"Yes. *Yes.*"

His cock lurched in her tight hold. He grimaced either in intense pleasure or feeling, Genevieve couldn't tell which. He firmed his hold on her wrists and hip.

"Good. Now hold still and take it."

"*Sean,*" she cried plaintively when he began to fuck her with short, hard thrusts, striving to ignite their flesh when previously he'd made them smolder and burn. He used his hold on her wrists to rock her back on him. They crashed together wildly, until the pressure and pleasure became untenable.

She felt him convulse deep inside her. His anguished shout of release struck her as poignant . . . beautiful. He reached around and massaged her clit bull's-eye fashion even as he continued to fuck her while he came. Her eyes went wide and she cried out as she plunged from the terrific heights of ecstasy to which Sean had taken her.

He leaned down and lifted her against his upper body. They shook into each other's flesh until Genevieve couldn't separate her bliss from Sean's.

Sometime later he led her over to their makeshift bed on the floor. They fell to the pillows, gasping. Sean grabbed the blankets and pulled them over their bodies. Genevieve's body slowly returned to equilibrium as she lay on her side, her back pressed against Sean's chest. She watched the snowflakes flying outside the window and experienced a strange paradox of uncertainty and utter contentment in her breast.

It'd been the most profoundly intense experience of her life. How could she let go so completely, release all of her inhibitions . . . give herself to Sean without reservations during the midst of desire, only to have doubt rear its head again when their passion was spent? Who *was* this man who had uncovered this foreign aspect of her own character?

Who was this man, who had killed in the name of their deep, boundless attraction for each other?

She thought of their volatile, powerful lovemaking. If their situation was different, she would consider the feelings she and Sean harbored for each other sacred and beautiful . . . *had* considered them that way not ten minutes ago.

But a human being's life had been taken in the name of their need for each other . . .

He nuzzled her neck. She shivered at the feeling of his lips on her ear.

"I love you, girl."

The moment to respond hung full and ripe.

And then it went, and she felt his warm, even breathing against her neck as he slept.

The falling snow turned into a wet, white blur before her eyes.

CHAPTER NINETEEN

Sean awoke the next morning feeling energized, refreshed . . .
good. For a few seconds before he opened his eyes, he wondered about his profound feeling of contentment. Then he pried his
eyelids open and glanced down. He smiled when he saw Genny's
head tucked between his chin and his chest.

He detailed the exquisite moments of their lovemaking last
night in his mind. Despite her uncertainties, she'd given herself to
him wholly. His cock grew hard against the sweet, warm curve of
Genny's ass as he recalled her complete surrender. It didn't help
things when he thought of making her shapely bottom blush pink
with his palm and the crop, or of how tempting she'd looked bend-
ing over the arm of the couch, submitting to her desire.

She stirred in her sleep when he reflexively thrust against her
firm, curving flesh. He groaned irritably. He didn't want to wake
her. She needed the rest, especially with everything she'd been
going through for the past few nights. He gritted his teeth when
he rolled away from Genny's warmth, resisting an urge to plunge
back under the covers—to drive his cock into her sublime heat.

His hard-on hadn't abated several minutes later as he stood in the shower with water beating down on his chest. He was considering bringing himself off; the memories from last night were so graphic and potent. He thought of Genny looking up at him with mixed anguish and arousal when he'd lifted the crop to her plump, suspended breasts, recalled how she'd given him her trust, and soon only desire remained shining in her eyes.

His cock twitched with excitement. He fisted it and began to stroke himself.

But then he thought of holding her afterward; recalled how he'd told her he loved her and felt the resulting tension in her body. He'd been too exhausted and sated after their lovemaking to make much of her reaction to his words.

But this morning, it struck him as depressing.

He let his diminishing erection drop and quickly finished showering. What he needed was a good workout. He'd go down to the Sauren-Kennedy gym. After he'd cleared his head, he'd sit down in front of his computer and go over his old files on the Max Sauren murder. He needed to relook at all the old evidence in light of what was happening to Genny.

He was missing something, and the longer it took him to figure out what that something was, the more Genny was left exposed and vulnerable.

He wrote Genny a note as to his whereabouts and quietly exited the penthouse.

An hour and a half later, Sean had worked out and showered again in the Sauren-Kennedy locker room. He sat at his computer in his office, poring over a secured file containing old photos, news articles, and his personal notes. He'd grown accustomed to compiling detailed files about cases for his work. Max Sauren's murder wasn't a case, but because of Genny, Sean had felt even more of a need to collect and organize the data.

To try to make sense of it all.

Max had been found dead in his car in early January. His motionless form had been spotted in the driver's seat of his silver Mercedes by a man who had pulled into the abandoned warehouse parking lot to change a flat tire.

The police had been stymied by the clean murder scene and lack of evidence or a clear motive. Not only had Max's gun not been on him, it hadn't been in the compartment where he'd sometimes stored it while he drove—a small container with a lock that Max'd had installed in his car. Because of his investigations and visitations with government officials, Max frequently had to pass through high-security buildings. He'd been paranoid about leaving his gun with anyone, preferring to lock it in his car versus hand it over to security. Sean had gotten Detective Franklin to admit that the gun compartment had been found locked and empty.

Max's keys had been missing along with his gun. The car doors had been left unlocked. His clothes had been mussed, indicating a struggle, but his wallet hadn't been touched. Max'd been shot twice. One bullet had collapsed a lung. The kill shot had pierced his heart.

Sean opened a file and stared at Max Sauren's face in death. He'd successfully procured some photos from an assistant coroner. Detective Franklin had become suspicious of a leak at the coroner's office, however, and Sean hadn't been able to get his hands on the official coroner's report.

He'd never gleaned much from the photographs other than the obvious bullet punctures of the chest, but he'd always been struck by Max Sauren's expression in death. It was peaceful, enigmatic . . . even slightly smug? Almost as if just before he'd died, the consummate spy had glimpsed the biggest secret of all.

The police had launched a massive search for the murder weapon, combing miles of city streets and foliage, dredging the depths of a nearby creek and checking hundreds of Dumpsters in the proximity. With Genevieve's permission, they'd searched the Sauren mansion and the grounds.

Nothing had ever been found, including—as far as Sean knew— Max Sauren's attaché case.

By the time they'd searched her house, Sean'd already doubted the police would find anything—unless Albert Rook showed it to them, that is. By that time, Rook had already planned his blackmail meeting and left Sean's office running scared.

Sean clicked on another file labeled ROOK. He opened some dated notes, and read one of his own entries.

October 6. MS said he wanted to meet about the Zeilerman case, but instead started asking about the quality of AR's work. Told him it was satisfactory, but had to keep on him—AR tends to cut corners and get sloppy. MS said AR is like a dog that obeys best with a choker. Asked what he meant, and MS said he had documentation that proved that while AR worked as a Navy weapons systems analyst he'd committed treason. It'd been AR's job to reveal certain military secrets to Taiwan, but he'd shared with the Chinese, as well. For a hefty price, of course. Asked MS why he was telling me this, and he said there may come a time when AR needed to be controlled. MS said the documentation was AR's choker.

Sean stared at the letters on the computer screen. The conversation that he'd just read marked the first time Sean had been one hundred percent certain that Sauren and Rook were lovers.

He'd suspected the two men were sexually involved before from the way that Rook stared at Max sometimes, while Max so studiously avoided his glances. But when Max casually told Sean about

Rook committing treason, it had been the last nail in the coffin. Max was the type to collect secrets about those who were close to him.

People who had the potential to hurt him.

Max's behavior had also revealed to Sean just how untrustworthy Rook was. His old boss may have enjoyed Rook in bed, but if he was telling Sean his lover's secrets, he didn't trust the man worth a damn. Max had probably sensed that Sean disliked Rook. If anything ever happened to Max, he probably wanted to ensure that Sean brought Rook to justice.

Unfortunately, Rook had come to Sean and laid evidence before him first.

He clicked on another file labeled GB/AR.

Rook had showed him digital photos of Max's gun and his keys. The only tangible evidence Rook had showed Sean on that afternoon were the shell casings. He'd claimed he found all of it on the wooded grounds of the Sauren mansion. Rook'd also claimed the gun was clean of prints, but he'd allowed Sean to pull a couple prints off the shell casings. All of them had been Genevieve's, a fact Sean was able to prove to himself thanks to the Sauren fingerprint archive.

Sean didn't necessarily believe Rook's allegations. It was just as possible Rook had murdered his lover. But as an ex–weapons analyst and military spy, Rook knew his stuff. The evidence he'd compiled was convincing, even if Rook would have to make up some cock-and-bull story as to why he illegally removed the evidence from where he "found" it. Rook had carefully documented the evidence with photographs, like any good intelligence operative.

Besides, the police already had Genny in their targets. They *might* switch their attention to Rook if Sean told them about the two men being lovers, and Rook was forced to admit how he'd illegally removed the evidence he'd supposedly found.

But *what if*? What if Max had showed Genny the tape, like Rook claimed he planned to do? She'd have been so disillusioned by Max . . . so hurt. Who's to say she couldn't have had an altercation with him? What if they'd struggled and Genny had shot him by accident?

Sean doubted it, but the possibility haunted him. On the few occasions he'd seen Genny following the murder, she'd certainly *looked* guilty and afraid, that much was certain.

But Genny was no cold-blooded killer. If she'd shot Max it'd happened in a volatile moment and by accident.

Sean thought it was much more likely that Rook was responsible for Max's death. He'd wanted something from Max, and had possibly threatened to reveal Max's bisexual tendencies—a powerful threat in the male-dominated, machismo world of espionage and intelligence. Max had threatened him in turn with exposure of his treasonous activities, and Rook had shot him to prevent that possibility.

But even if there was a good chance the police would poke holes in Rook's story, from Sean's perspective, there had been too great of a chance that Rook might be successful.

And it still nagged at Sean how betrayed Genny must have felt when Max showed her his true face after all those years of knowing him. Who knew what kind of an effect it had on her?

Rook had claimed that Max had showed him the videotape of the New Year's Eve ménage days before he was killed. Did Sean believe Rook? It was hard to say. It was the exact sort of thing Max would have done. Hadn't he done something similar when he told Sean about Rook? Rook most certainly *had* the recording, while Sean only had Max's report of his treason, not the elusive documentation.

All in all, Max had given his lover a better hand than he had Sean.

Sean sat back in his leather chair, exhausted from over-thinking.

The fact of the matter was, the videotape might have been mortifying for Genny, but the only blackmail effect it'd had on Sean personally lay in that he'd never want Genny to be hurt by it. It was an effective enough means of blackmail, but Sean didn't think Max had been counting on that to hold over Sean's head for future ammunition.

No. It'd been what he'd planned later that he probably had hoped to use as ammunition against Sean . . . after Genny had fallen asleep in exhaustion following their lovemaking on that New Year's Eve night.

THREE YEARS AGO

Sean felt the depth of his need like the pain from an unhealed wound as he worshipped Genny's breasts with his lips, tongue, and fingertips. Breasts had been created to provide nurturance, and Sean well believed that as he ran his lips over petal-soft skin and inserted a turgid, reddened nipple into his mouth.

He could have feasted on her for hours, and his selfishness was so extreme that he'd still want more—more of Genny's responsive flesh, more of her lush, firm curves filling his hands, more of her catchy sighs and whimpers of pleasure filling his ears.

More. Always more.

"*Sean*," she cried out when he pushed both distended nipples close together and laved them warmly with his tongue.

He inserted one turgid crest into his mouth and glanced up at Genny. A sharp ache stabbed through his genitals as he took note of her mussed hair, lividly pink cheeks, and shiny eyes. She whimpered shakily when he drew on her while his fingertips studied the topography of the other wet, beaded nipple. She panted as their stares held, but then her pleasure overcame her and she clenched her eyelids shut and tried to twist her torso away from his mouth.

Sean lifted his head as Max placed his hands on her shoulders and held her in place next to his body.

"What's the matter, girl? Does it hurt?" Sean whispered gruffly as he continued to mold her breasts gently to his palm.

Genny moved her head from side to side on Max's chest. Sean saw a tear leak out of her eyelid. "No, no," she muttered, sounding frantic. "It only hurts when you stop."

"Sweet thing," Sean said feelingly. He'd been so involved in making love to her breasts that he hadn't realized the depth of her arousal. He reached down between her spread thighs and slid his finger between swollen, creamy labia.

He reinserted a nipple in his mouth and suckled her a moment later as she cried out in climax. The expression of ecstasy on her face mesmerized him. He kissed her nipple warmly.

"I could eat you alive, girl."

He couldn't resist plunging a finger into her snug, juicy slit, needing to feel her shudders of pleasure from the inside.

Her sharp exhalations of pleasure fell in warm bursts across his mouth when he kissed her opened lips.

He reached for a condom while she panted in the aftermath of her pleasure. He was hardly even aware of Max at that moment, so totally enraptured was he by Genny. His arousal was so intense, his need so sharp, his entire world narrowed down to her.

His body shook with barely restrained desire by the time he pressed his cock to her entrance. Her eyes blinked open in surprise when he applied a firm, steady pressure with his hips and the tip of his cock dipped into paradise. She mouthed his name when he thrust into her farther.

A groan tore out of his throat. She gripped him in a tight, hot embrace. He needed to apply a firm, constant pressure to gain access to her succulent depths.

"That's right, girl. Let me in," he coaxed with his voice even as he slid farther into her depths, demanding total entry. By the time he pressed his aching balls to her damp, warm flesh, they both were breathing heavily.

And Sean had started to shake even more; his need had been so intense. He paused, completely sheathed in Genny's pussy, trying desperately to get control of his raging lust so that he could savor her. He leaned on his arms and panted while Max kissed Genny's ear.

"He has a nice, big cock, doesn't he, love? Does it feel good?" Max murmured. Sean noticed that he'd released one of Genny's wrists and was shaping one of her breasts with his hand, his thumb and forefinger lightly pinching a damp, distended nipple. His cock lurched deep inside Genny, making her moan. Her hips moved restlessly. Sean stilled them with his hands.

"Does it?" Max asked again, this time more forcefully. Sean saw the other man shift his hips, and knew Max was likely again aroused and pressing his erection next to Genny's ass. The evidence of Max's rearousal was just what Sean needed to reign in his nearly out-of-control lust.

At least it was until Genny opened her lips, her eyes on Sean's face, and whispered, "*Yes.*"

Sean clenched his jaw tightly and began to fuck her, long and thorough. Their gazes locked the whole time, despite the fact that not only their bodies, but the entire bed began to quake with his powerful strokes. When she began to shift her hips, matching his relentless pace, Sean felt himself quickly rising toward climax.

Too quickly.

"Hold her tight, Max. Don't let her move. She's all mine."

Sean didn't want anyone in that room to be left in doubt that Genny was *his*.

It didn't last for as long as he would have liked it, but given his forceful possession, Sean figured it was best for Genny that his tumultuous need crested sooner versus later. When her head went back and her face tightened in an agony of pleasure, Sean fell down over her, pressing his face to the side of her neck, breathing her scent as he pressed deep inside her clenching, climaxing pussy and orgasm ripped through him.

Sometime afterward, Sean became aware of Max's hands moving along the sides of their entwined bodies.

"Let me up," Max spoke intently. "I want her again."

Sean lifted his head and fell to his side on the mattress. He pulled Genny with him—all the way to the other side, putting his body between Max's and hers.

"Leave her alone," he told Max. "She's had enough."

Max just stared at him, his gaze hot and enigmatic. He heard Genny's muffled whimper, the small noise sounding distressed. He rolled toward her and removed the condom. He encircled her in his arms a moment later, turning his back to Max . . . doing his best to ignore the other man.

"Shhh," he whispered before he pressed his lips to Genny's damp brow. "You okay?"

She nodded. Sean covered her external sex with his hand in a protective gesture. He couldn't recall ever taking a woman so forcefully. His need had never felt so powerful.

But as usual, his need to cherish her was equally as great.

"Little sore?" he murmured regretfully as he kissed her lips.

"I'm fine." Her whisper had been so soft he'd barely heard her.

Regret swamped him when he saw the anxiety start to creep into Genny's gray eyes again. He swallowed thickly. Even though he'd always felt supremely comfortable talking to Genny, he realized he didn't know what to say to her at that moment. That was when Sean first realized he'd lost something. Burning in

Genny's fires had been the type of experience he'd have sold his soul for.

It began to dawn on him that was precisely what he'd done.

He'd kissed both of her eyelids. "You look so tired. Go to sleep, girl. It's all going to be okay, I promise."

He felt like a coward, knowing he'd only suggested it so he didn't have to consider his own reflection in Genny's eyes at that moment. He'd sagged in relief minutes later when he sensed the tension ease out of her body as she sunk into a deep sleep.

"I hope she was everything you thought she'd be." Max spoke quietly.

Sean lifted his head, removing his face from the fragrant warmth of Genny's neck. He turned and stared at Max. The older man looked entirely comfortable laying there naked on his back, his thick mane of gray hair resting on the pillow. Sean gave him an annoyed look. Some kind of defense mechanism had clicked on in his brain that night. Sean'd *known* Max was in bed with him and Genny, but he'd also been able to miraculously ignore the man's presence at times . . . block out the fact that he'd watched while another man touched Genny . . . while another man fucked her . . .

If he'd let the knowledge enter into his awareness too greatly, he wouldn't have been able to stand it. It'd been a kind of survival instinct. Not for *his* survival.

For Max's.

Max rolled over onto his side. Sean's gaze dropped to his groin. The other man sported quite an erection. Sean resisted an urge to get off the bed and leave the room. He didn't want to move away from Genny at that moment, though.

He didn't *ever* want to move away from her.

His just glared forbiddingly at Max instead.

A small smile pulled at Max's lips as he reached around Sean's body. The guy had balls, Sean'd give him that.

Sean held himself on a tight leash as Max Sauren wrapped his hand around his cock and began to stroke him.

Sean shook his head slowly. An old, primitive fury rose in his gut. He fought that ugly feeling, that old enemy—an anger born from a vulnerable child's instinct to survive. He fought it mightily, but Max's cocky grin only fueled it.

"So. This was what you had in mind when you offered me Genny?"

"We all have to pay for what we want, Sean," Max said warmly. "It's one of the unspoken laws of the universe." Sean felt Max's cockhead brush against his ass. All the defense mechanisms he'd acquired as an adult thinned. Ice flooded his veins.

He resisted an overwhelming, primal urge to murder the son of a bitch.

"What are you going to pay *me* for not killing you, Max?" The older man's hand paused in stroking his cock. "I assume you actually *want* to live?" Sean prodded.

Max's dark eyes met his. After a tense moment, he let go of Sean's flaccid cock. Max laughed softly as he lay on his back on the bed, his hands behind his head.

"You really would, wouldn't you? Kill me for something so meaningless," Max asked, humor filling his handsome face.

Sean's nostrils flared in fury. "If Genny wasn't here, I just might."

"Guess it's true what they say. Can't teach an old dog new tricks."

"I wouldn't try tricking me, Max. Period."

"We'll see," Max replied, his smile never wavering.

Sean suddenly felt like he couldn't breathe, like he was smothering in his own rage. He needed to get out of that penthouse, before he did something he regretted.

He tried his mightiest to ignore Max's stare as he gathered his clothing and rapidly dressed, but his anger threatened to explode out of his chest at any second.

"I wouldn't spare too many thoughts for any future dalliances with my wife. She may have enjoyed having you in bed, but she's a little out of your league, wouldn't you say?"

Sean just continued to dress methodically, realizing he was being baited at this point, although the knowledge was helping only minimally.

"Genny may have grown up in the roughest of circumstances, but as you know, nature shaped her into the rarest of jewels. Maybe you've imagined that the two of you have something in common because of your backgrounds, but don't kid yourself, Sean. Genny is about as different from the women in your life as an exquisite diamond is from a grain of sand. Your mother, for instance . . ."

Sean's fingers stilled in the action of buttoning his shirt.

"I understand she relapsed yet again, and had to return to that residential facility for addicts. Shame, really, that they actually have the nerve to call those places 'rehabilitation centers' when they serve as a revolving-door pit stop for the dredges of society. Genny mentioned your mother's circumstances to me once. Genny's so impressionable, you know. So kind. The pity I heard in her voice for your mother—and for you, as well . . ."

Sean closed his eyes and willed the red haze that had begun to cloud his vision to clear. When the raging surge of his heartbeat quieted in his ears, he opened his eyes and fixed his stare on Genny.

He finished buttoning his shirt, his gaze never leaving her still form. He walked toward her.

"Don't even think about trying to remove her from this penthouse. She's my wife. She belongs here, with me," Max warned quietly.

Sean's glance was full of loathing. He'd thought he'd understood

Max Sauren pretty well before that night, and he hadn't been wrong, technically speaking. But coming into firsthand contact with the dark void at the center of the man was different than speculating about its existence.

"I'm putting her out on the couch to sleep. Don't touch her. Do you understand me?"

Max merely shrugged before he peeled back the covers and slid his feet under them. He pulled the sheet up to his lean, muscular chest and yawned. "She doesn't even interest me if you're not in the picture."

He'd rolled over, turning his back to both of them.

Sean would have wagered Sauren was sleeping peacefully within the underside of a minute.

CHAPTER **TWENTY**

Sean grimaced at the memory as he clicked open another file on his computer. He *should* have awakened Genny on that night. He should have insisted she get dressed and come with him.

Instead, he'd left her with the devil.

The only excuse he had for leaving her was that he had no reason to suspect—to hope—that Genny would have wanted to come with him. Yeah, she wanted him—that had been made abundantly clear—but did that imply that she would have forsaken her life with Max because of one night of intoxicated, impulsive pleasure?

He'd settled her on the couch and retrieved a blanket from the extra bedroom to cover her.

If he'd known he wouldn't touch her again for three years, nothing could have made him walk out that door. If his brain hadn't been vibrating with fury, maybe he would have started to suspect why Max was playing with them like a cat with a couple of trapped mice.

* * *

Sean's head swung around when he heard a muffled dinging sound. His brows knitted together in puzzlement. It wasn't a familiar noise. He stared at the partially opened paneled door in his office. He sprung up from his chair and entered the small, six-by-six-foot room.

It hadn't been his preference, but he had eventually moved into Max's old office about a year after Max had died. As the executive director of the intel firm, Sean was responsible for getting new contracts and building business. Max's large corner office was much better suited than his old office had been for entertaining prospective clients.

It wasn't until after Sean had moved into the office that he'd realized that the wood paneling to the right of Max's desk was a disguised door. Inside the secreted compartment had been video monitors for camera feeds from various places inside Sauren Solutions—places that weren't on the more commonly used company surveillance. Max'd placed cameras in the reception area, the exercise facility locker rooms, the company break room, the firing range, and the elevators. Apparently, Max had liked to watch people *everywhere* in his domain.

Max had considered anyone that he had to deal with on a regular basis as a kind of opponent. Watching them while they were unaware of it was just one more way that Max acquired an upper hand.

A constant source of that rare commodity: information.

Sean had locked the compartment on a permanent basis, finding it a disgusting invasion of not only Sauren-Kennedy clients' and visitors' privacy, but also an infringement on their employees' rights. Besides, Sean had updated all the surveillance equipment for the premises, making sure that all video taken at points of entry and other key areas was sent to an external location, preventing an intruder from merely destroying the local server and any video evidence in the process.

Just this morning, however, in the midst of his preoccupation with Rook and worry about Genny, he'd entered the small room and activated some of the out-of-use cameras. He'd run a diagnostic on his own system earlier, and found that everything was in good working order. But he recalled that Max's cameras used a wider angle on the streets surrounding Sauren-Kennedy Solutions than his own. If Rook was, indeed, in Chicago, and if Genny or something she possessed interested him, he may very well be staking out Sauren-Kennedy. Sean wanted to observe some of the cars parked on the street. He was likely to notice anything unusual, as deserted as the Loop was with this storm raging.

Apparently when he'd used the equipment earlier he'd left on an audio-indicator for movement on the elevators. He hit a keyboard and a visual flickered onto one of the screens.

"*Fuck*," he hissed. He hurried out of the compartment and raced toward his office door.

A minute or two later, he waited in the dim, nearly empty Sauren-Kennedy parking garage, his hip leaning against the driver's side of Genny's dark blue BMW sedan.

"Going somewhere?"

Her muscles jerked reflexively and her brown leather carryall thumped onto the concrete floor.

"*Sean.*"

He watched as the color drained out of her face. With a quick glance, he took in her haphazard dress and mussed hair. She hadn't even bothered to run a comb through it, he realized as his anger built. She'd awakened, saw his note, and realized he was gone.

Then she'd grabbed everything and run out on him.

All his insecurities about not being good enough for her—and the inevitable subsequent surge of stubbornness—swelled in his chest.

After he'd seen the video of her on the elevator, he'd unsecured the lock on the stairs and plunged down the twelve flights to the subterranean parking garage. He'd arrived just before she'd hastened out of the elevator. His posture might look casual enough as he waited for her, but tension tightened every muscle in his body and fury boiled in his belly.

He straightened from his leaning position and bent over, shoving the nightgown Genny had worn just last night back into the bag— the same soft, emerald green, sexy gown she'd taken off, baring her beautiful body, before she'd given herself to him so completely.

Apparently she'd given herself on a short-term basis only.

He lifted her bag. "Let's go," he said simply when he met her wide-eyed stare again.

Her jaw dropped. Before, she'd just looked stunned, but now, anger entered her expression.

"Don't *tell* me what to do, Sean."

"All right," he murmured as he stepped closer to her. She took a step back before she held her ground. "If you'd rather I just picked you up and carried you back to the penthouse, I'm real fine with that."

Her chin went up. Her gray eyes smoked with rising anger. "Don't you dare threaten me with force."

He stopped within inches of her and stared down at her pale, upturned face. "It wasn't a threat. It was a fact. Haven't you been listening to a word I said? Have I been talking to myself this whole time?"

"Sean, I—"

"I have good reason to believe someone wants something from you, Genny, and I don't think they'll care one way or another if they hurt you while they're getting it."

She crossed her arms beneath her breasts. "That's just speculation on your part."

He heard the tremor in her voice. He leaned down until their faces were just inches apart. Her return glare conveyed anger and wariness in equal parts. "Are you so scared of what's happened between us that you'd risk bodily harm in order to escape it?"

He saw her throat convulse as she swallowed. "I'm not afraid. I just don't think it's smart for us to say here together."

"'S'at a fact?" he drawled.

Her eyes sparked defiantly.

"Well, I happen to think it's a brilliant idea," he said. "And since it's my business to know this stuff, we're going to go with my conclusion."

"'S'at a fact?" She'd been sarcastically trying to imitate his drawl, but it sounded like she was chewing gravel instead.

"Are you gonna walk inside?"

"*No.*"

Sean leaned down and swept her up into his arms.

"That's what I figured," he growled as he stalked toward the elevator.

She struggled and hollered in his ear, but very little penetrated the red haze of fury that fogged Sean's vision as he neared the elevator. For some irrational reason, all he could keep thinking about as he carried Genny onto the elevator was that this had all happened because last night, after they'd finished making love, Genny'd refused to tell him she loved him.

She'd refused him, period.

When he kicked the penthouse door closed a moment later, the loud bang startled him back into the present moment. Either that, or it was what Genny yelled furiously as he stalked down the hallway with her in his arms.

"PUT ME DOWN, SEAN KENNEDY. You told me all this

caveman stuff was only for the bedroom . . . that you'd never try to control me outside of it!"

Sean flipped the handle on the master bedroom door and strode into the room. She gasped when he tossed her onto the huge bed. She came up on her elbows and stared at him balefully.

"Well, look at where we are, girl," he said quietly.

She paused and glanced around, as though realizing for the first time just where they actually were. Her wary gaze flickered up to meet his.

"I don't want to stay here," she told him fiercely. He glanced down to the sight of her breasts rising and falling between pants.

"Right at the moment, I don't particularly care what you *want*," he told her before he turned and started to walk out of the room. "You're safe here, and that's all I care about."

"Sean? What are you doing?" she called out behind him.

She'd stood and was walking toward the door when he re-entered the master bedroom a few seconds later. He shot her a hard look before he slammed the door shut. She must have caught a hint at the magnitude of his irritation because when he stalked toward her, she edged back toward the bed. He saw her glance at what he held in his hands. Her eyes widened.

"I thought you said you didn't know the security code to the penthouse," he said as they edged toward the bed.

"I . . . I didn't when I first came."

"So, what? You watched me while I wasn't looking and memorized the code?"

Annoyance flashed across her face. "So what if I did? You can't *keep* me here against my will, Sean."

He rolled his eyes. "Haven't we already had this discussion?" He began to separate the four straps and cuffs he held in his hand.

"Wh- . . . what do you think you're doing?"

"I'm going to restrain you to the bed," he answered matter-of-factly. "If you hadn't been so sneaky and stolen the code, I wouldn't have to. But seeing as I have to keep you here until I figure out what's happening, and you're refusing to stay put . . ."

He held up a leather cuff and gave her a pointed look.

She looked stunned. "No. I refuse."

He gave her a glance that told her loud and clear he could care less what she did. He was restraining her to the bed.

Her expression collapsed. "Sean, you told me that all I had to do was refuse, and you wouldn't do it!"

He shook his head slowly. Her look of shock and hurt finally penetrated his thick fury. "I was talking about sex, Genny. I'm not going to restrain you right now for sex. Not at the moment, anyway. I'm going to do it because if I don't, you'll run again. Like you just did." They stared at each other in the taut silence. "I can't let that happen, girl. I wish you'd believe me. Something's not right. I think you're in danger."

She bit at her lower lip. He sensed her indecision. "All right. I won't run. You don't have to tie me up," she said, giving the restraints a scathing, anxious glance.

He reached up and smoothed a tendril of hair off her cheek.

"I'm afraid I do," he said as he tucked the strand behind her ear.

Surprise leapt into her eyes again, quickly followed by anger.

"Just for a half hour or so, Genny. I need to finish up a few things in my office, and I'm going to have to leave you here."

"I said I would stay!"

"You said that before. Just last night. In the parking garage: *'All right, I'll stay. I promise.'* Sound familiar?" Sean barked. He took a slow inhale when he saw her disquietude. "I know you're worried, girl . . . scared about what will happen if we stay here together." He held up a cuff significantly. "So I'm going to take the choice from you. Do you understand? You're *going* to stay here. As soon as I'm sure everything is safe, you can go. That's a promise you can bank on."

She swallowed thickly, her gaze glued to the leather cuff.

"Now . . . go ahead and get out of your clothes and get on the bed."

Despite his gentled tone, his words snapped her out of her transfixed state as she stared at the cuff. "Why do I have to take off my clothes? You just said this wasn't about sex!"

"I said I was going to restrain you so that you didn't run off again while I left the penthouse. But when I come back up here, I *am* going to make love to you."

He watched, mesmerized by the pink stain that spread on her cheeks and deepened the color of her lush lips.

"Go on, girl," he encouraged gruffly. "Slip out of your clothes and lay down on the bed. We'll get you all nice and comfortable, and I'll be back up to join you before you know it."

CHAPTER **TWENTY-ONE**

*W*e'll get you all nice and comfortable, and I'll be back up to join you before you know it.

Genevieve stared up at the ceiling and recalled those volatile words uttered in Sean's sweet, Southern accent. She pulled lightly on the leather cuffs affixed to her wrists and felt the strap tighten. She'd already tried to reach the buckle on the cuff with her fingers, but had been unsuccessful. Apparently whoever made the sex toys meant business.

Just like Sean did.

Her pussy twanged with arousal between her spread legs. The anticipation was nearly killing her.

Damn. How much longer was he going to *be*, anyway?

She'd been part anxious, part curious while she'd watched Sean go about the process of tying her down to the bed. There was no footboard on the bed where one could attach the straps of the restraint, and no posts on the custom-made cherrywood headboard. But none of that seemed to deter Sean. He just affixed the straps to the metal frame of the bed with calm efficiency.

His obvious expertise at restraining a woman irritated Genevieve even beyond his outlandish proposal to tie her down so she wouldn't escape while he worked. She'd considered fighting him on it, but then she'd looked into his eyes and sensed his determination. They might not be as furious as they had been, but the striking steel blue color still possessed a hard gleam.

Or had that been arousal she'd seen in Sean's eyes?

Hard to tell. He hadn't seemed as furious with her as he had been in the parking garage when he picked her up and carried her into the penthouse; his manner not unlike the way he'd hauled those grocery bags in yesterday. But despite that fact that he'd been extremely gentle with her as he'd restrained her naked body to the bed, there was no doubt in Genevieve's mind that Sean was angry with her for trying to escape.

And hurt.

Maybe it'd been that thought—the realization that he'd thought she was running because she didn't care—that had made her slowly start to undress while he watched her with a glittering gaze.

Why couldn't he see how potentially explosive it was for Detective Franklin to begin speculating they were lovers?

Sure, Franklin had questioned everyone at Sauren Solutions following Max's murder. He'd asked plenty of employees and family friends about Sean and Genevieve's friendship, but as far as Genevieve knew, no one had said anything that would have promoted the idea that Sean and she were lovers. Most people thought she and Max had an ideal relationship, and Sean had been dating Ava Linley. She believed him when he said that his relationship with Ava was casual and superficial, but Sean certainly wouldn't have been eager to correct Franklin if the detective thought otherwise. Ava had been Sean's alibi, after all.

Sean and she *hadn't* been lovers back then. Not technically. Unless being in love equated with being lovers—Genevieve wasn't sure about that. And they'd never even admitted out loud that they were falling in love.

I love you, girl.

Her body shuddered slightly as she recalled Sean's husky voice whispering those words last night in her ear. Her shiver hadn't come from being cold. Sean had carefully tucked the sheet and blanket around her naked body to protect her from the chill.

"Are you comfortable?" He'd asked when he had finished restraining her left wrist to the bed.

His face had been less than a foot away from hers. Genevieve had found it difficult to look into his eyes; she felt so vulnerable.

She'd forced herself to meet his stare anyway.

"I'm fine."

"I wasn't just talking about your position being comfortable." He'd given a significant glance around the master bedroom. "Are you comfortable *in here*?"

"I'm all right." She was glad she had spoken the truth. She might have been nervous and uncertain about allowing Sean to tie her up to this bed, but her solitary visit to the bedroom earlier had gone a long way toward exorcising the ghosts that resided in the penthouse master bedroom suite.

He'd considered her soberly for a moment before he'd straightened. "I want you to know that after I gained part-ownership of this property, I had the entire facility swept for any surveillance devices. The penthouse—including this bedroom—is clean, Genny."

She quickly averted her gaze. Her heartbeat began to throb loudly in her ears in the seconds that followed. It was the closest they'd ever come to discussing the volatile topic of Max taping them having sex on that night.

That meant Sean actually did know about the videotape, didn't it? Did that prove that Max showing it to him—trying to manipulate him with it—had lead to him murdering Max?

"Gen?"

"I said I was fine, Sean."

And she *was* fine—about being in the master bedroom again, anyway. Not about her anxiety-ridden thoughts regarding Sean committing murder. It *couldn't* be wise to get involved with Sean. To stay here in the penthouse with him.

To fall in love all over again.

Although, as he'd made a point of telling her earlier, he'd taken the choice away from her.

The last time they'd been in this room, they'd come together in a cataclysm of desire. Max's death had been the epilogue of that joining. What tragedy would occur this time? If it was Sean's arrest for Max's murder, Genevieve would never forgive herself.

That was why she'd run earlier.

Of course, Detective Franklin might just focus his sights back on her. It had never been pleasant, knowing the police suspected she'd murdered Max, but at least it had kept them distracted from focusing on Sean.

Her entire body went rigid a few moments later when she heard the front door close. She lifted her head off the pillow and stared at the bedroom door fixedly. Several seconds of silence passed. She held her breath as her ears strained to hear anything that would indicate what the hell Sean was doing in the penthouse. Minutes later, she heard what sounded like a piece of silverware striking the metal of the kitchen sink. The appetizing scent of toasted bread entered her nostrils.

Was he out there *eating* while she lay tied up to the bed? How *dare* he?

She resisted an overwhelming urge to shout out to him, to tell him to get his ass in there and untie her at that moment. She didn't treasure the idea of sounding like some kind of screaming shrew, however, so she bit her lip to restrain herself.

In addition to being nervous and uncertain, she was wildly aroused, anticipatory . . . and just plain *curious*.

A minute later, she heard a rustling sound emanating from the room to the left of her. Her face was still turned in that direction when the bedroom door snicked open.

Sean walked in carrying a plate and a glass of orange juice. A box was under his arm. He glanced at her, his face impassive, before he set the plate, glass, and box down on a desk. He whipped the long-sleeved cobalt blue sports shirt he'd been wearing over his head. She swallowed with difficulty.

She'd seen him nude now several times, but the impact of seeing his beautiful, muscled torso still left her stunned. He approached the foot of the bed. Genevieve thought he was going to uncuff her, and couldn't decide if she was relieved or disappointed. Instead, he lengthened the strap on her cuffed ankles about six inches. She shifted her legs restlessly beneath the sheet.

He picked up the plate and glass and came toward her. Genevieve steeled herself against his male beauty.

"You said you'd release me when you got back up here."

He gave her a "give me a break" look before he sat on the edge of the bed, his ass pressed against her hip. "I never said that. I said I was going to make love to you."

"I refuse," she challenged gruffly. "Release the restraints, Sean."

He sighed and set the plate and glass down on the bedside table. "Well . . . see, the thing is, we're not at the refusal stage yet."

"What's that supposed to mean?"

"We're not having sex yet, Gen. Actually, I was going to feed you."

Genevieve pried her gaze off his sexy mouth. "I'm not hungry," she muttered at the same time that her stomach growled. The toast smelled delicious.

"Liar."

Despite his calm tone, Genevieve noticed his firm lips were pressed together in irritation when he stood. Much to her surprise, he unhooked the left restraint from the strap. Still holding her wrist, he sat on the bed and lifted the sheet. He proceeded to slide his body beneath hers.

Genevieve's mouth was still hanging open in amazement a few seconds later when he attached the cuff to the strap again. Sean settled his back against the pillow and headboard, pulling her into his lap. When her right arm strained, he slackened the strap.

He kissed the top of her head while he tucked the sheet around her breasts. After he finished, he encircled her ribs. Genevieve gasped when she saw the way her breasts plumped on top of his forearms. His spicy male scent enveloped her.

She wasn't only tied up spread-eagle to the bed, but Sean held her in a warm bear hug while she sat in his lap, his groin pressed to her bare ass.

"I swear, the things you come up with," she muttered acerbically, perhaps trying to shield herself from the prickling, hot excitement brewing in her pussy.

"You nice and comfortable?"

"Yes." She was nice and excited, anyway.

"Okay. Time for a little breakfast," he murmured.

Her head shifted with his chest when he leaned toward the bedside table. He lifted a triangle of toast and straightened.

"Sean . . . I can feed myself," she said disparagingly when he lifted the buttered, yummy-smelling toast to her lips.

"Humor me," he rumbled. She felt his jaw move next to her temple and realized he watched himself press the toast to her mouth. Her lips parted instinctively when he pressed an edge to her lip. "Uh-uh . . . keep still, girl."

Genevieve paused, her heart beginning to drum in her ears, as

Sean slowly outlined her lips, oiling them with the warm, sweet butter. The fragrance of the toast filled her nostrils, making her mouth water. She felt his penis stiffen beneath her bottom. Her clit answered with a dull ache.

He inserted the corner of the toast into her mouth. "Go ahead . . . take a li'l bite," Sean said gruffly.

When she did, Sean moved the toast an inch away from her lips while she chewed.

The flavor of toasted fresh bread and butter filled her mouth. Genevieve wondered if she'd ever tasted anything half so good. It was as if her taste buds had become exponentially more sensitive . . . more expert at handling their task. Come to think of it, she realized as she swallowed the toast, her entire body felt the same way . . . hypersensitive, hyperaware, hyper*anticipatory* for the sensual pleasures she had no doubt Sean would bring it.

Sean kissed her temple warmly when she swallowed. "Open up," he whispered next to her ear. He pressed the toast between her lips again. They continued like that, neither of them speaking, until the slice of toast was finished and Sean reached for another. As he shifted in bed to get the toast, the forearm that cradled her breasts rubbed against the lower curves. When he straightened again with a new triangle of toast, Genevieve's hips moved restlessly in his lap. She'd experienced an overwhelming urge to grind her ass against the rigid column of his cock pressing against his jeans.

"Genny," he warned softly. He pressed the corner of the toast next to her lower lip and traced her mouth once again while their sexes throbbed in tandem. "Didn't your mama ever tell you not to squirm while you ate your breakfast?"

"She might have mentioned it, yeah," Genevieve whispered before she whisked her tongue along her lower lip, gathering butter. Sean gave a low growl of male appreciation. She felt his facial muscles tighten next to her forehead and cheek and knew he'd just smiled.

"Then be a good girl and keep still," he admonished before he pressed the toast between her parted lips. Genevieve ate this piece more greedily. Sean said nothing, but she could feel his gaze on her while she chewed. He was always ready to insert another morsel of toast between her lips when she parted them.

By the time she'd swallowed the last bite, Genevieve was panting softly.

"I don't want any more," she said when he leaned over to grab another slice. He went still, and she wondered if he'd heard the edge in her tone. It'd sounded like irritation, when in reality, Genevieve was only confused by her profound sexual reaction to eating *toast*.

Well . . . being *fed* toast by Sean while she lay naked and restrained in his lap.

He set the piece of toast down. "You sure? You seemed awful hungry."

"Yes. I'm full," she assured him.

"How about some juice then?" He started to reach for the glass of orange juice, but then grunted in dissatisfaction. He straightened on the bed, and Genevieve shifted with him.

"My fingers are all buttery." He held several fingertips before her lips. "Go on, girl. Clean them off."

Heat rushed into her cheeks and sex. She stared. The sight of his long, blunt-tipped fingers glistening with oil struck her as profoundly sexual. She thought of the times he'd pushed one of those thick fingers into her pussy. When he'd withdrawn, her juices had gleamed even more greatly on his skin than they did now with the butter.

"Yeah, that's it. Suck it nice and clean, girl."

Genevieve blinked at the sound of his raspy voice. She hadn't told herself to move, but suddenly she suckled on Sean's thick forefinger all the way to the knuckle. She pulled on him strongly while she ran her tongue over his skin, eager to find the traces of his flavor mixed with that of the butter.

Sean groaned and inserted his middle finger between her lips. She tightened around him and cleaned that one just as thoroughly. By the time he inserted the forefinger of his other hand, both of their breathing had escalated.

"You have such a gorgeous mouth," he murmured as he slowly sawed his middle finger back and forth between her pursed lips, and she drew on him tightly. He pressed his lips to her hot cheek while he watched himself penetrating her mouth. "Are you gonna suck that hard on my cock, girl?"

Genevieve moaned harshly even as she continued to suck on his finger. She wriggled in his lap, desperate to come into closer contact with the hard, hot cock next to her ass.

She whimpered in loss when he withdrew his finger and used both hands to still her squirming hips.

"Didn't I tell you? None of that," he drawled.

Genevieve realized she was panting hard through her nose. It stunned her, how aroused she was from eating toast from Sean's hand and then sucking on his fingers. How fair was it that he had such a profound effect on her?

But she could have cared less about the justice of her arousal at the moment. Right now, all she could think about was the unbearable, aching burn between her spread legs. Her nipples prickled beneath the soft sheet. As if Sean were a magician who could read her mind, he grabbed the top of the sheet in both hands and carefully folded it back, exposing her heaving bare breasts.

"Sean," she moaned. She began to shift again in his lap, desperate for friction on her tingling pussy. Once again, however, he stilled her with his hands, holding her immobile against his hard thighs, groin, and abdomen.

"I'm going to have to give you a good spanking if you keep that up."

Genevieve went still. There had been lightheartedness to his tone, but she'd caught the steel of threat in his warning.

He leaned over and grabbed another triangle of toast. Genevieve bit her lip in order not to cry out in wild arousal when he plumped a breast with his left hand and rubbed the buttered side of the toast against the beading tip. The rough surface of the bread gently abraded her nipple as he coated it with warm butter. He coated the erect crest until it glistened and turned his attention to the other aching nipple.

When he'd anointed both tips, he set down the toast and cradled her breasts in his large hands.

"Mmmm, look at that," he admired as he plumped them from below, making the dark pink nipples poke out in further pronouncement. She felt his cock lurch against her ass. Genevieve closed her eyes, overwhelmed. She thrashed her head on his chest, but he just continued to softly mold her breasts to his palms while he stared at the oiled, erect nipples.

"I used to think I was gonna go crazy if I couldn't touch your breasts, and I'm not saying that figuratively, either," he spoke quietly near her ear. "If I told you the number of times I jacked off while I thought about fucking them, you'd never believe me in a million years."

"Sean!" His name burst out of her throat in stark need. "Please don't. *Please* stop teasing me. Are you punishing me for leaving? Is that what this is about?"

His hands paused in their molding action. She felt his gaze on her even though she kept her eyes averted. "I don't want to make you suffer, Genny. I just don't like when you deny the obvious. Some things are too good to run from, no matter the circumstances. Some things are worth fighting for." His hands moved again, massaging her sensitive breasts. He pushed them up from below, sending the tips farther into the air. She grimaced in rising agony.

He refused to stimulate the needy nipples.

"I'm not a coward, Sean," she grated out.

"Show me you're not," he rasped near her ear. "Tell me what you want."

"You."

He kissed her heated cheek. "Can you be more specific?"

She lifted her eyelids slowly. From the corners of her eyes, she saw that his gaze was glued to her breasts as he molded the flesh gently.

"Touch my nipples," she whispered.

Once again, she felt his cock surge against his jeans and her left buttock. She watched, mesmerized, as he released one breast. He pressed his forefinger to the nipple of the breast that he still held, gently rubbing the melted butter into the turgid flesh.

Pleasure jolted through her. She jerked in his arms and moaned.

"Shhh," he soothed, even as he proceeded to do just the opposite of what would calm her down. He once again gathered both of her breasts in his hands, using the tip of his thumb to rub and agitate the oiled crests.

"Ohhhh," she moaned uncontrollably. His chin tilted.

"Open your eyes," he ordered gruffly. "If you don't watch, I'll stop touching you, Genny."

She slowly pried open her eyelids at that gentle threat. For a taut, delicious minute, they both watched while he expertly finessed her glistening nipples. When he lightly pinched both crests at once with his thumb and forefinger, his actions attenuated by the sensual glide of oiled skin against skin, Genevieve groaned in mounting frustration and once again wiggled in his lap. This time she pressed at a downward angle, trying to stimulate her spread, wet pussy.

Sean ducked his head beneath her arm. Genevieve cried out in protest when he shifted his body beneath her, and she was deprived of his hard heat.

She watched him as he stood by the side of the bed. He turned toward her. Her eyes widened when she saw the length of his penis pressing along his left thigh, the thickness of it stretching the denim tautly.

"Genny."

She glanced up at his rigid face.

"Breakfast is over. I'm going to make love to you now."

"Yes," she whispered emphatically.

His mouth quirked. "I was telling you because you've got the right to say 'no' now."

She pulled the restraining straps taut and stretched, curving her spine, her arching back causing her breasts to thrust toward him. His blue eyes blazed with heat. *You're acting like a freakin' cat in heat,* Genevieve thought wryly. But it was a distant thought that barely penetrated the sensual haze that enfolded her.

"Yes," she hissed once again.

Sean's nostrils flared as he stared down at her. Genevieve bit off her protest when he walked toward the foot of the bed instead of joining her. He removed the slack in her ankle restraints, and then did the same with her wrists. When he was done she was once again snugly restrained to the bed. She wished he'd make eye contact with her as he went about his erotic task with so much efficiency, but kept his gaze averted as he grabbed the sheet and blanket and bared her body.

He finally met her stare. Genevieve thought she understood why he hadn't looked before.

His gaze scorched her.

Her pulse leapt madly at her throat. Her anticipation had never felt so acute. She watched—mesmerized—as Sean unfastened the buttons of his jeans. He peeled open the fly as far as it would go and sunk his hand down the crotch of his underwear. Genevieve held her breath as he carefully revealed inch after inch of thick, succulent cock.

Then he released himself. The heavy cockhead fell, bringing the stalk down with it.

He straddled her on the bed, his cock jutting lewdly from his unfastened jeans.

"You're an exhibitionist, do you know that?"

Sean's smile was as innocent as warm milk.

"What d'ya mean, girl?"

"You know what the sight of that," her eyes flashed down to his erection poking between the fly of his jeans, "does to a woman."

He leaned down over her, his arms supporting his weight. His velvety smooth, deliciously heavy cockhead brushed the skin on her hip. He brought his face to within inches of hers . . . close enough for her to breathe his clean skin and spicy cologne.

"I'm only interested in what it does to you," he rumbled. His gaze skimmed down over her turgid nipples.

"Take a guess, Einstein."

Sean looked up into her face when he registered the edge in her tone. She couldn't help it. She smiled.

"Genny."

Something in his voice made her eyelids sting when she blinked. Or maybe it was that he lowered his burnished head and inserted an aching nipple between his lips. She stared up at the ceiling, tears blinding her as he agitated her nipple with his slightly rough, warm tongue, then ever so gently—ever so sweetly—suckled off the butter that he'd applied to the straining tips.

It was such a potent, precise stimulation that Genevieve could hardly stand it. It felt like too much . . . too much sensation, too much emotion . . . too much need. But her restraints kept her firmly in place and she couldn't escape her desire.

Later, Genny couldn't say how long he made love to her breasts with his mouth and hands, but by the time he lifted his head, she was mindless with need . . . right on the verge of climax.

Sean blinked as he stared at her face, as though he'd just awakened from a dream. The fact that suckling her breasts could transport him so utterly only sent her desire into unforeseen territory.

"Don't be cruel," she whispered.

"Aww, girl. I'm not being cruel. I love you. I want to make you burn."

"Then touch me. Make me come."

He considered her soberly for a moment. "You know, sometimes the burn is so much better if you push at the boundaries just a tad."

His blazing eyes flicked down to the juncture of her thighs and back up to her heaving breasts. Genevieve gave a tortuous moan when he softly kissed a wet nipple. Speech had left her. Her body trembled. "Look how red they are," he whispered. Even his warm breath kept her riding the crest of orgasm. "You have the sweetest nipples."

She gave a strangled cry.

He glanced up into her face as he gathered her breasts in both hands, pushing the distended crests together. "Hmmm, look at that girl. A feast." Genevieve made a desperate, gurgling noise in her throat, as if her desire could choke her. The hard glint of a challenge gleamed in Sean's eyes. "I think I'll fuck these beauties here in a moment. But first . . . do you think you could come for me?" Genevieve nodded her head eagerly, her breath stuck in her lungs. "Without me touching your pussy?"

Her eyes widened. She wasn't sure how to respond . . . couldn't respond, because then Sean lowered his head and laved both nipples at once with his warm tongue. Then he pressed her flesh into his hot mouth and suckled both nipples at once.

And Genevieve gave both of them her answer about whether she could come from nipple stimulation alone.

She cried out sharply, the orgasm having a tight, painful quality without genital stimulation. She was only vaguely aware of Sean's warm murmurs of praise.

A shout suddenly erupted out of her throat as orgasm blasted through her full force. She lifted her head, still shuddering in climax. What she saw made her cry out more sharply in blinding ecstasy. He'd parted her labia. His tongue slid over her clit, rapid, precise, and hard.

He'd been *so* right. Pushing at the boundaries of her desire had made the explosion exponentially more powerful.

When she felt Sean move on the bed moments later, her eyelids opened heavily. Her heavy panting stilled for a moment when she saw the rigid expression on his face as he came closer, eventually kneeling with his knees next to her shoulders.

His cock looked furiously aroused jutting from his fly.

His hand shook slightly when he fisted the stalk.

"You're so damned beautiful, Genny. Seeing you give yourself like that—I'm the one who's about to spontaneously combust. Open those pretty lips."

But Genny was already spreading her mouth to accommodate his girth. He grunted, low and feral, as he slid along her tongue, coating it with the pre-cum that seeped from the slit. His swollen flesh filled over mouth and overpowered her senses. His flavor permeated her awareness, making her hungrier. She closed tightly around him and sucked.

For all she was worth.

He'd given her so much pleasure just now. She was overwhelmed with a need to make him loosen his own restraints. She wanted to goad him into releasing his own inhibitions, to lose himself in pleasure . . . to ride her fast and free.

A harsh groan tore out of his throat as she suckled him deeper.

"Aw, girl. Do you want it that much?" he grated out.

Genevieve felt the tip of his cock brush her throat, but the palpable desire surging through her veins helped her quiet her gag reflex. Her throat convulsed, but she kept him deep, breathing through her nose.

She nodded once subtly.

"God, you're sweet," he muttered. He placed his hands on the headboard and began to thrust in and out of her mouth.

He wasn't exactly gentle with her. In fact, he bucked furiously between her lips. Tears ran down her cheeks, but Genevieve loved the rough treatment . . . loved seeing him release his inhibitions, relished in seeing him ride the wave of pure pleasure. All she had to do was look up into his face and see his grimace of intense ecstasy, see the wildness in his blue eyes as he watched himself fuck her mouth, and Genevieve became as transported as Sean had been while he'd made love to her breasts.

His grunts and moans of uncensored pleasure fell like the sweetest of music on her ears.

She felt his cock swell in her mouth. He glanced up into her face as he slid between her straining, tightened lips.

Her gaze must have matched the abandoned intensity of his, because he pushed his cock slowly into her throat until his balls pressed to her lips. It was the first time she'd ever taken him fully that way. Her throat convulsed around him, and for a split second, she instinctively panicked at the blockage. But then she heard him shout out his release, and she forced herself to breathe through her nose. Her eyes widened when she felt the spasm of his cock and she realized he came directly into her throat, making swallowing unnecessary.

He withdrew almost immediately, shooting the rest of his semen onto her tongue. She stared at his clenched face as she struggled to keep up with the volume of his ejaculations.

Her throat was raw by the time she cleaned the irregular spills erupting from his slit with her tongue. As always, those moments when the tension slowly left his muscles struck her as poignant. A little sad.

A reminder that, sometime soon, Sean would once again be absent from her life.

CHAPTER **TWENTY-TWO**

He withdrew and slid his knees down the bed. He collapsed on top of her, breathing heavily. She nuzzled his cheek and jaw while he attempted to catch his breath.

"You didn't have to, Genny," he mumbled between gasps of air. He lifted his head slightly, pinning her with a blue-eyed stare. "All you have to do is shake your head, and I'll always ease up."

"I wanted to, Sean."

He grimaced when he heard her roughened voice and buried his face in her neck. For a minute he said nothing while his body slowly regained equilibrium. Genevieve became hyperaware of the movement of his rib cage pressed against hers. She could feel his strong heart running fast in his chest . . . felt it slowing until it seemed to match the rate of the throb of her own pulse in her throat.

Her muscles grew deliciously heavy, not just with Sean's weight, but her own growing lassitude. She felt as if she could sink right through the mattress . . .

"I don't get how you could have so much trust in me that you give up your very breath to give me pleasure, but yet you were going to run away from me earlier."

Genevieve blinked open her leaden eyelids at the sound of his deep, rough voice. For a few seconds, she didn't reply, thinking about his volatile words.

"I thought it was for the best, Sean," she rasped eventually.

He raised his tawny head. Genevieve wished he'd release the restraints. She experienced an overwhelming need to touch him.

"You think it's for the best to deny how we feel about each other? How *you* feel about me, Genny?"

"We don't have a choice, Sean."

"You mean that *you* think *you* don't have a choice. I choose to be with you, Genny. I *always* have."

Tears filled her eyes. "Don't, Sean. Don't push it. Not now." Her lower lip quivered uncontrollably as she entreated him with her gaze. She felt so raw at that moment . . . so exposed. *"Please."*

"Why not *now*? *Why* can't we talk about it?"

"Sean, don't."

"Why can't we talk about it now, Genny?" he persisted.

"Because this time here . . . for this day, for this night, for these next few hours, it's *all* the time we'll have, Sean," she exclaimed. "Why should we ruin it, badgering each other and rehashing things that are over and done and we can't change, no matter how much we want it. No matter how much we wish it—"

She inhaled raggedly.

His face collapsed with regret. He kissed her cheeks while he murmured her name. "I'm *not* going to let anything happen to you. I'm not," he said as he pressed his lips to her burning eyelids.

Genevieve blinked open and pushed her head back on the pil-low so she could better see his face. A mixture of pain and determination pinched his features. He'd done nothing less just now than utter a solemn vow.

"Don't worry about me, Sean. I'm fine—"

"No, you're not. You're so worried your muscles are about to break from tension. The only time I see you release it is when I'm making love to you." His pressed his mouth to hers in a warm kiss. "Which means I'm about to do it again. But there's something I really need to ask you first, Genny."

Something about his tone made her muscles stiffen even more. God, Sean was right about her anxiety level. When Sean started to speak, however, she knew she had a right to be nervous.

"On the afternoon of Max's death," he began gently, "you tried to call me several times. I didn't answer because I was in a meeting, and I had my phone turned off. What were you calling me about, Genny?"

It felt like a fist inside of her stomach had just grabbed an organ and twisted. She flinched and turned her face away from Sean.

"I don't want to talk about that."

Sean exhaled slowly, but she could feel his stubborn determination like a steely blade pressed against her throat. He wasn't going to give up.

"You said we couldn't talk about New Year's Eve. This isn't about New Year's Eve. This morning I was down in my office, going over some possibilities for what could be happening with the fire and the break-ins. I opened up some old files concerning Max's death. One of the unanswered questions I have is why you tried to call me on that day. You never would tell me."

She kept her cheek pressed to the pillow, refusing to answer.

"Look at me, girl."

Something in his tone made her turn her chin. His blue eyes shone with feeling. "There's nothing you could do, nothing you've ever done, that would make me stop loving you."

Misery rose up in her, making her gasp. Tears sprayed out of her eyes as a tsunami of emotion crashed into her.

"Oh, God, Sean, *don't*. Stop it. *Stop* it."

His face twisted in shared pain. He leaned down and kissed the tears on her cheeks, as if he could transform those drops into something other than marks of sorrow by his love for her.

But he couldn't. Their love for each other wasn't enough to erase the sins of the past, and the knowledge of that wrenched inside Genevieve like a twisting knife. She writhed beneath him in a paroxysm of emotion. It felt unbearable . . . untenable, this swelling pain. But then in the midst of her misery she became aware of the friction of their rubbing, naked skin, the weight of Sean's hard male body pressing her down on the mattress. When Sean kissed the side of her mouth softly, still making soothing sounds, Genevieve turned and seized his mouth in a searing kiss.

She felt him go rigid as she ate at his mouth hungrily, and then penetrated his lips with a searching tongue. She knew why he stiffened like somebody who had been jolted with electricity; all the anguish he'd brought to the surface with his questions, all the love, found a conduit of release through that kiss.

She told him everything with it.

At first, he remained stiff, surprised by her onslaught of emotion. But when she began to slide her tongue in and out of his mouth in a sensual, bold seduction, he gave a low, feral growl. He placed both hands on the sides of her breasts, his fingers spreading across her rib cage, lifting her slightly off the mattress, holding her pounding heart in his hands. His tongue delved deep, taking her in the way she wanted . . . *needed* to be taken, possessing her as only Sean could.

In the distance, she heard her phone ringing, but she was so swept up in swamping emotion and pleasure that she couldn't have cared less. A montage of sensory information mixed and swelled in her brain as Sean branded her with his mouth, and she answered with her own boiling, frothing need.

His head lowered. He continued to hold her rib cage off the bed. Genevieve moaned roughly when he began to feed on her breasts, his hunger as wild and intense as that of a man who had been deprived of a woman's flesh for years. She twisted in an agony of pleasure, but the restraints and Sean's firm hold made escape impossible.

Not that she wanted to escape. It was just so damn difficult to exist at the white-hot core of so much pleasure. Of so much feeling.

"Oh, God. Uncuff me. I want to touch you so bad, Sean."

He glanced up at her with fiery eyes, his lips still shaped around the tip of her breast. His nostrils flared. Her vagina clenched, needing to be filled. She whimpered when his divine suction lessened and he slowly lifted his head.

Her phone began ringing again. Even though the volume level couldn't have changed, this time the sound seemed louder . . . more insistent somehow. She could tell by the way Sean watched her that he'd focused on the annoying, jangling notes as well. She thought of who might be calling. Her insurance agent? Jim? Her mother?

She sighed heavily. The intrusion of the outside world acted like a heavy, wet blanket, stifling the fires of her arousal and tumultuous emotional state.

"Maybe . . . maybe I'd better get it?" Genevieve whispered. "It could be something about the house . . . or maybe even my mother. She moved in with Aunt Roberta a while back. Both of them were so worried when I called yesterday."

Sean's mouth slanted in irritation. His gaze flicked up to the leather cuffs she wore.

"I'll get your phone."

The absence of his warm, hard body pressing down on her

made her feel like wailing in protest. She bit her lower lip to prevent moaning in thwarted longing when she saw his lean, muscular torso. His cock had grown erect again. The cockhead looked smooth and succulent as it bobbed in the air as he got off the bed.

A moment later, he came into the room carrying her still-ringing phone. Genevieve lifted her head from the pillow so she could see him. She noticed with a sense of disappointment that he'd tucked his cock back into his jeans and fastened two buttons.

"The caller ID says it's Jeff."

Genevieve blinked when she heard his hard tone. Christ. She'd forgotten that it might be Jeff calling. He'd tried to reach her several times over the weekend, but Genevieve hadn't answered. When she was with Sean, she forgot Jeff existed all together. She'd only left him the one message since they'd spoken late on Friday, just before she'd arrived at the penthouse.

So much had changed since then.

"It's all right. Just let it ring," she said.

Sean's stare seemed to bore into her.

"Is Jeff the guy you're dating?"

Genevieve swallowed thickly. *Was* she still dating him? She couldn't even call up Jeff's face at the moment. Sean's incising eyes seemed to demand an answer, though. She nodded.

His face stiffened. He stalked toward her, the phone still ringing in his hand.

"Sean? What are you doing?" she asked when he reached for the cuff on her left wrist. He unfastened it. He glared at her as he hit the receive button on her phone and shoved it into her now freed hand. She stared at Sean incredulously.

"Genevieve? Genevieve, are you there?"

Genevieve clamped her mouth shut when she heard Jeff's distant voice. She put the cell phone to her ear.

"Jeff? I . . . uh . . . hello." Her eyes widened in mounting amazement when Sean sat on the edge of the bed and placed his big hand on her belly. He stroked her along her side, from hip to breast.

Genevieve shivered. The intrusive phone call hadn't banked her fires as much as she'd thought. And from the hard expression on Sean's face, he seemed determined to prove that to her.

Jeff gave a bark of laughter. "Jesus, where have you been? I've been trying to reach you during every break I got, but you haven't been answering. Is everything all right?"

Sean's stare scored her as his hand slid down to her thigh, just inches from her spread pussy. A surprised cry popped out of her throat when he abruptly plunged his middle finger into her slit.

"Genevieve?" Jeff demanded.

"I . . . I'm sorry, Jeff," Genevieve sputtered as air rushed out of her lungs. Sean had spread his hand over her external sex and began to move in a tight, circular motion with his finger still inserted in her vagina. Her former arousal roared back into her flesh, the strength of her desire shocking her, given the circumstances. "I've been so preoccupied with the fire, and then this awful storm hit and—"

She gasped when Sean began to corkscrew his finger in and out of her while he continued to press on her clit.

"Genevieve, what the hell's the matter? Are you ill?" Jeff asked tensely.

"No! No, of course not. I'm absolutely fine. Please, don't worry. Please." She tried to shift her hips to escape Sean's precise stimulation of her sex, but of course it was useless, restrained as she was. Her glare at him was every bit as furious as his, despite the fact that he was making her burn. A drop of sweat ran frantically between her breasts. "Like I said, there's just been so much going on, Jeff."

"Well, I can understand that, I guess," Jeff said, seeming

partially mollified. Genevieve bit her lower lip to stifle a moan when Sean slid his forefinger between her labia and began to rub her clit. A wet, clicking sound reached her ears as he stirred in her abundant juices. Instead of trying to shift her hips away from Sean's attack on her senses, she began to press against the delicious pressure. She couldn't seem to help it. She knew she shouldn't, but the burn in her genitals felt too imperative to resist.

"I've been worried sick about you," she heard someone say from a distance.

"*Oh,*" Genevieve cried out sharply.

Her own voice penetrated her dazed arousal. She glanced around nervously, the bizarreness of the situation hitting her full force. Sean had her restrained to the bed, and she was having a conversation with the man she'd been dating, and she was about to have the mother of all orgasms while Jeff listened.

"Damn you," she mouthed at Sean, even as her hips bobbed more frantically against his hand and the erotic sound of his finger moving in her wet flesh escalated in volume.

"Genevieve? There *is* something wrong, isn't there?" Jeff said loudly, starting to sound both irritated and alarmed. Sean's nostrils flared as he stared at her and continued to stimulate her so precisely.

He was going to *force* her to come while she was on the phone with Jeff, Genevieve realized, aghast. It was humiliating, but she couldn't seem to stop pressing wildly against Sean's hand. The soles of her feet burned in sympathy with her clit.

She was panting now as she approached climax. "I have to go, Jeff."

"No . . . wait, Genevieve, what the hell?" she heard Jeff say before she fumbled for the button to disconnect. She was only vaguely aware of Sean taking the phone from her before orgasm slammed into her.

"Oh, God . . . *Sean*," she cried out sharply as she shuddered in climax. He nursed her through it, continuing to stimulate her as she came, making it last, coaxing every last shiver of pleasure out of her.

Only when the noise stopped did she realize she'd been keening. Her head fell back on the pillow. Her body sagged into the mattress.

Her panting ceased momentarily when Sean held up her cell phone. His eyes reminded her of flame trapped in ice.

He pressed with his thumb, disconnecting Jeff.

"So much for your boyfriend," he muttered.

CHAPTER **TWENTY-THREE**

Sean was furious. And jealous. And so damned pissed off listening to Genny try to placate her boyfriend that he really didn't care that Genny's sublime expression of satiation segued from disbelief to wild anger in a matter of seconds when he hung up the phone.

Ol' Jeff had apparently been stunned into silence by listening to Genny gush in orgasm.

"Sean, how *could* you?" she asked in a low, trembling voice. "How could you be so cruel? What's Jeff ever done to you?"

"He's touched you. That's what," he muttered simply before he stood by the side of the bed. "Don't think I didn't notice, by the way, that you got out of answering my question earlier."

She blinked in surprise at his accusation, but Sean had more for her. Having her boyfriend call had been the equivalent of popping the cork off his frustration. Genny was *his*. Precisely how long was it going to take to get her to admit that? He understood there were obstacles, but damn it, those obstacles were not going to follow them into bed.

Screw it, Sean thought bitterly as he walked over and retrieved the mini vibrator he'd ordered last week. It'd just arrived a few days ago, and he was going to enjoy breaking it in on Genny while he spelled out the consequences for withholding herself from him. His cock throbbed dully.

Yeah, he was going to enjoy it a lot.

Her wary stare when he returned transferred from him to the box he carried. Sean made short order of taking the orange vibe out of the packaging and inserting the batteries he'd put in the box earlier.

Genny's mouth opened, and he figured she was about to tell him *no*, so Sean went on the offensive.

"How do you think it makes me feel to be ignored when I tell you I love you?" he asked quietly.

The words on her tongue died a quick death. Sean began to unfasten her ankle restraints as she stared at him with her mouth hanging open.

"Sean, I'm not ignoring you."

He gave a small shrug, not caring to argue with her about it. It wasn't as if he didn't know she cared for him. She broadcasted it loud and clear in her luminous gray eyes whenever she looked at him. It was the fact that she wouldn't *say* it that pissed him off.

He unhooked her wrists from the restraining straps, but as he'd done with her ankles, he left on the leather cuffs. He liked the way they looked next to Genny's pale, flawless skin.

"Scoot over," he directed when he sat down on the bed next to her, bringing his feet up on the bed.

She scrambled several feet away from him and curled up on her side. She studied him warily. Sean slid closer to her on the mattress, and propped several pillows behind him on the headboard.

He pressed the button on the small but powerful vibrator. Genny's eyes widened as she stared at the buzzing sex toy. This particular model was the newer version of a favorite of his for providing stimulation in close quarters. It was about five inches long, with silicone ridges to increase pleasure during penetration. But Sean valued the clit-pleasing tip the most—or at least he valued the reaction it got when he applied it to a woman.

Just thinking about stirring Genny's incredibly responsive little clit with it made his cock lurch.

He patted his thigh.

"*What?*"

"Lay down in my lap," he said, not trying to hide the edge in his tone.

For about five seconds, he thought she might refuse him. He said nothing as she glanced at the vibe and then down at his lap, her gray eyes shiny with arousal—but shadowed by doubt, as well.

She scooted up in the bed and moved toward him slowly. He couldn't help making a low, satisfied groan when she draped her naked body over his lap. He caressed her hip and then a smooth buttock before he positioned her the way that he wanted her. When he was done, the bottom of her breasts pressed to his outer thigh and her bottom curved around the edge of the other thigh.

"Spread your legs a little," he ordered. He put the hand holding the vibe between her widening legs and went right for the kill, pressing the vibrating tip against her clit.

She moaned roughly and wriggled in his lap. He grabbed a handful of firm ass and stilled her against the vibrator. Her moan got louder.

"Feel nice?" he murmured.

"God, yes," she whispered. She'd turned her head slightly. He studied her profile as he continued to stimulate her clit.

"Good," he replied after a moment. "After I spank you enough times while using the vibe, you'll get nice and hot and wet just from the sound of my palm smacking your ass. You'll know from experience pleasure will follow."

Her head whipped around. He met her stare calmly. No matter what she was feeling in regard to what he'd said, the vibe continued to industriously do its job. A fine sheen of sweat covered her face.

He placed his left hand on a smooth butt cheek. Just the feeling of her firm flesh and satiny skin sent a pain of lust through his cock. He wondered if she felt the surge of heat in his genitals when she pressed down with her hips, stimulating them both. He gave her a brisk spank.

"Just one other thing, girl."

"What?"

"Rest your cheek on the mattress and put your hands behind your back."

She bit her lip, but she couldn't completely stifle a whimper of arousal. Knowing she was turned on by what he said made lust boil in his veins. She cried out softly in protest when he briefly removed the vibe from her clit.

She put her hands behind her back.

As soon as he'd hooked her leather cuffs together, he pressed the buzzing tip back to her clit.

"That's right," he said as he watched her shift her hips subtly and heard her soft moans. He moved his left hand, stroking her ass. He felt her muscles tense slightly and he swatted her. She gave a shaky cry.

He spanked her again.

"Not too hard, is it?" he asked as he soothed her buttocks with a gentle glide. "I just want it to burn, not hurt."

"It . . . it doesn't hurt," she mumbled into the mattress. She wiggled her bottom against his sliding palm and he popped her several more times.

"I know of a man who gives his wife a spanking like this every night before they fall asleep. Of course, it usually leads to other things," Sean said. He cracked his palm against the sweet lower curve of both buttocks. "I always said they seemed like the happiest couple I've ever met."

Her moan didn't sound so soft this time. From the vivid pink color of the cheek that wasn't pressed to the mattress, Sean could tell the clit vibrator was doing its job extremely well. Maybe *too* well. He pulled it off her, worried she might explode before he was ready.

He placed the vibrating tip back on her clit and smacked her ass several times. When she moaned in anguished arousal and squirmed in his lap, he grabbed an ass cheek, molding it to his palm greedily.

He loved her ass. He hadn't been kidding when he'd told her she possessed a butt that could make a grown man cry.

"Stop squirming around, girl," he admonished once he let go of a round, pink ass cheek. "You said it didn't hurt bad. What are you wiggling for?"

Her desperate groan was all the answer he needed. Despite his lingering irritation at hearing her try to alleviate her boyfriend's concerns, Sean smiled. Hadn't he said she suited him perfectly? Genny didn't need to be trained to enjoy being spanked.

He caressed her softly before he popped her several times with his palm, his swats designed to fire her nerves and raise blood below the surface, heating her flesh, making her lower backbone tingle and burn with sexual energy.

He kept spanking her, pinkening her ass, enjoying the smacking sound of his palm against firm flesh. Whenever he noticed the tension level in her muscles increasing, he removed the vibe from her clit.

"Sean, stop teasing me." Her roughened, desire-thick voice made him spread his hand over her entire ass and press her body down onto his erection.

"What do you want?"

"You know what I want," she returned acerbically.

He chuckled, ignoring her squawk when he removed the vibe. He leaned down over and spoke just inches away from her ear.

"*You* know what I want, Genny."

She glanced up at him.

"Your eyes always tell me the truth anyway," he said quietly.

"Then why are you forcing me to put it into words?"

"*You* know why."

Her throat convulsed as she swallowed. "It won't change anything, Sean. Some things just weren't meant to be. One of us has to be reasonable about this."

His mouth pressed into a grim line. "You're wrong. It would change *everything* if you felt free enough to tell me how you feel about me." He leaned over for the box he'd brought into the room. He'd put a few other things inside it besides the batteries. He glared at her while he withdrew some scented lubrication. "This isn't about *reason*. It hasn't been about logic since the first time you and I laid eyes on each other. You're just being stubborn by saying otherwise. And I have to say"—he popped the top on the lube—"it's kinda pissing me off."

She went rigid in his lap when he parted one of her hot, pink ass cheeks. She started when he poured some of the lube directly on the puckered rosette of her asshole.

"Sean . . ." she began, her voice carrying a hint of warning.

"Don't try to talk me out of it," he said, his tone even more forbidding than hers had been. He stared down at her blushing buttocks and oiled, puckered hole. Genny's was pink—prettier than most . . . delicate, like a tiny, tightly shut rosebud.

"You're *mine*, Genny. All that's left is for you to admit it."

Air rushed out of his lungs when she moaned roughly and the muscular ring of her rectum clenched. She'd gone completely still and rigid in his lap. The single gray eye that was turned toward him stared up at him with a mixture of wariness and arousal.

He felt a subtle tremor ripple through her flesh and quickly removed the vibe from her clit. She'd been on the brink of coming.

He smiled slowly.

"You're going to like telling the truth, aren't you, Gen?"

She clenched her eyelid shut and turned her forehead into the mattress.

"Okay. You want to play it that way?" he asked silkily.

He lifted his hand from between her spread legs. Her muscles grew even more tense when he spread her ass cheek even wider, further exposing her asshole. Her heard her muffled cry when he pressed the tip of the vibe to her rectum.

He left it there, allowing it to awaken that erogenous zone . . . letting it coax her into blooming for him.

He transferred his hand to her sex to encourage her even further.

This time she couldn't suppress her growing arousal. A shaky moan bubbled out of her mouth as he stimulated her clit and rectum at once. Sean shifted his hips up against her, incredibly aroused by the tempting feast laid out before him.

Still . . . it wasn't enough.

"Tell me, girl."

She moaned. Long tendrils of hair fell from her shoulders down to the mattress when she shook her head. "What difference will it make if I say it, Sean? It'll be under duress. You'll question later whether it was true, and you know it!"

Sean just continued to stimulate her clit while he pressed with the vibrator against her rectum without yet penetrating the clenching muscle. "It'll matter. Do you know why?"

She'd gone stiff again in his lap when he'd threatened to penetrate her ass. "Why?" she asked cautiously.

"Because I know you. Once you say the truth, you'll never be able to deny it again, girl."

He frowned when she remained silent. He pushed gently on the oiled end of the mini vibrator. She gasped when the end of the vibrating tip penetrated her rectum. Sean pressed firmly with his hand, not allowing her clenching muscles to eject the vibrator from her body. He stroked her clit rapidly, mixing her discomfort with pleasure.

Making sure pleasure ruled.

A second later she groaned in stark arousal. He felt her hips pressing down subtly on the slippery ridge of his finger. He pushed the mini vibrator farther into her ass.

"You've got a tight little asshole," he murmured, thoroughly captivated by the sight of the vibe burrowing into her ass between her pink, plump butt cheeks. "Did Max used to fuck you here?"

Her head sprung up on the mattress. Her cheeks glowed bright pink. She glared up at him balefully between strands of tousled brown hair.

"You don't know when to stop, do you?" she seethed.

Sean held her stare as he stopped stroking her, just applying a firm, upward pressure on her clit. He pushed on the ridged vibrator until only an inch of orange silicone poked out of her asshole.

"If you don't want to answer, that's your business. You better know I'm going to fuck your gorgeous ass. Regularly."

Her eye sprang wide as he began to fuck her slowly with the vibrator. Air popped out of her lungs. She shut her eyes and inhaled shakily when he began treating her clit to a slick rub with his finger while he plunged the buzzing little vibrator into her ass. She clenched her teeth.

"*Regularly*, my ass," she muttered under her breath.

"No." She gave a harsh groan of protest when he lifted the

hand that had been stroking her clit. He grabbed a hot, round buttock. "Regularly, *my* ass."

Her eye flashed up to his face.

He spread her ass cheek wide and pushed the ridged vibrator
into her as far as he could. He paused a moment and let the toy
buzz the nerve-packed flesh. She moaned, deep and harsh. Sean
suppressed a grin. He'd always prized the singular groan that a
woman gave while she was crazed with arousal and taking it in the
ass. It always had a primitive, stark quality to it.

No manners, no niceties . . . no *denial* could remain when taking it in such a private place.

Hearing that sound vibrating Genny's vocal cords made him
feel like he was about to lose it in a fit of mindless lust himself.

"Sean, please," she whispered hoarsely when instead of resum-
ing rubbing her clit, he left the vibe inserted in her ass and molded
her ass cheeks around it, enjoying the erotic sight. He watched in
fascination as her tight muscles slowly ejected the slippery sex toy
from her body. He put his finger on the tip of it and slowly pressed
the ridged plastic back into her ass. When her rectum began to
push it out again, he resisted the pressure until the vibe slid in and
out of her ass at an increasingly faster tempo.

"Ohhhhh," she cried out in rising excitement. But Sean also
heard the edge of frustration in her tone. She began to bob her
bottom up and down in a counter-rhythm to the vibrator, getting
extra friction along the sensitive channel.

"Does this turn you on, girl?" he murmured as he plunged the
buzzing vibe in and out of her ass.

"Yes," she hissed.

He took careful note of the vibrant color of her exposed cheek
and her rapid, uneven breathing. It looked as if she was one of the
rare women who could potentially climax from anal stimulation.

He regretted her broken cry of interrupted pleasure when he withdrew the sex toy from her ass.

He unbuckled her wrists cuffs. "Get up and stand beside the bed."

One of her hands fell to his thigh. He clenched his teeth together as lust gripped his entire body.

All that, just from Genny's touch on his leg.

He noticed that she'd propped her upper body on her elbow and watched him. Her hair fell wild and tangled around her sex-flushed face. She was stunning . . . jaw-droppingly gorgeous—

"Go on, girl."

He wondered what she must have heard in his tone when her eyes widened and she scrambled out of his lap. He followed her off the bed.

He pointed at the mussed bed. "Lie back down on your back."

She looked a little perplexed, but she followed his instructions, nevertheless. He saw the question in her huge gray eyes when he set down the vibe on the table and refastened her wrist cuffs to the straps attached to the bed, but she said nothing. Once her upper body was restrained, he moved to the foot of the bed, removing the ankle straps from the bed frame. Genny just watched him with a furrowed brow when he attached the straps to a hook on her leather wrist cuffs, then shortened them. He left the black straps dangling down her arm and got off the bed to remove his jeans and boxer briefs.

His cock had never felt so tight . . . so ponderous as it did when he freed it from the confines of his clothing. Genny's hot stare between his thighs didn't help matters a bit. He ignored the lust stabbing through him, determined to do things right.

Determined that Genny would shape the truth with those lips.

He grabbed for the mini vibrator and the bottle of lubricant, placing them next to Genny's hips.

She gasped when he reached beneath her thighs, opening them and pushing them back at once. Her hips rolled until most of her ass was exposed. He looked down at her, his hands behind her splayed knees.

"Try to keep your legs up for a second."

"But, Sean . . ." When he released her with his right hand and grabbed for the extension strap he'd added to her cuffs, however, she didn't let her leg fall. He heard her whimper when he attached the cuff on her ankle to the strap. He quickly did the same to her other ankle. When he'd finished, she lay on her back on the bed, her hips rolled back, bottom and sex exposed and her legs suspended in the air.

He examined her position critically before he got off the bed, reached behind her pillow on the bed, and pushed the knot on the wrist straps farther apart on the metal box string, widening the two restraints. When he knelt on the bed again, he couldn't help but give a small, satisfied grin. Her ankles and wrist cuffs were attached by about two feet of black extension strap. When he'd widened the knots on the box spring, he'd widened her thighs as well.

Luckily, Genny was flexible.

He stroked the back of a satiny soft thigh and palmed the lower curve of a buttock.

"Are you comfortable?" he asked gruffly.

He saw her swallow thickly. "I'm . . . I'm not *uncomfortable.* It just feels . . ."

"What?" Sean asked, even though he was completely preoccupied. He'd spread a round bottom cheek and was looking his fill at all of Genny's treasures—her pink buttocks, swollen, damp labia, and erect clit, her pink, slick slit . . . her well-lubricated asshole.

The position gave him access to everything, including the sight of her lovely face when she submitted to the truth. He had her precisely where he wanted her, but it was him who felt utterly cap-tivated by the vision of her beauty.

"I feel vulnerable, Sean. But I guess you already knew that. That was what you were going for, right?"

He held her stare as he leaned over and grabbed the vibe and bottle of lubrication from beside her.

"I guess vulnerable describes pretty well how it feels when you're in this deep. Not just for you. For me, too." He popped the top on the lubrication and poured some in his hand. He spread the silky liquid on his stone-hard, aching cock. When he glanced up, Genny was watching him with a fevered look in her eyes. "And you know what they say, girl—all is fair in love and war."

CHAPTER **TWENTY-FOUR**

Genevieve couldn't pull her eyes off the incredibly arousing vision of Sean rubbing lubrication onto his furious erection. She knew what he planned to do. Her experience told her that she wouldn't like it. Max used to have a thing for anal sex. He couldn't coax her into it often, because it'd always left Genevieve feeling unsatisfied and vaguely embarrassed.

It wasn't as if she'd been fastidious about the whole thing, but she'd definitely considered anal sex a bedroom activity that only men could enjoy.

Leave it to Sean to entirely flip the scenario. She'd never been so sexually aroused in her life, so *on fire*. Everything Sean did in the bedroom turned her on. Not just turned her on, made her want to scream and beg for the explosive release only he could give her.

When she'd lain restrained in his lap just minutes ago while he'd fucked her ass with that buzzing little vibrator, Genevieve had burned from her clit all the way up to her tailbone. It'd been unlike anything she'd ever experienced. She couldn't help but feel that if

Sean had just allowed her to come, her entire body would have ignited, not just her genitals.

He certainly seemed to know what he was doing, Genevieve admitted as she watched him apply more lubrication to the vibrator. Her bottom twitched restlessly. It was almost unbearable to lie there in this vulnerable position, completely at Sean's mercy, watching him prepare his instruments for torturing her with pleasure.

She moaned at the thought. He glanced up and smiled. He spread her buttocks with one large hand. Genevieve found herself shaking in anticipation when he flipped on the vibe and she heard the buzz. She groaned when he pressed the vibrating tip next to her rectum, and then pushed it into her ass. He held it inside her and flipped a switch.

Her head thrashed on the pillow when she felt a stronger vibration in her most private flesh. Sean just stared down at her for a minute while she whimpered and moaned, and the tension in her muscles grew unbearable. When she began to buck her bottom against the vibe and his firm hold with the inch or so of movement that the restraints allowed her, Sean cursed under his breath. He spread his hand over her thigh, his thumb keeping the vibe lodged deep in her ass. The fist of his other hand closed around his glistening cockhead.

Genevieve saw that every muscle in his torso was tight and delineated. He leaned forward slightly, and she cried out in mounting excitement.

"You want this cock in your pussy?" he muttered, glancing up at her with fiery eyes.

"Oooh, yes." It hadn't been what she'd thought he was about to say.

She gasped when he flexed his hips and the thick cap of his penis slid into her slit. She'd already been extremely wet from their former lovemaking and sex play. In addition, Sean had lubed his cock well. It surprised her that he still had to apply such a firm pressure to gain entrance to her vagina.

Sean grimaced in pleasure as he thrust several more inches into her, stimulating needy, hungry flesh. "The vibe is making your pussy extra tight," he muttered between clenched teeth. Genevieve's eyes widened in understanding, although she was too excited to speak. The vibrator in her ass took up space, thus constricting her vaginal channel. Sean pressed deeper and grunted in pleasure. His eyes flashed up to her face. "Not that you needed any assistance in that department to begin with."

Genevieve felt too filled to speak—too filled with emotion, not to mention the vibrator and Sean's cock. Instead of sheathing himself completely in her, he began to fuck her with the first half of his cock. She shut her eyes and focused on the delicious burn.

"Open your eyes, Gen," he ordered.

When she did, the sight of him between her suspended, restrained legs made her lips shape a plea. He looked magnificent . . . the very image of male sexual beauty, with his tensed, delineated muscles, blazing blue eyes, and teeming, thrusting cock.

"Sean, I can't take it anymore," she whispered helplessly. Her burn had increased until she required only the slightest stimulation in order to send her into mindless oblivion. But she couldn't get any direct pressure on her clit while he fucked her so shallowly. Nor could she get him to rub and stimulate that spot deep in her vagina with the thick rim below his cockhead. Meanwhile, the vibrator's buzz was creating a nearly unbearable tingling sensation in her ass that was quickly sending her into a sexual frenzy.

"Then tell me what I want to hear."

She clenched her eyes in frustration. "You know it's true. Why do you want to torture me, Sean? Torture *us*? What *good* will it do?"

He paused with his cock half buried in her slit. Her muscles squeezed him, instinctively trying to coax him into filling her . . . *overfilling* her. She made a choking sound when instead of fucking her deeply, he withdrew. Her eyelids popped open. Her mouth fell open in silent protest when he removed the vibrator from her ass as well. She watched him as he once again leaned forward. He tightened both extension straps several inches, propping up her bottom so it came almost entirely off the bed.

She'd feel ridiculous with her ass suspended off the mattress like this, nearly doubled over in a yoga pose, if she wasn't so horny she suspected a whispering breath on her clit would make her climax.

"I'll tell you what good it'll do, Genny." He came closer, draping her feet and lower legs casually over his shoulders. The crinkly hair that sprinkled his powerful thighs brushed against the backs of her legs and ass. He put his hands on the front of her thighs. She stared at him as the length of his cock throbbed next to the damp, sensitive tissues of her external sex. "It'll mean you *can't take it back*." He reached between their bodies and grabbed his cock. He used one hand to spread her buttocks, widening her asshole as well.

She moaned in unbearable excitement when he pushed the tip of his cock to her rectum. He looked up into her face. "I know you, girl. Once you've told me you love me, you'll have crossed the line."

He held her steady and pressed. Genevieve gasped, but she couldn't take her eyes off his rigid face and flaming eyes when his cockhead slipped into her ass. "And you're never going to return," he finished gruffly.

"Sean," she whispered when he began to pulse his hips—gentle, but firm. Her face tightened in intense feeling. It hurt a little— Sean's cock was much thicker than the vibe, not to mention longer. But Genevieve suspected the mild discomfort would fade quickly.

She pressed against his cock with what little motion the restraints gave her.

"That's right. If you press against it, your ass will take my cock better than if I push," Sean instructed. Genevieve saw that his ridged abdomen glistened with sweat. His muscles bunched tight. She knew if she touched them they would feel as hard as steel. She burned for release, but she could easily imagine how much Sean restrained himself at that moment . . . how much he leashed his desire to fuck her in this deeply intimate way, restricted himself from taking her fast and furious.

Just the thought made a groan score her throat. She pushed more firmly with her hips and cried out as several more inches of turgid cock filled her ass.

"You don't know how much you're tempting me."

She heard the warning in his voice, but the prospect of him losing control and fucking her hard tantalized her. Even the mild pain and discomfort of lodging something so large in her ass couldn't abate the illicit thrill.

She pushed against him, and he sunk deeper. He groaned gutturally and held her hips steady.

"You really shouldn't tease a man when his cock is in your ass, Genny."

She smiled even though her eyes stung with emotion. He was so damn cute, even in the midst of dominating her in bed.

He muttered a curse and withdrew his cock, only to sink back into her.

"Aww, yeah, that's good," he muttered thickly. "You're so tight and hot, girl."

He began to pulse his hips, gently fucking her ass. Her own body stunned her. How could anal stimulation cause her clit to sizzle with sexual tension?

She turned her cheek into the pillow. Her throat muscles

constricted, as though in protest to speech. "Oh, *God*," she groaned, the words escaping against her will. "I've got to come, Sean. I've got to." She cried out, but in mild discomfort mixed with intense arousal when he slid his cock deeper into her snug channel. He paused for a moment, allowing her body to grow accustomed to him before he began to slide his cock in and out, stimulating her with unbearable precision.

Genevieve groaned in profound sexual frustration and pushed again with her ass. A grunt tore out of her throat when his thighs pressed tight to her butt cheeks. He held on to her legs, keeping her securely against his body, as his fully sheathed cock throbbed furiously in her ass.

It took Genevieve a moment to realize the trembling she felt wasn't just hers. She stared into Sean's face as both her body and her emotions crested. She couldn't stand the torment on his face, the pinched look of sexual deprivation.

The idea of depriving him. Period.

"Tell me," he grated out between a clenched jaw.

"I love you. I always have, Sean."

His groan seemed to rip through his throat. He began to fuck her with short, powerful strokes. For a moment, it felt like more intense pressure and pleasure than her body could take. But then his thumb found her exposed clit, and Genevieve went off like a keg of dynamite. Her entire body exploded, every nerve firing and popping. She shuddered and jerked, completely at the mercy of electric ecstasy.

Of her desire for one man.

She eventually came back to herself because Sean gave her no choice. At the final moments before he joined her in climax, he held nothing back, fucking her ass every bit as he had her pussy in the past. Restraint no longer pinched his masculine features.

Instead, he looked like a man who saw the prize sitting next to the finish line and sprinted with wild exhilaration.

He growled and slammed into her. Genevieve cried out when she felt his cock jerk in her tight channel. A shout rocketed out of his throat. She whimpered, her mouth opened in awe. Her ass must be even more nerve packed than her pussy, because she could actually feel his warm seed filling her.

It was the most amazing sensation . . .

"God, *Genny*." He shuddered in the throes of bliss.

"Sean," she replied, her answering cry every bit as filled with need as his had been.

As filled with love.

CHAPTER **TWENTY-FIVE**

Genevieve awoke the following morning slowly, her consciousness rising up through a thick haze of delicious languor. She thought of hers and Sean's unbridled sexual exploration last night. She recalled how in between rounds, they'd cuddled and murmured softly to each other, asking silly questions and discussing topics only lovers found fascinating—when they'd first realized their feelings for each other, what they liked to do on a lazy Sunday morning, comparing tabs on their likes and dislikes for new restaurants and movies . . . whether or not this year would be the one for the Cubs.

They'd savored each other's company.

They'd taken a long, sensual shower. At around midnight, they'd eaten in bed, devouring Sean's muffuletta. They'd worked up such an appetite making love that Genny had declared it the most delicious meal she'd ever eaten.

Perhaps one day soon, she'd regret the fact that she'd told Sean time and again she loved him. She'd told him with her hands once he'd released her from her restraints. She told him with her seeking lips, and broadcast it again and again by trusting him enough to submit to her desire.

He never seemed to tire of hearing it on her tongue.

Maybe it was true what Sean'd said last night, because the more times she acknowledged her love for him, the less likely it seemed that she could ever walk away.

She suddenly felt an overwhelming urge to tell him yet again. She turned over in bed.

"Sean?"

She sighed in disappointment when she realized she was alone in the huge bed. She glanced at a clock on the bedside table. Much to her amazement, it was ten minutes after eleven. No wonder Sean was up.

The realization struck her that it was Monday morning—a work day.

In the distance, she heard a car horn beep.

She rose from the mussed bed and peeked around the drapery.

The snow had stopped. Pale sunlight broke through the gray, rapidly moving clouds. She inhaled, doing her best to stave off a rush of sorrow that weighted her chest. There were times over the sensual, entrancing weekend in the penthouse with Sean that she'd wished the storm would go on forever.

Strange, that the sight of sunshine could be so depressing.

She forced herself to shower and dress. While she was in the midst of speaking to her store manager, Marilyn, the residence phone rang. Genevieve figured it was Sean, so she told Marilyn she'd call her back, and they'd decide whether or not they should open the boutique tomorrow.

"Hello?" she asked, breathless at the prospect of hearing Sean's voice.

"Genevieve? It's Carol. You survived the storm, then?"

"Hi, Carol. Yeah, we really got dumped on, huh? You didn't drive into work, did you?"

"Yep. I just got here, though. They opened up the Skyway an hour and a half ago. I was one of the few people on the road, so it wasn't so bad. It seems like most people are taking the day off."

"Sean's lucky to have someone so dedicated."

"I tell him that all the time. He just went into a meeting, but he asked me to call you and see if you wanted anything. He said he'd come up for a late lunch. That man *will* go on about his cooking, won't he?"

Genevieve laughed. "If he's bragging, he's got good reason to. He made some awesome pasta the other night, and the muffuletta he made was out of this world." Her cheeks flushed when she realized she was admitting to Carol that she'd spent so much time with Sean.

What if Detective Franklin questioned Carol?

The old dread swept over her full force.

"Sean thought you might get bored waiting, so he asked if you wouldn't like a couple videos sent over from the place around the corner. They'll deliver them to the front desk, and I could run them up to you."

"Oh, that's not necessary . . ." Genevieve's voice faded off as she considered. Sean'd trusted her sufficiently not to tie her to the bed again. He clearly put a lot of stock into the fact that she'd finally admitted she loved him last night. Not to mention the hours and hours that had followed where they'd freely shared not just their bodies with each other, but their very souls.

It surprised her to realize he'd been one hundred percent right about her confessing her love for him. Now that it was out there, Genevieve would never . . . *could* never take it back.

But Sean was clearly a little concerned about what she might do if he didn't keep her occupied and entertained. She felt torn. Part of her knew she had to leave the penthouse and go about the business of getting her life back together, despite what Sean said about some kind of danger, which Genevieve seriously doubted. It wouldn't be running. Sean could accompany her if he wanted, but she couldn't just hole up here in the penthouse forever.

But she was also tempted to do *just* that: to put off all those difficult decisions in regard to the fire, her living situation, insurance claims, confronting Jeff . . .

Deciding what she was going to do about Sean.

That made up her mind. It was difficult right now to make any major decisions when it came to Sean.

"You know what? Maybe I'll take you up on that offer," she told Carol.

Carol gave her some advice on some new video releases she might enjoy, and they concluded their conversation.

It was with a slightly less heavy heart that Genevieve dug some velvet lounging pants out of her bag and slipped out of her black dress pants. Might as well get cozy.

If there was a weekend that needed to be extended for a day or two, it was definitely this one. Now that she'd made her decision, she found herself looking forward to the prospect of seeing Sean for lunch—of spending another night with him—more than she'd ever anticipated anything in her life.

She'd tried to call Jim on Saturday, but ended up getting his voice message, so she was glad to see his name on her caller identification when her cell phone rang a few minutes later.

Jim was immensely relieved to hear that nothing he'd done or hadn't done had inadvertently caused the fire. He explained to her that he'd returned to the scene of the fire on Saturday and the chief had asked if Jim would like to take a hodgepodge of items that had been removed from the ruins.

"There isn't much, and what there is seems pretty fire-damaged. Would you like me to drive it down to the city so you can take a look at it?" Jim asked.

"No, absolutely not, Jim. I'm sure it's just a bunch of junk."

"Well, some of the stuff may be something you value. It's a miracle, but one photo of Max and his father survived with only minimal scorching. I was so happy to see it."

Genevieve blinked burning eyelids when she heard the slight tremor in Jim's voice. Jim had taken care of Max for so long. He was sixty-seven years old, and he'd worked for Max in one capacity or another for forty of those years. He'd first been employed by Maximillian Sauren, Sr.—who had also held a high level position at the CIA.

Max'd learned secrets and Machiavellian machinations from the breast, no doubt.

It seemed that Jim's unfailing generosity and sincerity had never been dimmed by living in a house of secrets. Maybe Jim represented all that was good in Max.

"You keep that photo, Jim."

He protested loudly, but Genevieve was firm. He finally relented, but Genevieve couldn't stop him from insisting upon delivering the items to her. Even when she explained that she had nowhere to put the items here in the penthouse, Jim offered to take the items for storage to her mother's house in Gary.

"They've opened the interstates, and it'll be nice for me to get out after being holed up during this storm. Besides, I'd like to see Marietta and Roberta again," Jim said, referring to Genevieve's mom and aunt. All three of them were of an age and had met on many occasions, like dinners at Max and Genevieve's house, their wedding . . .

Max's funeral.

"No, Jim, it's really not necess—"

"I need to *do* something, Genevieve."

Genevieve sighed, hearing the subtle plea in his voice. "Of course, I understand. Do you have my aunt's address?"

"Yep. I've got it right here. Roberta Cline, 5437 Grove Street."

"And you're really going to go *now*?"

"Sure," he said, sounding more like the spry, energetic Jim she was used to.

She laughed softly. "Okay. Thanks so much, Jim. Please tell my mom I'll call tonight. And Jim?"

"Yes?"

"I don't want you worrying about your job or your pay. You have a position in my employ as long as you want it."

"That's nice of you to say, Genevieve," he replied gruffly after a pause. "Don't know that there'll be much for me to do, depending on where you decide to live 'n' all."

"Don't worry about that. I've come to rely on you too much for you to even begin to consider retirement. I'd be lost without you."

As she was saying good-bye to Jim she heard someone tap on the penthouse door.

"Hi!"

She caught a glimpse of Carol Fallia's short blonde hair when she opened the front door before Carol rushed her and gave her a tight hug. A moment later, Carol leaned back and studied her.

"You look fabulous. Only you could experience a catastrophe like you did this weekend and end up looking like you just returned from some kind of sexy vacation on a beach. Sounds like something from one of the plots of the movies I ordered for you," Carol said as she released Genevieve and jostled a white bag. She grinned widely. "Are you really doing okay, Genevieve?"

"I'm fine. It's so great to see you again," Genevieve said. "You've lost weight, haven't you? And I love what you did with your hair."

Carol smiled girlishly and fingered her jaw-length, asymmetrically cut blonde hair. "Jamie and I have a joke that he gains a pound for every one that I lose. Thank goodness for the Sauren-Kennedy workout facility." She glanced around the penthouse with curious green eyes. "Nice digs. I always wondered what this place looked like. I was going to come up with the maid once, just to be nosy, but Sean piled some stuff on my desk, and I never got around to it. The man's a tyrant." She gave Genevieve a wink. "He's such an adorable tyrant, I have no choice but to put up with it, though."

Genevieve laughed. "Come in and have a cup of coffee."

"Sure."

They sipped coffee in the living room and caught up. After twenty minutes or so, Carol checked her watch and squawked. "I better get going. I should check on Sean to see if he needs anything for his meeting."

"You spoil him," Genevieve teased as she stood with Carol. "I can't believe he talked you into coming in this weekend because of that big project. Good thing the snow kept you home. You'd think he didn't know you had a family."

"What big project?"

Genevieve paused in the action of picking up their coffee cups. "I thought Sean mentioned some kind of big project that made it necessary for him to . . ."

Stay in the penthouse.

She finished the rest of her sentence in her thoughts when she saw Carol's mystified expression. She obviously had no idea what Genevieve was talking about.

Sean Kennedy, Genevieve thought irritably. *You great big liar.*

Her frown seemed to cause understanding to dawn on Carol's face. She grinned. "Is *that* what Sean told you? That he was working on some kind of project, and that's why he needed to stay here? I was wondering what the heck you two were talking about on the phone Saturday. He'd have to hog-tie me to get me here on a weekend. Well, you know Sean. He always finds a way to get what he wants . . . one way or another."

Carol gave her a knowing glance.

Genevieve hid her irritation and anxiety. Great. If it wasn't bad enough that Sean had manipulated her to get her to stay in the penthouse with him, now Carol seemed to be getting ideas about their relationship.

"Carol . . . I wish you wouldn't mention anything about . . . this," she waved vaguely around the penthouse, "to anyone. It's not what you think."

Now Genevieve had taken up lying.

Carol waved her hand and made a pishing noise. "I worked for Max, and now Sean, Genevieve. I know how to keep a secret with the best of them. Besides, I don't really know anything unless you *tell* me, right?"

She quirked a plucked, frosted eyebrow at Genevieve significantly.

Genevieve laughed good-naturedly at Carol's subtle invitation to spill the goods about her and Sean, but she felt a little queasy as she showed her out of the penthouse. Carol's casual comment about Max, Sean, and secrets had unsettled her deeply.

She wasn't really mad at Sean for lying about needing to stay there. His lie indicated his degree of desperation—and determination—to be with her, after all. It'd irritated her, but she understood why he'd done it. She'd been dead set against them staying there together, after all.

But the promise of the day had been dimmed somehow, Genevieve realized with a sinking feeling.

She wandered into the living room and checked a clock on one of the tables. Sean wouldn't be up for a while. She listlessly picked up the white bag of videos, figuring she'd watch one of them and try to relax. Sean was right. She had been strung as taut as a high wire ever since she'd seen Sean. He was also right about the fact that the only time she wasn't rigid with stress was when he was holding her in his arms.

Or making her insane with lust.

After examining her two movie choices, she picked the romantic comedy, thinking Sean wouldn't mind missing that one as much as he might the suspense drama.

She inserted the disc and picked up the remote control. As she cuddled up on the velvet couch, she wondered if she was joking herself about relaxing when Detective Franklin was out there somewhere, relentlessly doing his job.

And potential witnesses like Carol accumulated.

She was about to hit the PLAY button when the penthouse phone rang.

"Hello?"

"What'cha doing?"

Warmth flooded her at the sound of his deep drawl.

"I was going to watch one of the videos Carol brought up."

"Uh-huh. And what are you wearing?"

"I guess you'll just have to come up here and find out."

She could perfectly visualize the slow spread of his potent grin.

"I'm gonna do exactly that." He dropped his voice volume. "I worked up quite an appetite last night."

"Is that right?"

"Gawd's truth. Mike Butler might have been talking Swahili while he updated me on his case this morning. All I could think about was burying my nose in your—"

"*Sean.*"

"Neck," he finished innocently.

Genevieve snorted. "Carol and I had a nice visit when she delivered the videos earlier. She had no idea what I was talking about when

I mentioned that big project you were working on." A taut silence followed. "You remember? The big project that made it so imperative that you absolutely *had* to stay in the penthouse this weekend?"

"Don't be mad about that, Genny You were in shock. I had to think of something to stay with you here. I was desperate."

"You got that straight," she muttered under her breath. Still, a grin tilted her lips. It was a relatively minor lie, after all. And he'd only been doing it because he cared about her. Besides. What right did she have to judge him?

They all had their secrets.

The thought amplified her anxiety all over again. She *wanted* just to forget everything for a while. She *wanted* to glory in Sean, in the richness of their burgeoning relationship. Why did the harshness of reality have to keep interfering in her thoughts when she was trying so hard to keep it at bay for a while?

"When are you coming up here, Sean?"

"So . . . I'm forgiven?"

"*When?*"

He chuckled softly. "I guess that means 'yes.' I just need to look over a few things and I'll be up in an hour and a half or so."

"That long?"

"Less than an hour, most likely."

"Come quicker."

A pregnant silence ensued.

"Are you teasing me, girl?"

She closed her eyes and smiled. She could perfectly imagine him leaning forward with his elbows on his desk—the familiar hard gleam entering his blue eyes.

"If I am, it's all for a good cause."

"Forty-five minutes. Tops," Sean growled softly before he hung up the phone.

* * *

As soon as Sean set down his phone, Carol knocked and entered. She gave him a funny look as she stepped into the office.

"What?" Sean asked.

Carol shrugged. "Who was on the phone? You look like you're about to kick some butt and take no prisoners."

He laughed as he flipped open his laptop. "Don't worry. I'll show mercy to this particular captive."

"I'm off for lunch. Do you want me to pick anything up for you and Genevieve while I'm out?"

"No, there's plenty of food in the penthouse."

"It sure was nice to see Genevieve again," Carol reflected with a smile. "She's so calm, so elegant, you know? I remember how contained she was at Max's funeral. She actually comforted *me*. I felt like a real heel."

"She disguises her anxiety extremely well," Sean murmured as he opened a file. Personally, he'd always been able to read Genevieve's nerve level like bold, neon print.

"I guess so. I mean . . . her house just burned down, and she chatted with me this morning as if the only thing she had to worry about was getting a dress to the dry cleaner. I'd be a basket case if my house had just burned down. Do you suppose *everything* is gone?"

"I don't see how much could have survived that blaze. The insurance report indicated it was a complete loss of property."

"That's just awful. I'd freak out if I lost all the kids' baby pictures . . . or our wedding photos. What a shame. You'd think *something* could be salvaged," Carol muttered with a sigh before she left Sean's office.

Sean found himself staring unseeingly at his computer, seeing another screen in his mind's eye.

"*Carol*," he shouted.

"*What?*" Carol asked a second later as she poked her head in the door, a harried look on her face.

"Call our contact over at WGN News. Ask him to send over the footage of the Sauren mansion fire—the same clip they broadcast on the news."

"What? *Now?*"

"Ten minutes ago," Sean muttered at the same time he hit some keys on his computer.

Maybe they had the news clip on the Internet . . .

A little over an hour later, Sean rushed into the penthouse, adrenaline pumping through his veins. He hadn't been able to find the news clip on the Internet, and their contact at WGN hadn't returned from lunch until a half an hour ago. He'd sent over the video attached to an e-mail. Sean had just finished watching the clip on his computer minutes ago. After a few terse phone calls, Sean'd hurried up to the penthouse, eager to see Genny.

Anxious to see that she was okay.

"Genny?"

Silence.

"Genny?" he called more insistently. He strained his hearing for the sound of the shower running, but the penthouse was quiet.

Empty.

He stalked into the living room, then down the hallway. Of *course* the penthouse wasn't empty. Hadn't he just talked to Genny? Hadn't her voice gone all sexy and husky with need when she'd told him to *come quicker*?

Where else would she be but right here, waiting for him just like she said she would be?

"Genny?" he bellowed loud enough to startle her if she was anywhere on the entire floor of the high-rise.

The guest bedroom door bounced against the doorjamb when he opened it. He checked in there, the master bedroom, and both bathrooms. Her purse, clothing, and toiletries were nowhere to be found. Neither was Genny.

Not believing his eyes, he checked again.

He experienced a profound sense of incredulity when he walked back out to the empty living room.

She'd left.

How the hell could she have *left*? After everything?

After he'd just come to understand the threat against her with perfect clarity?

He pulled his cell phone out of his pocket and speed-dialed Carol. She picked up on the second ring.

"Is Genny with you?"

"What? No. I haven't seen her since I was up at the penthouse."

Sean started to say something when he noticed the television. It was a blue, blank screen. The television was turned on, but the DVD player had been switched off.

"Okay, Carol," he mumbled before he disconnected. He lunged toward the remote control that lay on the coffee table next to what appeared to be Genevieve's cooled cup of coffee.

He switched it on and stared, his incredulity mounting.

She straddled him, her bottom in the air, wearing nothing but a pair of thigh-highs and ivory-colored leather pumps, her pale, bare breasts crushed to his chest. He held her jaw and kissed her like she supplied him with the breath he required to survive.

A naked man moved behind her. He gave the two of them a slow, knowing grin before he pushed back one of the woman's ass cheek and slid his cock into her slit.

His harsh groan of arousal tore Sean out of his stunned trance.

Max.

How the hell had that volatile video of the New Year's Eve ménage à trois gotten *up here*?

Jesus.

Is *that* what Genny had seen before she'd raced out of here?

CHAPTER **TWENTY-SIX**

Sean gripped the remote control so hard in his hand the plastic made a cracking noise.

He clenched his eyelids when he recalled his suggestion to Carol to have some videos delivered to keep Genny entertained. Obviously Albert Rook had intercepted the delivery boy and inserted his own movie. It'd been the bastard's subtle way of informing Sean that he couldn't keep Genny completely off limits.

But Rook's gambit had gone one better than that. It'd driven Genny out in the open.

She was exposed.

A profound sense of frustration and helplessness went through him when he realized he didn't even have Genny's newest cell phone number. For the past three years, she'd insisted upon any communications with him going through her lawyer.

He'd just have to call her attorney on the way to his car.

He rapidly rolled down a list of names on his phone and pressed the number of one of his top operatives—a man he knew was doing surveillance in the Loop that afternoon.

"Mike? Kennedy. I've got another job for you. Yeah, right this second. The Misseli case is going to have to wait."

A minute later, he grabbed his coat and rushed out the door.

The unexpected site of the video must have sent Genny spinning in a cyclone of emotion. Where would she have gone in her anguished flight?

Minutes later he barreled west on Madison Street, his attention divided as he tried to find Genny's attorney's phone number on his cell phone and maneuver through a traffic-laden street that had been narrowed by snow piled six feet high on each side. The ramps to the Kennedy Expressway were approaching, but Sean couldn't decide whether to go east or west.

One of his operatives, Mike Butler, was checking out the Sauren property in Lake Forest. Paul Dershiwitz would probably be arriving at her Oak Street boutique any minute now. For the life of him, Sean couldn't recall any of Genny's old friends' names.

One question kept plaguing him. How long would it take Rook to catch up with her, now that she was exposed? He must have been in the proximity at around the time she'd left, or else how could he have interfered with the video delivery? Surely he'd seen her as she pulled out of the garage.

He jerked left on the wheel in a spur of the moment decision to head east toward Indiana—Genny might have fled to her mother's—when his cell phone rang. His forehead crinkled when he glanced at the number at the same moment that he had to merge into traffic. Hope flickered through him when no caller identification showed. Maybe it was Genny?

"Hello?" His desperate bark was almost drowned out by a loud horn. Apparently he'd cut somebody off.

"Kennedy? Sean Kennedy?"

He recognized that mellow, Southern-accented baritone.

"Franklin?"

"Right. I wasn't sure who else to call, so I thought it wouldn't hurt to try you. The station got a call from a squad car about a half an hour ago. Currently, that same officer is on the 31st Street ramp on the Dan Ryan headed eastbound, pulled up behind a dark blue BMW sedan."

"Genny?" Sean croaked as he rapidly switched three lanes and pressed his foot to the accelerator.

"That's right," Franklin said.

"I'm on my way. I'm not far from there."

"No—*wait*, Kennedy. That's not why I was calling. Ms. Bujold has been taken to Northwestern Memorial. I'm almost to the hospital as we speak. I was calling to see if you'd meet me there."

Sean cursed under his breath and zipped back through the three packed lanes he'd just maneuvered out of, barely making the Roosevelt Road exit.

"Is she hurt?" he shouted as he flew up the ramp.

"I can't say for sure," Detective Franklin rumbled, not unkindly. "All the officer said is that she was dazed and unsteady, possibly sustained a head injury. Doesn't look like her air bag deployed like it should have when the guy rammed her car, both from the side and the rear. Her car had been searched, and whoever forced her off the road also stole her purse. Bit strange he didn't just take the entire car, seeing as he searched everywhere, including the trunk. Not your typical carjacker, it would seem."

Sean grunted, not really paying attention as his mind churned and he navigated traffic.

"You think you know who might have attacked her, Kennedy?"

Sean blinked, his focus narrowing once again to Franklin's mellow voice. He hesitated only for a few seconds before he chose the lesser of two evils. Franklin might pose a threat to Genevieve, but Albert Rook was a greater one at the moment. He was certainly the more *immediate* of the two. Sean required that the entire Chicago Police Department look out for Rook, not just a handful of very skilled operatives.

"I have reason to think it might have been an ex–Sauren-Kennedy Solutions operative named Albert Rook," Sean began at the same time that he turned down Jefferson Street and zoomed northbound.

A woman's screams in the distance seemed to cleave right through Genevieve's head like an ax.

"You want to sit back here, Ms. Bujold?" a heavyset nurse in her sixties asked. She had a square, stern face and short, dyed blonde hair. Despite her no-nonsense manner, she'd been nothing but kind and solicitous to Genevieve from the moment she'd entered the emergency room.

The nurse nodded toward a relatively secluded alcove that had been separated by a filing cabinet and several heavy curtains. Genevieve doubted the curtains would serve as much of a barrier to the poor woman's screams, but it afforded her a measure of privacy that the bustling emergency room couldn't. She was feeling dazed and vulnerable enough without sitting in the midst of a public arena with a bandage on her forehead.

She followed the nurse into what looked like someone's makeshift office, given the desk piled with papers, the man's pair of shoes beneath the desk, and the disposable food container on top of the filing cabinet.

"The attending still needs to examine you," the nurse explained amiably. She nodded in the direction of the screaming woman. "As you can hear, he's a little preoccupied at the moment, though. Chances are, the doctor will want you to stay overnight for observation, given that bump on your head."

Panic and irritation flared in Genevieve's gut in equal measure. The last thing she needed was yet another medical professional asking her how many fingers they were holding up and who the president of the United States was.

"I can't stay here! No one even knows what happened to me. The man who robbed me took my cell phone."

The nurse glanced around cautiously and nodded at the phone on the desk. "Go ahead and use that phone after I leave, but don't let on I said it was okay. We're not even supposed to let people back here—it's the psychiatrist's office, and he gets furious when we let people use it—but Lord knows he's busy enough today. These big snowstorms bring out all the crazies." She glanced at Genevieve's head wryly. "Not that I have to tell you that, of course."

The nurse had helped the resident dress the wound Genevieve had received when her head had become very familiar with her steering wheel, so she'd heard the skeletal explanation Genevieve had given during the examination.

Not that Genevieve really *had* any more than a skeletal explanation. The whole incident seemed as bizarre and surreal as the experience of sitting on the couch in the penthouse and seeing the images of Sean, Max, and herself on the television screen.

She'd already wondered a dozen times if she was dreaming. She sunk into the chair in front of the metal desk, wondering who she should call. The simple question should have been easy to answer.

In fact, it was so complex that she began to shake with the receiver clutched in her hand, frozen by indecision.

She knew who she *wanted* to call. She wanted to call Sean more than anything. But as that flagrant display on the video screen earlier stated loud and clear, what she wanted when it came to Sean and what she allowed herself to have should be two very, *very* different things.

Who had sent it to her, and why? The same person who had been breaking into her property? The same person who had run her off the road?

Genevieve didn't have the answers to those questions, but if there was one thing she understood, it was that this whole fiasco was somehow associated with Max's murder. Sean thought so. Detective Franklin did as well.

She herself was starting to believe it, although she was stumped as to *how* it was all related.

She sat in the grubby office chair, immobilized by doubt and fear. The nurse suddenly stuck her face around the curtain.

"Miss? There's a Detective Franklin here to see you. He says it's important."

Genevieve felt as if her head had been slammed into the steering wheel all over again.

"Ms. Bujold," Franklin greeted her in his deep voice. He parted the curtain and joined her in the cubbyhole, a concerned expression on his round face. He looked enormous in the tiny space.

"What are you doing here?" she asked him shakily. When he opened his mouth to explain, Genevieve interrupted him. "Oh. Right. Following the tracks."

He shrugged his wide shoulders and gave her an apologetic look.

"Sometimes a detective's got so little to go on, he's got to hover and try to see the lay of the land, if you know what I mean, Ms. Bujold."

She smiled grimly and set the phone receiver back in the cradle. "Like a vulture?"

His white teeth flashed in his dark face. "Well, that doesn't make it sound too pretty, but we've all got to get our supper somehow. Are you all right?"

"I'm fine. I'm ready to go, but they want the attending physician to look at me first. I suppose you heard about what happened? From the police officer that found me?"

Franklin nodded. "Did you get a look at the man who did this to you?"

"He was wearing a black ski mask. He drove an older model, white SUV. I never got the license plate. I was too busy trying to keep my car from wrecking when he forced me off the road."

"Do you know who it was?"

Genevieve glanced up at the blunt question. "I'd be the first to tell you if I knew who had just run me off the road, threatened to shoot me if I didn't unlock the door, and then slammed my head into the steering wheel before robbing me. Unfortunately, I don't have a clue."

"You didn't notice anything that might help to identify him? Didn't recognize his voice?"

She shook her head.

"What about his height and weight?"

She scrunched her forehead and winced in pain as she accidentally agitated the bruise and cut on her head. "Maybe six foot? Maybe more? I couldn't really tell about his weight, because he wore a black overcoat, but he wasn't overweight. He seemed in shape . . . athletic."

"You said he had a gun?"

Genevieve nodded.

"I don't suppose you noticed what type of a gun it was? If I recall correctly from the investigation, you know a bit about guns."

She paused in the action of reaching to see if the bandage on her head was secure. "It was a Beretta nine-millimeter."

"The kind of gun Kennedy carries?"

She smoothed her face into impassivity even though her heartbeat began to drum in her ears. "Yes, I suppose so. Many people that have a history in intelligence work use that type of weapon, Mr. Franklin."

"Including your husband."

This time Genevieve didn't respond. She just watched him with affected calm as he lifted a long leg and propped himself against the corner of the metal desk.

"May I ask where you were going when the man forced you off the road?"

"I was going to my aunt's house. My mother lives with her now. I believe when I saw you on Saturday evening, I might have mentioned that my stay in the penthouse would be short—just until the storm is over. My mother lives in—"

"Gary. I remember," Franklin said in a friendly fashion. He whistled and shook his head. "Sure seems like someone's got it out for you, Ms. Bujold."

"Someone had it out for my purse, that's for certain."

He tilted his head and studied her like a curious puppy. "You really think this was just a random incident? After everything else that's happened to you over the weekend. Doesn't that strike you as a bit unlikely, Ms. Bujold?" When she didn't answer, Franklin continued. "Kennedy doesn't think it's any more of a coincidence than I do."

"Everyone's entitled to his opinion." Genevieve stood. "If you have any more questions for me, maybe I should call my lawyer, Mr. Franklin?"

His eyebrows went up in a guileless expression. "I wasn't cross-examining you. I just came down here to make sure you were all right."

"Really. I thought you came down here because you still suspect I killed my husband, Detective."

He leaned back when he heard her frank appraisal, a woebegone look on his puppy-dog face. "I assure you that's *not* what I think, Ms. Bujold."

Her throat tightened. She had to struggle to get out words. "Surely you don't suspect *Sean* of anything, do you? That's *ridiculous*, he was—"

She started in shock when she heard someone call her name from the other side of the curtain.

"Sean?" she cried out breathlessly.

A second later Sean whipped the vinyl curtain aside and plunged into the makeshift office. The already small space shrunk even further. She felt as if she hid in a closet with two extremely large men. Sean gave Franklin a cursory glance before he pinned Genevieve with his blazing eyes. She gaped at him, mesmerized by the unexpected sight of him. She stilled an overwhelming urge to run into his arms.

"Are you all right?" he asked tensely.

"I'm fine, Sean."

"What did the doctor say about your head?"

"It's just a bump. They might want to keep me overnight for observation, but I don't plan on agreeing to that. Sean, what are you *doing* here?" The anxious question popped out of her throat.

"I called him." She blinked at the sound of Franklin's mellow, Mississippi-accented baritone. The detective glanced blandly between her and Sean. "I figured he'd want to know if something happened to the woman he cares about so much. I see I was correct in my assessment."

CHAPTER **TWENTY-SEVEN**

Nausea rolled through her. She must have swayed slightly, because suddenly Sean was there, easing her down into the chair. Genevieve wanted to shout at him to quit touching her—to stop giving credence to Franklin's benignly uttered volatile statement, but she was too busy fighting off the nausea.

"I need to talk to her alone, Franklin."

"Sean, no—"

"Sure thing," Franklin said politely before he stood. "I'll be out in the waiting room, Ms. Bujold. There are a few other things I'd like to ask you."

Genevieve closed her eyes at the sight of Franklin ducking through the curtain. Why did Sean insist on digging a bigger hole for himself? Why didn't he just hand over a written confession to Franklin here and now?

"Sean, you're acting like a fool—"

"Not now, Genny."

At least he used a hushed tone. What if Detective Franklin

lingered outside? Both of his hands cupped her jaw. They stared at each other in the dim, grubby space. His blue eyes flickered over the bandage on her head. She read the rigid set of his features and sensed his anxiety and his frustration with her. She sensed his love most of all.

Genevieve tensed, thinking he was about to lay into her for leaving the penthouse.

For leaving him.

"There were some things that were salvaged from the fire," he began. "We saw the firemen start to retrieve them and set them out on the lawn when we caught that news clip last Saturday. Do you know what happened to that stuff? Did Jim take it to his daughter's house in Niles?"

Her mouth gaped open. It'd been one of the last things she'd have expected him to say at that moment. "How did you know about that?"

"Just answer me, Genny. It's more important than you know."

She clamped her jaw shut. "Yes. Jim took some salvaged items to Niles."

"Do you have Jim's daughter's address?"

"I . . . yes, but that's not where that stuff is anymore, Sean. Jim called me this morning and said he was going to take them to my mother's for storage today. Sean, what's this all about?" Genny asked when Sean released her jaw. Dizziness waved through her once more. She wished he'd put his hand back on her. She wished he'd hold her. As always, his touch steadied her. Instead, he grabbed a scrap of paper from the desk and a pen.

"Your mom moved in with your aunt a while ago, didn't she? Write down her new address."

"Buy *why*?" She asked as she clutched the pen and started to write the address.

"I was wrong to think the fire related to all the other stuff that's been happening to you. Well . . . *it* does relate, just not in the way I thought. In fact, that fire was what set this whole thing rolling." He must have noticed her confusion broadcasted loud and clear on her face. "The fire wasn't set by anyone. But all those news cameras caught something on film that meant a hell of a lot to someone who saw it."

"Who?"

"Albert Rook."

"Albert *Rook?*" Genevieve exclaimed, her amazement growing. She hadn't heard the man's name in years. Since he was friends with Max—they used to golf together, she recalled—the police had questioned him during the investigation. But they'd questioned every employee at Sauren. Rook had attended Max's funeral, she recalled, and then left the company soon after. She'd never seen him since. But there had been that time . . .

"Genny. What are you thinking?" Sean whispered tensely.

"It seems so strange to hear his name again. I'm just stunned. Do you think that was *Albert Rook* who broke into my boutique?" Her eyes widened. "That it was *him* . . . in the SUV that ran me off the road?"

"I'd bet money on it."

"He was such a strange man. So cold . . . so intense all of the time. I was just remembering that after the funeral, he said he wanted to meet with me. At the time, I thought he wanted to personally give his condolences in regard to Max." She searched Sean's face. "He didn't want to give his condolences though. Did he?"

Sean shook his head, a grim expression on his face. "No. He wanted to blackmail you, Genny. He wanted to blackmail *us*. But I ran him off before he got the chance. He stayed away for three years. But a couple of days ago, he must have seen a news clip about the fire—WGN is broadcast on cable in Indianapolis, where Rook lives."

Genevieve wanted to ask him how he knew where Rook lived, but another question flew to her tongue first. "What did he see?"

"A briefcase. The carbon attaché case Max used to carry. Do you remember it?"

Another wave of dizziness rolled through her brain. She shut her eyes and it passed. "Yes. Of course. I don't recall it being in the mansion, though. I thought it was with the things that were cleaned out of his office. I never went through them personally—"

"The briefcase wasn't in his office. I checked," Sean said tersely. "He probably had it hidden somewhere in the mansion. Max loved hidey-holes. I wouldn't be surprised if he had a compartment or a room installed somewhere in the house—some place where he could stash what he held most dear to him. But the fire brought some of Max's precious secrets to light. That hidden attaché case survived the blaze. They build those things to survive an apocalypse," Sean muttered under his breath. "Albert Rook got firsthand proof that I'd been lying to him three years ago. I didn't possess the evidence he feared I had. Genny, there's something important I have to ask you."

She sensed his almost palpable tension; *shared* in it.

He leaned down so their faces were only inches apart.

"Did you kill Max?"

The hissing sound of his last whispered syllable seemed to linger in her ears.

"*No,*" she mouthed. Her brain had short-circuited, depriving her of the power of speech.

Sean studied her with a lasering stare. His expression suddenly shifted. Incredulity shadowed his features.

"Christ. You thought *I* did, didn't you?"

Genevieve grabbed onto his shoulders as though she were drowning and he was the one solid object in a sea of uncertainty. "You didn't?"

His face collapsed with emotion for a brief moment before he glanced away, his eyes glistening.

"I might have thought about it a time or two—especially after New Year's Eve. But the answer is no. I didn't kill Max."

He straightened. Her hands fell uselessly in her lap.

"I have to go, Genny."

"What? *Where?*" She felt just as disoriented as she had when Albert Rook had shoved her head into the steering wheel.

"I have to get that briefcase."

"No, Sean. Don't go *now*," Genevieve pleaded. She couldn't believe he was planning to leave after what they'd just told each other.

He hadn't killed Max.

He'd thought *she* had.

She stood and lurched toward him. He caught her before she fell to the floor.

"Genny, sit down," he said sternly.

"But . . . I can't believe . . . I . . ."

He set her down in the chair. She felt his firm lips brush against temple that wasn't bandaged. He turned and parted the curtains.

"*Sean,*" she called out shrilly.

But he was gone.

She was starting to stand and go after him when the curtains moved and the heavyset nurse swept inside. She gave Genny a blazing glance and pointed at the chair.

"Sit down, young lady. You're about to pass out," she proclaimed. "Stay right there while I find a place for you to lie down."

Genny sagged into the chair. Despite her wishes to go after Sean, her body didn't seem to be cooperating. Black spots occluded the edges of her vision. She saw the messy office through a thick, dreamlike haze.

*   *   *

Detective Franklin stood when Sean approached him in the crowded emergency room waiting area.

"Albert Rook killed Max Sauren," Sean stated bluntly. The whites of Franklin's eyes showed as he gaped in amazement. "I'll be able to show you in a few hours the motive for the murder. In the meantime, he's still out there somewhere. He's a threat to Genny. Would you stay with her?"

Franklin looked hesitant. "It'd be better if you just told me where you're off to, Kennedy. I can help you get the evidence you're talking about."

Sean shook his head even as he started to back away. He needed to get that briefcase, and quickly. It was tangible evidence that not only proved Rook's criminal character, but also provided a powerful motive for murder. Now that he'd looked into Genny's eyes point-blank and knew the truth—that she hadn't murdered Max—Sean wouldn't hesitate to help the police arrest Rook. Rook could malign Genny all he wanted. He could show Franklin the evidence he'd shown Sean three years ago.

But Franklin wouldn't be so likely to trust his claims once they saw the solid proof of Albert Rook's treasonous activities. Once he knew Max had been blackmailing him with that knowledge.

Once Franklin understood that Rook and Sauren had been lovers.

"I have to go. Just promise me you'll stay with Genny."

Franklin didn't look happy about it, but he nodded his head grudgingly.

"Good. I'll have my secretary phone you with Rook's description," Sean told Franklin before he turned and rushed out of the emergency room. He thought of Genny back in the ER, her face as white as newly fallen snow, her body sagging limply in his arms.

He fought against a powerful instinct to race back in there. To hold her. To comfort.

She'd thought he'd killed Max. No wonder she'd avoided him. No wonder she'd winced every time he looked at her in those weeks after Max's death.

Of all the damned things, Sean thought bitterly as he shoved open the metal door and jogged out onto the icy sidewalk.

It was like the cards had been stacked against Genny and him from day one.

Genny blinked open heavy eyelids. Her brow crinkled in confusion when she saw a dark brown face looming over her. She strained to focus her vision.

"Detective Franklin," she mumbled. She started to sit up.

"Whoa, not so quickly. You fainted. You were out of it there for a few seconds when the nurse brought you over to this cot. Your knees folded like an accordion underneath you."

"Where's Sean?"

"Off on a mission to save the world, apparently. Or at least on a mission to save you, I'm guessing."

"What do you mean?" she whispered as she leaned back on her elbows. Things seemed a bit clearer now, less hazy. Still, her head pounded with pain.

"He said he was going to get something that would help to prove that a man named Albert Rook killed your husband."

"The briefcase."

Franklin's features hardened. Suddenly, the puppy dog disappeared and a hard, formidable man took its place. "What briefcase?"

But Genevieve stared to the left of him, deep in thought. "He'll have gone to my aunt's and mother's house."

"Hey, *hey*, now. What are you doing? That nurse is worse than my grandma Flora used to be. She'll skin me alive if I let you get up." Genevieve ignored him—fierce scowl and all—and swung her feet to the floor. She sat for a second or two, assessing how she felt. No dizziness crashed into her like before so she slowly started to stand. Franklin put out his hand to help her.

"I need to go to my mother's."

"You're not going anywhere. Look at you. You can hardly stand. You can't operate a vehicle. Besides, have you forgotten? You don't *have* a vehicle at the moment. The officers probably had your car towed to one of the city facilities by now."

Genevieve bit her lower lip. She hadn't thought of that. She studied Franklin speculatively. He looked somber and genuinely concerned. She wondered if he suddenly seemed so much less threatening because she no longer believed she had to protect Sean from him.

"You could drive me there."

"Why would I do that?" Franklin asked skeptically. "You're not even supposed to leave the hospital yet."

"I thought you were the cop who wasn't going to rest until Max Sauren's murder was solved."

Franklin pursed his lips together and considered her thoughtfully. "You do know the right buttons to push. Are you sure you're okay?"

Genevieve took a deep breath and nodded. "The faint must have done me good. I feel much better." If it wasn't exactly the truth, it wasn't precisely a lie, either. She did feel better than before, when Sean had said he was leaving.

Of course, she'd felt so awful then, to say she felt better wasn't really saying much. She realized something crucial at the same moment she took note of the continued doubt on Franklin's face.

"You *have* to take me to Gary, Detective," she said firmly.

"Why? What are you thinking?"

"Sean told you about Albert Rook?" She put her hand on his upper arm and started to urge him out of the semi-private examination cubicle. Franklin didn't exactly go along with her willingly, but he didn't plant his feet either.

"Yeah. He thinks Rook murdered your husband."

"Right. Well, I just realized—Rook stole my phone when he forced me off the road. It's got all my addresses and phone numbers in it."

Franklin stopped dead in his tracks, halting her as well. She gave him an entreating glance. "We *have* to go. Rook likely remembers I have a mother in Gary. The only reason he probably hasn't broken into her house like he has everywhere else associated with me is because the house is under my aunt's name. Not my mother's. He probably didn't know her correct address before he stole my phone. He'll go there to find that briefcase."

"Okay. There's still no reason for you to go. I'll go alone."

"Not if you don't know where to go, you won't."

Franklin gave her a narrow stare. "I can play poker with the best of them, Ms. Bujold. You wouldn't put people you care about at risk just to make a point, would you?"

"You want me to beg? All right, fine. *Please* take me to my mother's in Gary, Detective. Maybe we can find out a few things from each other along the way."

He considered her for a long moment, and then nodded decisively. "Okay. Let's go. Keep an eye out for that nurse though. She'd kick my butt from here to Biloxi if she knew I was making off with you."

Genevieve couldn't help but give a small smile at the evidence of such a huge man—a homicide detective who dealt with the toughest elements of society—being intimidated by a short, plump, and fierce elderly nurse. She was beginning to realize it wasn't an act. Franklin really did have both a smart, relentless police detective and a cuddly, kind man residing inside that big body.

"Detective?" she asked as they moved hastily through the bustling emergency room.

"Yes, ma'am?"

"How come you never call me Genevieve?"

"I 'spect it's because you never asked me to."

"Oh. I thought it was because you thought I was a murderer," she mused as he pushed open a door and held it for her.

Franklin smiled. "I might have thought it once. For about ten seconds three years ago."

Genevieve gave him a surprised look. "I thought I was your primary suspect."

They left a long corridor and walked into the enormous welcoming hall for the entire hospital. Bright winter sunlight streamed through floor-to-ceiling windows. Genevieve squinted in the brilliance.

"I'll admit I thought you were guilty of something. You're one of those unfortunate people who wears her heart on her sleeve, I'm afraid. But feeling guilty and committing murder are two very different things. As Max's wife, you were in a position to know things about him that others didn't. Things about the state of his health, for instance."

Genevieve came to an abrupt stop just feet inside the sunlit hall. Franklin halted along with her. They locked gazes for a few tense seconds.

"An autopsy was performed on your husband's body, Genevieve. It's normal procedure, in cases of murder."

She shook her head slowly.

"You never told me you knew," she whispered. "You never said anything about it to anyone."

"It's not uncommon for us to hold certain things back in a case like this."

Maybe she'd experienced so much shock earlier that it was impossible for her to feel even more. Genevieve just felt numb as she stared up at Franklin.

"I'm guessing from your reaction that you were one of the only people besides Max's doctor that knew he was dying."

"Max told me for the first time on the same day he was killed," she admitted through leaden lips after a long pause. "He . . . he said that he planned to taunt Sean . . . to goad him with the knowledge that he would never have me. He planned to whip Sean into a rage so that . . ."

"What, Genevieve?"

"So that Sean would murder him," she whispered.

After a tense silence, she glanced up into Franklin's face. His features had settled into a hard mask, but compassion shone in his velvety black eyes.

A giant knot had formed in Genevieve's throat, but she fought past it. It was time for these toxic secrets to be released into the open, time for their power to be diminished by the blinding light of the truth. She believed Sean when he said he hadn't murdered Max. If *he* hadn't, and *she* hadn't, there was no longer a reason to shelter Max's manipulations.

"I tried to warn Sean on that day, even though Max had already told me he would be conveniently unavailable. Max had sent him in his place for an important meeting with the Assistant Secretary of the Treasury about some important government business Sauren was trying to procure in regard to a counterfeiting operation."

"Why didn't you call the police?"

"How many people do you know who would plan their death in such a ruthless, heartless fashion, Mr. Franklin?" she countered defensively. "I wish I *had* called the police. More than you could ever know. But the fact of the matter was, that afternoon was the first time I'd ever seen Max behave that way. I didn't really believe he could be capable of such ruthlessness. Such selfishness. I was a fool not to take him at his word."

She inhaled heavily and sighed. "He was dead within three hours of our conversation."

Franklin glanced off into the distance. After a pause, he whistled softly. "I see your point. Well, if *this* ain't something. Sauren wanted to go out with a bang not a whimper. You'll pardon me for saying so, but your husband was a singular son of a bitch, Genevieve."

"Sean *didn't* kill Max," Genevieve stated fiercely.

"I don't think he did, either. I was convinced of it at one time, but my captain was always betting on you. It seems now as if Sauren manipulated this guy Rook to do his dirty work for him—or at least that's what Kennedy thinks. Sauren got his abrupt, dramatic death and managed to keep you and Kennedy apart in the process. He just kept pulling those strings."

"All the way from hell," Genevieve murmured.

The knowledge that Franklin didn't believe Sean was a murderer seemed to cause relief to sink all the down to her bone marrow.

"Let's go," she urged. "Sean's got a good twenty-minute lead on us."

CHAPTER **TWENTY-EIGHT**

Sean drove slowly down the narrow, residential street lined with well-maintained bungalows. He'd tagged along with Genevieve on two different occasions to visit her mother. Both the neighborhood Genevieve had grown up in and this one were inhabited by blue-collar families, but this one was a bit more respectable than Genevieve's and her parents' had been—a little less shabby.

The bungalows had been built back in the 1920s and '30s, and only had single-car garages. As a result, cars lined both sides of the street. Sean parallel parked a half-block away from the address Genny had written on the piece of paper. The cold winter air struck him like a slap when he got out of his SUV. The storm clouds had completely cleared. The sun would be setting soon enough, but for now it shone fiercely, as if it were trying to make up for its absence for the past few days.

As Sean made his way down a narrow opening in the hills of shoveled snow on the street, he realized he should have asked Genny for her mother's phone number. It'd've been nice for Mrs. Bujold to get some kind of advanced warning of his visit. The trip from Chicago to Gary had been pleasantly short, considering the recent bad weather. He'd been so busy talking to Carol the whole time, and then contacting the operatives he'd sent in search of Genny, that he hadn't even considered how odd it was going to be for him to just drop in like this on Genny's aunt and mom.

He'd asked Mike Butler and Paul Dershiwitz to follow him out to Gary. Until Rook was found, Sean wanted Genny's aunt's house watched.

He grew hyperalert as he approached 5437 Grove Street, taking in the neat house with the freshly shoveled sidewalk and steps, scanning the area for anything out of place . . . looking for the vehicle that he knew Rook drove.

He saw nothing unusual.

He sprung up the front porch, his gaze flickering over the mailbox with the gold lettering that read Cline. His fist drew back in preparation to knock on the front door when he heard the muted sound of glass breaking from the interior of the house. He shifted quickly away from the door, pressing his back to the brick separating the front door and a large bay window that overlooked the street. He eased down the small front porch toward the window as he reached for his gun.

At first, the bright sunlight prevented him from seeing anything in the dim interior of the house. Then he made out the profile of an older, attractive woman with short, graying brown hair and a delicate face sitting rigidly in a chair near the window. He inched farther down the porch, peering around the edge of an ivory scalloped drapery into the living room.

A tall man with white hair was standing near a couch set against the far wall. On the table in front of him, a broken coffee cup lay shattered just inches from a phone. Sean made out another woman who sat on the couch, her gaze fixed on a second man who stood just to the right of the couch holding a gun.

Albert Rook.

And the man who'd obviously tried to reach for the phone when Rook had entered the room was Jim Rothman, the man who worked for Genny and had previously worked for Max. Rook waved the gun and the three adults all stood and moved out of Sean's vision, Rook bringing up the rear.

Sean moved stealthily off the front porch and vaulted over a hill of snow into the front yard. He plodded through the thick snow toward the back of the house.

Detective Franklin reached across Genevieve's lap and stilled her hand from reaching for the release on the car door.

"I'll go and check things out at your mother's house first. I'll let you know once I see everything is okay. If I don't come back out in thirty seconds and wave for you to come up to the house, you call the local police, okay? I carry two cell phones. You take one."

Genevieve started to argue—that was her mother and aunt in there, after all, not to mention Jim.

And Sean.

She noticed how Franklin's expression had gone hard and implacable again. She nodded in agreement, although she secretly wondered if she'd be able to handle the anxiety of sitting there, waiting to hear if everyone she loved most in the world was safe. She wished she'd have been able to reach Sean or her mother on the twenty-five-minute trip from the city, but neither of them had picked up. Franklin's scowl after she'd told him of her futile attempts had made her all that much more nervous.

"All right, but *hurry*," she charged Franklin.

She watched Franklin's bulky, but graceful form as he walked toward her aunt's house. The sun had begun to set, casting the neighborhood in a pink-hued haze filled with shadows. She sat forward in the seat tensely when she saw Franklin knock. Her heartbeat began to thrum in her ears when, after a pause that seemed like it lasted for an eternity, the detective turned the front doorknob and entered the house.

Just before he was blocked from her view, Genevieve saw him reach for his gun.

She opened her car door, the throb of her heart now a hammer in her head. She wasn't sure if she had waited Franklin's prescribed thirty seconds or not before she heard a sound like a muted firecracker.

She rushed out of the car, fumbling for Franklin's cell phone.

Sean winced when the heavy oak door opened with a squeak of protesting hinges. Picking the ancient lock had taken him longer than he'd have expected. He must be losing his juvenile delinquent skills.

He quickly shut the door behind him, not wanting the cool air to warn Rook of his presence if the squeaky hinges hadn't already. He couldn't be sure where the others were in the house, but the rear door entered into the basement.

He found himself in a narrow room that contained neatly arranged plywood shelving and a washer and dryer. The room was dim, but through the crack of a nearly closed door he saw a light and heard what sounded like a heavy object being scooted along the old cement floors.

"I don't understand. Who are you? What do you want?" a woman asked shakily.

Sean went still, surprised that Rook had ordered his captives down into the basement. He couldn't be sure if it was Genny's mom or aunt who had spoken.

"That's not for you to worry about. Just keep your mouth shut and

I'll be gone before you know it. There's something here that's mine."
Sean heard a grunt of satisfaction. "Here it is." Sean moved closer to
the door and peered through the crack into the outer room.

He saw Rook in profile, the three other adults facing him. Rook
stood in the midst of a pile of fire-singed items. He held up Max's
attaché case. The supple leather sheath that used to cover it had
been burned off. The fire had scored and dulled the metal, but it
remained largely intact.

Sean tensed in preparation to spring into the room when he saw
Rook crouch.

"What's this?" He held up what looked like a scorched picture
frame.

"Get your hands off that. That's none of yours, Rook. You take
what you came for and go," Jim shouted angrily.

Rook glanced up. A viperlike grin spread on his thin face. "You
want to be able to set this photograph of Max next to your bedside
table, Rothman, so you can stare at the love of your life every night
before you fall asleep?" Rook's voice rang out sarcastically in the
empty basement. "He used to laugh at you behind your back, you
know. Max knew what you were, even if you didn't, old man. You
thought it was loyalty, but Max knew the truth—that you're a pitiful old fag hopelessly in love with his master."

Jim drew himself up proudly. "You're the pitiful one, Rook.
You killed him, didn't you? You murdered Max."

Rook's smile looked a little demented. He tossed the picture
frame onto the floor. Glass tinkled as he cocked his weapon.

"Yeah, I did, old man. And you're as stupid as I always thought
you were for asking me to admit it in front of you. Now I'm going
to have to kill all three of you."

"Don't move, Rook. You're gonna get a bullet right in your
brain if you so much as twitch," someone barked from the other
side of the room. Sean saw Detective Franklin hurrying down

the stairs, his gun drawn and trained on the side of Rook's head. *"Drop the gun."*

Rook's eyes popped in disbelieving fury. Sean saw the subtle movement of Rook's hands tightening on the gun. He moved around the door, aimed and shot at the same time that Rook started to swing his weapon in Franklin's direction.

Rook fell to the basement floor clumsily, finally collapsing onto his back. He cursed in pain and rolled onto his side.

Sean stared down at Rook as he kicked his fallen gun across the room. Rook's green eyes widened as he struggled to breathe; he winced.

"Kennedy." The single word seemed to carry all the hatred that Albert Rook possessed in his wiry, strong body.

Sean didn't say anything. Instead he picked up the carbon attaché case and dangled it over Rook. An ugly snarl twisted Rook's face as he stared impotently at Max Sauren's treasure chest of secrets. Out of the corner of his eye, Sean saw Franklin approach.

"Thanks," the detective said as he withdrew his cell phone from his pocket while still training his weapon on Rook.

"The pleasure was all mine," Sean drawled, his gaze locked with Rook's. No one spoke as Franklin put in an emergency call for an ambulance and backup. When Franklin hung up, Sean handed the fire-scored attaché case to Franklin.

"I think you'll find a *fine* reason inside of that case for why Rook here decided to kill Max Sauren. You see, Rook here sold military secrets to the Chinese while he was a weapons systems analyst for Navy intelligence. Max had proof of his treason, and it's inside that attaché case. I'd bet my life on it. Do you want to tell the detective here about that evidence you contrived to try to make it look like Genevieve Bujold had killed her husband?"

Marietta Bujold made a sound of distress. Her sister put her arm around her shoulders and made soothing noises. Sean gave Genny's mother an apologetic glance. He was about to suggest that Jim take Marietta and Roberta upstairs when he noticed a pair of white tennis shoes coming stealthily down the basement stairs.

He recognized those shoes.

"Genny?" he bellowed.

"Sean?"

He gave Franklin an incredulous, irritated glare.

"You told me to watch out for her, and she *insisted* on coming here. Refused to tell me where her aunt and mother lived if I left her at the hospital." When Sean didn't seem pacified, Franklin added sheepishly, "I *did* warn her not to get out of the car."

Genny vaulted down the stairs, all caution forgotten.

"Mom? *Sean?*" Her huge gray eyes took in Rook lying there on the floor. Her gaze darted to Sean's face. She rushed over and embraced her mother and aunt, asking them and Jim repeatedly if they were all right. Once she'd satisfied herself that they were fine, she went over to Sean and gave him a fierce hug.

All the icy coldness that had flowed through Sean's veins from the moment he'd seen Albert Rook standing in the living room upstairs melted. He shut his eyes tightly and inhaled the sacred scent of Genny's hair.

He cracked his eyelids open a few seconds later when he heard Rook make a raspy sound of disgust. He continued to hold her tightly as he met the man's stare over the top of Genny's head.

"Jealous, Rook?" he asked softly.

"You're welcome to her," Rook replied scathingly. "Max used to watch you two carry on. Do you think he didn't notice?"

"I doubt there's much Max Sauren *didn't* notice," Sean said wryly. He heard the sound of sirens in the distance. "Go ahead, Rook. Why don't you tell the detective about the trumped-up evidence—your clever scheme to frame Genny for Max's murder?"

Rook just gave him a disgusted look as he held a hand over his side and panted.

"It was clever enough to keep your mouth shut, Kennedy. You didn't seem to have much problem believing your girlfriend had murdered her husband."

He felt Genny stiffen in his arms. Sean rubbed her back in a soothing motion.

Rook groaned as a spasm of pain shook him. "What the *fuck*," he muttered bitterly to himself a few seconds later.

Sean thought he understood the acid in Rook's tone. "Treason pretty much trumps any crime you've committed, Rook. Including murder—which you just admitted to in front of everyone in this room, by the way."

Rook's furious glance told him that particular reality had just come crashing down, as well.

"Max and I used to watch you and Genevieve shooting at the Sauren firing range sometimes. He would joke about how long it would actually take before you cut the crap and just nailed her like you did every other woman that came within ten feet of you." Rook paused, wincing and clutching his side.

"All I had to do was collect some of the casings you two left after shooting at the range. You taught Genevieve how to load her own gun. Her prints were all over the shells. It was Max's idea." Rook's lips twitched. Sean couldn't tell if he was in pain or recalling Max fondly until he continued. "That was Max for you. He always wanted to be ready with a plan for extenuating circumstances."

Sean distantly recalled that Genny and he had practiced at the firing range early on that fated New Year's Eve. It'd been the holidays, and the company had been closed. It would have been easy enough for Rook to retrieve the casings they'd left behind, either on that day or any other day during the holidays.

"So you're saying it was Max who masterminded your whole blackmailing scheme?" Sean said.

Rook looked insulted. "I came up with most of that on my own. What do you think? That Max planned it from the morgue?"

Sean recalled that smug expression on Max Sauren's face in death. "You never know, with Max," he muttered under his breath. He wondered if Genny had heard him when she slowly lifted her head from his chest and turned to look at Rook.

"We used my nine-millimeter to practice at the firing range, so the shell casings could have conceivably come from either Max's gun or your own." Sean continued, wanting to get as much out of Rook before he had a chance to recover and retract or alter his story. "So whose gun did you actually use to kill Max?"

Rook was starting to respond when a fit of coughing struck him. Sean heard the dull thump of several vehicle doors shutting in the distance.

"I'd better go meet them," Franklin said, referring to the approaching police and EMTs.

"No. You stay put," Sean said, still staring at Rook. "Jim? Can you go? You might find a few of my operatives up there along with the police. Tell them we're safe, will you?"

Jim nodded willingly and headed up the stairs. Everyone else in the chilly basement stared at Albert Rook with tense expectation.

"Go on, Rook. Whose gun did you use?" Sean prompted.

"Max's. I knew where he kept it in the car. Afterward, I policed my brass and destroyed the evidence. After I'd collected the shell casings with Genevieve's prints on them, I—" Rook gasped, his face clenched with pain.

"You cleaned Max's gun of any prints and planted it along with Genevieve's shell casings on the Sauren mansion grounds," Sean continued for him. "Then you photographed all the evidence and brought it to me, hoping to blackmail me into giving you money or

Sauren stock in exchange for your silence during that pivotal time during the police investigation."

Sean noticed in the periphery of his attention that Genevieve turned her head again and was staring incredulously up into his face.

Rook shot Sean a look of pure loathing. "But you fooled me with that fake briefcase and your stories, didn't you? You said you'd give it to the police if I came near your sweetheart. But you were a damn liar, weren't you, Kennedy? I knew that when I saw Max's briefcase lying on the Sauren mansion front lawn after that fire destroyed his house."

The sound of pounding feet emanated down through the ceiling.

"So why did you do it, Rook? Why did you shoot Max?"

Rook's face suddenly crumpled with anguish. It shocked Sean. Albert Rook was the last person on the planet he would have expected to show such intense emotion. To see him suddenly transformed by misery was damned unsettling.

"I don't know why he did it," Rook wailed. "He just turned on me all of a sudden—out of nowhere. He said I'd gotten too clingy . . . too needy. He said he wanted me to leave the company . . . that everything we had was finished."

Sean glanced down at Genny when he felt her muscles jerk. She once again turned and stared at Albert Rook at the same time a man shouted down the stairs. Franklin went over to the foot of the staircase and held up his badge, identifying himself as a CPD homicide detective.

"Everything is under control. A man has been shot. Send down the EMTs, but have your men stay put for a moment. It's crowded enough down here," Franklin shouted in his authoritative, deep baritone. There was a sound of men calling out and shuffling feet.

"And then Max threatened to give the documents in that attaché case to government officials, didn't he?" Sean prodded, ruthless, even in the face of Rook's misery to see the truth exposed.

Rook's low growl was no longer furious, only defeated and pitiful. He rested his cheek on his upper arm. Sean could almost see the energy draining out of him.

"Yes. After everything we had together, everything we shared. He used to say I was the only one who truly knew him. But that night . . . he said I was nothing more than a convenience. He didn't *want* me anymore."

Sean started when Genny lurched out of his arms and staggered toward Rook.

"He wanted you to do it. That's why he purposefully made you so angry. Max *wanted* you to kill him," she said hoarsely.

Sean paused in the action of going after her, surprised by her words. He noticed that Franklin watched the unfolding scene with an expression of sadness and compassion on his face. Rook went entirely still, his eyes pinned to Genny, his expression taut . . . incredulous. A man and a woman pounded down the stairs carrying medical bags in their hands.

"He'd discovered he had an inoperable brain tumor. He was dying. He goaded you into murdering him," Genny told Rook. Sean saw a tear skitter down her cheek. The EMTs hastened over to Rook's side.

"You were as much a victim of Max's machinations as Sean and I were," Genny finished softly.

Rook let out a howl of pure suffering as the female EMT began to attend to him. Sean realized, with a distant sense of pity, that Rook's misery at that moment had nothing to do with his bullet wound.

CHAPTER **TWENTY-NINE**

The last thing Genny wanted to do was sleep, but that's what she did almost immediately upon returning to the penthouse with Sean. She lay on the velvet couch with her head in Sean's lap, the only source of light in the living room coming from the gas fireplace. Sean ran his fingers through her hair, very careful to avoid her bandaged forehead. A heavy, profound sense of exhaustion and relaxation overcame her.

She wanted to glory in her newfound freedom. She'd been released from a prison of sorts that evening, and so had Sean. But even though she wanted more than anything to celebrate the fact that she no longer had to avoid the one person that her soul craved like her body did air or water, her woozy head would not cooperate. She found herself drifting off as she stared up at Sean's ruggedly handsome face.

He smiled when she started, forcing herself back into wakefulness. He'd been unusually quiet ever since they'd made their statements at a Chicago police station located on Racine. Earlier, in her aunt's basement, Sean'd seemed hell-bent on making sure that everything was said that needed to be said . . . determined that every last ounce of toxin be expelled from the wound.

Now he seemed subdued and thoughtful.

"Are you all right, Sean?"

"I'm great." He brushed a fingertip over her eyebrow and caressed her eyelid. Genny shivered at the featherlight touch.

"You're not . . . you're not upset with me for leaving here today?"

"No. Not anymore. I know how much seeing that video must have brought it all back to you while your defenses were down . . . made you remember the reason you thought you should avoid me for all of those years." He met her gaze. "You were trying to protect me. Because you thought I killed Max."

A heavy sensation settled on her chest. "I'm sorry. I'm sorry for believing him and not trusting you enough just to ask you. Please forgive me."

He grimaced before he resumed stroking her hair. "I'm just as much to blame, Genny. I suspected Rook was lying about you shooting Max, but a small doubt in me remained."

"But when I came here last Friday, you seemed so set and determined about us being together," she whispered. "How could you have been so sure we should be together, even suspecting there was a chance I was a murderer?"

He shrugged slightly and his expression hardened. "I'm not like you, girl. I've seen a lot in my life . . . done a lot. If you had killed Max, I figured you hadn't done it without good cause. Like I told you in the emergency room today, I might not have shot Max, but I won't kid you that I hadn't thought about it—especially on that New Year's Eve night . . . after you'd gone to sleep."

"I know."

Sean's eyebrows quirked up. She told him about the portion of the tape Max had insisted she watch in his study on the day that he'd died. She felt Sean's muscles tense beneath her cheek.

"That *bastard*," he hissed. His blue eyes blazed with anger. "He must have done a nice editing job on the tape, because what he didn't show you, apparently, was him grabbing my dick and telling me that the price of having you was to become his play toy in bed."

Genevieve closed her eyes. How could one man have spread such a great degree of pain that it lingered for years after his death?

"I was such a fool. Why couldn't I see what he was?"

Sean smoothed his fingertip over her eyelid, as though bidding her to open her eyes. When she did, she saw what was perhaps Sean's defining characteristic stamped clear on his rugged features; she saw his stubborn, fierce determination.

"You couldn't see it because what Max Sauren was is completely alien to your nature, Genny. I saw it, but even *I* underestimated the degree of his narcissism and ruthlessness. Everything was a game to him; every person in his life was just a tool in one of his manipulations or a plaything for his pleasure. Albert Rook is scum, but even *he* wasn't capable of understanding what Max Sauren really was."

"How long did you know that Max and Rook were lovers?" She felt like such a fool for not realizing Max's bisexual nature. The clues were there, if only she hadn't been so naive.

"I guessed it for certain when Max made a point of telling me he had evidence of Rook's treason. It was Max's way of keeping Rook in check, so I figured Rook had some kind of inside position with Max that made Max feel vulnerable."

Genny just shook her head. She knew someday she would come to terms with what Max had done . . . with who the man she'd married had *been*, but for now it just felt too overwhelming to try to make sense of the intricacies and darkness of his character.

The fire had warmed the room comfortably. Sean's fingers in her hair both soothed and stirred her. Her weighted eyelids fell slowly before she started herself into wakefulness once again.

"Why are you struggling not to fall asleep, girl?"

She stared into his gleaming, firelit eyes. "I don't know. Maybe I'm afraid if I fall asleep, when I wake up tomorrow, it'll all be gone."

He leaned down and pressed his mouth softly to hers. She could smell the remnants of his spicy cologne mixing with the singular scent of his skin and the fragrance of the peppermint gum he'd been chewing while they waited at the police station. Heat swelled in her belly and genitals. Even though she could hardly keep her eyelids open, he created a havoc of sensual need in her body.

"You believed I'd murdered Max in cold blood, but part of you always trusted me despite all the evidence. You trusted me at your core. Isn't that right, Genny?"

Her throat knotted. She thought of what it had been like seeing him again that first night in this penthouse, all the emotion that had come crashing down on her in a tidal wave. She thought of his fierce lovemaking. Would she really have allowed him to restrain her during sex, have given herself to him so wholly if she believed there was something elementally missing inside him . . . something that had made him a killer?

"That's right," she whispered.

"Then I want you to listen to me now. I'm going to be here with you tomorrow. And the next day, and for as many days and nights after as you want me to be around. Nothing is keeping us from each other anymore. I won't allow it."

A feeling of happiness unlike anything she'd ever known swelled in her chest upon hearing his words. "I suppose you plan on keeping me tied up here in this penthouse."

"Whatever it takes." His blue eyes gleamed in the firelight. "Now go to sleep, girl."

He must be part magician, because Genevieve found herself doing precisely that.

*   *   *

Her eyelids opened heavily the next morning at the sound of the shower being turned on in the master bathroom. She sat up on her elbow in the king-sized bed and looked around sleepily. Sean had carried her to bed last night, and she'd never awakened even slightly. She still wore the velvet lounging pants and knit top she'd had on since yesterday.

Her head didn't pain her when she rose from the mussed bed, and no dizziness struck her while she took a quick shower and rebandaged her head with the supplies she and Sean had picked up last night at a twenty-four-hour pharmacy.

She was walking back into the master bedroom wearing a towel secured at her breasts when the bathroom door opened and Sean walked out in a cloud of steam.

She paused just inside the threshold of the door as sensual desire flooded through her flesh. The sight of him took her breath away. His short, wet hair spiked up at odd angles. Her gaze trailed over his naked, golden body. A powerful hunger grew in her. It seemed like a carnal decadence to be allowed to look her fill at all those delineated, gleaming muscles. She stared at the white scar on his hip and sent up a prayer of thanks for his life.

Her eyes lowered to the sight of his genitals resting between muscular, powerful thighs and another fervent prayer of thanks went up for being gifted with such a marvelously beautiful man. His penis was flaccid at the moment, but still long and firm where it rested along his left thigh. His round testicles were the image of masculine potency.

As she studied him, his cock stirred.

She glanced up into his face. Her vagina tightened and ached when she saw the familiar, feral gleam in his steel blue eyes.

"You know something?" he asked in a low, husky voice.

"What?"

"I used to wonder if your eyes alone could make me come. Back then—before we ever touched each other—I swear I could feel your stare on my skin."

"I felt the same way," she whispered as her gaze traveled back down over his body. "Sean? Would you do something for me?"

"Anything."

Her gaze darted up to his face when she heard the complete, unconditional truth behind the single word.

"I know how you like to be in control when we make love." She walked farther into the bedroom and dropped her towel to the floor. She gloried at seeing the spark that flew into his eyes. Her nipples tightened as he stared at her bare breasts. "But for right now, would it be too much to ask for me to touch you . . . to make love to you?"

He stepped toward her slowly, his manner reminding her of a stalking panther about to pounce.

"You mean you want to restrain me?" he asked.

Genevieve nodded, not sure how to interpret his rigid expression. She relaxed a little when he gave her his small, sexy smile.

"I suppose I could endure it."

"Will it really be that difficult?" she asked in a hushed voice when he neared her. He reached out and caressed her shoulder softly. Her breath caught in her throat when she saw that his cock had grown hard, and that he'd paused so that the shapely, tapered crown came within a half an inch of brushing against her naked hip.

Liquid heat surged between her thighs.

"Difficult? No, not too much," Sean mused thoughtfully as he continued to stroke her shoulder and upper arm while he stared hotly at her breasts. His light, elusive touch drove Genevieve to distraction. Her nipples pinched in pleasure as she inevitably thought of his fingertips on them instead of on her shoulder. He pulled his gaze off her breasts and met her stare. "But only because it's you. I wouldn't trust anyone else in the world enough to do it."

"Sean," she whispered feelingly.

He leaned down and she strained upward. They shared a lingering, carnal kiss that stirred both her heart and flesh.

"Come sit on the edge of the bed," she whispered next to his lips when he sealed the soulful kiss moments later. When he'd done what she asked, she opened the bedside table and drew out the leather cuffs. Her glance at him was a little uncertain, but he merely raised his eyebrows jauntily and stuck out his hands.

She laughed as she put them around his wrists. "Now put them behind your back." When he followed her instructions, she got onto the bed and fastened the hooks, restraining his arms. His impressive back, shoulder, and arm muscles flexed. Genevieve realized with a trace of trepidation and excitement that he could probably rip the hooks from the leather if he tried hard enough.

She eyed him cautiously as she stood next to the bed. "You're not going to try to break loose, are you?"

His expression was worthy of a choirboy. "Now, would I ruin your little experiment, girl?"

She smiled. She'd liked his answer. It warmed her to know that he did this willingly. He seemed to understand she wanted to glory and cherish without constraint everything that had been denied her for so long.

She was in the process of molding his dense deltoid muscles in her palm, scattering hungry, tiny kisses on his neck, jaw, and cheeks and drowning in his delicious, clean male scent when he spoke.

"You know I'm going to have to pay you back for taking such liberties with me," he murmured as she brushed her lips next to his mouth.

"Is that a promise or a threat?" she asked as her hands moved to his chest and her fingertips explored crisp, curly hair and smooth skin tightly gloving muscle. He made a hissing noise when she circled her forefinger over a flat nipple and he beaded tight for her and groaned roughly.

"It's just a fact of life, I reckon."

She bent and continued her exploration of Sean's copper-colored nipple with her tongue.

"Hmmmm," she purred. She pursed her lips around him and created a light suction while her curious fingers mapped out the fascinating contours of his ribs and muscular abdomen. His muscles leapt beneath her touch, thrilling her. When she finally lifted her head, she wore a smile of sublime satisfaction. Sean watched her with a fixed, feral expression.

"Maybe this isn't such a great idea," he said.

"It's a wonderful idea," Genevieve corrected as she opened the bedside drawer and extricated the scented lubricant Sean had used on her several days ago. She put her hands on his knees and parted his long legs. She knelt between his thighs and stared up at a magnificent landscape of virile, aroused male.

His nostrils flared, but he didn't speak when she glanced down at his erect cock lying on his thigh. She then held his stare while she ducked her head and placed a chaste kiss on the smooth crown. His cock leapt at her touch.

"You're asking for it, girl," Sean growled softly when she lifted her head and regarded him soberly.

"I only want to make you feel good, Sean."

She saw the flicker in his blue eyes and knew he remembered how he'd said the same words to her while he tried to reassure her on the first night he'd touched her.

Genevieve flicked open the cap of the lubricant and poured some of the silky liquid into her palm. She rubbed her hands together and then cradled her breasts from below. Sean stared at the movements of her hands fixedly as she liberally coated the valley between her breasts with the lubricant.

He groaned, deep and rough, when while still holding both breasts in her hands, she lifted his stiff cock with two fingers and positioned him in the crevice between her breasts. She leaned forward and squeezed her flesh around his protruding penis.

She glanced up uncertainly into his face. He watched her with almost palpable intensity as she begun to bob her torso up and down, sliding his cock up and down between her breasts.

"You said you wanted to . . . the other day," she whispered as she straightened enough so that only his luscious cockhead stuck out of the valley between her breasts. His face clenched when she plunged down again, sliding his swollen cock through her oiled flesh. "But then you never did. I thought you'd like it."

A spasm tightened on of his cheeks as he continued to watch her. "You thought right. Touch your nipples."

Genevieve's eyebrows went up in a wry expression at his demand, but she supposed a simple pair of cuffs wasn't going to change his dominant nature even remotely. She paused in her movement with his cock embedded almost entirely between her breasts save the glistening crown. She ran the tips of her forefingers around the areolas of both nipples, flicking the sensitive center nubbin softly. She'd started to do it to titillate Sean, but touching herself while Sean watched with such focused intensity aroused her more than she thought it would. Her clit twanged in arousal as she lightly pinched both nipples while she once again moved, sliding his cock between her breasts.

A groan scored Sean's throat. He began to shift his hips slightly, moving in a subtle counter-rhythm to her strokes. A light sheen of perspiration glistened on his taut belly.

It did something to her to see him so uninhibited in showing his need.

"It feels good, doesn't it?" she asked as she watching his face raptly while he watched his cock burrow again between her breasts. His hips moved more restlessly as he tried to increase the rate and pressure of his stimulation.

"You know it does," he mumbled. "You have the most beautiful breasts I've ever seen. It's going to feel so good to come on them."

Genevieve groaned as her clit pinched in painful arousal at his words. For several seconds, she was ruled by the rough need in his voice. She bobbed up and down over him more rapidly while she rubbed and pinched her nipples with more force.

She paused when the realization penetrated her thick lust that she was doing precisely what he'd suggested, even though that hadn't been her plan. He grunted in protest when she straightened in her kneeling position. His heavy erection batted against his thigh with a soft whapping sound of flesh against flesh.

God, he took control of their lovemaking so easily . . . even when he was the one restrained.

"What are you doing," he asked quietly. She saw his shoulders and arms flex and knew he was testing the restraints. She saw his strong throat muscles convulse as he swallowed and suspected he had barely stopped himself from ordering her to keep fucking him with her breasts.

The knowledge sent a thrill through her for some reason. Her pussy throbbed in excitement. She licked her lower lip anxiously.

He stilled as he trailed the movement of her tongue.

She grabbed the thick root of his penis and held him up for her consumption. She watched him as she dragged the smooth, fat cockhead over her closed lips.

"I thought I'd suck on our cock a little. Would you like that?" she asked gruffly.

Every muscle in his magnificent body had grown tense and defined. His nostrils flared as he inhaled through his nose.

"I'm gonna turn you over my knee when you're done, Genny. And that's both a threat and a promise."

She just smiled in the face of his sensual dare before she pushed the crown of his cock between her lips. The lubrication was flavored, and tasted fruity on her tongue. Her eyes closed in sublime satisfaction as she sucked him deep and strong, and his grunts of pleasure, softly hissed curses, and tense groans resounded like magical incantations in her ears. She loved when Sean set the pace of their lovemaking; became outlandishly aroused when he used her body to deliberately and precisely stoke the inferno of his passion.

But this . . . this delicious abandonment of her senses as she drowned in his taste and fed on his flesh and grew drunk on his pleasure . . .

This possessed its own sort of carnal magic.

She'd waited so long for him, desired him so greatly. Now he was hers, and she wanted . . . no, *needed* to assure herself that the elusive dream had become a reality; that he was *right there* for her to touch and taste and pleasure.

Moments later, she felt him subtly swell in her mouth as she pressed his cockhead into her throat.

He groaned harshly when she slid him out of her mouth. He watched her with blazing blue eyes and the shadow of a snarl on his firm lips when she stood next to the bed.

A frisson of excitement mixed with anxiety went through her at the sight of him.

She'd had the temerity to handcuff a wild beast . . . to restrain a force of nature.

She propped several pillows next to the headboard, doing her best to not be affected by his hot stare on her.

"Can you come all the way onto the bed and rest your back against the pillows?" she asked.

His handsome mouth twitched, but whether it was in amusement or irritation, Genny couldn't tell.

"Why don't you uncuff me first?"

She shook her head apologetically.

He stood. For a few seconds, he just stared down at her from his towering height. "Only for you, girl," he said pointedly before he sat back down on the bed and stretched his long legs in front of him.

Genny experienced the strangest, most powerful brew of emotions as she straddled his narrow hips and lifted his cock to her slit: intense arousal, swamping love, a poignant sense of sadness for all the years Max had robbed them of each others' presence . . .

A profound sense of *rightness* at being finally joined to Sean.

A tear trickled down her cheek as she pressed with her hips, and her vagina slowly stretched to accommodate his cock. When she rested in his lap, her teeth clenched in pleasure at the sensation of being full of throbbing male flesh—of being inundated with Sean—she reached around him and found the clasp on the cuffs.

His hands came around to her hips. He began to lift her subtly up and down on his cock, grinding her sensitive external sex against his pelvis in a taut, circular motion on the downstroke.

Genevieve cried out as pleasure became her universe.

She hadn't been giving in by freeing him . . . by letting him take control of their lovemaking. It'd been as natural as breathing at that moment for her to let go . . . to release herself entirely to him, just as Sean always abandoned himself to her in his own fashion.

"Open your eyes, girl. Look at me," she heard him mutter

tensely a while later while he held her down tightly in his lap and his cock throbbed deep inside her.

She lifted her eyelids and stared at him while she panted, existing on the very precipice of climax.

"You love me, don't you?" he rasped.

Something shuddered deep inside her . . . a prelude to bliss.

"From the very first moment I saw you, boy," she whispered before she tumbled headlong into ecstasy.

ABOUT THE AUTHOR

Beth Kery grew up in a huge house, built in the nineteenth century, where she cultivated her love of mystery and romance. When she wasn't hunting for secret passageways and ghosts with her friends, she was gobbling up fantasy and adventure novels, along with any other books she could get her hands on. Currently, she juggles the demands of two careers, her love of the city and the arts, and a busy family life. Her writing reflects her passion for all of the above. Find out more about Beth and her books at www.bethkery.com.